WHEN THE COIN
IS IN THE AIR

"I loved John Young's wise and moving novel. A young man is forced to navigate the difficult choices of early adulthood while protecting his own life and his mother's from a violent, abusive father. Reminiscent of the novels of Pat Conroy, *When the Coin Is in the Air* explores the complexities of the pull between duty and self-determination, tempered by love."

–Susan Neville, author of *Invention of Flight* and Professor at Butler University.

When The Coin is in the Air is a riveting story of adversity, destruction and transcendence. John Young weaves a gritty but ultimately uplifting tale, sure to speak to anyone who has wrestled with demons. From the start, Young's debut novel will grab you, and it won't let you go.

–Don Tassone, author of the novel *Drive*.

In John Young's *When the Coin is in the Air*, there is clarity about who the characters are, especially Jason's nuclear family, which includes his charismatic and successful older brother, his abrasive father, and his artistic, quiet mother. As Jason tries to find his place in the family and the world, he finds pieces of each of his family members within himself.

The book is also a page-turner. I found myself grabbing it to read a few chapters here and there, laughing at the characterization of the Indiana Teacher's Conferences during the nineties, nodding my head in recognition....

–Kelly Blewett, NPR/WVXU.org/AroundCincinnati.

WHEN THE COIN IS IN THE AIR

A Novel

by

John Young

Golden Antelope Press
715 E. McPherson
Kirksville, Missouri 63501
2019

ISBN   978-1-936135-70-7 (1936135-70-1)

Library of Congress Control Number: 2019944276

Published by:
Golden Antelope Press
715 E. McPherson
Kirksville, Missouri 63501

Available at:
Golden Antelope Press
715 E. McPherson
Kirksville, Missouri, 63501
Phone: (660) 665-0273
http://www.goldenantelope.com
Email: ndelmoni@gmail.com

This book is dedicated to
the four strong women
who made me who I am:

My mother, Charline
My sisters, Sandy and Marty
My wife, Lauren

Acknowledgements

Bringing a book into the world is a bit like raising a child. There's a lot of blood, sweat, and tears. Plenty of mistakes and stumbles. But there's also love and wonder and laughter.

Through all of it, I've had the support and encouragement of so many great friends, I cannot list them all here. But some warrant a special thanks for being early readers of this book and for offering guidance. These include:

Jeff Bell, Paul Kroner, Ron MacLean, Caroline Leavitt, David and Elizabeth Burstein, Ken Bennett, Don Tassone, Tripp Eldridge, David Young, and David Clifton.

I'm also grateful for the team at Golden Antelope Press, especially Betsy and Neal Delmonico for their guidance and partnership in bringing this novel to life.

Finally, I want to acknowledge the unwavering love and support of my family. Lauren, I deeply appreciate you and how you've inspired and encouraged me from the start. Nick and Tess, a guy couldn't ask for better kids; I admire the people you've become. And a quick shout out to Nick for great design work on the book cover.

Thank you all.

Contents

CONTENTS   v

WHEN THE COIN
IS IN THE AIR

Fire in the Field

It was a hot day, the day I burned the field. Chores filled the morning, and I hurried because Mom said when I finished I could ride my bike the three miles to see my friends in the nearby suburb. One of the last chores was to burn the trash, and I lugged the barrel to the fire circle at the edge of my grandfather's field.

The field, which surrounded our yard, stood in hay that year, drying in the relentless, August sun, about due for a final cutting and baling. Within a minute of my lighting the fire, the wind picked up, lifting a piece of flaming paper out of the fire ring into the field. I ran to stomp out the small fire, but when I turned, three or four more pieces took flight, blowing past me to scatter in the field.

Like an unleashed pack of foxhounds, the fire rushed into the dry hay. I ran to the garage and grabbed an old blanket to put it out before anyone saw, but by the time I got back, it was out of control. Flames raced across the grass, as the sound of fire rose from a faint whoosh to a loud rushing and crackling like something alive, pumping heat and smoke into the hot air. Oh no, everyone would see. Everyone would know of my giant mistake. I sprinted back to the garage where my old man was pounding wrinkles out of a fender–and told him.

He ran out of the garage. "Goddamnit!" he yelled. He snatched up my t-shirt. "You're gonna pay for this." He shucked me aside and ran back to the garage. He snapped off a broom handle over his thigh, then snapped it again, cursing me under his breath. At first I thought he'd club me with the broken handle, but instead he tore rags and made slapdash torches and splashed kerosene over them. His hand shoved me. "Grab some blankets and get them wet!"

We had a stack of wool army blankets. I grabbed two and ran to the hose.

What had I done? How could I have done this?

He was yelling at me, and I ran with the heavy, dripping blankets. He waited in his pickup truck, engine revving. I started to go to the door but thought better and jumped in the back with the wet blankets. The truck fishtailed through the gravel and across the yard and then bounced into the field. I struggled to keep my feet and squatted, pressing myself into a corner of the truck bed. He took a sharp turn, racing around the fire, and I almost fell out.

Was he trying to toss me out?

Would he shove me into the fire?

It was what I deserved. How did I do this? You can't fix this, I thought.

He slammed to a stop at the far end of the field. I grabbed a cold, wet blanket and jumped out. He snapped open his lighter and held up the torches with their crude petroleum smell. I knew what to do—he'd told me before: fight fire with fire, one of the oldest rules in the book. We sprinted into the hay ahead of the flames, choking on the smoke, tears flowing from my eyes, and we started back-fires with our torches. I started for the woods to keep the fire from the trees, from the birds and animals.

"NO! Save the corn first, you idiot!" my father screamed.

I was an idiot. How stupid can you be, Jason?

The corn, an 80-acre field, and nothing protected it but an old wire fence, a man, an eleven-year-old idiot, two blankets and two lousy torches.

I looked up. Flames tall as a horse now galloped toward us. Smoke and heat blowing, rolling ahead on the wind. I sprinted ahead to protect the corn.

The hastily made torches allowed flaming kerosene to run down over my hands, burning me and leaving a burned-hair smell on my forearms, but the pain wasn't bad enough to pause for. Besides, this was no time to make a fuss. Once we got the backfires going, we had to control them against the wind with the wet blankets–to keep them from spreading into the fence row and the dry cornfield behind us. I still worried about the woods, the birds and animals. We threw the wet blankets down, stomping the fire out, then threw them on the next patch of flames. We worked as fast as we could, a few feet at a time.

Dad stayed at the east end of the field to watch the downwind backfire. I was on the run again, starting backfires to protect the woods. Behind these fires was a blackened waste, a ruined 12–acre hayfield, but I didn't pause to look at it. There was more fire to put out. I choked on the smoke but ran hard anyway.

As I ran to save the woods I loved, the woods I'd put at risk, I thought of the first time I was in this field. It was six years ago. I was five. My grandparents had offered my mother and father an acre to build a house. It followed a reconciliation between my father and his parents.

It was a beautiful spring day, endless blue skies. Nothing like the day of the fire. The field had been plowed and disked, ready for planting. Mom led the way. My older brother, my father, and I followed. She took her time. At several points, she stopped and turned slowly, holding out her arms as if framing the view.

"April," Dad said, "come on, let's just pick a spot."

She ignored him and continued her survey, tromping through the dusty field.

"April–"

She spun on her heel, hands on her hips: "Walt, this is where we'll raise Walter and Jason. I will walk this field and choose the spot for our home. If I want to walk it five times, then I'll walk it five times."

Dad stood nearly a foot taller than Mom and was twice her weight, but she stared him down. I was afraid it might get ugly. But it didn't this time.

He smiled and held his hands up as if to stop a bus, "Okay, Ape. Okay. Take your time, you're right."

"Darn right, I'm right," she said in a lighthearted way and gave

Walter a playful shove, which made us boys laugh. Then April Blake went on about her business, and we followed her. She picked a spot at the opposite corner of the field from the white, Indiana farmhouse where Dad had grown up.

Just before Christmas of 1978, we moved into our simple new ranch house at the corner of 86th Street and Mud Creek Road. After our string of cramped rentals, it felt like a mansion carved out of a corn field.

But this year, the field was in hay–and the hay was on fire, and the cornfield next to it was in danger.

Fire rolled toward my uncle's driveway and the woods. I had to stop it.

I sprinted ahead of the closest flames, the hottest flames. My lungs forced a cough in the smoke, and I put the flaming torch to the hay, starting the backfire. Once that section was controlled, I started the next spot, and the next.

On and on I worked without looking for my father. It was hard to see, my throat and eyes burned. I was parched, my hands now bleeding after the blisters burst, but I dared not complain or ask for water. It was a long afternoon. Eventually, Dad brought me a shovel to help bury the remaining fire. He threw it on the ground at my feet.

He growled, "Damnit, son, sometimes you're more trouble than you're worth," and he spit to the side.

"I'm going in for supper," he said. "You finish what you started." And he left me to work alone. His words replayed over and over in my head as I chased down final flames and shoveled smoldering areas of the field and pounded out embers.

When Walter got home from his summer job as a house painter, he brought me water and helped me put out the sparks. My seventeen-year-old brother tried to joke with me about it.

"Jason, I didn't know you hated baling hay this much."

But I couldn't laugh it off, not the loss of twelve acres of hay. My brother went inside to eat. I made another check, walking the perimeter of the field with the shovel and a wet blanket, shoveling out and stomping on smoldering clumps.

From the hedge, my mother called me for supper, but I waved her off. I couldn't believe the trouble I'd caused. What would my grandparents think? What would they do? I couldn't quit until every flicker of fire was out. It was dusk before I finished.

I sat on the pile of rocks at the top of a small hill in the field, surrounded by charred earth, still smoking and smoldering in places. The sky going purple promised to hide what I'd done, at least until dawn. My hands were burned and bloodied, the hair on my arms singed off, bloody blisters forming on my forearms, too. The rubber soles of my workboots had melted, and my lungs hurt from breathing smoke for seven hours. I was fall–down exhausted. But I couldn't go inside and face my parents. Especially my father.

"Jason," my mother's voice close and soft at my shoulder surprised me. I hadn't heard her coming across the field. "Come on inside now."

I couldn't speak to her or look at her. I felt so ashamed and stupid for the fire and for having complained about chores earlier in the day. "I got to make sure it's all out."

"You put it out," she said.

I still hadn't looked at her. I couldn't. How could I tell Mom I was afraid to face my father, afraid to be in the same house? I felt embarrassed beyond words. What kind of person caused such destruction? Not Walter, that's for sure. I was just a dumb eleven-year-old boy. A stupid kid. More trouble than I was worth.

We stood silently in the blackened field for a bit, my head down. Smoke smoldered nearby. Then I felt Mom's hand rub my back and up to the back of my neck and across my shoulders. I swallowed down the knot in my throat. I wanted to fall down on my knees and bury my face against her skirt, but I was too old for that.

"It was an accident," she said. "Could've happened to anybody."

"But it happened to me," I choked out, unable to imagine it happening to my older brother, the star athlete about to start his senior year of high school. Walter had burned plenty of trash in the same fire ring without incident.

"Oh, Honey, it was an accident. It's okay, nobody got hurt. Nobody's going to say anything about it. Nobody's mad at you."

I found this hard to believe. Besides, I was angry with myself.
"Come on inside now and get cleaned up and have some dinner."
"I got to check a few more spots."
"Okay, but you come in soon."
I nodded. "Okay," I whispered.

She went back to the house, and I went to the far end of the field alone with my shovel. I zig-zagged around, turning over and stomping out any last smoldering clumps.

When I came back into the house, Dad was sitting in his Lazy Boy, the television on while he read the paper. He didn't acknowledge me. But he never mentioned the fire again, and neither did my grandparents.

I lay in bed that night exhausted, my arms sore and sticky with antiseptic Mom had applied, and I wore a long-sleeved t-shirt like a bandage over my arms. I couldn't sleep. My lungs and eyes hurt. Walter slept in the other bed. The fan hummed in the window, blowing warm air over us, that and the smell of the charred field.

Crash Courses

Something happened in the burned field. Almost immediately, small green sprouts sprang above the black. Millions of them in bright green. More and taller every day. It was beautiful. A little rain, and the field sprang to life. I had done something terrible, but in one week, it turned into something beautiful. At dusk, deer drifted into the field and rabbits materialized around the edges to eat the soft, lush shoots.

I stood at the edge of the field on Friday night and thought for the first time how resilient nature was. The earth was made for life.

"Hey," my father bellowed to get my attention. His shout spooked the deer out of the field. "Tomorrow morning," he said, "we're going to clear rocks from the field."

"Okay." This was no time to complain.

In the morning, I went out into the field early to look for rocks. I'd often marveled how new ones bubbled to the surface every year. My dad came out with a couple of shovels and a wheelbarrow. "Just three loads today," he said. I had expected more.

As we dug and pried rocks from the field, I felt bad about tromping on the new green sprouts. While I worked, I remembered two years before, when Walter and I were out here with Dad picking up rocks after plowing, and I'd found an Indian grinding stone. Designed to be gripped from the top with two hands, it weighed seven pounds and was perfect, a museum–quality artifact. It sat on my dresser, and I often picked it up and ran my hands over it, imagining Native Americans grinding corn with it. When I wandered the woods and creeks around home, I'd imagine myself as an Indian boy five hundred or a thousand years earlier, and dreaming about life with no plowed fields, just old-growth forest. Walter, who knew of my Indian-boy musings turned the grinding stone over in his hands and said, "Jason, you–and only you–had the eye and the spirit to find that stone." The grinding stone was a touchstone to the past. Someone else had grown up in this field–in the age of stone tools.

Now, I held the rock I'd pulled from the ground and looked at it–the top black from my fire. I dropped it in the wheelbarrow with a clang. Then I tried to pick up a bigger rock. It was too heavy for me, but I was trying to prove my worth.

"Leave it," Dad snapped, the way you'd speak to a dog. "You're just going to hurt yourself. Get those smaller ones over there."

I picked up the big one again. I got it off the ground, took about three steps. Then I dropped it and tried to roll it toward the wheelbarrow. The old man shoved me aside. "I said, get those small ones." I noticed my father's muscles as he hefted the big rock into the wheelbarrow. I wanted to be powerful like him. Dad rolled the first load up the small hill at the center of the field. (There was a rock pile in each corner and this one in the center.) He stopped about forty feet from the pile and asked if I'd ever tried to shot putt. Then he demonstrated his high school shot-putting form, spinning and launching hunks of feldspar high in the air toward the rock pile. Black soot from a rock marked his neck. He handed me a rock–told me to push it, not throw it. I tried to imitate him.

"Your form stinks," he said walking to my rock and tossing it on the pile. Then he added, "But not that bad for a first try."

I decided to keep working on my baseball pitching with Walter.

The second wheelbarrow load went to the rock pile near the house where my father grew up–the opposite corner of the field from our place. We could see Uncle Roger's big house from this corner. He owned car dealerships and made a lot of money.

"One more load," Dad said. "You bring the wheelbarrow." I followed him across the field toward our house. We loaded up a dozen rocks and added them to the pile at the corner of our yard.

"This afternoon, I'll need help at Zoreman's," Dad said.

"Okay." Rats, I'd have to call my friend Brian Jackson and cancel plans to ride my bike to his neighborhood.

Speaking of rats, that was my first thought when I heard "Zoreman's." It was a junk yard with plenty of rats. Dad didn't allow us to use the term "junk yard," though. It was a salvage yard. He sometimes took me to local yards to find parts for cars he rebuilt in the garage. Sometimes autobody work was his job, sometimes his hobby—depending on whether he had an insurance adjuster job or not.

That hot and sticky afternoon, we parked under Zoreman's sign: "We Meet By Accident," it said. My dad got out and flicked his cigarette butt into the gravel. I went over and stepped on it with a twist—thousands of butts littered the gravel parking area. Inside, the office was dark and smoky, but Dad kept on his aviator sunglasses. Country music twanged from a yellowed clock radio. Hot and sticky outside, but almost cold inside as an oversized window air conditioner droned on and on.

Judy sat in front of Zoreman's dispatch radio, which looked like something salvaged from a World War II battleship.

"Hey, there he is, best-looking man around here." Judy's cigarette bounced in her mouth as she spoke, sprinkling her ample bosom with flecks of ash.

"Not saying much, is it, Judy?" Dad said, eyeing the man behind the desk.

"Especially not when Jimmy's the other lug in the room," Judy cracked.

Always a Jimmy, Bobby, or Billy at salvage yards.

Judy perched her red-lipstick-stained cigarette atop similar butts in her ash tray and slowly blew smoke across the face of the radio. A plume rose and curled from the ash tray until the a/c blower mixed it into the general haze of the room.

"How's it hangin', Big Walt?" Jimmy said, extending his hand to my father.

"Little to the right," Dad answered, meeting the outstretched hand.

"Hey, I'm looking for a right-front on a Cutlass," Dad said. "I'd like to pull it and a few small parts off that red one, about six aisles over, halfway up, on the left."

"Sounds good," Jimmy said. "But it's orange."

Judy chimed in: "You're both color-blind as dogs. I know that car—it's rust-colored."

"Bust colored?" My old man boomed. Judy laughed and shook her head.

"Course GM calls it titty-tone," Jimmy added.

Embarrassed by the turn of conversation, I studied the smashed-up race car photos mounted on the cheap paneling. Zoreman's Wrecker worked the Indianapolis 500, so there were plenty of pictures of crumpled speedsters from The Old Brickyard.

"Color blind and deaf," Judy muttered.

"May as well add dumb," Dad said.

"Didn't think I had to," Judy shot back.

"Ouch, nothing worse than a woman with a sharp tongue," Dad said.

"Oh, I don't know," Jimmy said. "She could have a big butt."

"Hold on right there," Judy said.

My father chimed in: "Well, you know what they say: the bigger the cushion …. " And the three of them laughed. By then, they probably thought I'd memorized every wrinkle in the smashed-up race cars, but I tried not to listen.

Finally, we left the office. Dad drove around the building, past the gray aluminum fence which hid acres and acres of wrecked cars. We splashed through mud puddles in his truck. There could be a mid-summer drought, but broad, rainbow-covered puddles always awaited us at Zoreman's.

Six rows down, Dad halted. He fished a scrap of paper from his pocket and handed it to me. "Down this aisle or the next one, you'll see that red or rust-colored Cutlass. Those'er the parts I need." I looked over his scrawl as he lit a cigarette and got out of the truck. I heard him load the small tool box with wrenches and screwdrivers for me. "If you can't get a part off, wait for me." He handed me the box and a spray can of Liquid Wrench for stuck bolts. "Do NOT damage any parts, especially the right front fender."

He climbed up in the truck. "I'll be at the shed if you need me." The shed was a metal garage, a gravel-floor shack that listed to the east as if shoved by a strong wind. Dad stored parts and a couple of wrecks there, and he ordered me to keep it a secret from my mother. She'd put her foot down that we could have no more than one, okay, sometimes two, wrecked cars at home. But her rule didn't stop Dad from buying, selling, trading, and swapping other wrecks and parts, without her knowledge.

I watched him rumble away in his four-by-four pickup and stood there for a minute. God, it was hot, not a breeze, not a cloud. Just a hazy-white Indiana sky overhead and a blaring sun. The air of the salvage yard carried a familiar scent of gas and oil, stronger in summer than winter, supported by the ever-present smell of mud, but not a smell like the mud of the fields around home. Wrecked cars of every color and size stretched out in every direction. Toward the back, wrecks were stacked two, three, four high. I started down the lane to find the Cutlass.

Three car-lengths away, a pair of rats emerged in the lane and paused to consider me. I looked for a rock, but by the time my boot nosed one out of the ground, they were gone. Still, I picked it up and carried it. Stinkin' rats. That was the worst part about Zoreman's. That, and the blood. And the hair. And the shoes.

There was a lot of blood–dried blood–in the wrecked cars. On windows, on steering wheels, on seats and dashboards and floors. After a while, you kind of got used to it, like a doctor maybe. The hair was worse. You'd see a spiderweb crack in a windshield, and you couldn't help but look. There was hair, often a woman's long hair, dangling from the crack, or pasted by blood. The shoes completed the story in my mind. Some collisions hit so hard they knocked people right out of their shoes. Men's shoes–sneakers, wingtips, even workboots. Women's shoes–pumps, flats, sneakers. Kid's shoes. Even baby shoes. Not always both shoes.

I saw these things often at salvage yards like Zoreman's, and often up close, because my father encouraged me to collect S&H Green Stamps from the wrecks as a kind of pay for picking parts. People still collected the stamps as a bonus from grocery stores, stuffing them in gloveboxes or center consoles. Any I found, I kept. I pasted them in the little books and saved up to buy fishing gear from the S&H catalogs.

I paused in the lane by a rollover gold Firebird. I'd never checked it for Green Stamps. A spiderweb marked the windshield. Long blonde hair dangled from it. Couldn't open the doors but the windows were all smashed out, so I held my breath and leaned in. Beige interior showed blood everywhere. To open the glovebox and avoid the hair, I put my right hand on the dashboard. Something rough there. I snatched my hand back. Teeth were stuck in this dashboard. I'd seen it before, but it was always unsettling. Had to tug my eyes away from the teeth, her teeth. Her one red pump lay on the floor at an unnatural angle. It was bad in there. I wanted out, but I was in, so I checked the glovebox. No stamps.

I stepped back to the lane and took a couple of deep breaths to clear my head. There wasn't a smooth piece of metal on the Firebird. Nothing to salvage. A story built in my brain, and I tried to keep out the death of the driver and passenger, but I knew it happened. I felt it. As I walked on searching for the bust-colored Cutlass, I scanned the thousands of wrecks at Zoreman's. Hundreds of people had lived their last seconds—suffered their last seconds in messy and painful... you stopped there if you could. You mentally backed out of the demolished Firebird and blocked the stories of the other wrecks around you. You walked on down the lane in the heat, keeping an eye out for rats.

Where was that stupid Cutlass?

Growing up with wrecks in our garage—accidents seemed not only possible but probable. No one had to sell me on wearing seatbelts. When I worked at a local farm, the old farm truck didn't have seatbelts, and it made me nervous. Its metal dashboard waited like a threat.

I found the Cutlass. Judy was right, rust-colored. Found a wad of Green Stamps in the glove box. I checked the crumpled trunk before I got to work. A nice Rawlings baseball glove floated in water, right-handed, but ruined.

Then I started on those parts.

Halfway through, I heard something moving near me and picked up the rock I'd kept handy, expecting to throw it at a rat. Instead a little Carolina wren hopped around. I froze, watching her work. She got within three feet of me. I loved her rusty-brown color with the beige stripe by the eye, the narrow, striped tail, and her sharp beak. The wren was one of my favorite birds. I always thought of wrens as female because they reminded me of my mother; quick, small, beautiful, always busy-busy-busy, and they stood their ground against bigger birds. When I sat up to watch her, she scolded and flew off.

*

Parts lined up, I went to find my father. As I neared the shed, I saw Judy slip out the door, smoothing her hair and blouse as she went. It felt weird to see. But at eleven years old, I found Judy overweight and creepy. My mother was thin, classy, and sophisticated, so I dismissed any suspicion.

When I walked in, Dad was over at the workbench. He stuffed something in his pocket. The shed, like his garage at home, overflowed with tools, and smelled of autobody putty, oil, and automotive paint. These odors permeated my youth the way the smell of cut grass did for suburban kids.

I told him I got all the parts off the Cutlass and lined them up to pick up.

"Jason, think fast," he said and rifled a football at me.

I tried to catch it with one hand to avoid dropping the tool box, and it hit my hand, ricocheted off my shoulder and tumbled across the gravel floor of the shed.

"You won't make receiver this year," my father said. I felt the jab since my brother was prepared to star as wide receiver for the high school. I scooped up the ball and studied it. A Spalding University, kind of beat up, but still, the second best ball to the NFL Duke.

"Wow, a U-ball," I said. "Where'd it come from?"

"Jimmy found it in a wreck, and no one claimed it, so he said you could have it."

The only kid I knew who had one was Brian Jackson. His dad was a high school coach and had given one to Brian and his brothers. I never thought I'd own a ball like that.

"Do I have to share it with Walter?"

"Nope, Jimmy gave it to you. It's yours." I admired the ball, and then my father added, "Jimmy said you seem like a hard-working kid who didn't complain much, so he wanted you to have it." He was quiet for a couple of seconds. "I told him he was full of crap." Looked like he was cleaning up at the bench. "But you did work pretty hard today."

I didn't answer. Sometimes it was best not to answer with my father. Just kept admiring the football–a real University Ball.

We went to get the parts I'd lined up. Dad looked each one over, and we loaded them in the truck. On the way out, I asked: "Can we stop at the office real quick, so I can thank Jimmy for the ball?" I went inside to thank Jimmy for the ball, but he was out on a wrecker run. I asked Judy to thank him for me. "You bet, Honey."

When I got back in the truck, I realized how tired I was, hot and tired. At a stoplight, Dad said. "Milkshake?"

"Really?" I answered. I meant because I was excited, and it was rare.

"What the hell you mean, 'really?' Like you don't think I'd ever buy a goddamn milkshake?" I didn't know if I should answer. "So you don't want one? Well I'm going to get one for myself. You don't need anything."

He whipped into Steak-n-Shake, got out and slammed the door. "You wait here."

I really wanted a shake, but I wasn't going to get out of the truck. What I wanted even more than a shake was just a big cup of cold water. I hadn't had anything to drink since lunch, hours ago. I rubbed my hands over the football, wondering if using oil on it would work out the scuffs. I fell asleep leaning against the door waiting for Dad.

"Hey," Dad said at my open window, startling me awake. "Here's yours."

He handed me a white bag–inside a large strawberry shake and a tall ice water.

"Hey, thanks," I said. I held the ice water in one hand, the milk-shake in the other, the cold felt good against my hands which still felt tender from my burns in the fire the week before.

We didn't talk for a while. Just rode down the highway with windows down, radio up loud. It was the best strawberry shake I ever tasted. Then my father clicked off the radio.

"Football starts soon," he said. "You still want to play middle linebacker?"

"Yeah. And guard on offense."

"Thought you might want to play some fullback this year."

I didn't want to say why not. Dad had played offensive guard in high school, and I thought he'd want me to play guard too. I didn't want to tell him I was too big for fullback. But of course he asked.

"Weight limit for ball carriers in sixth grade is 105 pounds," I said, "and I'm 115."

He didn't say anything for a minute. Then he hit the steering wheel. "Goddamit. You and Walter could run ten pounds off, make you lighter and faster. You'd be a terror as a fullback."

A Terror

Although my father imagined me as a terror at fullback, I became a terror at middle linebacker and pulling guard my sixth-grade year. I had played poorly in third and fourth grades. As a fifth-grader, the game became more clear, and I played better. Then three things happened. First, I had a growth spurt. Second, Walter became my personal coach (with Big Walt tutoring on toughness). And third, the principles and nuances of the game finally clicked. One more thing marked a new beginning, a new school: Mary Castle Elementary.

Heading into the football season, Dad drilled me on how to shuck off a blocker to make a tackle, and how to get down the line as a pulling guard and smash the defensive end before he saw it coming. But it was Walter who really became my coach. While I took after our father with a thick build, Walter was skinny and fast. At my age, the track coach had nicknamed him Quicksilver, and he'd become something of a hero in our school (and with our father) when he won the sixth-grade 100 meter dash in Indianapolis–and more the hero because he was the only white kid in the finals. But he gave up track to focus on baseball, where he crowded the plate like a young Ty Cobb and turned singles into doubles by stealing second on the first pitch, daring catchers to throw him out. Walter brought intensity to every sport–but more to football, where he clawed for every inch when he had the ball.

My father celebrated Walter's drive and success. And Walter intended to infect me with it–times two. I was an eager student. I wanted to be like Walter, maybe better, at least at football which was the most important sport in our house and our high school. Walter played wide receiver, but he aimed to make me "the meanest motherfucker on the field" as a middle linebacker and offensive guard for the local traveling team. Walter drilled me in tackling and keeping blockers away. He taught me how to avoid a straight arm by driving me into the ground several times. How to wrap up the running back's legs by running over me when I went high. For offense, Walter trained me to explode out of my stance and get into the body of the opposing middle linebacker. If I made a mistake twice, he'd punch me in the facemask or throw me to the ground and kick me if I didn't get up quick enough–because getting up quick meant you might make the tackle or get down field for another block. Plus, I didn't like getting kicked.

One crunching lesson after another made me tougher, meaner, hungrier. When my season started, I was ready. I was bigger and stronger than most players my age. To those who outsized me, I was faster, and to guys who were smaller, they'd better be faster, a lot faster. Because while I played clean, I raged around the field wanting to kill someone.

That year I was defensive captain of the sixth-grade team, and our defense dominated across the state. We went unscored-upon while winning all ten games, and I was named Defensive Player of the Year in Central Indiana.

Though I never got carried off the field, never scored a touch-down, I felt proud about my year and the award. What I didn't know was that I'd just finished my most successful year in football–at eleven-years-old. I dreamed of playing in the NFL.

But what mattered more to everyone on my team, and my town, was Walter's Lawrence Central team. He led the Marion County Champions in receptions and made First Team All-County–vastly overshadowing my accomplishments. He was a hero. I was just a kid playing in a kid's league.

*

Walter received football scholarship offers from several small colleges to play wide receiver. Dad's dream come true. But one night, I listened from our bedroom as our parents argued:

"...like hell he's not, April," Dad said. "Can't walk away from a full ride."

My mother's voice came in slow and firm: "Walt, sports are for boys. He's ready to be a man. This is his time."

"Just think about the money it would save."

"Just think about the cost to Walter," she said. "The cost of him going to some little, second-rate college and wasting hundreds of hours playing football instead of learning."

"But he can learn from playing sports."

"He already learned what he can from playing sports. It was good for him. As a boy."

"He loves football."

"He always will," Mom said, "but no one plays forever. He's done with football, and you need to let him move on. He wants to study art and literature."

"Art and—Christ," my father said. "Such a little prince."

The gridiron had been common ground for the three of us, and Walter now turned away from it.

At eleven, I'd failed to grasp that Walter's athletic abilities and interests had been eclipsed by his artistic ones. For years, he'd shown artistic talent with uncanny draftsmanship, drawing constantly, sketching in the margins of his math book and filling art tablets. And I knew his paintings had won Gold Keys in the National Scholastic Awards two years in a row. He took his art seriously, spending hours and hours drawing and painting, bringing more imagination into his work, turning to abstract art, studying Picasso and Klee.

By then Mom had become a fashion designer with her skirts and blouses hanging in the windows of Indianapolis's finest women's shops. We even heard radio commercials touting April Blake Originals. She encouraged Walter's artistic side and helped him get into college classes at the Herron Art School.

*

Sixth grade at the new Mary Castle Elementary separated me from Brian Jackson and other friends for the first time. Though it felt weird, it was also fun to be in a new place with new desks, new gym, new library.

In its first month, my school held a contest among sixth graders to present names for the school mascot. Then the whole school would vote. I said we should be the Knights, the Mary Castle Knights. Brilliant. Painfully obvious, even for an eleven-year-old, but hard to beat. Because I came up with it first and the rest of the class got behind me, I was asked to present the idea at an all-school assembly. The three other sixth grade classes came up with their own mascots.

We drew straws to determine presentation order. I had to go last.

The other kids brought presentation boards with pictures of their mascots and had little speeches with note cards.

Not me.

That made me nervous at first, but having the best mascot name gave me confidence. And I had a plan. When my turn came, I took the stage with no props and explained how the Knights would guard the castle that was Mary Castle School. Then I stepped out in front of the podium and said quietly but firmly:

"We Are The Knights."

Then I said louder, "Come on. We are–" pointing to the students.

In the back, my classmates, as planned, hollered back, "–the Knights!"

"Yeah." I said and stepped back and forth, raising my arms like a TV evangelist. "Now everybody!" This time I bellowed it like a pro wrestler:

"We are–"

And the entire gym, teachers, kids, even Mr. Bates, the principal, cheered back: "–the Knights!!"

My work was done. We were the Mary Castle Knights.

*

That winter I played forward on the Knights basketball team while Walter did the same in a losing season for the Bears. As the days got longer and graduation approached, he couldn't wait for baseball. On weekends, we practiced after he got back from art classes at the Herron Art School.

Though art was replacing sports in his career plans, Walter was still my private baseball coach. He set out to make the most of my size, teaching me to bat like a heavyweight boxer. He reminded me of my father who had boxed in Chicago fight clubs while driving for Greyhound Bus in his twenties. Dad used to boast about his three professional bouts, and chuckle about how his brief career had ended when a quick-handed heavyweight knocked him cold. I imagined my father coaching Walter to bat like a boxer. Although my father had taught my brother much about sports, by the time I was twelve, Dad was gone from home a lot. He disappeared for days, sometimes a week or more, and Mom saying he was on a business trip no longer seemed believable. But she stuck to that excuse, and I wasn't going to embarrass her with a challenge.

Anyway, that spring Walter determined I would be a slugger, and a switch hitter who crowded the plate, a first baseman since I was bulky and left-handed, and a coming-at-you pitcher on the order of Bob Gibson. Walter and I played a lot of Pepper, a game where the fielder tosses a ball to the batter who bunts it back. The fielder and batter begin about eight feet apart, and the game quickens as you go—at least the way my brother played it—to sharpen eye-hand quickness for both players. After several seconds at the eight-foot distance, the players step back, without stopping, and play at that new distance, step back and play again, until reaching about thirty feet, and then work in close again. Then they switch roles and do it all over.

Fielding practice followed Pepper. And fielding was the right word because our yard remembered all too well its years as a corn field, making every grounder an adventure in wild hops. I hated the way my brother barked at me as I took bruising bounces off my shoulders, forearms, and shins: "Hustle in front of it. Get down and meet the ball. Bend your knees. Rush the slow ones. Take it on the hop." But I loved his praise when I snagged a tough one, and I felt myself getting better.

For batting practice, we went out into the grassy field with two old balls because balls still got black, picking up charred bits from my old fire. Walter never delivered fewer than 100 pitches to me. If I hit a pop-up he raced after it, stumbling across the rough ground– never, never losing sight of the ball. Even if he fell, which he rarely did (his baseball hat flying off), he scrambled to his feet, trying to make the catch, even diving for it as if the World Series depended on it. Then he'd spin on his heel and rifle an imaginary throw to second. If I tipped an easy pop-up, he'd get under it and catch the ball behind his back–and laugh.

He laughed a lot.

He laughed more often than he screamed at me for getting lazy with my stance or for letting my back elbow drop, laughed more often than he tried to hit me with a pitch for making the same mistake twice. If I really smacked one, one that might clear a home run fence, he cheered and laughed, "All right! All right! All right! Way to go, Moe!"

Moe was a family nickname I'd shed when I went to first grade, but when it resurfaced at moments like that, I never minded. No one before, or since, relished my successes more than my brother. If seldom to me, often to others. So when I made the All-Stars that summer, Walter never said a word to me. But his friends told me how much he talked about my play and how proud he was of me. And it was Walter who showed me the clipping of my All-Star performance in the *Lawrence Topics* weekly newspaper.

Another Season

Because Walter had left for Indiana University—left home and the playing fields—the glare of my father's intensity shone on me alone. I was twelve, seventh grade. Leaving football fundamentals to my coaches, Dad emphasized the need to deliver pain to the guy across the line. Especially on the first play of the game.

"Give him something to remember," he said as his eyes glistened and his mouth worked his dentures. He encouraged me to target the neck with a forearm shot. Hitting the point of the chin could cause a blackout. A hard elbow or, if necessary, a punch under the ribs could knock someone's breath away. A helmet to the kidneys in a pile... Never play dirty, just push the edges, he'd say. Use toughness to your advantage. Hit someone until you hear the whistle. And never let anyone play dirty against you. If someone goes after your balls, or tries to claw an eye in a pile, all bets are off.

Lessons of the lineman.

My father also took breaks from rebuilding wrecked cars in the garage to teach me about street fighting. He held out his hand with a glove on it. "Punch my hand. Be quick." I did as he said. "Okay. Now, do it again." This time he waved his hand around. I swung. And missed. "Again." I got up on my toes and took a short, quick jab. I grazed the edge of his hand.

"What did you learn?"

"It's hard to hit a moving target."

"Exactly."

I thought of Walter saying the hardest thing in sport was hitting

24

a baseball–hard to hit a moving round thing with another moving round thing.

Dad leaned in, focusing his blue eyes on mine. "You get in a fight or you think it's about to start. Keep your head moving because it's tough to hit a moving target, and it's easier to duck if you're already moving."

That was the day's lesson.

Another day he said: "In a fight, edge away from a guy's right hand to gain a split–second more reaction time, and to reduce the power of the punch if it connects. You're a lefty so edging to the right also opens your power alley."

One lesson after another:

If you hit someone, hit hard.

Win fast with a blow to the nose.

A driving punch under the ribs will end things fast, too.

Or land a knock–out punch to the chin.

If you get knocked down get up by rolling.

And if the other guy gets up wrong, end it with a boot to the face.

After a fight scene on TV. "See that? See that?" he jumped to his feet. "If a guy ever starts to take his jacket off like that, POW, take him out. Never take off your jacket. It's padding. That's important. If the other guy's got a knife, a jacket could save your life." He paused, "If you know you're headed for a fight ahead of time, put on a second jacket for protection."

Dad's lessons in street fighting were not new, but they intensi-fied, growing more nuanced. Like understanding the importance of quickness, of footing and bringing a punch from your toes, through your hips, all the way through delivery.

One night, we were watching some bad cop show on TV while Mom worked in her sewing room. On TV a guy pulled a gun. "No, no, no," my father said. "Turn that stupid thing off, and come with me." I followed him out to the garage. He went to his truck and pulled out a .38 revolver. I'd never seen it.

"Whose is that?" I said. I had gotten my first hunting rifle, a .22, the previous Christmas. But I was opposed to hand guns.

"It's mine. Sort of. I'm probably not keeping it," he said. "Don't tell Mom. She doesn't need to know. It'll just upset her." He didn't seem to mind upsetting me. "Look, I'm trying to teach you something here, something important. How to hold a gun on someone."

"What?" I said. "Why would I have to do that?"

"You never know. But you better know what you're doing if your life depends on it. Right? Well you don't do it like those idiots in Hollywood movies." He held the revolver out straight armed. "You hold a gun out naked, and someone will take it away. Or maybe his friend will."

He looked at me. Why was he telling me this?

"Pay attention. You hold it like this. In close, elbow in tight where you have muscle mass and strength. Then you hold the other arm across and above. See, like this. Keep your knees bent a little." He held his left forearm across to protect the gun. Like a lineman protecting his running back.

"Here, try to take it." Then he turned toward me.

"Don't point that at me!" I yelled. "It might be loaded."

"Calm down. It's not loaded."

"Loaded or not, never point any firearm at a person," I shouted. "You taught me that."

His expression was both angry and shamed. I knew he didn't like being called up short, or shown up. But I didn't care. I was right, and I wanted out of there.

"Here, you hold it," he said.

"No way."

"Don't be a baby. I'm just trying to show you something."

"Forget it," and I started toward the door.

He caught me by the neck of my sweatshirt and pulled me backward. "You listen to me, you little spoiled brat," he growled–his face near my ear. He pulled the neck of the sweatshirt tighter, so it choked me a little. "You don't walk away from me. Got it?"

"Got it," I whispered. But I just wanted to get away. He started to release me, then pulled me up short, choking me harder.

I knew this for what it was, this was bullying.

I knew because I'd been a bully.

*

In fourth and fifth grades, I was a big kid, more powerful than most, with a father who extolled the virtues of violence. My father and brother were disappointed in me for my lackluster football performance. They called me weak and meek on the field. I felt disappointed in myself too. Ashamed. I was angry about it.

My bullying started as a playground ruffian. I managed to avoid a physically awkward, gawky stage. My awkwardness was psychological. I was a reluctant bully. I'd grind some kid into the playground dust, then feel bad about it and help him up, and become his protector for a week. Some of my bully acts reflected my older brother's, the way he roughed me up, pinned me to the ground and forced me to eat grass or dirt, rubbed my face in the mud, held me down and slapped my bare stomach until it glowed red, and performed other big–brother torments from Dutch–rubs to towel snapping. Yes, I'd had effective role models. Much of my playground bullying focused on intimidating other kids, as I had observed my father intimidate us to get his way. It might start with a glare or a couple of sharp words from a jutting jaw, supported by closed hands at his sides. Maybe grabbing a collar and pulling it tight enough to hurt a little, to leave a red reminder in the mirror. When he was ready to explode, Dad's mouth worked at his dentures as if preparing to bite. Now, when I got physical, it was just as my father had taught me: if someone called me a name, a quick punch to the stomach or slamming a head against a wall put an end to it. If one of the other big, rough kids tangled with me, a jab to the nose or throat usually brought conflict to a quick conclusion. But bullies are wary of each other, we knew we were both dangerous–and cowardly. We understood that about each other and typically sought easier targets. Yet the slightest infraction in this bully–to–bully wariness demanded rapid action. The instinct was: I will be the aggressor to keep you from being the aggressor.

Most of my bullying took place on the playground or in play with other boys. In games of tag or dodgeball or red–rover, I went beyond normal boyhood roughhousing. I wanted to inflict pain.

That was all but impossible, though, with those big, soft red rubber balls. And knowing I couldn't really hurt someone badly freed me to try all the harder.

I must've learned a dozen ways to trip someone. A favorite, because it required teamwork, was what I called A Pair of Jacks (short for a pair of jackasses): One jackass gets on all fours behind a guy and then the second jackass gives the standing guy a shove backward. Heels up.

Worst of my inventions was The Headhunter: During touch football or tag with suburban kids, I ran down boys and when I caught them, I'd reach out, feel their skulls fill my palm and sense their balance vulnerable. Then I'd give a shove. Already running at full tilt, it launched the kid headfirst into a heap. In the moment of predatory instinct, I didn't care if the kid was younger or smaller–it usually meant a more acrobatic crash.

Afterward, regretting what I'd done, I'd keep it a secret from my mother, who, I knew, would be ashamed. But next time on the playground or some suburban backyard, it was more of the same. I got pounded into the ground a time or two as well, but that was part of the fun. Once my eyebrow smashed another kid's head. It hurt like hell. I struggled not to show it. Everyone stood silently looking. I lifted a liquid running down my face, afraid it might be an involuntary tear. When I saw blood, I smiled and tasted it. "Yep, it's mine," I laughed. "Let's go." Laughter at the sight of one's own blood went a long way toward establishing a personal brand. (Uh-oh, this kid doesn't feel pain like the rest of us.)

My favorite game during those years was "Smear the Queer" (not a very politically correct name–and most of us didn't even know what "queer" meant–at least I didn't). The rules of the game were simple. Everyone try to kill the kid with the football. When tackled, the ball carrier had to fumble and another boy would take up the football to be chased by the mob. There was no goal line, and no goal except to see how long you could keep your feet, or to crush the kid with the ball.

The Headhunter maneuver was ideal for Smear the Queer. There I'd be chasing Phil Sperry, the roundness of his skull filling my palm as I reached out.

Wait! I'd say to myself. Don't do it. You don't have to do this–you could hurt this friend. In the next brain wave came: kill him! And, wham, I'd dump Phil to the ground with everything I had.

Gathering up the rolling football, I'd turn toward the other boys who had been chasing Phil and, imagining my father cheering me, I'd charge screaming right into the pack like a Bronko Nagurski gone mad–only to be pounded by the mob of rowdies.

*

I felt conflicted and unsure about why I bullied. I did not like myself for it, and most of the time, I remained the sweet reflective kid who still studied nature and took long walks in the woods with my dog. Yet I liked the power and status bullying afforded me. Arguments were short, and I won them. More: bullying was an outlet for my anger and hostility.

I think that's why I quit being a bully when I found success in sixth-grade football. I loved the controlled aggression of football, the framework for violence, the license to deliver a blow, to battle until the whistle. There was no feeling sorry for smashing a kid. That was the whole point. That, and winning. Besides, the equipment prevented most injuries. It was perfect. I even liked practice and would have played year-round if possible.

Success with football meant I no longer needed to prove myself with a cheap shot to another kid on the playground. I still loved rough games (especially dodge ball), but rough within the rules. I still didn't take crap from anyone. But I no longer started scuffles. In fact, I stopped other bullies as if in recompense for my past. Silently I thought myself a force for good. And I developed a hatred for bullies.

So when Dad yanked my sweatshirt collar tight the second time, choking me–that pissed me off and made me hate part of him. Made me want to stand up to him.

And I think he sensed it.

*

Actually, I know he sensed it. One night after a seventh-grade football win, a teammate's father dropped me off, and I followed the gravel out back to the garage where I heard Dad working on a car.

"How'd the game go?" he asked from under the hood. The question surprised me because he seldom missed a home game, but I shrugged it off.

"We crushed 'em."

"Good. How'd you play?"

"I had a pretty good game."

"All right," he said absentmindedly, and drew back from under the hood wiping his hands on a pink shop rag. He wore a white v-neck t-shirt, and I liked the way it showed his muscles.

"Recovered two fumbles," I said and playfully punched him in the shoulder.

Bam, his hand struck like a snake, snatching me up by the throat. The other ripped away at my shirt, buttons popped off, books and papers skittered across the concrete floor. He slammed me against the tall, metal toolbox. My back rammed shut the drawers, jarring tools inside, and the metal handles pounded into my back. Then he spun me around and up against the car where he grabbed my flannel shirt and tore it right off my body, wrenching one shoulder and burning my neck.

Then he grabbed my curly hair and pressed my head against the roof of the car as he leaned in. Cigarettes and coffee on his breath as he growled, "Don't you ever hit me unless you're ready for a fight. Got it?"

He bounced my head on the roof and let go.

Just as I thought it was over, he snatched me by the neck and shook me. Then he held up a wrench close to my head.

"I said, 'You got it?!'"

I nodded, and fought back tears, "Yeah. I got it."

But it didn't soften him.

"You think you're ready to take me?" he said, and shook me again by the neck. "Huh? Huh?"

"No." I forced out, shocked by his reaction and scared of the wild-animal glare in his blue eyes. For a moment, I really thought he might bash my head in with the wrench.

Then the warning: "I don't ever play fight. With me, it's all or nothing. And don't you ever forget it."

No, I wouldn't.

"All or nothing," he said again.

When he released me, I gathered up my books and what was left of my shirt, which I threw in the trash barrel, and went straight to my room.

My mother called after me in a sweet tone, asking about the game. I cut the answer short. Then she came into my room, "Everything okay?"

"Yeah."

"You sure?"

"Yep," I stared down at my math book.

"Nothing happened at school?"

"*Mom*," my voice full of exasperation, "*nothing* happened. Okay? We won the game, and I've got a math test tomorrow. Don't you want me to study?"

She withdrew and lingered at the bedroom door. "If you want to talk later—"

"There's nothing to talk about, Mom." At least nothing I was willing to talk about, or knew how to address.

I kept asking myself what I had done wrong.

And then, what was wrong with my father.

Enter Debbie Devore

"Hey, you!" a girl's voice yelled.

I was on my bike, riding fast for the lake to go fishing. It was close to 9:00, getting a late start. But I hit the brakes when I heard her voice and circled back. I knew who it was, Debbie DeVore. She was sixteen. I was fourteen, just finished eighth grade. Debbie wore a tight, orange t-shirt–no bra. It ended at the waistband of her cutoff blue jeans, cut short to show off her long, thin legs.

"Where are you going in such a hurry?" she asked.

She had these intense blue eyes, and her dark-brown hair hung straight down in a hippie style. I had trouble keeping my eyes off her nipples which rose up in the cool morning air, pointing right at me.

"Well?" she repeated, hands to her hips. "Where you heading?"

"Up to the reservoir to go fishing. Then maybe a swim." I imagined her swimming in those short-shorts and that little t-shirt–no bra.

"Ever go skinny dipping?" she asked.

I couldn't believe she asked, asked like it was nothing. I'd never heard a girl ask a question like that, and I couldn't answer. I did go skinny dipping, most fishing days. Mom didn't want me to swim alone, but I did, skinny dipping because I couldn't wear wet shorts home. There were no houses around the lake, just woods. A couple of times fishermen saw me skinny dipping and hooted, but I didn't care. A girl though ... Debbie DeVore, skinny dipping? Only in my dreams.

"Jason? You okay?"

Jason? Debbie DeVore knew my name?

I guess it made sense, we'd ridden the school bus together for a year. We rode together in the morning, first ones on, last ones off, because we lived out in the country. We junior high kids rode to the high school to drop off Debbie and the other high schoolers, then rode to our school. On the way home, we got on first and then picked up the high school kids. My ride was close to an hour each way. Debbie and I had talked a little on the bus, but not much, mostly me calling out a fox I might see at the edge of a field or a deer, or saying goodbye at the end of the day. She never spoke to me in the morning.

"Sorry, yeah, I'm still half asleep," I answered.

"Tell me about it," she said.

She did look like she'd just gotten up. But I was lying. I'd been up for over two hours, to, as Mom said, "finish chores before fishing."

"How do you like it out here?" I asked, changing the subject. What a stupid question, I thought. The DeVores had moved from the suburbs out here to the country the previous summer. I was sure Debbie hated it.

"It's all right," she said. "If I don't die of boredom." Then she leaned in close, with this sexy look in her eye: "But in July, I get my license, so I'll be free."

She crossed her arms, and I realized I was looking at her nipples again. Hard not to—because I was a horny fourteen-year-old, but also, they pointed at me like two fingers. "Double-D," guys called her. She was not busty, but they called Debbie DeVore that anyway, because, well, because we were junior high idiots. Horny little idiots. Some of the crude dudes from Oaklandon even called her "DeVore the whore."

People called Oaklandon kids "hillbillies," but I never did. When my mom was a kid and her family moved up from south-eastern Kentucky, people called them hillbillies, and she hated that term, so you never heard it in our house. My mother shook off the Kentucky accent, but when she was tired or ticked off, you'd hear it come back.

Anyhow, Debbie DeVore was no whore, and no DD bra size, but something sexy emanated from her. She knew it, and she used it. Within a week, Debbie and I were an item. I couldn't believe my luck. But I kind of could. Like me, she was bored, curious, and horny. Her parents both worked. Her older brother worked. Her other boyfriend–who was eighteen–worked. She hung around reading magazines and watching lousy daytime TV.

Jason Blake was the perfect distraction.

Unless I had to work at one of the local farms or pick parts for my old man, I got up early to go fishing. Afterwards, I'd sneak in through the DeVore's back door using the key Debbie had given me, and head up to her bedroom to wake her up. And we went skinny dipping at the lake a couple of times.

I learned a lot that summer.

I stole a copy of *Everything You Wanted to Know about Sex but Were Afraid to Ask*, and Debbie and I took turns reading it out loud to each other. We laughed and cringed and experimented. Then I stole a copy of *The Happy Hooker* and that made Debbie crazy mad. Was it the "DeVore the whore" connection? She snatched it out of my hand and threw it at me. I ducked. Then she grabbed it and rammed it in the garbage. Okay, message received.

That was also the summer I gave up baseball–which pissed off Walter–because I wanted to spend more time fishing. I also worked part time at two farms, Korn's Christmas Tree Farm and the Parker farm. Occasionally, I also worked at a small orchard near home–although I was paid in apples. Ever since I was five, Mom had snapped a paper bag to signal me to walk the half mile to the orchard where I could pick apples off the ground. We'd have apples every night from the early, gnarly green ones to the final red ones that hung on until they turned mealy under December snows.

That summer I also worked out at the high school gym, nine miles away, to get ready for football. Some nights I got a ride. Some nights I hitch-hiked, and sometimes I rode my bike. More than once, I had to walk one direction or the other. I taught myself to run two telephone pole lengths, walk one, run two, walk one, to get home faster.

My main preoccupation that summer was Debbie DeVore.

When she got her license, we began to venture farther and farther from home. She'd drop her mother off at work, swing by and pick me up down the road from home, and we were gone. We drove to Butler where we walked around campus and pretended to be college kids (I'm sure I fooled no one). Then on to IU where Walter went, and up to Purdue where Debbie's parents had met. One day in early August, she picked me up at a meeting spot down Mud Creek Road.

"Where to today?" I asked.

She kissed me. "Cincinnati, Ohio!"

"What?" It hadn't dawned on me we could cross the state line. My mom would kill me. But only if she found out.

"Let's go," I said. And we had an adventure, exploring the city, walking the serpentine wall along the Ohio River and watching the barges pass. We went uptown to the University of Cincinnati and had a late lunch of Skyline Chili.

Coming home, we knew we'd cut it close. We stopped for gas and a pop in Batesville, Indiana–"Casket Making Capitol of America." Debbie still had to pick up her mother at work. When we came out, the back tire was flat. Debbie immediately started crying. "My mom will kill me. I'm dead."

"At least we're in the Casket Capitol of America," I said, but she saw no humor in it.

"Why are you crying?"

"We don't know how to change a tire!"

"I do," I said, and got busy. I thought I was her big hero, but when I leaned across the seat, hand on her thigh–

"Don't," she said. "Your hands are filthy."

She was right, but I thought dirty heroes were sexy to girls. "Let me run in and wash up," I said, but she was already rolling.

The car was quiet with the air conditioner humming, but we didn't talk much as she drove fast. The radio played. I could see she was worried about meeting her mom late. But it felt like something more.

When we got close to Indianapolis, Debbie said, "Where can I drop you off?"

"What?"

"I can't take you home," she said, "I'm already late to pick up my mom."

"Right, but I can't ride with you?"

"No," she said. "She doesn't know I see you."

That put me off. Not about her mom, but I got the sense I wasn't good enough for Debbie DeVore. Like her family would think poorly of me. Would they? Did they?

I didn't say anything, and she kept driving. We were close to downtown. "Can I let you off here?"

"I don't even know where we are." I said.

"You're smart. You'll figure it out," she said.

"What?"

"Just get out, Jason! I'm late to get my mom, you idiot!"

So I got out, and she sped away from the curb. That was how it ended.

I saw Debbie a few days later. I stopped by to return her house key and we went out on the back deck. She was cool to me. I was cool to her.

"Guess it's over?" I finally said.

"I think so," she answered. She came up close and leaned in with those killer blue eyes looking up at me. "But it was fun while it lasted, right?" Her hand went to the front of my jeans and rubbed lightly. "Mmmm," she said to the rise in my pants. I was confused and thought we were back on or ready for some fun. "I have one favor to ask," she whispered. "Let's keep this summer fling between us. It will be better for your freshman year if people don't know."

Better for me? Or better for you? I wanted to ask, but I didn't have the guts.

We had one long, long, deep kiss—like she'd taught me. As I tried to go to the next step, she gently held me off. "No, Jason." She smiled. "I have to go now." She stepped away. "Hey, good luck with football." When school started, Debbie DeVore was a junior. I was a freshman. She drove to school. I took the bus. In the halls, she regarded me as the friendly neighbor kid.

High School Football

Sweat-soaked at the end of a steaming August football practice my freshman year, my teammates and I were clomping for the locker room in cleats when a huge hand gripped the back of my neck. It froze me in my tracks.

I turned to see the leathery and age-spotted face of Mr. Samuel Oliver Bachman (Old SOB we sometimes joked, though he was no SOB). This tall man, oldest teacher in the school, was also athletic director. He'd been at our school since he graduated as a three-sport letterman from Butler University an eon before. His other nickname was Poppa Bear since we were the Lawrence Central Bears.

"You're a Blake aren't you?"

"Yes, sir, Mr. Bachman, Jason Blake."

His hand slipped around my shoulder pads. "I thought so." To my friends he said: "You fellas go on, I need to talk to Mr. Blake." I wondered if I was in trouble, but he smiled and patted my shoulder. "Your mother, April, still ranks as one of my all-time favorite students, smart as a whip, probably the best math student I ever had. And I coached your dad–Big Walt was a tough nut, a little wild. More than a little." He chuckled at the thought of my father. He said he knew Walter too. Mr. Bachman didn't mention my many aunts and uncles and cousins who had passed through the school before me, but I felt them.

"You come from a fine family, Jason Blake–you did say Jason?"

"Yes, sir, Mr. Bachman."

He held out his mitt of a hand, and I shook it. "I wanted to welcome you and encourage you to leave a positive mark on Lawrence Central like your family has."

As he spoke, I felt proud of my family, but I also felt a long shadow stretch over me. I doubted I could match my mother in academics. I could match my father's wildness perhaps, though I didn't want to. I realized I'd never compare to Walter as a three-sport letterman, and even if I was as good on the gridiron, there'd be no touchdown-catching glory.

More daunting than living up to family history with its attendant expectations was the harsh reality that several of my teammates had grown bigger and stronger than I was. However, few carried my on-field aggression and passion for collision. Still, while I remained the middle linebacker and defensive captain, I no longer shucked aside offensive linemen with ease, and, for the first time, I came to know the pain of a hard hit, and the shame of leaving a practice or a game with grass stains on my butt or the back of my jersey.

Practices were harder. Coaches were less happy with my performance.

The freshmen team practiced apart from the varsity and junior varsity. Once in a while we'd face the JV and get knocked around–it was their relief from weekly pounding by the varsity.

*

I lay on the ground, blue sky of an Indiana fall above, black starlings streaking south, my helmet touching the helmet of the other guy, listening for the coach's whistle to get up as quickly as possible and smash the other guy. The drill was Head-to-Head. When the coach blew the whistle, you were to get up and collide with the other guy. The offensive player was to protect the coach behind him. The defensive player was to get through the blocker and tag the coach, who didn't move. You were supposed to get to the coach in less than three seconds, but Coach Mason let it run

until someone was flat on the ground or he got tagged. The drill,
performed in front of all the linemen and linebackers, established
a pecking order. Coach Mason–freshman head coach and a former
lineman himself–loved it, and it was a daily drill. I lay there, sweat
running into my eyes on this hot day in late September, the day
after our third game and first loss. I'd gotten banged around pretty
badly by a tough fullback and a good offensive guard, and I felt
drained. It showed in practice. I barely held my own against guys
I'd normally cream.

Coach Mason started barking at me in practice. Now for Head-
to-Head, he matched me against Kenny Jonson, a guy I used to
knock around, but who was now bigger and stronger than I was.
The whistle blew and I was up just ahead of him, I tried to shove
past, but he held me and we wrestled. After two seconds I got low,
got leverage and shoved him aside to tag the coach.

I started back to the end of the line.

"Blake, get back here!"

Normally you clashed and then went to the end of the line.
Sometimes, Mason made you repeat, either with the same guy or
another, after instruction. But I thought I'd done pretty well, and
I'd expected Jonson to get yelled at for holding.

"Get down here and do it again. Jonson won that round." I
didn't argue. Then he matched me against another big, strong kid.
Then another, and another. No instruction, just: "Do it again, Blake."

"You better keep Blake away from me," Coach Mason yelled at
the other guys. "For his own good." Not a hint of play in it. "Blake
touches me, and you all run."

Over and over, I got on the ground, Head–to–Head. The whistle
blew. I was up and fighting. Again. Whistle. Scramble up. Fighting.
Again. Again. Again. Sometimes I reached the coach. Then he
stared backing up and trying to duck my tag. More than once he
grabbed me as I tagged him and threw me to the ground, yelling
at the offensive lineman, "Why didn't you cut him down?" And so
the game stretched. After getting past my man one time, I shoved
the coach instead of tagging him. Mason responded by adding
two offensive linemen to pound on me. Next time I got to him, I

tagged him hard again, and he threw me to the ground and kicked me in the ass before I got up. He wore me down. Then Coach called over the rest of the team, backs and receivers, to watch, and it continued. He kept me going, a twelfth time, a fifteenth. I could hardly stand up. When the whistle blew, the guys were blasting me before I could get off my knees. After one tough double team, I got up slowly and Mason yelled at the team:

"We need a middle linebacker who has endurance, who can get past the block, who can get into the backfield and stop a play. Where is my middle linebacker?"

"I'm right here." I said and not very loudly, standing as tall as I could.

"What?" Mason screamed. "I don't see anyone stepping up to lead my defense. I don't hear a leader. Where the hell is my middle linebacker?"

"Here!" I said before all my teammates.

"Blake? You? The way you played yesterday, you pussy, you better get a lot tougher. And fast." He spat on the ground in front of me. "You see these guys? They count on you to fill the hole and make the tackle. If you're not up to it, just say so right now, and I'll find someone who is."

Fuck you, was all I thought. Fuck you. I hated Mason. I wanted to take off my helmet and hammer him with it, wanted to quit. But I couldn't.

Blakes played football.

*

One Saturday, near the end of my uneven ninth-grade season with Coach Mason, the season of my discontent, our team traveled an hour south to Perry Meridian for a game. I'd been told my parents would miss the game, but as I returned from the coin toss as one of the captains, there my father stood near the bench in a yellow golf jacket and a navy blue cap. At the sight of him and his odd expression, I thought something had happened. Perhaps my mother, or brother, had been in an accident. I hesitated when he called me over because we were about ready for the kick-off. But I ran to him.

He seemed to vibrate with a nervous, violent energy. "You go out there and hit some people today. Hit them so hard they think about you every time they step on the field. I mean it!"

"Okay, right." I tried to sound like he'd fired me up and sprinted to join my teammates, but he was more of a distraction. I wondered why he seemed so agitated and angry. Had I done something wrong?

From the first set of downs, he paced the sidelines barking at me to "Get in there and hit somebody!!" His hands on his hips, his arms cocked at his sides clenching fists, lighting a cigarette and throwing it down half-smoked in disgust. He wouldn't stop.

On the sidelines my teammates said, "Man, what's with your dad?" and "Bet you don't want to go home tonight."

I couldn't figure out what I'd done to cause him to rage up and down the sidelines. I saw him do this to my brother once from the stands during a basketball game, but when Mom arrived late, she'd made him leave the gym before the game was over.

Where was she now?

On offense I played guard, and we pushed down the field near the goal line. When I went to the line of scrimmage, I looked up and saw him in the end zone screaming at me. All I could see was his dark mouth. I couldn't hear him. I couldn't remember the play or the snap count. I couldn't hear our quarterback.

The harder I tried to play, the less it seemed to satisfy my father.

Late in the game, Perry Meridian came with a reverse and I read it. I read it as well as Butkus or Singletary of the Chicago Bears ever read a play in their lives. Slashing through a hole off tackle, I met the ball carrier in the backfield with everything I had, and I felt a moment's hesitation before his leg gave with a snap under my shoulder.

His scream was chilling. He writhed on the ground beneath me, mindless as a dog hit by a car. His hands tore up bits of grass, his good leg kicking, kicking, his helmet rolling to the side and grinding into the turf as he howled. Over the sound of my teammates' congratulations for such a tackle, slapping my shoulder pads, I heard Dad bellow from the sidelines. "That's it! That's the kind of hit I want to see on every play." While I called the defense into a huddle, I couldn't help but watch the Perry Meridian trainer wrap an air cast around the shattered leg and pump it up to the kid's screams. Then they lifted him onto a stretcher, and carried him to an ambulance. That kid would never forget that hit. Neither would I.

But it wasn't enough. My father continued to scream from the sidelines.

We won the game going away, but I felt as though we'd lost. Jogging from the field, I saw my father waiting near the bus with his hands on his hips. Keeping my helmet on, I crowded into the middle of my teammates. But he saw me and barked my name. I stopped in the flow of freshmen boys celebrating a victory and went to him.

He grabbed my facemask and pulled me in tight where I felt the warmth of his smoky breath. I also felt the eyes of my teammates on the bus. "I've seen about all I can take of your candy-assed play," Dad snarled. His eyes flashed from one of my eyes to the other, back and forth. He gnawed his lips like a madman. When he let go of my facemask and grabbed my jersey, I wanted to run but, I knew better and there was no place to go. I had to face him. He snatched up my facemask again. "Do you want to be a football player or not?" He jerked my head in the helmet and twisted my neck. "Huh?" I'd heard the last of my teammates' cleats mount the steps. They were on the bus, watching out the windows. I felt their eyes on me, the coaches' too.

"Walt?" I heard Coach Mason say gently. "I need my team on the bus."

Dad let go for a second, then snatched my facemask again, yanking my head close. I smelled the tobacco. "Look at me when I'm talking to you!" he said. My eyes returned to his, but they looked so strange, glassy and small, shifting. It was hard to face him. "I asked you a question!" I couldn't remember the question.

He jerked my head by the facemask and let go. I would cry if I answered. So I would not answer. "You had two good hits the whole goddamn game. You better get tougher in a hurry. I won't have it."

"Walt?" Coach Mason said to my father. "Time for us to go."

"I'm taking him back," Dad said without looking up.

"School regulations, Walt. We have to take all of the boys back to the school."

"Okay, Coach," my father said. Then he whispered in a growl to me, "Just wait till we get home."

I climbed the steps of the bus and Coach Mason clapped me on the shoulder, "Good game, son." Don't talk to me. Don't touch me, I thought. The guys quietly studied my face. Near the back of the bus my friend, Tim Parker, had saved me a seat and waved me back. After I sat with him, my two other best friends came back. Brian Jackson switched with the kid across the aisle from me, and Mike Lattamore swapped seats with the guy behind me. When the bus rumbled out of the parking lot, the team took up the familiar, happy, post-victory chatter. But I kept my helmet on, my head down. Tim's hand rested on my kneepad. I felt Mike's hand grip the back collar of my shoulder pads. And Brian sat sideways in the aisle, elbows on knees, his head bent close to mine.

The four of us rode in silence.

These three guys loved my old man. Tim's father taught high school biology and was the basketball coach. Brian's father taught high school history and was a football and track coach. Mike's father chaired the sociology department for Indiana University's Indianapolis branch. But mine could fix smashed-up cars in his garage, making them look good as new–almost. Sometimes he worked out there until three in the morning. Years ago, he had driven the bus route from Indianapolis to Chicago to St. Louis and back. He'd been a boxer. He'd gotten in street fights and had job offers from the mob for strong-arm work. In his school days, among many other exploits he shared with my friends, he'd gotten in trouble for setting a raccoon free in the principal's office. Endless stories of wildness and near-tragic experiences about growing up on the farm. The stories thrilled my friends when they visited my house. Beyond the vivid tales, my father directed us to all the illegal swimming holes in the old gravel pits in the area; told us how to get out of a speeding ticket; and warned of clingy girlfriends. During his stories, which kept my friends laughing, and which they recounted at school for our classmates, I felt an uneasy blend of pride and horror.

But my friends had never seen this side of my father, had never imagined it, so their silence was probably as much for themselves in witness of a fallen hero, as it was in support of me.

Halfway home, the bus stopped at a farm stand. The coach wanted to buy apples and cider for the team. Everyone got off but the four of us. Coach Mason got on and ordered my three friends off. Then he came back to me.

"You played a good game, Blake."

I shook my helmet. What would my brother say if he'd seen the game? Walter's evaluation I could trust. I wanted to believe my coach. Had I missed tackles I couldn't remember missing? I hadn't cost us the game.

"Your dad was wrong. You did fine. I'd tell you if you didn't, you know." Yeah, he would. "Come on out and have some apples and cider."

I shook my head again. I wanted to, but I couldn't face the guys.

"Okay, I'll have Brian bring you something. But, Jason, hey," I looked up at him. I couldn't remember Coach Mason ever calling me Jason. "I want you to stop by my office to get my home phone number before you leave. If there's ever a problem, you just call me. I've got a comfortable couch with your name on it. Okay?" He tapped me on the shoulder pad. "One more thing, Jason, your dad was wrong. I'm the coach, and I'm telling you, you had a good game today. You got it?"

I nodded with a shrug. I decided to believe him. But it didn't make me feel much better. Because what did it say about my father? Why had he acted like that?

A Broken Year

Sophomore year, the football coaches, who all remembered my brother, held high expectations. I didn't get the middle linebacker job for the junior varsity squad. It went to a junior who played backup on the varsity. They moved me to defensive end. Until I broke my left arm in practice three days before the season began.

For eight weeks the plaster cast kept my arm at a ninety-degree angle. After a summer of weightlifting, I helplessly watched the muscles of my arm atrophy as the top of the cast grew slack. I avoided friends and scorned anyone who wanted to sign my white plaster. At football practice, I sulked up and down the sidelines in street clothes, feeling forgotten. Or I dressed in sweats and ran laps and stairs, more in an attempt to impress coaches than with dedication to my conditioning. If I'd broken my arm in a game, at least I would have established myself as a player, but now I felt like a nobody.

Bored with watching practices and games, unwilling to help the managers carry equipment for fear of being seen as a manager, I felt my frustration and anger mounting. In the past, football was the outlet for my anger. Now it was gone. One day, while my teammates practiced on the field, my rage broke loose and I repeatedly smashed my cast against a locker room wall until the plaster softened to a pulp the length of my forearm. The doctor replaced it with a heavier cast. Another day, after practice, I discovered Terry, a third-string player, a mild-mannered and likable guy, had swapped his helmet for mine. I attacked him for it, slamming him against a locker and shoving him to the floor before my friends dragged me out of the locker room. My friends, my team-mates, shoved me into the hall and told me to stay out of the team locker room.

The next day I wanted to apologize to Terry, but every time I saw him, he ducked off in the other direction. When people heard I was looking for him, they warned Terry I was hunting him down. It took me three days to corner him and properly apologize.

When the cast finally came off, I got back on the football field for the last two games, but my rage split the seams, and I was thrown out of both games for fighting. The season, the whole year, was shot as far as I was concerned.

I had identified myself as a football player the way a physician identifies himself as a doctor. Without football, who was I? What was I worth to my school, to my friends, my family, myself? When I broke my arm, I lost more than my spot on the team, I lost my sense of place, my sense of self. Feeling the pull of my father, I gravitated toward a world of rough-neck, boisterous, macho pos-turing and hallway scuffles. My grades, never too important to me anyway, slipped, and I didn't care. I ached for my place in this high school with nearly 2,800 students, almost 800 in my class, six times larger than when my parents had attended in the old brick build-ing across the street, nearly twice as big as when Walter walked these halls six years earlier.

*

The week after the football season ended we cleared out our lockers. I tried to feel like one of the guys, like part of the team, but I wasn't. None of them regarded me the same. Then the varsity head coach called me into his office.

"Blake, I'm moving you to offensive guard next year." I started to object, because I'd always played defense better than offense. But he didn't want to hear it. "It's decided. You'll still have to earn a starting spot, no guarantees, so hit the weights and bulk up. Study the position and get better at it. Your job is to protect the quarterback and running backs."

Over time this idea of protector set in for me. Something about it felt right. I came to see it was my place. I could be good at it.

*

The bright spot of my fall semester without football had been speech class. I had dreaded it, but to my surprise found I liked it. My speech teacher, Mr. Goodenough, who was also head of the theater department, saw potential in my entertaining speeches and took an interest. He'd never even heard of my brother or parents. His interest in me was about me. In several ways he reminded me of my father: a big, energetic, and loud man, quick to joke and laugh. Mr. Goodenough was passionate about literature and theater–openly passionate about it–reciting lines from favorite plays and poems. In speech class he challenged me, dismissing good when I could do better (Some kids nicknamed him "Never" for it's Never Goodenough), and he suggested I start doing homework again for my other classes. Most teachers grew frustrated by my milder imitations of my father, but Mr. Goodenough seemed to enjoy my pranks and tried to redirect my energy.

Because the school district continued to expand, half a dozen portable classrooms were lined up outside the gym to manage the overflow. Mr. Goodenough took one for his noisy speech and theater classes.

One day during demonstration speeches, I sat at the back of the room next to Mr. Goodenough. Before class, I'd put my wrist watch in my pocket, anticipating that he might ask me to time the speeches. When he did, I said I'd forgotten my watch and asked to use his. He gave it to me and after a few speeches, I set his watch forward ten minutes. Then, when he stepped outside to help a student get props for her speech, I climbed up on a desk and set the classroom clock forward ten minutes. Quickly and quietly, I got everyone in the room wearing a watch to advance the minute hand. Even Shelly Gardner complied.

As the clock on the wall said class was nearly over, Mr. Goodenough said, "Is it really that late? I'd planned to do another speech."

He shook his head. "Shelly?" he said–Shelly, sweet Shelly, trust-
worthy Shelly–"what time do you have?"

She looked at her watch and read the time, same as the clock
on the wall, and I loved her for it. "Okay," he said, "we'll have to do
the rest tomorrow."

After a couple of minutes, I said, "Mr. Goodenough, the bell
must not be working. It's time to go." He looked at the clock,
checked his watch which I'd given back, and let us go. We ran
into the school like a bunch of third graders heading for recess. A
couple of goofballs caused a ruckus in the hall and were caught
by an assistant principal, the one whose ties were all variations on
the school colors: maroon and gray. Instead of turning me in, as
they should have, the goofballs gave up Goodenough.

The following morning, a girl who worked in the office said she
saw the assistant principal and principal "yelling" at Mr. Goodenough. I imagined the administrators going nuts over twenty-five
kids wandering the halls for ten minutes as if it lay a foundation for
school-wide anarchy. I felt bad about getting my favorite teacher
in trouble. When I went to class, I was ready to admit what I'd
done, willing to accept his wrath.

Instead, "Welcome back, my prodigal pranksters," he said. I expected this performance to turn dark, as it might with my father,
but it didn't. "Those ten minutes didn't change the world much,"
he joked, looking right at me. "But if it happens again, I assure you
the world will change."

I stayed after class to confess. But he knew I was responsible. I
apologized anyway, and he laughed and said it was a pretty good
joke.

When time came to choose schedules for the coming year,
Goodenough told me to take his acting class. "No way," I said.

"Oh, yeah, you're going to take it, and you're going to love it."

"No I'm not." Football players did not do drama. We did drafting, small-engine repair, and Zoology.

At least a couple of times a week after he started in on me,
Goodenough pressured me to sign up for his drama class.

"Why do you want me to do this?" I asked.

"Because you'll be good at it, and it will be good for you. I've seen you in speech class all year. You have what it takes. Trust me."

When I told Walter how Goodenough nagged me to sign up for his acting class, he all but forced me to sign up for it. With both of them on my case, I caved.

Like my brother, Mr. Goodenough pushed me. He even yelled at me on occasion, but it was always clear he did it to improve me. He made me memorize passages of Shakespeare's *Othello* and recite the lines ten different ways to appreciate the richness of the language and to understand the art of an actor. Shakespeare's language sucked me in. I read the whole play, checked recordings out of the library and listened to variations from great actors. In the violent, powerful character of Othello, a great warrior and leader, tragically tormented and undermined by his flaw of jealously–I saw myself. Strength and weakness. Courage and fear. Love and hate. I too felt tormented–not from jealously–but for being emotionally hyper–sensitive in some respects while living to fulfill my father's expectations of the rugged football player.

Walter Returns

At the end of my sophomore year, I was sixteen and Dad helped me get my first, formal summer job with the school system painting classrooms. Walter returned from his junior year at Indiana University for the summer. He came home every few weeks during the year, but now my cool college brother was home for summer. Though he still encouraged my love of sports, Walter also began to share his new-found love of learning. After hating the dogma of an art instructor, he rejected formal art study and became an English and philosophy major.

On his first Sunday back for summer, he and I sat in our room the entire day and listened to every album the Beatles ever made. He talked about and explained the poetry of the lyrics.

During the *White Album*, when "Mother Nature's Son" came on, Walter said, "This song always reminds me of you and how much you love the outdoors." Then he turned it up and sang along, "Born a poor young country boy, Mother Nature's Son. . . ." From then on, every time I heard that song, I thought of how it made my brother think of me.

I did love nature, and my love of it led me to fishing and hunting. Mr. Garner, one of the local farmers I worked for baling hay and doing odd jobs was an outdoorsman, and he introduced me to hunting. He loaned me my first shotgun, an old, single-shot 20-gauge, and taught me gun safety and shooting skills. Mr. Garner also gave me a seven-year stack of *Field & Stream* magazines, which I read cover to cover. He taught me to deer hunt, and I loved my time in the woods, but I never shot a deer because I never got a clear enough look. I preferred bird hunting for quail and pheasant. I trudged along fencerows, my attention drifting off to daydreams and thoughts of nature, only to be shattered by a covey of quail exploding from underfoot. Mother Nature's Son.

To make money for college, Walter painted houses. On weekends, when I wasn't working at one of the local farms, he hired me to help, mostly to scrape peeling paint and to sand. He'd hand me a scraper and say, "Get after it monkeyboy!" And up the ladder I'd go. He paid me what then seemed a vast sum of five dollars an hour, fifty bucks for a ten-hour day. It was more than the school system paid or local farmers paid me for baling hay, clearing brush, or repairing fences. I loved working alongside Walter.

Then, one night Walter came home the day after I'd actually been trusted with a paint brush, and found me in our bedroom reading *Field & Stream.* "You owe me fifty bucks," he snapped. I saw his jaw muscles flexing and the anger in his blue eyes. I sat up. "When I got to work this morning, Mrs. Shivers showed me where you slopped paint all over the brick next to a window."

"I did?"

"Damn right. I wasted almost two goddamn hours sanding it off thanks to you."

I was stunned. How could I do that and not even remember? How could I miss it? I would have cleaned it off. "I'm sorry. I didn't see it."

"You're paying for it. Give me back what I paid you yesterday."

Rolling to the edge of the bed, I reached underneath for my cookie-tin bank among the dust bunnies. I pulled the lid off and handed him five ten-dollar bills, unable to meet his eye for letting him down after he'd trusted me. To relieve my guilt, I would have given him two days' pay, but I wanted the money. For the rest of the summer, I worked only one more Saturday with Walter, ten hours with a scraper in my hand.

*

Walter graduated from IU in May of 1990 and promptly married Missy, his high school sweetheart. I was his best man. Never one for tradition, my brother rejected tuxes. Instead he had my mother make light-blue, puffy-sleeve pullover shirts with huge collars and a yoke neck, a 1970's style which made us look like swashbucklers. The groomsmen joked that they wanted swords. He also wanted no church and no mention of God in the ceremony, but Missy's parents, devoted Catholics, prevailed on that point. Still, Walter did manage to find a radical priest instead of her family's standard.

My brother planned to become an Indianapolis fireman, working three days around-the-clock duty at the fire station, so he could paint and write poetry during his four days off. A bright guy and a good athlete, Walter topped the physical and written tests for fireman candidates. But between affirmative action and preferences for veterans, he didn't get a position. He was furious. "Just because these guys are black or killed people in a war, they get the job. To hell with hiring the best candidate. To hell with public safety!"

It took him years to get over it–if then.

Instead of putting out fires, my brother found a job as a graphic designer and writer for the publications office in an Indianapolis bank. Almost instantly, the bank recognized his talents and gave him more responsibility.

*

Throughout the football season my junior year, Walter pressured me to break up with Nancy, a girl I'd dated for nearly a year. "You're wasting your best high school years dating one girl, man. Don't blow this chance," he said. "If you don't start dating around, I guarantee you'll regret it."

Like you? I wanted to say, but held my tongue.

He assured me it wasn't about Nancy, that he liked her. It was for my own good–I had to get out there and play the field. As I considered my brother's recommendations, I wondered why dating his wife Missy through high school and college was okay for him, but not for me. Still, his coaching did help me note other girls and opportunities. Yet I didn't want to hurt Nancy, and I was afraid to leave the security she offered.

Eventually, Walter convinced me, and I tried to break up at the end of the football season. She wouldn't let me. Don't be weak, be a man, I told myself. Before Christmas, I called it off. Absolutely no turning back. The night I made it clear was tough. Nancy knelt on the floor while I sat on the sofa. She hugged my knees and sobbed, my jeans wet with her tears as she begged me not to break it off. Even as I hurt her, I loved her, and it tore me up.

In one of those great stupidities of youth, I decided being cruel would make it easier for her to get over the break-up. If I spoke to her at all in the following weeks, my words were curt, my tone harsh. But for the most part, I ignored her over the next months, even when she spoke to me. If she phoned, I told her I didn't want to talk to her and told her not to call me. Honestly, I was afraid I'd confess how much I missed her and go back.

Although I maintained the front of ignoring Nancy and pursued other girls, I noticed her growing thinner. And she was already thin. Then she vanished from school, and one of her friends approached me in the hall and said, "You've put her in the hospital. I hope you're happy, you asshole."

"What?" I said. But the girl ran away from me into the girls' restroom. What was this about the hospital? I asked another friend of hers, but she wouldn't talk to me. Hell with it, I walked into the girls' restroom and told her to come out and talk to me.

"You put her in the hospital, you son-of-a-bitch," the girl said shoving me.

"I haven't even talked to her for two months," I responded, stepping aside to let a couple of girls leave the restroom.

"Exactly, you big idiot," she shouted at me. "How could you do that to her?"

About then, a woman teacher came into the restroom and ordered me out, threatening detentions, and I left.

I was confused. I didn't know what had happened or comprehend how I had caused it. I stopped at Nancy's house on the way home to find out. When her mother came to the door, I asked if Nancy was there. She said Nancy was resting. When I asked what happened, her mother leveled a look at me and said she didn't want me stopping by the house again or talking to Nancy. No calls. No visits. They were going on a vacation to Florida, and Nancy would be fine after some rest. But she didn't want me seeing Nancy when they got back either.

A month later I heard Nancy's parents had moved her to St. Mary's. I felt terrible and had to see her, had to find out if she was okay. I had to tell her how sorry I was, that I hadn't meant to hurt her, and that I loved her, still loved her. But I was ready to break and move on, so I didn't want to confuse her.

Though I didn't know what I'd say exactly, I skipped a play rehearsal on a beautiful spring afternoon and went to St. Mary's to find her after school. I waited in the parking lot and ran over to her when I saw her. "Nancy, Nancy," I called as I ran. She looked thin but beautiful.

"What do you want?" she asked, her look, her tone stopping me cold.

"I just wanted to see if you're okay."

"Like you care," she said.

This chill and anger was not the quiet and gentle Nancy I knew.

"I'm sorry. I never meant to hurt you."

"Yes you did. You, Jason Blake, are a bully. You liked hurting me. And you did hurt me. So congratulations to you. But never again." Her anger, her words put me on my heels.

"I'm sorry," I said quickly. "I loved you, and I still care about you."

"You didn't love me. People who love don't act like that. You, Jason, are fucked up. You are a fucked up person." I'd never heard her use the word 'fuck,' and it hit me like a roundhouse to the ear.

Her eyes narrowed at me: "I loved you—that was a mistake. You were not worth it. You are not worth this conversation. I am over you. I'm done with you. Never come here again. Do not call me. Do not ask my friends or sisters about me. Do not bother my parents. I wish I'd never met you, Jason Blake." With that, she turned and strode away.

I was stunned. I watched her get in her car and drive out of sight. Nancy never so much as glanced back. I felt like crap. Part of me blamed Walter for my pain and Nancy's and her friends' and her mother's. It was his fault.

But no, it was mine, and I knew it.

She was right, I'd been a bully.

And I hated bullies.

Becoming Christian

After the school play, and after the school year, and after Nancy stomped on my heart in the parking lot of St. Mary's School, my football coach offered me a free trip to the Fellowship of Christian Athletes camp in Black Mountain, North Carolina. And I jumped at it, more for a free trip to a sports camp than from a desire to learn more about Christian life.

Mom had taken Walter and me to church when we were young, until Walter argued well enough and hard enough to stay in bed and watch football on TV. I continued going with her for a few more years, until I could talk my way out of it. But church never took for her sons, and eventually Mom gave up.

During my junior year of high school, several friends became Christians through Young Life, most notably Brian Jackson and Tom Clinton (as well as some interesting girls–Nancy had been a regular too). So I looked into it and listened to their talk of the Christian life. With skepticism, I attended some of their gatherings, and while I found them fun, they didn't move me.

Walter, a professed atheist, objected to my spiritual search. He described how he'd gone to a meeting of "Jesus freaks" when he was in college. "They spent as much time praying for a guy's hangnail as they did for a girl's father dying of cancer. Can you believe that? Shows you how warped those people are. You don't want to hang around people like that, do you? Christians are idiots."

His episode didn't jibe with anything I'd observed at Young Life. Nor did I believe Christians, or any other group of people could be summed up by one stupid experience.

If anything, Walter's disapproval of Christianity fueled my desire to discover something to believe in. I saw bad kids changed by faith and saw pained ones find peace in it. Besides, as much as I was looking for something to believe in, I was looking for a way to differentiate myself from my brother (and my father), to be seen as Jason Blake at my school, and not just another Blake. After my treatment of Nancy and her putting a fine point on it, I also longed for a way to relieve my guilt and redeem myself to myself.

*

As soon my teammate Ty and I pulled into the parking lot in North Carolina, we were met with a force of determination. While Young Life's playful approach soft-sold Christianity, the Fellowship of Christian Athletes, or FCA, was all about conversion, man. We played hard and prayed hard.

Professional athletes from every league came and spoke to us kids, witnessing how they'd asked Jesus Christ to be their personal lord and savior. They spoke of how faith had changed their lives. How they'd found their way. How they'd discovered inner strength and courage and power and peace.

I wanted all of those things too.

And they asked each of us to cross the bridge and join them in the faith.

The counselors were college athletes who spent time with each kid, talking about faith and discussing the Bible and encouraging us to ask forgiveness and take Jesus, the redeemer, as our savior. For me the quiet time, above all else, moved me. I always sat on the same hill with a long view out over the Blue Ridge Mountains. It was stunning to see so many young men silent, not a sound on campus during two forty-five minute quiet times, and hardly any movement. I looked at blades of grass, at trees around me, out across the Blue Ridge Mountains. Patterns in nature had always interested me: the grain in wood related to the design of bird feathers (individually and collectively) or to the lay of fur on a deer and even to the ripples of a river, the pattern of soil erosion, and the sedimentary layers in limestone. Sitting on the hillside seeing the repetition up close and in the distance–large and small–I could imagine, could feel, a single creator designing the world after a series of patterns, a direction given to land and air and water and life that united them, united them under one God.

By the end of the week, I was sold, converted.

*

"You gotta be kidding," Walter said when I told him. "Tell me this is just a silly summer lark."

I assured him it wasn't.

"So you're joining the people who want some preacher or some Bible-rule telling them how to live?"

I didn't know what to say. "No. That's not it," I finally said. "I want to be part of a community." I wanted to add, "a community of love," and I wanted to feel forgiven, but I feared he'd mock me. "I want to believe in something larger than myself."

He walked away saying: "I thought you were stronger."

When I told Dad, we were on our way to Zoreman's Salvage Yard to pick parts for a car rebuild, and he did the kind of scoffing laugh he reserved for nitwit lawyers, doctors and professors–"Some guys think they know everything because they know a lot about a thimble-full." But he didn't say anything for a few breaths. Then, "Yeah, your mom told me."

"What do you think?" I asked.

He kept his eyes on the road. "I think your mom seems happy about it."

"And you?"

Now he clicked off the radio. We were quiet for a few beats, listening to the humming tires of his four-wheel drive pickup. Then he spoke: "I wonder if you'll be happy about it." After another beat or two, he added: "But what I think doesn't matter. It's your life, and you can live it up or screw it up however you want."

We rode in silence for a few miles. "But I don't want to hear a lot of Jesus talk."

And the radio went back on.

I didn't care what Big Walt or Walter thought. I wanted to be a man who believed in something. I wanted to be different.

*

Yet doubts swirled. My Christian friends called me Thomas, for Doubting Thomas, because of my endless questions and doubts. Dogged by it, I constantly challenged the Bible, as well as the faith of my friends and the leaders. Often I heard:

"Some things you have to accept on faith. It takes a leap of faith."

"Why can't you just accept it?"

"It's in the Bible, man. It's the Word of God, Jason."

"If you really believe, why do you question everything?"

"Man can't know the answers to everything. We can't hope to understand the ways of God."

The more firm my friends and religious leaders were, the more I doubted them and their conviction. It all seemed way more complex than they tried to make it.

I rode the swing of faith out over the abyss, but I couldn't quite let go of the rope and fly out into the unknown.

*

In the fall, I was named captain of our school's Fellowship of Christian Athletes chapter, and on Columbus Day weekend, six of us were taking a Greyhound bus to Chicago for an FCA regional meeting. I went down to the Greyhound station early to make sure our reserved tickets were in place. The driver heard me getting the tickets and he kept looking at me. "You say Blake? Not related to Walt Blake are you?"

"That's my dad. I'm Jason Blake."

"Yeah, you look like Big Walt. Used to drive with your old man, long time ago."

"Really?" I said, "I've heard a lot of stories, but I never met anyone who drove with him."

"Yeah, we used to meet in Chicago and go to the fight clubs. I never boxed but your dad was pretty good, more mean than good really. Walt was tough."

"Until he got beat up and quit," I said.

"You mean until he got kicked out." He read the question in my face. "That guy that beat your dad once, about a month later, your daddy got back in the ring with that big black dude and knocked him down and kept hitting him while he was on the canvas. Broke the guy's jaw. After the fight, they found your dad had a roll of nickels taped in each hand. The Midwest Boxing Federation suspended him for life."

"You mean he cheated?" I said. I was shocked.

"Well, that kind of stuff happened all the time in them fight clubs, but that dude was tuning up for some big pro fight, so the bastards made an example of your dad."

"But he did cheat, right?"

The old driver could see what he'd said now, "Well, strictly speaking, yeah, I suppose you could say that." He paused, "But he was tough, your daddy was. Good guy too. Just wouldn't want to be on his bad side, that's all."

Yeah, don't get on his bad side, I thought.

The Last Big Game

My senior year of football, Lawrence Central rolled through the first six games with an average winning margin of 36 points, and it could have been higher. Our coach refused to score after we got 50 points ahead. In one game it was 56-0 at half time. The last six points came on a defensive interception. My father and brother, Walt and Walter side by side, attended every game. My mother went to a few home games.

For the seventh game, we headed to a clash with our arch rival Carmel High School. Coming into the game, we were ranked number two, Carmel number one.

If we were the best team ever from Lawrence Central and the best team in the state, we'd have to prove it now.

The year before, the Carmel game on our field had set an Indiana record for attendance, nearly 20,000. The game had matched our All-American, Notre Dame-bound Ty Davidson (my FCA buddy) against their All-American quarterback who later played at Purdue and in the NFL. Carmel took that game 50-43 in the last minute. After they executed a successful onside kick that bounded over my head.

Then they went on to win the state title while we watched from home.

And we hated them for it.

We also hated them because we saw them as the rich kids. While our community spanned families–from those who lived in old mobile homes or houses with dirt floors to those who lived in mansions–Carmel was more uniformly affluent.

So in my senior year, we were hungry for Carmel: number one against number two, payback time. The Indianapolis newspapers and TV crews covered the matchup the entire week before the big game.

Because of an expansion project at Carmel, our fans were asked to ride fan buses to the game. One game night, our team bus with a Lawrence Police escort led the way. Twenty-six, fully loaded fan buses followed. We players couldn't believe how long the line of yellow buses stretched behind us.

Both school bands pounded away in the stands. The field was in a hollow, so as the bleachers overflowed, and people blanketed the hills around the field. It was a thrill to be there, to be at the center of it.

Carmel was tough. Well-coached. Big, strong kids. But we were winning the battle. No one wanted this win more than Tim Parker, and we kept running him to my side over and over. In the first half, he gained over 100 yards. Near the end of the first half we led 21 to 10, and we marched down field, pounding it inside. We drove to the five-yard line.

Then, on a pass play, they blitzed two linebackers and smashed our quarterback, bruising Ridley's shoulder so he had to leave the game. Two plays later, on third down, Carmel ran a stunt, causing me to miss my block as Tim Parker tried to round the corner. Three of their players made a spectacular gang-tackle and broke Tim's ribs. It ended his season. We went for it on fourth down, last play of the half, and Carmel held, stopping Tim's brother Tom Parker as he dove for the end zone.

That shifted the momentum. We lost two key players, and they made a critical goal-line stand. They came out for the second half like wild horses, and we came out flat. We couldn't move the ball.

As our offense faltered, under the second-string QB the defense slaked as well. Their QB picked our secondary apart, and their larger linemen wore down our team. They whipped us in the second half. For the second year in a row, they killed our shot at a state title.

We lost to a better team, better coached, better players—the future repeat state champs—but we couldn't see it then. It just hurt like hell. The long trail of buses was a painful reminder we had let down our town, not just our teammates and school.

When the team bus pulled into the parking lot, coach held us on the bus while the fan busses emptied. "Hold your seats a minute, men," he said, "and you are men. You played like men tonight. I couldn't be more proud of how hard you played. You showed real courage and never quit. You didn't win the game, but in my eyes, you're winners." He lifted his hat and rubbed his bald head. "In my opinion, there's only one team in all of Indiana that could beat you, and that was the team we played tonight. And they needed every blade of grass their home-field advantage gave them."

By the time he opened the doors, our fans had lined the path to the school clapping for their fallen team. I pressed through and jogged to the gym. I loved them for clapping for us, for calling out: "Good game, boys," through their disappointment. But I couldn't stand my own disappointment and had to get out of there. Usually one of the last guys to leave the locker-room, that night, I was among the first.

Tim Parker had been injured coming to my side. Since sixth grade, I'd opened holes for him, chased him down the field trying to get another block, and celebrated with him in the end zone. My man was among the three that clobbered him. I was close—still trying to shield him. When he didn't take my hand to help him up, I was shaken. When the trainer helped him to the sidelines, I felt guilty. And when we got home, and they had to help him off the bus, I was ashamed. Not only did it end his season, we never played another snap together.

We lost a second time to Ben Davis on a fluke call. Tom Parker took the hand-off and followed me. I sealed the linebacker and Tom blew past me, romping into the defensive backfield—I was right behind him—one player to beat. Tom tried to hurdle the tackler, but the defender hit his feet. Tom turned a full flip and landed on his feet in a squat position. He sprang forward and raced for the winning touchdown. But the referee, no doubt to protect Tom, had blown the whistle. The play was ruled dead. It cost us the game and the county championship.

Funny how the losses linger more than the wins. We ended with eight wins and two losses. The same record my brother had in his senior year and my father in his. But Walter's team had won the county championship. Though he freely admitted my team was better than his, it left a bitter taste in my mouth. And I didn't make the All-County Team as he had.

I was a good high school football player on one of the best teams in Indiana, but my growth had stalled at six feet, and I was not bound for glory at a division-one college. When a few small colleges offered me scholarships, six years after they had for my brother, I passed too. If it disappointed my father, I never heard about it because, like my brother, I was smart enough to tell Mom first.

*

After football season, I took to the stage in Mr. Goodenough's winter and spring plays, and it didn't take long to discover girls liked the curiosity of a poetry-reciting football player. And I wasn't afraid to arrive at high school parties wearing my letter jacket and, completely out of context, rage a few lines from *Othello*.

Starting College

Walter and I finished playing pickup basketball at Fort Benjamin Harrison on a November Saturday afternoon. There were always good players there, and we walked back to the car feeling spent.

"Hey, we need to talk," Walter said. I looked at him and waited. "About college. You're not thinking of playing football are you?"

"I thought it would be fun, but–"

Walter jumped on it. "Jason, you need to leave that behind. It's time for you to grow up and dedicate yourself to learning–"

"Hey, wait a second," I said. "You didn't let me finish. What I started to say was I thought it would be fun, but I'm not interested in the few schools that are interested in me. Besides, I decided to join the Army. I can always go to college on the GI Bill later–"

"What!!??" Walter screamed.

I was already laughing. "Yes, I'm going to college, and no, not to play football. I know I need to hit the books. It's time."

"Good. It would kill Mom if you didn't go," Walter said. "Yeah, it's time to hit the books as hard as you hit the linebackers this fall. Where do you want to go and what do you want to study?"

I wasn't a hundred-percent sure. For several years when I loved hunting and fishing, I thought I'd study forestry at Purdue and go out west to work in the National Parks System or something. But now my interest in theater and literature had taken over. I knew I could only afford a state school, so I was leaning toward IU or maybe Ball State.

"Theater? English? That seems to be your big interest these

days," he said. "So IU is the best school in the state for that, one of the best in the country."

"Yeah, I was thinking about Indiana. Maybe Ball State," I said.

"Apply to Ball State for a back up, I guess, but why bother if you could choose IU?"

His tone made it sound so stupid to even consider the smaller university. And IU has the beautiful campus, the reputation.... So in the end I only applied to IU.

In the fall of 1992, I headed for Bloomington, Indiana. I was ready to go, ready for a new adventure, ready to shed my skin and meet new people. Despite the university's being the largest in my home state, none of my close friends went there. Under Walter's direction, I had applied for and been accepted to the academic dorm, the Collins Living Learning Center. My brother also went with me for freshman orientation, and once again took on the role of coach, encouraging me to schedule his favorite classes as well as ones he wished he'd taken. And I appreciated the help.

As I finished packing, Mom came into my room. She sat on my bed and said, "For the first time in a long time you don't have any football or any job taking up your time. So your real job now is to focus on your school work. You study, and read, and think. It's time to learn."

When she got up and put her hand on my back, I knew to stop what I was doing and turn to her. Her eyes were glassy, and I gave her a big hug. She squeezed me back hard, like she always did.

"I'm so proud of you, Jason," she whispered.

Part of me wanted to ask why, since I hadn't done anything yet, but I knew better. I just kept hugging her and feeling her strong embrace.

*

The next weeks were like nothing I'd ever experienced. The world of books and brilliant classmates threw open windows in my life, and light poured in from every direction: anthropology, geology, biology, literature, history, political science, physics, philosophy. I was gulping from the fire hose.

When Professor Bloomstrom had us read Nabokov's *Invitation to a Beheading*, I was stunned. I didn't know people wrote like that. I had a similar response in theater classes when I read plays and acted scenes from Ionesco, Pinter, and Beckett. Before my cultural anthropology class, I never knew anthropologists studied current sub-cultures–the gangs of New York and LA, the homeless of Seattle.

There was so much to learn. Every day excited me, and I felt changed almost daily. In the first few months I dropped the twenty pounds I'd added for football. I could hardly sleep from the excitement of it all–"the thrill of the new" waiting at every turn.

Part of the new was that I learned about other religions. I saw similarities and differences, observed intolerance between sects who sought a higher spiritual meaning in different ways. This was the final sockdolager for my skeptical faith, and I threw up my hands. Christianity and other faiths were too limited and rigid for me to embrace any one fully. Yet the *possibility* of some higher being or some spiritual dimension beyond life seemed plausible: in nature there seemed to be a spiritual force at work. Spirituality seemed too plausible for me to join the ranks of atheists, and so I shrugged and said, I don't know. For some reason, I couldn't quite give in to my brother entirely, so I continued for a time to defend beliefs I no longer held. Perhaps that was because I respected the faiths of my friends, Christians and Jews as well as Buddhists and Muslims, and I supported them because I saw how their faiths lent them direction and provided a sense of peace.

But more likely, I couldn't give in to my brother because it galled me to have been wrong about myself. That he was right. That I had followed a neatly pruned path, trying not to notice the thicket and thorns all around, and then it had become all too clear to me.

Another bounty of college was the girls. My god, the beautiful girls seemed endless. I managed to date some of them, but most of the relationships lasted no more than a few dates. I guess I was experimenting and learning, just as I was in class.

Then, at the end of my freshman year, I took up with a girl named Diane, a design student at the University of Cincinnati, a classmate of Brian Jackson's. He introduced us. A sexy, spunky and fun-loving blonde–and I fell hard for Diane. A designer and artist, a ballet dancer, she was so different from other girls, certainly way different from my high school girlfriend, Nancy.

Rentless Walter

My brother frequently made the hour-long trip from Indianapolis to Bloomington. We'd take in a ball game on a Saturday afternoon and go to the theater or play basketball that night, and he'd drive back home to Indianapolis late. We debated which was Bloomington's best book store or second best pizza joint (Mother Bear's was a clear pizza winner, we agreed). As we walked through the wooded, pastoral sections of campus on brick sidewalks, passing the limestone buildings, we discussed literature and philosophy. Then he would inevitably ask, "Have you read *Ulysses* yet?"

"No, just *Portrait of the Artist* and *Dubliners*."

"What are you waiting for? You don't know James Joyce until you've read *Ulysses*. And you have to read part of *Finnegan's Wake*. Nobody reads the whole thing, but you have to look at it just to see what Joyce was doing with the language. He might have been as great a genius as Shakespeare."

When our discussion turned to philosophy, I'd soon be in over my head. I had only dabbled in it: a little Nietzsche, Camus, Sartre, Plato, the Transcendentalists, as well as Hobbes, Mills, and Marx.

"Jason, the Transcendentalists!?" He said with his familiar frown of disappointment. "Jesus, Jason, didn't you get past that in high school? You should be reading Whitehead and Wittgenstein."

Walter continued to urge me toward certain classes and professors, delivering advice. Lots of advice. Always my coach, he wanted me to take in everything he had, as well as to plow every field he had missed, the way he'd tried to make me a switch-hitting power hitter and a coming-at-you pitcher in little league baseball.

I had mixed emotions about Walter's coaching. I did thrive under it. But might I not thrive without it? His presence had become a staple in my life, as hard to question as air. From pushing me to date around more–since he'd married his high school sweetheart–to signing up for the *Ulysses* seminar he'd taken years before, he pushed. I resisted *Ulysses* in favor of Chaucer.

*

After two years in the Living Learning Center, I wanted to live in an apartment near campus for my junior and senior years. Walter went to his former landlady, Frances Fieldstone, and lined up his old apartment for me. When he took me over to see the place, Francis shrieked at the sight of him and enveloped him in broad laughter as well as her huge arms, and then, when Walter introduced me, she pressed her soft self into me. "Oh, Jason, it's a sure good to meet you." She stepped back to look at my curly hair, and then at Walter's straight hair, and said, "How'd you'uns end up with such different mops?" Her southern Indiana or Kentucky accent, her country-woman size and manner, the lingering odor of fried food throughout her side of the house, the sagging couch–she was a familiar type. She opened a door in her living room to show me the apartment on the other side. It was a dive, with more cracks in the walls and ceiling than our old rented house on 38th Street, and the stained linoleum floors sloped at ridiculous angles, causing my roommate, Howard Rosen to deem it a skateboarder's paradise. The wafer-thin rug in the kitchen/dining room/living room was a family discard my brother had put there six years before. The range, leveled with bricks under one side, was an old 1950s galley-kitchen model, a skinny little space-saver, which stood alone on a fifteen-foot wall, looking as lonely as an underfed, stray cat. The slump-shouldered relic of a refrigerator had been leveled with two-by-four boards, but not well enough because when you pulled the latch, the door swept open on its own and banged the wall. But the two-bedroom apartment was

two blocks from campus and cost just $220 a month, utilities in-
cluded, furniture too ("Anything you don't want, Honey, just put
out at the curb for the trash," Frances said.)

The apartment was as perfect for me as it had been for Walter.
Howard and I took it.

Escape to the Cape

Once I had the apartment lined up, thoughts turned to summer, and I was keen for an adventure rather than returning to Indianapolis. To be honest, I just couldn't see living around my father again, couldn't imagine a fun summer there. I also still sensed I was following in my family's footsteps–confirmed by my brother's securing his former apartment for me–and I wanted to break free and succeed or fail on my own, out where no one knew me or my family. I had loved New England when I went there with Mike Lattamore and his family on a camping trip out east when I was fourteen. I knew a lot of college students spent summers working on Cape Cod, and it seemed like a fun place. So I set my sights on it. I also figured with all of those summer houses, there had to be jobs for a college kid with some carpentry and house painting experience.

I went home for one night, just enough time to drop my junk, do a couple loads of laundry, and visit with Mom. Nothing but a quick hello with Dad. "Drive careful," was all he said, as he headed out to the garage. In my first two years of college, Dad had never made the 60-mile trip to visit. As Walter and I grew closer during my college years, my father and I experienced a steady distancing. Maybe because he never went to college. When I called home, he was seldom there, and if he was, he never wanted to talk to me, saying hi and quickly passing the phone to Mom. If Walter and I quibbled about the poetry of Wallace Stevens or my recent interest in Spinoza's philosophy of God in nature, we'd quickly change the subject to sports if my father entered the room. But I always felt the weight of his disapproval. I'd quit football. He thought I'd become soft. I was another little prince. When his glances of disdain hit me, it felt like he wanted to follow with a punch. When he lit a cigarette, he looked at me as if daring me to tell him to quit–as I had in junior high. So the thought of going home to live with him seemed impossible. We had become strangers. With a simmering hostility and little in common but a complicated history.

Next morning my father was gone. Mom handed me a bagged lunch and a travel–mug of coffee as I loaded up my tools and tossed in a duffel bag of clothes. I stopped at the bank to empty my vast savings ($295) and headed east.

As I drove alone in my little orange pickup, I thought of my father. At my age he was driving for Greyhound Bus, having adventures of his own in Chicago and St. Louis–drawn to the rough spots, the cheap hotels, taking up boxing. I couldn't imagine that life for myself. At the same time, part of me longed for something like it. He and my mother married young, at age twenty, and Walter had married Missy right out of college. Here I was twenty years old, and I had no prospects of following those role models. And a part of me felt good about that. All the more reason to head out for the tall–and–uncut.

Leaving felt good, especially since I'd just broken off with Diane, the girl I'd dated for about a year, the friend of Brian Jackson's from the University of Cincinnati. Brian studied graphic design and she studied interior design. Rambunctious, flirtatious, and sexy, Diane was an enticing, exciting inverse of Nancy. Coming from a prominent, and conservative, Catholic family in central Ohio, she was anxious to cut loose. Especially sexually. And I was more than happy to do my part. Yet we held back at the edge of intercourse, of penetration, exploiting the narrowest definition to comply with Catholic warnings against premarital sex. At least for a while. When we finally broke through that dam, she was flooded in guilt and began listening to her mother, a woman who hated that I was not Catholic and had no intention of becoming one, that I was from a lower–middle–class family, and that I was more interested in artistic expression than amassing wealth. While I dated Diane, we'd agreed to date other people, but only each other steadily. Whatever that meant. While it eased the pain of a long–distance romance, and resulted in a few more Julie–dates, it ultimately spelled our end.

At the Ohio state line, I was jolted by the memory of a weekend when I went to see Brian Jackson in Cincinnati. Diane had said she was too busy with an interior design project to get together until Sunday. But on Saturday night, when Brian and I walked back from Skyline Chili, there she was in a beautiful dress, climbing out of a new red–and–black Corvette. The guy was a Joe–handsome blond, in a well–tailored suit. I didn't even own a suit, let alone a sports car. Diane pranced around the sleek car, her wavy blonde hair jouncing around her shoulders in a way that always crippled me, and clashed with him in a crushing hug and an unabashedly passionate kiss. The kind of kiss I thought reserved for me. The sight of it had split me in two. The lovely blonde couple made their way up the sidewalk draped over each other, pausing to neck every few yards.

Brian had done his best to distract me, but short of setting me on fire, the best he could do was keep me from charging inside and making a fool of myself. I phoned a friend of hers who told me she'd been seeing the guy for a while. He was a successful, twenty-eight-year-old IBM sales rep. And he was Catholic. I hated him. Bad enough he was rich and better looking than I was. But Catholic too! Her mother must have been in bitch heaven.

When I saw her the next day, I resolved to see if she'd continue her lie to me.

"How're your projects going?"

"I'm behind, as always, but I'll get done."

"Make good headway last night, did you?"

"Not much but some."

"Work late?"

"Yeah."

"I'll bet you did."

"What's with you?"

"Nothing was, until I saw you getting out of a Corvette last night all dressed up."

Caught in her lie, she burst out laughing.

Until that moment, I'd never been tempted to slap a girl. Now I wanted to stop this laughing face. To slap. To punch. It scared me, this echo of my father in my instinctive wanting to lash out. I held back, gnawing my lip in a way similar to my father mouthing his dentures when he was about to explode.

"I hear you've been seeing that rich asshole for a while."

"He's not an asshole."

"Just rich."

"So what? You think having money is so terrible?"

"Root of all evil."

"Give me a break, Jason. Lighten up," she said. "It's fun to go out to a nice restaurant once in a while. Is that so bad?"

To me, it was. Why? I asked myself. Because I couldn't afford it, simple. I hadn't been to one since high school prom, and then I'd ordered by lowest price, not entrée of choice.

Later that day I decided I couldn't compete if Diane wanted what that guy offered. His straight blond hair and good looks, his sports car, job and money–they all stood in horrible contrast to me, me with my dark curly hair and acne, my little orange pickup and penny-pinching ways. I felt forced to end the relationship. I found her that night in her studio space at the university working on her final interior design project, a Laundromat.

I wanted to keep it simple. Wanted to make it hurt her the way I hurt. The emotional equivalent of my father's lesson of a quick jab to the nose.

"Hey."

"Hey, big boy," she said in a bad Mae West way. She slid from the stool and clamped one of her full-bodied hugs on me and grabbed my butt, pulling me tight against her hips. I didn't return it. A couple of her friends watched us.

"You're cold," she said.

"Whatever you say. Let's go outside and talk."

"I've got too much work to do."

"You didn't have too much work to stay in last night, but you have too much to talk to me now? That's bullshit. What I have to say won't take long."

She agreed to go outside but stopped in the dark and unpainted concrete stairwell. "Just say whatever you have to say right here."

"Beautiful spot for it," I answered. "It's over, Diane. We're finished."

"Just like that?"

"That's what it boils down to. I don't want to waste your precious time."

"Because you saw me kiss some guy? Like you don't kiss the girls you go out with at IU?"

I hadn't expected her to punch back. Of course I had kissed those girls and more.

"Because you lied to me. Because you've been dating this guy a lot and you put him before me when I was in town. Because you're starting to show your true colors."

"I already had that date when you said you were coming to town. And what the hell does that mean, 'true colors'?"

"You're becoming your mother. With priorities to eat at nice restaurants, join the country club, ride in comfy cars, and join the right church."

"My mother has nothing to do with this."

"Doesn't she?"

She opened her purse and took out her key chain on which she had a brass plate that said *VIRGIN*. She'd carried it half as a joke, half as a badge of honor. She took it off and handed it to me, with a dramatic flair. "This is yours," she said.

"I don't want it."

"You sure did before, and you got it." Again she laughed. The toll of this break up didn't seem to carry much weight with her. Certainly not the weight I intended or expected.

I took the key fob. And on my way out of the building, I dropped it in the trash. The truth was she and I had been growing apart for some time, but without me really seeing it or without me being honest with myself. If we'd gone to the same university, the relationship would have burned out in a few months. I'd kept trying to make her be something or someone she wasn't. She'd played along with me for a while. While it was fun. But after joining a sorority, she'd grown more interested in expensive dinners and nice clothing and the traditional Greek social life. Being the superior, judgmental jerk I could be, all of these interests drove me crazy, and I railed against them. Instead of reining her in, my complaints drove us apart.

As I steamed into Ohio on my way to Cape Cod, I had to own my role in it, my flaws, my biases. None of it made me feel good. But I decided to learn from it. Diane was gone, Nancy was gone, but the lessons stuck.

*

So, in addition to setting out on my own away from my family's long shadow, going to Cape Cod was also about getting headspace from Diane. I played a James Taylor's tape over and over; one song, a lyric kept surfacing as I drove: "Nothing like a hundred miles between me and trouble in my mind. Nothing like a hundred miles to make me forget about you."

How about a thousand miles? I hoped a thousand miles was enough to make me forget about Diane—as well as my brother and father. Far enough for a fresh start.

*

Driving across Upstate New York, I resolved to change my name for the summer. Just to do it. To break with my past, with myself. And I entertained myself for miles with name choices:

Jake, Jake Blake? No.

Jackson, Jackson Blake.

Montgomery, Montgomery Blake. Yeah, not bad.

Montague Blake. Where's the ascot?

Miles Blake. My friend Jane might like that one.

Constantinople Blake? Sure.

Rocky Blake? Only if I wanted to get in a lot of fights.

Colin Blake. Curtis? Watson? Lincoln?

Eventually, by the time I crossed the Massachusetts line, I came back to my own name, dull as it was, and decided to be Jason Blake for the summer. But a new Jason Blake, one made of wet clay, open to re-shaping.

I skirted Boston on 495 and headed on to the Cape. Driving up the high arching Bourne Bridge (1933–1935), soaring over the Cape Cod Canal, I felt I was climbing out of something, and–easing down the other side of the bridge–sliding into a new world.

A Cape Summer

With feet on sandy Cape Cod, my luck had changed, or so I thought, and I stopped at the first business I saw to ask for a job. The big fruit stand just over the bridge buzzed with customers and college-aged kids racing around helping and stocking food. It looked perfect. But the manager said she had all the help they needed. So I hit the road, checking out a few towns on the Cape, searching for tourist-type jobs at restaurants and gift shops along the way without luck. The first two nights I found quiet side roads and slept in the back of my truck. The second night, deep into the fuzzy hours, I was awakened by a sharp rapping on the aluminum shell over the back of my pickup.

"Hello, in there," came a big voice.

"Hello," I said.

"Can't sleep here, son." The guy was probably my brother's age.

"I was falling asleep at the wheel," I lied, "tried to drive straight-through from Indiana but couldn't quite make it."

"Where you headed?"

"Wellfleet."

"Okay. You go back to sleep, but I don't want to see you sleeping on the streets here tomorrow night, got it?"

"Got it. Thanks."

"And out of here by 8:30 in the morning."

"8:30. Right, I'll be gone."

With that he drove off, and I hunkered down in my sleeping bag for the rest of the night. But there was no question I needed to find a job and a place to live.

In the morning, I drove to Falmouth. I liked it and went to a lumber yard to ask for a job or to see if any carpentry crews were looking for help. The assistant manager wanted my address, and I confessed I was living out of my truck for the time being. She said she knew a man who sometimes helped young people and gave me the name of a Daniel Standish, a Falmouth insurance man.

With nothing to lose, I went to see this Daniel Standish of the pilgrim name. His business sign incorporated the Christian symbol of the fish. After we talked for a few minutes, I asked if he was a Christian and told him I was (though my doubts were already getting the better of me). In his next breath he asked me to come and live with his family until he could find me a job and a place to live. For the next two weeks, I lived there–free room and board as Standish refused to take my money. He hired me to work around his house, building a fence, putting up a basketball goal for his son, painting the trim on his house, even had me answering the phone at his office.

*

I had heard Standish badmouth a place in Falmouth called Two Brothers, a giant bar and dance club on the beach. I think he referred to it as a "den of sin." But I figured since I'd gotten to Cape Cod before most of the New England college kids–their summer started mid-June–I'd have a chance to get a job working nights at Two Brothers. I walked in the door and there was a big guy behind the bar. I'd guess him at six-feet two and 240 pounds. He looked at me and said, "Yo, you looking for a job?"

"Yeah."

"Bouncer?"

"Maybe."

"Follow me," he strode past me out to the big deck. I paused to admire the view of the beach, the bluffs of Falmouth Heights and Vineyard Sound, before running down the stairs to the sand. When

I caught up to him, he whirled around and took a roundhouse swing at my head.

I ducked it and, using his momentum shoved him and locked up his arm from behind. As he tried to break free, I felt his weight shift and threw him to the sand.

"Stay down," I ordered and was ready to kick him in the face or punch him in the back of the head depending on how he moved.

Instead he held out a hand and laughed. "Want the job?!"

I didn't take his hand, but backed away a step. "Good move," he said. I still doubted I could trust him, prepared in case he made another move at me. I could feel my heart pounding in my neck and ears, the adrenaline tingling in my arms and back.

He got up and dusted off the sand, "I'm Mick."

"Jason," I said. "Jason Blake."

"I wasn't going to hit you," Mick said. "Just testing your reactions. You're not very big for a bouncer, but you're quick. Are you smart?"

"Most people think so."

"Smart enough to defuse a fight rather than get into one? Because the job is simple, Jason: protect the patrons from the problems." Mick said.

That got my attention.

"Every time there's a fight, I lose money. Every time you bounce some jackass in a big scene and his buds follow, I lose money. Every time you smooth ruffled feathers, prevent a fight–protect the patrons from a problem–by getting a ruffian to leave quietly, this place is a money–makin' machine."

"Makes sense," I said. "I'm not really a fighter anyway."

"Good."

Now that I realized he really wasn't going to jump me, the adrenaline leached out of my muscles and the shakes set in.

"Come on inside. I'll go over the details." He laughed and patted me on the back as he held out his hand to shake.

Inside, Mick gave me a Two Brothers jacket made for the bouncers. Thick cotton sweatshirt inside (good padding for a punch to the ribs or kidneys), and rip–stop nylon shell (which would slow down a slashing knife).

"Here's how it works," he said. "Pay is forty bucks a night, fifty for every night without a fight or a rough bounce. Hours are eight to midnight, and it includes dinner while you work. All the soda and coffee you want. No beer or booze while on duty. No touching the waitresses or patrons while on duty or in Two Brothers uniform. Got it?"

"Yeah," I said.

"After you get some experience, you'll go until two in the morning for seventy–two a night plus twenty if there's no fights or rough stuff. All cash—no contracts, no checks, no benefits. We'll train you in a few afternoon sessions and have you shadow a couple of the other guys. We work in pairs. And I'm here most nights too."

I'd never made close to ten or twelve dollars an hour, so I didn't bother to tell Mick I was twenty years old, legally underage to even be in his bar.

Over the next few days, I got detailed training in bar fighting and how to diffuse it from Big Dave, a guy who'd played defensive end at Nebraska and had grown up in a rough part of Miami, a tough white kid among Cubans and blacks. He was six-foot four, thickly muscled and held a karate black belt. A twenty-year veteran as a bouncer, Dave taught me ten ways to stop a guy. The goal wasn't to beat anyone up, just stop them quickly, and get them out the door with minimal distraction or damage to anyone. He taught me where to hit a guy if he moves this way, that way. How to wrestle a guy to the ground. How to call for backup. How to watch out for the drunk buddy who might bust your head or your partner's. How to clear the crowd. How to disarm a guy with a knife. What to do if someone pulled a gun. A gun? It wasn't likely, Big Dave assured me. But it had happened. It was both thrilling and scary to learn all this. Would I really need to know it? Did I want to know it? What had I signed up for?

In the end Big Dave reiterated the rally cry of the bouncer at Two Brothers: "Protect the Patrons from the Problems."

After my training, I was ready to shadow Dave. It was an eye-opening, non-stop lesson. He taught me how to watch the crowd, and he could spot the guys who were likely trouble the second they walked in the door.

Dave graded them on an estimated danger level 1-5 and "nitro." He only gave numbers to those already deemed risky. A one was a bad drunk, not a real physical threat but mean and likely to start a fight over a girl, an odd glance, or a Yankees hat. A five was a guy who was an ex-athlete or current one, often a big guy who could crush you if things got out of hand, and things could get out of hand in a hurry. Or he might be a lean-muscled stud, quick and vicious. A "nitro" was a number four or five who was drunk, angry, high, or armed—a dangerous guy who made you want to dial 9-1- and hold your finger over the other 1 until he left. Dave warned me to watch a "nitro" all the time and stay close. The best you could hope for with a five or a nitro who started trouble was that they were drunk enough to have impaired coordination—that and that you had a good partner.

Dave called out girls who attracted trouble. They were all "shark bait." I never told Dave I was attracted to these girls myself—which I found unnerving.

Dave also told me Mick had bought out the brothers who'd started the place after his baseball career ended. He'd played first base for the Red Sox and Mets. Mick was a good guy who could hold his own if trouble broke out.

There were three bars in the Two Brothers. The bars were named ABC.

A–Bar was the main one. It was out in the middle of the building, a large rectangle, and we all kept track of the customers by their positions on the clock. "There's a 4 and a nitro circling shark bait at two-o'clock."

B–Bar served the disco. It was less trouble because there were no stools and people drifted back and forth. Around B–Bar we relied on the bartenders and waitresses to help us spot trouble brewing, guys getting too drunk or getting too physical with female customers.

C–Bar was the easy one. It was mellow. Down the hall, with

ample soundproofing, and removed from the rest of the club by a breezeway, it was basically a folk music venue. I liked it there, but Mick didn't want us hanging out at C-Bar. No trouble to control. Still, we wandered down there from time to time.

Every bar was outfitted with alarms, and each bouncer had to keep an eye on the wall monitors, a series of lights which identified where there was trouble. Red was the east end of A-Bar and yellow the west end. Green was B-Bar. And there was no light for C-Bar.

My first two nights came off without a single ruffled feather, and I was feeling flush with a hundred bucks in my pocket. Only one guy had to be asked to leave after he patted a waitress on the butt. There was no discussion when Big Dave eased up next to him, slid his beer aside and quietly explained his night was over, but he'd be welcomed back if he could keep his hands off the staff and customers. The guy never said a word, just put ten bucks on the bar and walked out. I stuck close to Big Dave, hanging on his nonstop chatter about who to watch and how to avoid trouble. After twenty years, there were few things Dave hadn't seen. A migrant worker really, Big Dave floated up and down the east coast with the tourists and the weather. Winter through spring he enforced the peace at bars in Miami and Ft. Lauderdale. After the annual insanity of Florida's spring break season, he'd take a month off to visit friends, working a few nights in North Carolina and New Jersey as he drifted toward the Cape and Two Brothers–which opened in May and closed in September.

On my third night bouncing, two guys squared off. One threw his glass of beer at the other, prompting Dave to say, as we rushed to the east end of A-Bar: "Showtime." When we got there, the dry guy was staggering to his feet, his nose looking like an "S" curve and gushing blood. Dave took the puncher and told me to take the mess. I held him back, as he made a show of going after the other guy, but he didn't put in much of an effort. He didn't want any more, just trying to save face (or what was left of it). I gave him a bar towel for his bloody nose. After Dave got the other guy out, with Mick following to make sure none of the group messed with Dave, I escorted the mess out with Dave following. It really was teamwork. But that didn't keep Dave and Mick from teasing me for getting blood on my jacket, Mick reminding me to wash it before work the next night. Mick's last words were, "No bonus tonight boys. The job is to protect the patrons from the problems."

*

While I kept my night job quiet around Daniel Standish, I'm sure he suspected I was out carousing with girls or getting into some other trouble, and he redoubled his effort to find me a job and a place to stay, probably to get me away from his kids.

He did find me a job. A carpenter friend of his, Sonny McCoy, hired me to join his Christian crew for $5.50 per hour. Not much money, especially in light of bouncing, but jobs were scarce, so I took it. And the Christian leaning appealed. I'd worked for some crazy crews before. (Once on a framing crew, the crew chief got high in the morning before climbing up to walk on the rafters of a three-story house. He quit smoking on the job after he got blown off the top-plate of a garage we were building and broke his arm.) So if Christ made the crew sane and respectable, that was fine by me. Standish also found jobs and places to live for players on the Falmouth Clippers baseball team, a team in the Cape Cod League. He found a place for me and one of the baseball players to share.

We rented a small bedroom and kitchen access for $40 per week each, from the Stone family. Really from Mrs. Stone because she ran things. A college-educated woman, she was bright and full of energy, but shackled by her family. Mr. Stone, a very nice man, was as dull as his name. Conversation, to him, meant talking about the weather. In a 30-year military career, he never rose above sergeant. Their oldest boy was a high school dropout who messed with drugs, had gotten a girl pregnant and married her, and couldn't keep a job. So he frequently borrowed money from his mother. Their youngest boy was fourteen and on the fast track to follow the older, sneaking off to smoke pot and booze it up with his buddies. There was a daughter too, though we knew little of her–until she returned from the mental institution.

Mrs. Stone loved my roommate and me because we were, like her, energetic, interested in life, and mentally engaged in it. My roommate played baseball games almost every evening, but I spent time with her before heading off to the Two Brothers. While the rest of her family huddled like stone-age men around the television, watching *Jeopardy* or reruns of *Gilligan's Island* as if they held the secret of fire, Mrs. Stone and I sat in the kitchen and talked about life, favorite books, and, since she'd graduated from the University of Iowa, the Midwest. Stuck in her blunt household, I felt sorry for her. The thing that kept Mrs. Stone sane that summer was planning a visit to her friends in Norway with her husband and younger son. I looked over maps and picture books of Norway with her, listening to details of the trip.

My day job as a carpenter left me exhausted many evenings, so I didn't really want to go to Two Brothers. But the money was too good to pass up, and I liked the new skill I was developing under Big Dave's tutelage. I liked my slowly evolving sense of trouble brewing, the ability to discern the vibe of whether to spring or slide into a situation.

The Christian carpentry crew circled in a different orbit than the staff and customers at Two Brothers. McCoy's carpentry crew met at 8:00 each morning in the church parking lot, with Sonny handing out coffee as people arrived. Once all eight of us were there, we had a quick prayer, and Sonny assigned the four junior carpenters to the three senior carpenters for the day's work. Sonny checked in at each job site every day, lending a hand if needed, solving problems, talking to home owners and meeting with or estimating for prospective customers. We mostly worked on the old stick-and-shingle summer homes along the water. They belonged to wealthy or once-wealthy families of Boston and New York.

The guys on the crew included me in their activities. Carl and his lovely wife invited me to dinner and took me to hear folk music at the coffee shop in Woods Hole. We also played tennis on the Oceanside, on a clay court at a big house. The old woman who owned it sat and watch us play doubles in our dirty work clothes and told stories about "famous" New York people we'd never heard of. My favorite activity was a Friday ritual of crab hunting after work which ended with all the crew's families in a crab feast at Sonny McCoy's house. Boiled corn and crabs and a giant salad bowl. We crowded around two large picnic tables or sat in the grass, laughing and joking around. I was the butt of many jokes from both the guys and their wives.

"With all the pretty college girls on Cape Cod," one wife said, "why can't you get a date?"

"Who says I can't get a date?" I said, though it was true. I'd only had one date with a girl who said she'd finished her freshman year in college, a year younger than me. But when we went for a walk on the beach after a movie and kissed, she confessed she was seventeen and in high school. I took her home and never saw her again. The other two girls I'd asked out had deferred.

"He's just too picky," another wife said.

"Lower your standards and up your fun," said a third. They all laughed at that.

*

One Monday we were rebuilding a sun porch on a rambling old house and Sonny was there working with us. I cut the replacement floor joists. These were a big, expensive boards, two-by-twelve and twelve feet long. When we went to put the new ones in, I discovered I'd cut one two inches short. Crap. The board was suddenly waste. It also put a stop to the work. Someone would have to go get a replacement. Sonny called a break and sent one of the other young guys to the lumber yard.

Sonny said, "Measure twice..."

"Cut once," I finished the carpenter's maxim. That was as close as he ever came to scolding me.

I sat there looking at the short board and noticed I hadn't even cut it square. Was this the result of working until after 2:00 a.m. over the weekend at Two Brothers? The least I could do was cover the second mistake–cutting it short was bad enough. I pulled out my square, marked the tail of the board and re-cut it.

Sonny watched and said, "No matter how many times you cut it, Jason, it won't get any longer." And he laughed and laughed at his joke. At the end of the day, I asked if I'd have to pay for the board, like another crew I'd worked on, but Sonny just laughed and said no. Not unless I made a habit of it.

But I did get reassigned to two tough jobs for the rest of the week. The first was to spend two days climbing up and down the ladder, bringing 80-pound bundles of asphalt shingles up to the crew which was putting a new roof on a house out by one of the kettle-hole ponds in Woods Hole. On a bet for coffee, one of the guys said I couldn't carry two bundles up, 160 pounds. I won. The next two days, I was assigned to work alone at an antique house next to the old Quaker Meeting House in East Falmouth. The stone foundation of the old house had collapsed and someone had to dig it out. Guess who? The cellar was too low to stand up in, so I had to stoop, crawl or squat. First I had to drag out the boulders. Then I had to shovel out all the dirt—one five-gallon bucket at a time. Actually, I'd fill two of them and drag out two at a time to dump on the driveway. I knew I'd have to eventually shovel that pile into a truck. Over and over I filled the buckets. It was back-breaking work. Then, in the middle of the afternoon, I was startled by the sound of a second shovel next to mine. It was Sonny. He didn't say much, just kept shoveling.

It made a big impression on me that he showed me, without telling me, that he wasn't above doing the grunt work, wasn't above the dirty work. Right then, I decided if I ever owned a company I'd do the same thing.

After about an hour, he said he had to go, but it helped me a lot. Both for my morale and for getting the job done.

"Let's take a break. I got you a Gatorade."

While we sat on the tailgate of his truck, he told me he'd heard I was working as a bouncer at Two Brothers.

"Yes sir, that's right." I answered.

"If you need the money, Jason, I'll pay you another dollar an hour. But only if you quit."

"Sonny, I really appreciate it, but I need the money. It will really help me and my family when I'm back at college."

"I'm just worried about that place."

"I'm not getting in trouble. I don't drink or anything like that."

"Good luck finds you in a good place, and bad luck finds you in a bad place." He patted me on the shoulder. "Simple as that, really. You're a good kid, and I want what's good for you."

I didn't answer for a few seconds. "I'll be careful," I said.

*

That night, after working to dig the foundation, I showed up at Two Brothers early to get something to eat. It was busy, heading into the July 4th weekend. During my six weeks as a bouncer, we hadn't had much trouble. A couple of guys took swings at me, but I was able to duck or block them and wrap the guy up until help arrived and off he went. My worst encounter came when a huge guy grabbed me and lifted me up like a rag doll, crushing my ribs. Dave stepped in quick. "Stop," he said. The guy tossed me aside and took a wild swing at Dave. Then Pow. Dave hit the guy so fast and so hard his head snapped back, and he just crumpled. Bam and down, like a roll of wet sod. Big Dave had shielded me from most of the bad stuff, but that night, heading into the July 4th weekend, Dave was out sick. I got assigned to work with Ted, a guy whose father was a friend of Mick's. Ted was a couple years older than I, a tennis player at Tufts. A tennis player?!

And wouldn't you know, in swaggers the big dude who Dave had taken out when he grabbed me. With two oversized buddies. He wore his number-five nitro full-bore. I wished Dave was there. I almost quit on the spot. One drink in, the guy glared and pointed at me from across A–Bar. I asked Mick to help keep an eye on him, and Mick gave him and his friends a no–hard–feelings beer from me. I'll admit I was scared. This guy was every bit the size of an NFL offensive tackle, probably six-five and easily 310 pounds. I was six-foot and 185, and Ted was taller than I, but soft. Besides Ted was chatting up a new waitress and not paying attention.

The big guy disappeared into the dance room. After awhile I checked in at B-Bar to see if they'd seen him. Oh, yeah, he was knocking them back with his two buddies. I went back to pull Ted away from his own shark bait, and to warn Mick and tell him to have the cops nearby because this was feeling like a powder keg. Almost instinctively I reached past Mick into the cash register and took a roll of nickels ($2 worth) and put it in my left pocket, a lesson from my father's boxing cheat. It was a waiting game now.

And it wasn't long. The number-five nitro grabbed a B-Bar waitress who had a tray of drinks, reaching down the back of her shorts. She dropped the tray, screaming, but he held tight.

"Hey, let her go," I said. "Not cool." I didn't want to be too firm, which he'd take as a challenge, or too light and he'd mock me.

"Hello, Pigeon Shit," he said.

"Let's not have any trouble. It's time to go."

"You going to throw me out? Where's your big brother?" His friends, one on each side of me, laughed. I reached into my pocket and locked my fist around the roll of nickels.

"Look," I said, holding out an open right palm. "let's keep this simple. The boss already called the cops, and they're outside–"

"I'm gonna kick your ass." He flung the waitress aside like a doll.

"Those cops would love to toss you in–"

"I'm gonna kick your ass right now."

Everything went into slow motion. He pulled back that hammer of a fist, reaching for Nantucket, and I exploded into him with everything I had, with an inside right jab, hitting him square in the throat. (I aimed for the chin, but at least I connected.) He gasped for air leaning forward, and I hit him again with my weighted left hook right where the jaw joins the skull. It broke with the same pause and give as the kid's leg broke on the football field when I was in ninth grade. Nickels exploded from my hand, as he went down.

Then the room tilted as I heard screaming.

The next thing I knew I woke up in the hospital–or so I thought. It was a nursing home run by one of Mick's friends.

Turned out, one of the big guy's buddies had grabbed a whisky bottle from the bartender and cracked it over my head. Mick was sitting there when I woke up. He stuffed a hundred bucks in my hand. "Tell me you got health insurance."

"I got health insurance." Wait. Did I? I wasn't sure. I wasn't sure what day it was or where I was. But, yeah, I had health insurance of some kind through the university.

One of the nursing home residents, an old woman, thin as a fork, kept coming in every hour or two to wake me up, take my pulse, and check my eyes. I don't know if she'd been a nurse in her youth, but at least someone was checking on me. I worried about how badly I might be hurt. I knew my head was messed up. Big Dave came by late that night to make sure I didn't need to go to a Boston hospital. In the morning the nursing home doc checked me over again and said I'd be fine–other than a five–day headache and a warning not to bounce my head around for a few weeks.

Sonny McCoy came by too. "Jason, I warned you about that place. When you get close to trouble, it finds you. That's a lesson you just learned the hard way."

I didn't say anything.

Sonny drove me over to Two Brothers to get my truck. When we stopped, he said "I want you to take an extra two bucks an hour and quit that bouncer job." I didn't tell Sonny I'd already decided to leave, but I told him I would, that I'd go in right then and tell the owner. I saw Mick's BMW in the parking lot.

Inside, I told Mick I was done. He knew. He said Big Dave had decided for me. Mick bought me lunch and gave me another two hundred bucks. "Use it for your textbooks this fall."

And so ended my life as a bouncer.

I never went back to Two Brothers.

*

For the next week I did have wicked headaches and couldn't use a hammer, so Sonny put me on soft duty: cleaning up, running errands, painting a porch, and straightening up his office.

The good news was I got plenty of sleep for my first time on Cape Cod, read more, and spent evenings after work walking on the beaches instead of preventing bar fights. I also hung around the Stones' house where I spent time talking to Mrs. Stone about books. To repay my attention and to help me out with the loss of dinners at Two Brothers, Mrs. Stone often cooked an extra potato at dinner, or somehow had a little extra pasta or salad. It upset her that my dinners now usually consisted of either peanut butter and jelly sandwiches, or cans of Chef Boyardee Ravioli, heated on the stove with me forking food straight from the can.

The Stones left to spend the last six weeks of the summer in Norway, leaving my roommate and me alone with their daughter. As soon as her mother left, Carla Stone lost her cashier job at Stop-and-Shop and spent her days in front of the TV, wearing her bathrobe from the time she got up, around noon, until she went to bed, around midnight. By all appearances she stopped bathing as well. Living off our rent money, which Mrs. Stone had instructed us to pay to Carla, she tried to raise our rent a few days after her mother left. She went into an incoherent rage, shrieking wordlessly through the house, when we refused. Then Carla did not speak to us or acknowledge our existence for days—until something like a telephone call for one of us after ten o'clock would set her off screaming at us again. By the end of the first week, my roommate couldn't take it and moved out to live with a couple of baseball teammates. I wanted to do the same, but I felt a responsibility to Mrs. Stone as a repayment for her kindness, to help support her daughter. I wondered what my brother would do. I knew Dad would quit her as he'd quit many jobs. What would Mom do? I imagined her bearing it out, telling herself it would end soon, and then walking away having fulfilled her sense of obligation. That's what I decided to do.

But it got worse.

As the sole target of her imbalance, Carla tilted toward me. I pitied her when I woke in the middle of the night to the sound of her sobbing in her bedroom. Then she'd hurl something against the wall—the sound of china or glass shattering. Then silence. Some nights it was impossible to sleep when Carla simultaneously played the TV and the stereo, raising the volume of both as if the devices were in competition. Once in a while, I came home late and hearing this competition from outside the house, I lingered beside my small pickup debating whether or not to go in. Twice, I slept in the back of my truck rather than face her and the racket. Carla had done herself some sort of violence before being institutionalized, I knew, and I feared she might hurt herself. Or worse, turn on me. Especially after I awoke to the sound of a doorknob rattle and saw her slowly crack open the door to peer in on me with one eye. With images of her sinking a knife into my back as I slept, I put a bolt on my door and locked myself in at night. Next time I heard the knob rattle, the door didn't yield, and Carla Stone went into a rage yanking at the knob and pounding on the door, again shrieking wordlessly at me. Then collecting herself in a seething anger, she hissed, "I will kill you. You know that? Oh, yeah. I'll do it."

That did it. I decided to get the hell out and not ruin my last month on the Cape. Running an asylum wasn't part of the bargain. I'd live out of my truck if I had to.

I drove over to Old Silver Beach. It was a foggy night, cool, the air damp. I could hear the ocean from the parking lot but couldn't see it. I felt relieved after my decision, but down deep I also felt uneasy, wondering if it made me the kind of man who left when things got tough. I refocused on the practical. It would be hard to find an affordable place for just four weeks. And I didn't want to cut into my meager savings plan. Despite my paltry take-home pay, I set aside $75 per week for college. (It wasn't enough, and I'd have to take out a student loan to survive the school year.) After rent, I had about $35 a week plus any overtime for food, fun and gas. When I worked for Two Brothers, I had money, but no time. Now that I had time, I wouldn't allow myself the money.

I mentioned my living situation to Dale McCoy, a painting contractor and the younger brother of my boss, Sonny McCoy. Dale had become a good friend that summer though he was more than twenty years older than I. A very funny and happy-go-lucky man,

Dale was also a deep thinker about life and religion and friend-ship. I had resolved to live out of my truck and asked Dale if I could shower at his outdoor shower behind the house after work, and maybe park my truck in his turnaround. Instead, Dale insisted I move in with his family for the same amount of rent I'd paid the Stones. I hedged, giving him a chance to discuss it with his wife and back out of the offer, but he was emphatic. And I accepted.

That night I told Carla I was moving out. She blocked the door. She said I couldn't leave. She threatened me again if I tried.

"I'm sorry. I've decided."

Then she began to cry, to wail and blubber as she followed me up the stairs and back down while I carried my books and magazines. She begged me not to move out.

"I can't stay," I said, and went upstairs for the last of my things.

Then as I turned, she pulled out a kitchen knife and I slammed the door on her and locked it. She jabbed the knife into the door again and again. I threw the last of my things out the second-floor window and climbed out on a porch roof. I had to jump to the lawn. I picked up my stuff and snuck around the house, expecting her to spring out of the bushes with that big knife. But when I came past a window, I saw she was already back in her chair, watching TV, as expressionless as a reptile.

To assuage my guilt, I took out my wallet, doing it fast because I knew I'd stop myself if I reconsidered, and slipped another week's rent, $40, under the front door. Then I sprinted to my truck and raced away.

I wanted to call Mrs. Stone and tell her what happened; it felt cowardly not to, and irresponsible. What if Carla hurt herself? But I didn't know how to reach her in Norway, so I just ran.

Living with Dale McCoy, his wife Gail, and their two daughters–May, 12, and Beth, 15–was life in a playground compared to the Stone house. Dale and I sat up late in discussions, sometimes about religion, but more often about how to live a life or about dreams, and we joked around a lot. He was like an older brother, but easier-going than Walter, and like Walter, Dale was a kind of father figure too.

At the end of the summer, Dale asked me to go with his family, and two other families, to spend four days at his father's cabin in New Hampshire. It was a perfect end for my summer. We hiked in woods of the White Mountains, went swimming in ponds and icy-cold mountain streams, and hung around campfires. At the end of the night, everyone else would go to bed inside the little cabin, but I slept outside under the stars.

These eight adults and seven kids, all friends I'd made that summer, felt like family to me. And when it was time to leave for Indiana, it saddened me to say goodbye. Dale and Gail made me promise to come back and stay with his family the next summer.

As I drove my bright-orange Nissan pickup across the mountains toward Vermont, New York, Pennsylvania, Ohio, and twenty hours later finally to Indiana–I reflected.

I had driven a thousand miles from home, ended up in a town none of my family members had even visited, and carved out a life for myself. I'd earned a living, found places to stay, and made life-long friends–I could have stayed the rest of my life in Falmouth. And I did it all alone.

Another fact crept up on me: except for college, my brother had never lived outside of Indianapolis, and even then, with friends or family. In this act of independence, if in few other places, I gave myself permission to mark that I had surpassed Walter.

More Wrangling with Walter

Back at school, living in the battered old apartment, Walter came down to visit and we locked horns over literature, going a bit beyond our old erudite banter. I relished the opportunity to mirror his superior frown of disappointment and turn the tables on him. "You mean you've never read a single novel by William Faulkner?" I let my jaw slacken in dramatic astonishment. "Not one? How did you miss the American challenger to Joyce?"

"Until you've made a study of *Ulysses*, don't compare anyone to Joyce."

"Never read any Faulkner," I muttered, shaking my head. "He won the Nobel Prize, you know? Something Joyce didn't do. And many serious scholars consider him the better writer."

As a reader of modern poetry, I became his equal. But I knew Chaucer and Donne and Shakespeare, as well as theater and modern American fiction, better than he did.

In painting, sculpture, design, and art history, Walter was a true scholar, largely self-taught. Whenever we went to an art museum together–and these visits seemed to follow one of my "You never read Faulkner?" discussions–he grew as pedantic in pontification as any professor. Like a lecturer, he *did* enlighten me about the artwork. But I also learned to keep my mouth shut, other than to admire a painting, because if I was wrong, Walter made me feel like an idiot: "No, no, no, he's not an impressionist. He's a *post-*

impressionist."

Fine, so I conceded art to him.

In retaliation for his pedantic art lectures, I occasionally became the bombast-master of theater, spouting off to him about Ionesco, Pinter, or the Stanislavski Method.

In my junior year I learned of a graduate program through Indiana's School of Education which sent students overseas to teach. This graduate program accepted some undergrads, and I decided to apply for a spot in England. When I told Walter, he didn't think I should do it.

Why?

"To get a teaching job, you need to interview in spring and summer," he said. "How can you do that if you're in England and then backpacking around Europe all summer?" He shook his head like I was a clueless dolt.

I told him I'd talked to the dean who ran the program, and they had a very high placement rate. A lot of schools held positions open so they could interview young teachers with this unique experience.

"Bullshit," he said. "You'll miss the hiring cycle and end up living at home and selling shoes at the mall."

"First of all, you don't know anything about the teacher-hiring process. I do. Second, this is a great life experience which will put me ahead of other teacher candidates. And third, even if there is a risk that I'll miss some jobs, I'll land on my feet. That's what I do, Walter. Who do you think you're talking to?"

He stewed for a minute, "And you still have undergraduate classes to finish. How are you going to manage grad school and undergrad at the same time?"

"It will be hard," I said. "But I know how to work hard, and I'm ready to make it work. Just watch me."

It jolted me, him trying to hold me back, the guy who'd always pushed me and challenged me. What was that about?

*

I was twenty–one–years old and he was just twenty–seven, yet he was confident he knew what was best for me. And he'd been right often enough, so I found it difficult to argue with him as he attempted to steer my life. I'd told him about the Overseas Program because I thought he'd joyously support me. Now, instead of deterring me, his opposition strengthened my determination.

Still, there was no denying I'd taken classes and read books as much for him as for myself. Was that because he steered me to what he liked, or because he understood me well enough to know what I wanted and would enjoy? I did enjoy my studies, loved them, so I made no sacrifice. But without Walter's pressure on the wheel, would my direction have been the same? Without an older brother, where would I be? Might I have tried to play football at a small college? Or studied forestry at Purdue as I had planned years ago? Questions without answer. Pointless in the asking because, for my life, it challenged something as real a part of existence as water. From my first days alive, Walter had exerted his influence. Yet I asked: Who would I be without him?

Walter's visits to Bloomington seemed to include more and more walks past his old haunts, with him pausing to tell me again about a class he'd had in one building or another, a girl he went out with from one dorm, a girl he wished he'd dated from another one, reminiscing about his days in my apartment. At times a fog of ennui seemed to hang on him like one of the old alumni retracing a lost youth–but Walter was still young.

I was just a kid, but I wondered if Walter had married and set-tled into a stable Midwestern life too young.

On one of his visits, we passed a pretty girl on campus, and exchanged a hello.

"Who was *that*?" he said.

"I don't know. We keep passing on the sidewalk. She must live in the neighborhood."

"Dude, you have to ask her out."

"I'm not going to go up to a strange girl on the street and just ask her out," I said. "You're nuts."

But the thought stuck, and after seeing her again, I stepped in front of her and said: "Hey, we keep passing on the sidewalk, and I thought I'd introduce myself. I'm Jason Blake. And I wondered if you'd want to grab a cup of coffee sometime."

She blushed when I stopped her, but she said yes. Although nothing came of our couple of dates, they gave me confidence and on three or four other occasions, I did end up asking out girls right off the street or from women's clothing stores. (It had dawned on me one day that pretty girls worked in women's clothing stores but they never saw guys, so I went in to ostensibly shop for a birthday gift for a cousin and often left with a phone number.) Probably because of the sheer boldness of these approaches, the girl often said yes to a first date. And I kept the stakes low with a request for coffee or tea.

I did get into the overseas teaching project, thus becoming simultaneously a graduate student and an undergraduate in my last fall semester of college. I had to carry twenty-four credit hours (nine hours of graduate level) when the typical full-time undergraduate load was fifteen. I didn't sleep much that semester, and didn't goof around much, but I survived.

That fall, my mentor in the Education Department, Professor Anne Pain signed me up for a meeting of the Indiana Council of English Teachers. I didn't want to go, but fearing "Severe Pain," as we jokingly called it, I went with another future English teacher and friend, Ken Lincoln. About fifty teachers mingled in the dingy old Howe High School gymnasium in Indy. The six of us student members: me and Ken from IU, two girls from Butler, and two girls from Ball State clustered together in awe of the real teachers.

I met one of the young women from Butler, a sophomore. Waiting in line for coffee, she admitted she came for extra credit in an education class. We poured coffee into styrofoam cups; she sprinkled in powered creamer and handed it to me.

"De-Lite Non-Dairy Creamer," she said. "Think it will delight you," she made a goofy, dramatic show of looking at my nametag, "Jason?"

"I'll be totally delighted, Katie." I almost mirrored her goofy gesture, but her nametag was over her breast.

"What do you think that stuff really is?" she asked. "'Coffee whitener'? Doesn't that sound delicious?"

"Better living through chemistry," I said.

"Good chemistry is important," she replied and smiled.

I liked her and wanted to see Katie again, but I didn't have time that fall with so many classes, and then there was student teaching and off to England.

Goodbye Bloomington

At the end of my last fall semester, I had to complete an eight-week student teaching stint before flying to England to teach for the ten-week spring term. My British assignment would be in Devon, at the Exmouth Comprehensive school. My preparatory student teaching assignment was in Indianapolis, an hour away from my beloved Bloomington.

Leaving the campus of the university that had so transformed me—intellectually, socially, spiritually—pained me, and the fog of ennui I'd seen floating around my brother quickly formed around me. When I packed the last of my things, I went for a walk around campus. There was a smell here unlike that of anyplace else. Even in December there was a fecund smell. The smell of hope? Of promise? It seemed to rise from the damp and rotting leaves along the walkways or the limestone walls. Every building held memories. Sitting on the limestone steps of Maxwell Hall with my first college girlfriend. Sneaking into the unlocked office on the fourth floor of Kirkwood Hall to call Brian Jackson at the University of Cincinnati. Watching the sunset from the roof of the Geology Building with Jane Kirkwood. The historic Well House where couples were supposed to kiss at midnight. One limestone building after another, various patches of woods on campus. I'd come to feel I owned something there, just as I felt it owned something of me.

Through my studies and through my experiences, at some vague time, I had stepped off any neatly defined religious path altogether. I didn't know about God and didn't think it knowable. That decision had liberated me from a struggle to rationalize a belief I couldn't quite cotton. And I had become a comfortable agnostic here.

Part of me was ready to move ahead, but part of me wanted to join the legions who stayed and tried to restart their clocks in Bloomington. An uncle of mine once said you couldn't swing a cat in Bloomington without hitting a Ph.D. There was no doubt I was moving on. I knew I had to, but I also knew I'd miss this place.

All of this departing also meant a return home to Indianapolis to live with my parents for eight weeks. I was not the same kid who'd left nearly four years before. I looked forward to seeing my mother, who I knew had worked outrageous hours for years to make possible my education at a great university. From early morning cutting to hemming while she listened to evening television, she had designed and made skirts and blouses to help me and my brother get through college. She'd done that since I was about nine years old. I admired and appreciated Mom more than ever now that I neared graduation, and I understood how my completing school would fulfill her long-term goal of creating opportunities for her family. A certain bonding over this accomplishment–her youngest child making her long-held dream come true–was close at hand.

My mother's fashion designing continued to grow in popularity, making her something of a local star, with more frequent radio and print advertising for shops touting April Blake Originals. Occasionally, I had delivered skirts or blouses to shops when home from college. On one occasion, I'd parked outside the gray metal door at the back of the mall and rung the bell. "Friend or foe?" came the muffled call through the metal door.

I leaned toward the seam, "Friend." The store's assistant manager let me in and checked my mother's shipping list and invoice against the order.

"This is wrong," she'd said.

Before I could respond with surprise that my detail-oriented mother might screw up the paperwork, the owner happened to come in, and she said to the assistant manager: "You better double-check our order because April Blake doesn't make mistakes."

Sure enough, Mom had gotten it right. On the way home, I had to laugh with some pride at what the owner had said, "April Blake doesn't make mistakes." And it was true that my mother was buttoned up, especially about her business. I found myself trying to recall her life mistakes. Twice she'd misjudged snow-covered roads and slid her car into a ditch. She'd burned a few meals. Perhaps she hadn't noticed me falling under my father's influence while she worked hard to earn money to help Walter get through college. But I couldn't blame her for focusing on priorities. Then I hit upon her one great mistake, her getting pregnant and marrying young. As one who loved school and excelled at it, she'd dreamed of attending college and becoming a lawyer. Since she was part of a large family, eleven kids, there was no money for college–so she decided to work for a couple of years, to save money. But then she met and fell in love with Dad. That was her big mistake.

Thank God, I thought, or I wouldn't be here.

Once, when my brother said I'd been "a mistake," born six years after him–Mom overheard him and roared a laugh: "You were both mistakes! Neither one planned. My great mistakes. My wonderful, beautiful, brilliant mistakes." And she kissed me and my brother on the head. Then she lightly cuffed my brother.

*

I looked forward to spending time with my brother too. He and Missy were expecting their first child. Though just twenty-eight, Walter had built a new home on a hill just across the pasture from my parents' place. And his professional life had begun to soar. After he won awards for his designs and illustrations, he'd left the bank to join an advertising agency as an art director. Walter and I also would have fun watching IU basketball together. Unabashed, we'd laugh and cheer and boo at the TV–all of which I anticipated as a release from the pressure of living with my parents, as well as from the stress of student teaching, of trying to stay on top of every lesson, every paper, every kid.

*

It was my father I felt uneasy about seeing.

Not in my first two years, and not in my last two at IU did he ever make the 60-mile trip to visit me.

The one time Big Walt made the trip it was not to visit:

WHAM, the fat-tired, four-wheel-drive pickup truck hit my little Nissan pickup from behind, causing my head to rebound off the glass behind the seat. The big pickup kept shoving my truck ahead. I rubbed the back of my head and looked in the rearview mirror to see my old man laughing.

A truck tire was tied to the front of his big Dodge Ram, another was slung over the tailgate of my Nissan to keep the trucks from damaging each other as he rammed me back toward college.

I'd had my clutch repaired in Bloomington three days before going home for Thanksgiving. At home the clutch gave out. To get me back to college and my truck back to the Bloomington repair shop, I had to be pushed up to a speed where I could get the truck into second gear. From there, I could speed-shift without using the clutch. It's something race car drivers do all the time, but I was no race car driver, and I didn't even have a tachometer to help gauge the correct RPM to switch gears. So there was a lot of jamming the stick shift and tooth-rattling grinding of gears.

My father followed me all the way to Bloomington. Every time I was stopped by a traffic light or stop sign, he had to push me back up to speed with his truck. After I dropped my truck off at the garage, Dad gave me a lift toward my apartment. We were on the main road out of town when I told him where to turn.

He asked, "How far's your apartment?"

"About a mile, maybe twelve blocks."

He pulled to the side of the road, "I got to get home. You can walk from here, can't you?"

"Well, yeah, I guess." It threw me. After coming this far, how much longer could it take to drive a mile? But he'd done me the favor of getting my truck back to the Bloomington shop, so I got my bag, my books, and thanked him for his help, then hoofed it to my apartment. That was as close as the old man ever came to visiting me while I was in college.

*

While my mother's success as a fashion designer accelerated, my father had lost his job teaching auto body repair at the Warren Central vocational school–for reasons that were never shared beyond a blur of angry blame he threw toward administrators. Still, because he had helped the superintendent from my old school system rebuild a vintage car, he landed a post teaching auto body at Lawrence North.

As fate would have it, that was the very school IU had assigned me to for my student teaching. So, not only did I live with my father for eight weeks, I had to work with him too.

The car I had begun driving some months back in place of my old pickup was another of my father's nearly completed rebuilds from crumbled tin. It needed some repairs, though, and more body work. He suspected the suspension or frame was out of whack, judging by the way it dog-tracked down the road and sheered the edges off tires. So he left it at the vocational school to repair while I lived at home. He promised to finish it while I was in Europe. That left me to borrow Mom's car or my father's "new" four-wheel-drive pickup, another multi-colored patchwork of used parts and body putty awaiting time in the paint booth.

It was in this handsome truck that we rode to school every day, Mr. Blake and young Mr. Blake. Two teachers, one from Auto Body Repair, one from the English Department. One in a jumpsuit, one in a tweedy sports jacket and club tie. When I got out, I dusted off my trousers and jacket, yet the chemical smell of body putty and cigarettes lingered in my nose through the morning. If people saw me riding away from the school, a passenger in my father's truck, I hated the impression we made, and the feeling that I still lived under my parents' wing. At the end of the day, though, Dad and I rode home together. After dinner he'd say he was going back to school to work, and he'd be gone until late at night, ostensibly to rebuild cars, including mine. Yet I never saw any progress. On nights he stayed home, he'd read the paper or a magazine with the TV turned up loud. The couple of times I asked him to turn off the TV if he was reading so I could work in the adjoining dining room, he got his hackles up.

"Don't come back here and start telling me how to live," he'd snarl. "If I want to listen to the TV while I read, I'll do it. If you don't like it, go work in your room."

I'd never mentioned the nickels in the boxing gloves story, but when he spoke to me as if I were a child, I almost brought it up.

Instead, I went up to my room to work.

*

Yet, on another day, as an English Department meeting wound down, I sat with the teachers. Someone brought up my father. I wanted to hide, but here's what I heard:

"Jason, he is one proud papa," the department head said.

This surprised me.

"Oh, yeah, last fall when he found out you were assigned to our team, Walt was down here bragging about your 4.0 grades and showing pictures of you walking the stage and shaking the governor's hand at the IU Founder's Day."

I didn't want to say anything, but my father wasn't even there for Founder's Day. My mother took those photos.

"Walt told us to just go ahead and hire you now," one of the women laughed.

One of the male teachers added, "I told him you couldn't be as smart as he says if you still want to be an English teacher." He laughed and punched me in the arm.

They all laughed as I hid behind my styrofoam cup, taking slow sips of cold coffee with powdered creamer.

I felt both surprised and proud–my father had never mentioned anything about my being honored at Founder's Day. He'd never told me he was proud of anything I'd done. No, he never said he was proud of me. And he never uttered a word to me about my college academics.

Faculty Meeting

The nadir of my student teaching came at a faculty meeting.

Because Lawrence North was a big high school with over 2,000 students and about 120 teachers, faculty meetings filled a small auditorium. At my first such meeting, I sat with the other English teachers. The room brimmed with happy chatter, the pleasure of camaraderie and adult conversation, things teachers were starved for. Perhaps that's why faculty meetings always started late. From the back corner of the room, where the vocational teachers stood, time and again I heard my father's laugh boom over the chatter.

Finally, the principal called the meeting to order. Everyone quickly got quiet. Except my father. The loud and rancorous voice of the staff Falstaff continued his jesting, oblivious to the quiet settled around him. "Walt," the principal said, "can we get started?" I was horrified that my father had been singled out. Rather than straighten up, he muttered an irreverent wisecrack that caused a wave of sniggers among his colleagues. The principal waited. The rest of the faculty waited. I withered under the weight of every quarter-second. Like a high school mischief-maker or class clown encouraged by laughter, my father pressed on with another remark muttered to his mates. My eyes, glancing from colleague to colleague, registered rolling eyes, shaking heads, and huffs of exasperation. These people–teachers in academic disciplines whom I had worked hard to join over the last three-and-a-half years– included some of my former teachers as well as Brian Jackson's father, who had been a father figure for me. Finally, a couple of the more conscientious vocational teachers whispered to my old man to pipe down and he did. The principal's waiting had grown to a glare and, fixed on my father, he asked if it was okay to begin. "Don't mind me, Chief," my father smirked.

I'd shrunk ten inches by the time the meeting began. Nothing from the meeting stayed with me except that mortified feeling. When it ended, I lingered over my notes as if absorbed, waiting for the room to clear so I could slink out unnoticed and without overhearing the rancor my colleagues felt for my father, whose voice I could already hear crowing in the outer hall.

On another occasion, at a school convocation, I watched him crack a joke among a few vocational teachers during "The Star Spangled Banner." Their laughter disrupted the music and I noticed a few colleagues frown in his direction. I also noticed how his students, the kids who lived on the fringe of academic life, grinned and nodded, as if to say: "He's one of us." I was too far away to hear what he said, but the color guard had a couple of buxom girls in skimpy outfits and I suspect it had something to do with that.

There were other such embarrassing moments: Dad laughing too loudly or making off-color comments in the halls of the English department or in the teacher's lounge. "The guy tried to Jew me down," he'd say, "and I told him, 'Forget it, I wouldn't sell the car to you if you threw in your daughter.'" To avoid such moments, I found myself eating lunch in the English office and hustling down to the vocational wing at the end of the school day to meet him so he wouldn't come looking for me in the English department.

*

After school one day I went down to the auto body shop to meet him–the harsh odor of auto spray paint made the huge room claustrophobic–and my father said, "I heard a rumor that one of the teachers in the voc wing is selling drugs. You hear anything about it?"

"No," I answered, surprised at the thought. "What kind of low-life would do that?"

"I don't know," he said from under the hood of a car. "But you haven't heard the rumors down in the academic area?"

"No, but if it's true, I hope they catch the guy and throw his ass in jail. A teacher who's a drug dealer?"

He didn't respond but this had happened all my life when he worked on a car–questions unanswered because of a seized bolt, grunting yanks of a socket wrench ending conversation. I could see he'd be awhile, so I went into his office to grade papers.

When he came in to take off his coveralls, he said, "I heard the guy was just selling marijuana mostly. But you haven't heard anything at all about it?" I assured him again that I hadn't and wondered why he kept asking.

"Probably just a rumor down in this wing," he said.

"Who told you about it?"

"Just somebody down here."

"A kid or a teacher?"

"Ahhh, it was a kid. Who knows–maybe he made it up." He grabbed up his things, "Let's get home."

We didn't talk much on the way home, which was typical. He played the radio loud. As we crossed Mud Creek Valley, he said, "If you hear anything in the academic area about a voc teacher selling drugs, let me know ASAP, okay?"

I was glad to see him concerned for his students.

*

But something about it made me a little suspicious. Like he might be covering for someone.

From Indiana to Europe

After a year of preparation and eight weeks of teaching in the same school as my father, time finally came for me to head for England. To teach English to the English for the ten-week spring term.

I loaded my bags into the trunk of Mom's car Friday morning, including the new duffel she'd bought for me a week before, and we headed for the airport. Running late. In the rush, I kept thinking, "I won't get to say an appropriate good-bye," and then I wondered how I ever could. We exchanged small talk, with long silences full of thoughts about what lay ahead as well as a familiar pre-departure dread. I missed her already. At the airport, my mother said, "I'll drop you off and head on home." I noticed the strain in her voice and looked over to see her eyes filling, but she wasn't going to cry. She wanted to send me off with a smile. I sat in the car with her for an instant before jumping out. "Thanks for everything." I meant for my thanks to reach back into my youth, with a special emphasis on the last four years, but it couldn't carry the proper weight. I got out of the car and unloaded the trunk. We stood on the sidewalk and embraced. She squeezed me hard.

"I'm proud of you, Jason," she said. "You have a wonderful trip." She raised her fist up between us and shook it: "Make the most of it."

"I will. I love you."

"I love you too. Now hurry up," she said, "or you'll miss your plane."

I shouldered my heavy bags and rushed into the airport as best I could. (When we trained to teach overseas, one of the demands from the IU staff had been that whatever you took to Europe you should be able to carry by yourself for at least five blocks.)

I missed my plane.

They put me on the next flight to Boston, which left in two hours. The rush only to wait left me feeling empty. I went to the pay phone and called Brian Jackson, who was in Boston doing a graphic design co-op. I was flying through Boston so we could hang out for the weekend before I flew to London. My being two hours later was fine with him. I went to the airport coffee shop and sat at the counter to ponder leaving for England. The two waitresses were a mother–daughter combination.

Daughter: "He only wants seventy-five hundred for that RX7." There's a pause. "What you think I'd get for my car?"

Mother, after a moment, no hurry to answer: "What you want a new car for?"

Daughter: "I don't know. Just a thought is all."

Mother: "You'll need your car if, or when, you move to another state."

Daughter: "Another state?"

Mother, taking up a dishtowel and wiping the counter: "Well, you said you'd like to move to another state."

Daughter, hand on hip: "I would. I'd like to."

Mother: "Okay then."

Daughter: "But where? There's no place to move to. Heck, I don't know where to go. What would I do when I got there?"

She began a new pot of coffee despite the two full pots waiting. Enough for one per customer in the place. "No place to go," she muttered to herself.

Mother: "I just thought you said you wanted to move some-wheres, that's all."

Daughter: "Well, I'd go if there was somewhere to go."

I certainly had somewhere to go–Boston. Then England.

*

When I landed in Boston, Brian Jackson and his bear hug met me at baggage claim. He seemed bigger. Always taller than me at six-feet, three, he now felt thicker as well. And I noticed a blond streak in his hair, though I decided not to mention it. He drove an old, battered convertible VW Beetle. Brian of course drove with the top down despite the fact that it was early March, twenty-eight degrees, with snow flurries.

"Why own a convertible," he bellowed, "if you're going to keep the top up?"

"Couldn't agree more," I said as we heaped my bags into the back seat.

He and his roommate had gotten wool throws for their legs and goofy wool hats and big furry mittens to wear while driving around Boston and Cambridge in the winter with the top down. They'd become a 'thing' which we three were all drawn to. There was a thrill to being seen as the eccentric, fun-loving guys reaching for extremes. Convertible top down in winter? Absolutely. I'd been to Boston a few times while living on Cape Cod, but Brian knew it better and gave me a loud, hilarious romp around Beacon Hill, Back Bay, and Fenway before rolling into Harvard Square. We dropped my bags at Brian and Rod's apartment. It was a three-bedroom, rent-control unit in an old brick building on Wendell Street, less than a mile from Harvard Square. The dining room table was a card table, and the three chairs were old aluminum and nylon-web folding lawn chairs–all from a yard sale. Books and magazines were piled around the floor. The beds were mattresses on the floor, and their clothes were in milk crates they'd stolen from behind a supermarket. But they had rented a big-ass TV because they both loved Boston sports.

In total, it was an awesome place.

They'd gone ahead and leased it for a year even though they had to go back to the University of Cincinnati to finish their senior year. They were committed to coming back after graduation. A group of four UC girls were subletting it for the spring quarter.

Although I didn't say anything, I couldn't help imagining my-self with Brian and Rod, taking the third bedroom and teaching school in the area. I longed to join them on their adventures. Every weekend, they went somewhere and did something–skiing, ice climbing, hiking, as well as hitting parties and shows. I knew an adventure awaited that night. And I was right.

We headed out to Concord, Massachusetts to pick up Rod from his co-op job, then skirted Walden Pond so I could check off a literary stop, before heading north. As it got dark, it was shockingly cold on the interstate with the top down, but rules were rules. We arrived in Newburyport and drove to the beach on Plum Island, not much of an island, connected by a causeway and a short bridge. I'd been here before and knew it was famous for bird watching, even got a mention in Rachel Carson's *Silent Spring*, but I'd never been here in winter. It was cold. Freezing really. They wanted me to see the giant chunks of ice that had flowed down from Canada and landed on the beach. Chunks of ice as big as the VW Bug, a couple as big as a school bus. The moonlight turned them into glowing blue–white ghosts in the sand. While walking through the dunes back to the car, we spooked a snowy owl. It rose up before us on huge, white wings that gave it the feel of an angel. It certainly felt like a religious moment in nature, and it gave me pause to think of its possible symbolism, plague of the literature student. Back at the car, we wrapped up and went into the wonderful brick village of Newburyport, found Delaney's Pub, and had a beer and a cup of chowder to warm up. Then we headed back toward the city along the coast, freezing and screaming our asses off all the way. But none of us will ever forget that drive.

Back at the apartment we warmed up and got ready for a party in Back Bay. To get there, we left the car and took the T, the subway. It was fun to walk in Boston, crossing the Commons and the Public Garden. (We cut across the ice on the duck pond, which cracked and complained under our weight, making us spread out and run for it.) There were beautiful, fit–looking people everywhere, and everyone seemed about our age. Maybe a little older and better looking, wealthier for sure, but close in age. It felt like a giant college campus. On the way to the party, Rod admitted he had a monster crush on the art director who'd invited us, and when I met her, it was easy to see why.

Cassy was gorgeous and sexy, an athletic little fox. It didn't hurt that she lived in a fabulous Back Bay apartment on Marlboro Street, in a very cool brownstone. The apartment had plush oriental rugs, real furniture, dark wood bookcases jammed with interesting books, and stark white china. Cassy, an art director where Rod worked in Concord, and her live-in boyfriend, were probably twenty-eight years old, and cool as hell, "New York cool," Brian said, and we were duly impressed. We wondered if we had a shot at being as hip as this pair in the next six years. Impossible.

We'd been at the party for a while and it was getting both warm and crowded when Brian suggested we go up on the roof. From there, we froze as we looked across Back Bay's old chimneys, capped by decorated ceramic cylinders like beautiful pottery vases. Beyond that lay Beacon Hill in one direction and the Prudential and John Hancock towers in the other. We sat up on the roof and talked, catching up, musing about what lay before us. Me heading to Europe until July or August, him about to finish school, and both of us about to embark on careers and adulthood.

Then we noticed below us, in a building across the street, a nude woman beautiful as a dream, passing a window. She paused, as if on display for us, dark brown hair flowing over her shoulders. She turned toward the room's interior, speaking to someone. We were breathless–and for a moment, I wondered if it were a dream. She got into bed. Then here came a naked man, also well built. Was everyone in Back Bay beautiful? Were we going to sit there, a pair of dumbstruck troglodytes, to watch the two of them have sex?

Then a most remarkable thing happened. There was a second woman. Also nude. Also beautiful. A second woman? A blonde. I'd thought this only happened in porn, but here stood a second woman as beautiful as the first. "Oh, god," I whispered, "is this real?"

"Can't be," Brian choked out.

The second woman stood before the other two talking for a moment, then gave a little laugh and climbed on the bed.

"Can't believe it," I whispered.

"Me either."

Then the first young woman reached up and turned out the light.

"NO," we gasped simultaneously.

"I can't believe we saw that," Brian said.

"What's about to happen right there, I never even let myself imagine."

We sat there whispering and watching the window for several minutes, both saying what we saw could never happen to dorks like us. "Even if the opportunity was there," Brian said, "I'd find some way to blow it."

"Yeah, you'd blow it," I said. "Of course, I would have blown it before I had a chance to recognize I'd blown it."

We watched the dark window, silently imagining.

"Well," Brian said, "you are a perv."

"Takes one to know one."

All this time, we still hadn't taken our eyes off the window across the street. Who knows how long we'd have stayed there, like a couple of dogs watching to see if a squirrel returned. Finally Rod burst onto the roof with beers. "Here you are. I thought you'd left me." When we told him, Rod refused to believe us at first, then grumbled, "I'm always late for the show."

Before we finished the beers, we realized we were freezing again and went downstairs to the party. A lot of people had left and only a handful of cool, designer-types lingered. Cassy and her man held court in this casual, unaffected way that somehow managed to own the room. I didn't understand it, never had, this cool and distant magnetism. It left me feeling on the outside looking in. I thought Brian and Rod felt the same, at least judging by how hard they seemed to be working to get on the inside with this group. Brian was juggling bananas and apples with Rod, and not very well. Cassy kept telling them to cool it, while laughing in a languid way and threatening Rod that she'd take the cost of the fruit out of his next pay check if he dropped an apple or banana again.

A smart friend of mine once said, "Leave a party at its height. Don't overstay it." But that assumes you can recognize the peak.

I never quite developed a knack for it, but I did start trying to leave when I first noticed a party slipping. That night in Boston, we hung around too long, riding the party right down into the embers and then ashes. Eventually we left, after midnight, and walked through Back Bay and up Newbury Street, where plenty of fashionable people made the scene. Glamorous. Rod told about an unseasonably warm day, sitting at a cafe on Newbury Street and just dying as the gorgeous girls paraded about like it was summer. After that day, he said he couldn't imagine living anywhere else but Boston.

Back over in Harvard Square, we stopped at Club Passim, the famous folk cafe. Neither Brian nor Rod went for folk music much and hadn't heard of Passim, but I had and wanted to stop. We found the narrow stairs down in the alley entrance, and entered the surprisingly small room, not much larger than a typical high school classroom, to see what was up. Not much by then, nearly 2:00 a.m. The show had devolved into a jam session with some locals and a couple of troubadours. We sat and listened for a little while, just long enough for me to soak up the spirit of the place where future folk stars had played since the time of Pete Seeger (about the time he dropped out of Harvard), Joan Baez, and Bob Dylan.

At Brian's apartment, Rod crashed while Brian and I stayed up to talk until after 3:00. Exhausted I fell into bed.

Sunday morning Rodney was up and making breakfast for the three of us. He and I hung out until we had to wake up Brian to play pick-up basketball at the playground around the corner. Games started at 10:00. Then at noon we walked down to Nick's for double cheeseburger platters. Finally, we watched the Celtics basketball game that afternoon at a local pub, and the Celtics won in overtime to table-pounding cheers. It was another jam-packed, memorable weekend of fun, and then Brian and Rod took me to the airport that evening–freezing in the open convertible again–for my overnight flight to England.

England Arrival

I woke up just before the jumbo jet touched down. It was light and as we descended, a vast sea of green surprised me. After the brown winter colors of Indiana and Boston, England looked so alive.

Of course it was drizzling when I finally got outside. It rained at least a little and poured often during my first month in England. Still, I loved it.

As the first member of my family to go overseas, I felt the charge to seize each day, and I embraced that charge enthusiastically. There was no doubting why I was in England or for whom I had come–this was for me. I knew it was a transformational adventure, and I wasn't going to blow it. Almost every weekend I hitch-hiked around the country, living cheap. On Fridays, I only taught until noon, so I brought my weekend bag to school, and after class simply walked out to the main road and put out my thumb.

The students appeared at open windows and called out to me, "Safe travels, Sir." "Good luck, Sir." And then some smart-ass would call out, "You crazy Yank," and I'd laugh and shake my fist at the windows.

Once, trying to get back from a weekend on the coast of Cornwall, I caught a lift (you don't say "a ride" in England because that's slang for sex) from an evangelical minister who proselytized for Jesus. I went along trying to stretch the ride. And it worked. At his exit, he decided to continue on, bearing witness to convert me.

As he inculcated, I noticed eyeglasses in his jacket pocket–with a broken lens.

On these weekend trips, I stayed in youth hostels if rain threatened. On clear nights, I bivouacked in pastures or in woodlots on the outskirts of towns or villages, living on one or two meals a day to save money. I told myself every night spent outside and every day with one meal meant another day in Europe because I had an open–ended, standby ticket to return to the States. My one–meal rule meant a meal paid for because I met a lot of people who, after some conversation, offered to feed me. Not that I begged or bragged about my one–meal rule; they were simply generous to a young, solo traveler who seemed to love their country and their company. To cover room and board, my mother deposited $150 per month in my checking account, and I kept track of it, planning to repay all of it to her.

*

Not long after I arrived in England, I had an inkling, a premonition, that my father had died. This notion hit as I stood at my bedroom window, admiring a bright, gibbous moon on a March night. A chill shook me, and I pulled a chair up to the "electric fire" and held out my palms to warm myself. The few times I'd called home, Dad was never there. When I asked about him, Mom said he was working. I never got a card or letter from my father as I did from other family members, nor did he sign the letters or birthday card from my mother. And when she sent photographs from a gathering at Easter, Dad was absent from all but one which I recognized as a snapshot from another year. Would my family keep his death a secret from me? Yes, because they knew I'd come home right away and miss traveling in Europe when there was nothing I could do to help. Yes, it was possible. Likely. But it wouldn't work to ask. How could I segue into that question in one of my letters or in one of my rare and brief trans–Atlantic phone calls? And if it were true, a part of me didn't want to know because I did not want to end my adventure prematurely. I knew I would return home, and then be stuck unable to afford to come back to England–and fail to finish my program and graduate in May.

I also received a card from Missy with photos of my first nephew. Walter's son, born just a couple of weeks after I left, made me an uncle. I got only one letter from my brother. I'd excused his neglect because he was busy with his new job in an ad agency, and with his first child. But I also knew he hadn't supported my decision to go to Europe. So the opening paragraphs from his letter surprised me:

> Well I couldn't ignore your absence long enough today, so I'm writing. It's odd not to hear you weep over some disastrous romance in over two months, and odd not to have your energy around to tap, and odd to be without a literary companion. What is most strange is the absolute joy I have in knowing you are doing ecstatic things. I take (or rather steal) a piece of your glory in experiencing England. When you love someone as we do each other, it is a curious reward of that relationship that we quite literally share the experience, share the achievements, of the other person. I somehow enjoy like mad the fact that you are in England. It's absurd, but I do. I brag about it. I should be sending English postcards to friends.
>
> Be sure to keep in touch with the IU Placement Office and get back in time to find a teaching job. That's the priority. You'll have more summers for Euro adventures *after* you get a job. Enough on that. I assume you are sleeping with your eyes open. That is my only request. No souvenirs, just keep your eyes wide and take in every image until you are as cluttered with those strange lands as the old blue Nissan pickup was when we moved out of infamous Germa's house at 3 a.m.

The "moving from Germa's at 3 a.m." is a self–effacing reference to the first place he and Missy had rented after they got married.

Walter fancied himself an urban pioneer, moving into a marginal neighborhood. On the first night, after he and I had spent the day moving them in with our matching Nissan pickups, Walter, Missy, and I were sitting on the floor surrounded by moving boxes, eating pizza, when we heard two gunshots down the street. By the end of the first month, Walter was done. So we heaped our small trucks high with all of their belongings the night before his next month's rent was due, and escaped back to a safe suburb four miles from the ranch house where we grew up.

The second time I read the letter, I lingered over the snarky comment about me weeping over a disastrous romance. Right then, I resolved to never again share emotional details of a romance with him.

Mom's letters–and she wrote frequently, more than when I was in college because then we spoke on the phone a couple of times a month–provided family news, made reference to my last letter, and mentioned how much she missed me. She always ended with, "Soak up everything!" or "Do everything you can and enjoy it!" In one of her letters she closed with, "I'm afraid my news is not as exciting as yours, but give me time and someday I'll write to you from England!"

And I knew she meant it.

*

What Cape Cod had done for my confidence two years earlier, England elevated to another level. I was one of a few Americans in the small town of Exmouth in Devon. "Young Mr. Blake, our favorite Yank," my colleagues and soon my students chanted from time to time. Eventually, that became the call I heard from the school windows when I left on Friday afternoons to set out on an adventure.

My colleagues became friends who took me to their favorite historic and cultural sites, including obscure country pubs. The teaching itself was not so different than in the states–with the exception of occasional glitches in language or spellings.

For example, with a class of fourteen-year-olds:

"...and here's another way to write the date," I said. "You write 3 for the third month of the year. Then you put a slash after it . . ."

There was a titter behind me, an awkward silence, a whispered: "Did he say, *slash?*" and then a roar of laughter.

"What's so funny?" I asked.

Belly laughs all around, "He did. He said, 'Put a slash in!'" a boy gasped, and the laughter roared again. The kids were completely out of control, pounding their desks, pushing each other out of their chairs.

"Ellen?" I asked a reliable teacher's pet, who cupped flushed cheeks in her hands.

"Please, Sir, don't make me say."

And the rest of the class exploded again and kept it up until the bell rang and they boiled out of the room on giggles, "*Put a slash in. He said, put a slash in,*" echoed down the corridor. I hoofed it down to the English office to find out what I'd done.

Jason Battle, head of the department, had always gotten a kick out of my faux pas and reliably guided me through many a cultural morass–although he did post a running list of my quotable blunders on the wall of the faculty lounge for ready sport. When I described the dialogue, he went into hysterics, raising dust as he pounded a stack of books next to him and coughing on the dust. Jill Hanson, another English teacher, walked in and Jason, with tears rolling down his cheeks, told me to tell her. "No, no, wait," he said. Then he told Jill, "Go get Peter and Shaun first." I didn't mind if these other people knew; Jason had told Jill to fetch my friends in the department. Soon Jill, Peter Thomas, Shaun Mc-Carthy, and Isabel Pearson came into the room, all ready to hear the latest blunder from Young Mr. Blake our favorite Yank.

Though I didn't understand the punch line even as Jason Battle made me retell it, I delivered it, laughing along as my friends hung on each other's shoulders in gaffaws.

By then, Battle had composed himself enough to explain that "slash" was the most crude term for urinating. What American's call a "slash" in punctuation, we British call an "oblique stroke."

"How dainty you Brits are," I said.
Oblique stroke indeed.

Knocking Around Europe

When my ten-week teaching stint came to an end, I was sad to leave the school, and Jason Battle said he'd hire me in a minute if he could, but laws required him to hire English citizens first. The school held a short convocation to wish me off, chanting "Young Mr. Blake our favorite Yank" as I went up to say goodbye.

I left early the next morning before anyone would head for school, the sun just rising. When I put out my thumb, a bread truck headed for Exeter picked me up. From Exeter I hitchhiked through Wales, or tried to. Actually, I spent three days mostly hiking through the Wye Valley. But eventually, I reached Holyhead and took a ferry to Ireland. Most of my time in Ireland was in the west country, around Galway. I was struck by the beautiful but sad scenery–those fields lined with stone walls and cluttered with endlessly more stones, the abandoned stone houses which had fallen in on themselves. In Galway I met Cormic Molloy, who showed me the tremendous sea cliffs of western Ireland and took me to an ancient country pub where Gaelic was still the first language. After a few pints, Cormic waxed poetic about his love-hate for Ireland. He spoke of the wonders, then railed about how Ireland allowed its best young minds to go abroad because there was too little opportunity at home.

This last point made me think of my home state and my brother. Indiana produced its share of talent, but talent was the state's top accidental export. The best leave. When my brother's advertising talent gained national recognition, he could have, and perhaps should have, gone to Chicago, New York, Minneapolis, or San Fran-cisco. But he stayed. By keeping his talent at home, Walter became one of the city's stars. But he admitted he wondered what might have happened if he'd gone to New York. He also struggled to recruit and retain top talent.

On the way back to Galway, Cormic Molloy stopped his bat-tered old VW Microbus at the top of a high hill. The star-filled Irish night with a small moon seemed to press down on the dark landscape where hints of white stones melded into the black of the sea. Cormic clicked on his CB radio. From there, on the west-ern edge of Ireland, we heard the crackle of American voices, of truckers hauling peaches up the Carolina coast. Melodic, south-ern accents. Voices from home, from three-thousand miles away. At first I tried to call back to them, yelling into the microphone, but they couldn't hear me across the sea. Cormic and I slid open the side door of the bus and sat there, looking at the sea and the waning moon on a star–filled night and listening to the far–away voices.

*

From Ireland, I took a ferry to France, and a train to Paris where I met three other young American travelers, and we crashed in a rough little hotel in the Latin Quarter near the Sorbonne. After a few days of great art museums, good coffee, and cheap wine, I headed south on an overnight train to Milan. In smaller cities, like Pisa and Florence, I returned to the practice of hiking out of town and sleeping in fields or under low trees to extend my trip. I also maintained my one full meal a day frugality. I'd have a crusty roll and coffee for breakfast, then buy cheese, bread and fruit from the open–air markets for the larger meal. Living on the cheap was more than a necessity, it was fun, a kind of game for me–and more than a little self–consciously bohemian.

In Florence, I shouldered my bag and walked across the bridge over the Arno River and climbed into the hills on the far side. I found a beautiful spot overlooking the city, under a low palm-like tree, and slept under the stars in my sleeping bag. In the mornings, I hiked back to the train station, checked my bag and explored. I discovered my favorite piece of art in Florence when I visited the breathtaking David by Michelangelo and saw his Slaves in Stone. I saw these not as unfinished–which the museum label stated–but as the first works of Expressionism. How better to convey a slave than to leave him half-captured in a block of marble? Genius. On my third night in Florence, I was crossing the bridge when a pretty German girl, an art student I'd met at a cafe earlier that day, saw me. She was alone, waiting for friends from the University in Aachen, and suggested we have a glass of wine. Before long, she invited me back to her pensione to shower and ended up scrubbing my back. That night I didn't need to hike into the hills. In the morning, I thanked her, kissed her goodbye, and caught a train to Venice.

As I went from city to city visiting one great art museum after another, I often thought of my brother, wishing he could see these treasures, and wondering again why he hadn't wanted me to take on this adventure. Was it because he wanted to do it first? Maybe. Because he didn't want me to surpass him in another area of life? His letter had encouraged me to get the most out of it, so long as I came back in time to get a teaching position. Weird. I knew I would have to job hunt–but this adventure was far from finished.

Though I met and traveled with English speakers (a Canadian, an Australian, a Brit) for a day or two, much of my time was alone. I spoke no foreign languages, so in French, Italian, German, and Spanish, I could do little more than apologize, ask if someone spoke English, ask how much something cost, and ask where the bathroom was.

By the first of August it was time to return if I hoped to land any of the last teaching positions available for the fall. Still, I lingered a few days in London before heading to Heathrow Airport, weighed down with bags. I had a backpack, duffel bag, weekend bag, and book bag–yet I still managed to meet the demand of my mentors at IU: to carry all of my bags for five blocks.

I carried other weights too. Weights that easily offset the bulk on my back.

Homeward bound. What would it be like to return home to the land of huge cars and whopping refrigerators, of immense wardrobes, overweight people, and wanton commercialism? So much would be the same, and I felt so changed. Yet I looked forward to being among loved ones again. Would my father be there? Would my brother and I take up where we'd left off, with closeness or distance? Would I end up in Indiana, or make it to Boston to live with Brian Jackson and Rod Kittle?

Homeward Bound

As the 747 rose over London heading for Boston, I felt myself separated from something dear. Looking out the window as England's green vanished from view in clouds, I thought about how exciting it had been in the last days of February to leave the brown, snowy world of Indiana and arrive in the lush green of England.

When I landed in Boston, I planned to stay with Brian and Rod for a couple of days. They had graduated from the University of Cincinnati and were working in Boston as graphic designers. The jumbo jet touched down late, and I caught the airport limo shuttle to Cambridge. The "limo" looked like an ancient Checker Cab stretched eight doors long and appeared to sag in the middle. But I piled in with a bunch of businessmen, surprised there was no competition for the seat by the door. We squeezed three abreast on the tattered bench seat, and rumbled toward the tunnel where six lanes funneled into two. Completely knackered, I soon fell asleep leaning against the door.

I woke up when the limo hit a big interstate bump, and I felt my self sliding sideways. The door had popped open and I had a startling, close-up view of pavement! I caught myself on the open door with one hand, snatched up a handful of business suit with the other, and hauled myself back in, slamming the door after.

The guy whose suit I'd grabbed straightened his jacket and smiled. "How's the weather out there?"

I could've clobbered him. But, heart still lodged securely in my throat, I merely hacked out a laugh.

"Happens all the time," he said. "These things get to bouncing, the frame sags, and something's got to give. Usually the doors pop open, but I've seen a window blow out."

Welcome back to the states, Jay-bo.

"Somebody could get killed," I finally said.

"Could. But you know, I been riding these things three times a week for eight years, and I've never seen anyone fall out. Your little maneuver there was about as close as I've seen."

"Me too," the next guy chipped in.

"Thanks," I replied, "I feel honored."

*

When I arrived at Harvard Square, Brian and Rod were there in the convertible bug. In costume. They wore three musketeer outfits–like something from a 1960s musical. Crazy wide-brimmed hats with giant white feathers arching out of them. The third costume waited on the back seat for me. Rod jumped out of the car and grabbed a couple of my bags. Brian grabbed me in a monster hug. Despite the nutty outfit, the sight of the six-foot-three swashbuckler nearly made me cry. He was a link to home, to our shared past stretching all the way back to Story Book Kindergarten, to a mutual understanding that our futures would take us far from where we'd come. He was also a solid link in the long chain of love from friends and family.

"Hey, bro," he said, "let's roll," and he snatched up my heavy bag and slung it into the back of the car.

Rod jumped in the back. "You're up front," he said. "Returning hero and all that nonsense." With that, he jammed a big hat with the feather on my head and handed me a blue, shiny jacket.

"What? No sword?"

Turned out we were on our way to a costume party in the South End. A funny, crazy night, and I, who had not driven in six months, hadn't slept much over the last two days, addled by jetlag, and unfamiliar with Boston, was named designated driver.

Perfect.

Next day, Brian and Rod encouraged me to move to Cambridge and live with them. It sounded great, but there were realities. Like getting a job. Two schools in Indiana had agreed to wait for me to return from Europe for interviews. Still, I had decided to head East if neither came through. After all, the Massachusetts school year started later, and there might be some last-minute openings.

Later, Brian and I went into the city to knock around. At an early evening party, we went up to the roof of a high-rise overlooking the Charles River, imagining we'd see more beautiful naked people. But no. After a while someone Brian knew came up and took a picture of us sitting on a wall with the gold dome of Beacon Hill lit up in the gloaming behind us. We'd pulled ourselves up on the wall, sitting precariously. Right behind our butts the building dropped straight down six floors to the sidewalk. A foolish risk, perhaps, but it made for a great photo.

*

Hanging out with Brian and Rod in Boston, I felt like I was where I belonged–in this historic yet youth-oriented and energetic city. A place of fun and great intellectual pursuit. And with these guys.

But I had to get back to Indiana. At least for now. The next morning Brian drove me to the airport. I hefted all my junk and lugged it to the ticket counter. Midwestern storms delayed the plane for two hours.

I'm Going Back to Indiana

The paint shaker of a plane finally dropped below the storm clouds, revealing my home town stretched out flat and green in the rain. The jet descended, hit the runway hard, and I was home.

After six months of teaching English to the English and knocking around Europe, I was back in Indianapolis, a new college grad and ready to find my first paid teaching job. Would my family see me differently now? Would I still be the kid brother, despite being the first in my family to seek adventures in Europe?

I got off the plane fantasizing about my family holding up a "welcome home" sign for the conquering hero. But no one waited. I made my way down to baggage claim. No one there either.

Had they forgotten about me?

Here I was, an adult, age twenty-two, and that old fear fluttered like it had in the department stores of my youth.

Then I saw my father. He stood alone. Where was Mom?

At the same instant, I felt relief that he was alive. Here he stood looking young at 50, a baby-face still, somehow looking younger than I did at that instant. As I approached Dad, I said without thinking, "Where's Mom?"

"And hello to you too."

"Sorry," I said, "Hi, Dad," and shook his hand. "I just thought Mom was picking me up and you'd be working."

"She'll be here any minute. We drove separately."

This jolted me. We lived forty-five minutes from the airport. They wouldn't drive separately. Something was wrong, and I could see it in his eyes. He said he'd been working, getting car parts at a salvage yard west of the city–though he wasn't dressed for picking parts. I suppressed the urge to point out his obvious lie. It made me want to ask why I never heard from him the whole time I was gone, but I let it go.

As we started for the baggage claim carousel, here came my mother. When our eyes met, her rapid walk broke into a graceful stride ending with a skip and a crushing hug for me. Mom's eyes brimmed as she apologized for being late and gave me another crushing hug, so strong for such a small woman.

I mentioned it was odd that she and my father drove separately.

"We were off doing our own things," she answered. And this carried the immediate ring of weighted truth. I wanted to sort out what was up, right then, but Mom's ebullience lifted me off in another direction. She said some of my aunts and uncles were coming to welcome me home as well as Walter and Missy with Connor from across the pasture.

Waiting for my bags, Mom stood on one side of me, my father on the other. The two forces that came together to create me. Here I existed between them again. An odd, yet familiar energy flowing.

Now home from my long trip, I listened to the happy, airport voices around us as I quietly stood between my parents and watched the empty baggage carrousel turn. Because I'd been so immersed in English accents, these voices, these accents of home, rang as quintessentially American to my ear. That Hoosier twang. A confluence of north and south, the hard vowel from Chicago, the drawl borrowed from Kentucky. And the people. They looked more overweight than I'd remembered, as supersized as their SUVs.

Finally bags began emerging from a dark hole and sliding down to circle the carrousel, each bag a block of experience. Where had they been? What had they seen? How were they different? How had their owners changed? When my backpack (purchased in England and carried all over the Continent) appeared, I had the sense of myself lifting my European experience, yet another rebirth, from a steady flowing motion and setting it down hard in Indiana.

The three of us silently waited for my next bag. I felt Mom

put her arm around me and I hugged her again. She punched me lightly in the shoulder with an open palm. "I can't believe you're home," she said and laughed.

My father stood at my other side, strangely quiet.

Once my bags were off, Dad grabbed my duffel bag, Mom took the weekend bag, as I shouldered the backpack and carried my briefcase, and we started for the parking lot.

I felt an awkwardness growing as we stepped from the air conditioning into the familiar heat and humidity of an Indiana August. The rain gone, the asphalt steamed into the hazy, white-blue sky overhead. Who was I going to ride with? My instinct was to go with Mom, but I knew Dad was more easily wounded by minor slights. At the parking lot, my father started to hand me my duffel, even though I was weighed down with my backpack, daypack, and small duffel.

"I'll get it from you at home," I said.

"No, take it now." He paused, "Just in case I'm late."

"I won't need–"

"Just take it, okay?" His voice sharp now.

After another pause, his voice softened as he added, "I'll see you later."

"Okay," I said, juggling my bags, and then I followed Mom to the car.

She asked me to drive.

*

On the way she said she wanted to stop for a cup of coffee. This was as wacky as my parents driving separately to the airport because, while my mother loved coffee, she had a routine, a discipline, about it the way she did about most everything in her life: she only drank coffee with meals and never between. Clearly, this wasn't about coffee–she had something to say.

I stopped at a Perkins and cut the engine. Before we got out, I finally said, "Something's wrong."

She sighed. Without looking at me, she said: "Well, yes. Not long after you left for England, Dad moved out. We separated. And we plan to get divorced." Now she looked at me.

What she said registered both quickly and slowly. Like the tumblers of a combination lock falling into place, this answered a whole series of questions.

Quickly registering: Why they'd driven separately. Why there'd been an odd reserve from my father. Why his lie was so transparent. Why my mother's "doing our own things" carried a weighted resonance.

Slower to register: Why I hadn't heard from my father while in Europe. Why he was never there the few times I'd phoned home. Why Mom had sent an old Easter photograph of my father with the new ones of everybody else.

Slower still to register: Why my parents, so different from each other, had stayed together. Of course–until I, the youngest, finished college. (And the truth of this would emerge to be: Why my mother had stayed with my father . . . and the debt I owed for her sacrifice, a debt for which she would neither request nor expect recompense. She took her reward in watching her children succeed in the world.)

A world of questions lay ahead. The first came out: "What happened?" I felt myself making sense of all of this and trying not to let my face express too much, even as my gut tightened.

"We haven't been close for a long time. We lived together peacefully, but nothing more, really," Mom said. "And he found someone else."

"Really?" I nodded, taking in this point. Naively, I had imagined my father as being faithful to my mother, although I'd seen him flirt with women over the years.

"But that's fine. You know, I really don't mind," she said. "This may be hard for you to understand, but I think it's all for the best."

Again I was surprised by my lack of surprise. "It really isn't that hard to understand," I said. "You two have always been so different." This was true: by physical size, by interests, by emotional maturity, by any measure. What puzzled me was why Dad left my mother and not the other way around.

"That's right, very different," she said, "and now we can each go our own way." She went on to insist I not harbor any ill will toward my father. If anyone should, it was her, she said, and she didn't.

Who was this other woman? Was she the reason he left? But I couldn't ask now.

We sat in the car for a moment. Without any overt sign I understood she was content and pleased with the separation. She was happy. And I knew she'd make the best of it.

"Are you okay with this?" she asked.

"Yeah, I am," I said, hedging a bit. "It doesn't surprise me somehow, and yet it's still sinking in."

"It's got to be a shock. I'm sorry," she said. "I hope it doesn't spoil your homecoming."

"No it won't. It doesn't," I said. "You still want a cup of coffee?"

"Oh, not me. I never drink coffee between meals, you know that."

*

We pulled into the driveway off Mud Creek Road, and there was our little brick box on the flat, Indiana landscape. I hefted bags out of my mother's car and paused to look at the house. It seemed so small now. Shoved into the corner of the field.

Of course, my father did not meet us back at the house after the airport. But the rest of the family was there: Walter and Missy with baby Connor, a few aunts and uncles, a couple of cousins. When I entered, everyone cheered and slapped me on the back. I said hello to everyone and told them I'd be right back after I lugged my bags to my room.

I paused there to collect myself. Back from Europe, hit with the news of my parents separating, thinking about my first interview, and wishing it were in Boston, and my visiting family members waiting for me to come out and share my stories. I leaned against the window and looked out on a changing landscape. When I was a kid, this view stretched for about a mile with farm fields and woods in the distance, two farms and another ranch house visible. But now a scatter of suburban boxes encroached beyond my grandfather's field. The spec-house-beige color and 10/12 pitch rooftops reflected a mundane, affluent sameness while their pointlessly curved streets and bulbous cul-de-sacs assured congestion like a badly designed sinus cavity.

Although I'd never thought the suburbs would get this far, things were changing. My grandfather pondered offers to sell his land, including the field surrounding our place. I wondered if Mom would stay after the divorce. This humble house had been her beachhead for the family, her masterpiece of reinvention. She had succeeded.

A soft knock at the door and Mom entered. She came to me at the window and rubbed my back as she looked out. "Things are changing here, Jason. Lots of change."

"Yeah," I said.

"That's the nature of things," she said. "Come on out and see the family."

As soon as I entered the room, two of my uncles let out another cheer.

While flattered, I felt out of place as the center of attention. Unworthy in a way. But their interest felt genuine. People hung on my first story as never before, so I told another.

"One weekend I hitchhiked up to Stratford for my Shakespeare Pilgrimage," I said. "There I was waiting on an old wooden bench for a tour of Anne Hathaway's Cottage—she was Big Bill's wife—and the tour guide pointed at me to start the tour and said, 'And this young man is sitting on the very bench where William Shakespeare asked Anne Hathaway to marry him in 1582. I jumped up like someone stuck a pin in my butt!" They all laughed.

Someone asked for a story from Germany, and I told about my haunting walk around the Nazi concentration camp at Dachau, sensing the weight of the hundreds of thousands who lost their lives in that murder factory. Then how I couldn't find a place to stay in Munich, and walked around the beautiful city all night, how every time I passed a beer garden, some local would send a waitress out with a pint of beer for the wandering Yank. What little sleep I got that night at the train station was shattered every hour by police with snapping German shepherds straining their black leather leashes. They left me alone when I showed them my Eurail Pass and told them I was headed to Innsbruck, Austria on the 5:30 morning train.

"I woke up when the train stopped at a mountain village six miles from Innsbruck," I said. "The conductor tried to keep me from getting off the train. 'Innsbruck next stop,' he told me, 'Innsbruck next.' But it was just too beautiful to ride, so I hiked through the mountains on the trail along the tracks. I'll never forget the view over the beautiful city of Innsbruck before I descended to spend the day there."

Someone asked for stories from Italy, and my head was instantly full of them. I told of reading Shelly's poems on the Spanish Steps in Rome and visiting the ruins and walking among the vast artistic plunder in the Vatican as well as visiting the Sistine Chapel. And about Florence and Venice—leaving out the parts about a few lovely girls I met.

Where else did I hike? "My twenty-mile hike along the sea cliffs in Cornwall, England was amazing, but the winds threatened to blow me over the edge and signs warned hikers of the danger. I also climbed up to the glaciers in the Swiss Alps. And I marched through a driving sleet storm on Hadrian's Wall built by the Romans in Northern England." I told them about the cliffs of western Ireland and the many art museums of Paris.

I was flooded with memories and stories. At one point I said I must be boring them, or sounding like a show-off, but they said no and peppered me with more questions. They laughed at the story of the date with a slash, and they wanted to hear what it was like to play rugby. And was the theater in London better than New York? And what were the youth hostels like? Was Geneva really as beautiful as they'd heard?

It dawned on me as I spoke into the evening that I really had seen and experienced a lot in my six months in Europe. It gave me confidence that I had the teaching and life experience to make a high school better.

First Teaching Job

The morning after the welcome home party, I woke up to a Monday without a job or a future. I called the placement office at IU. They had two prospects lined up for me, high schools that had waited for my return, based on my letters of recommendation and my overseas teaching experience. Only one issue–and I had mixed emotions on this point–both schools were in Indiana. On one hand, I'd be close to family and the comforts of home; on the other hand, I'd be close to family and the comforts (or complacency) of home.

The first interview was in a small town bordering Bloomington, a position as an English teacher and assistant football coach. I could live near Indiana University, a place that had been magical for me, and the most liberal and intellectual city in the state.

The second school was Cathedral High, a Catholic prep school in Indianapolis. This position was as English teacher and head of the theater department.

I went into both interviews with confidence. Although a twenty-two-year-old rookie, I brought the unique experience of teaching in England. I felt ready to claim a post and make a school better. The day after my interview with Cathedral, both schools called to offer me a job. In some respect, the news was almost too good. There'd be no national job search now. (Not enough time for it, and I had to question myself if that wasn't too convenient. No chance to join Brian and Rob in Cambridge, Massachusetts.)

The big positive was Bloomington for the first school, and in some ways I thought it would be fun to coach football. In other ways, not. The Cathedral job fulfilled my desire to direct plays, a chance to do for some unconventionally bright kids what Mr. Goodenough had done for me.

It was difficult. I called on Professor Anne Pain, one of my mentors at IU, and her advice was simple: "Flip a coin."

"Right." I laughed.

"No, really," she said. "I know it sounds absurd, but it doesn't matter if the coin comes up heads or tails. In fact, don't even look at it. What matters is what your heart says when the coin is in the air."

She waited for me to say something, but I waited her out, not concealing my doubt at her 'flip' suggestion for deciding my future.

Professor Pain leaned forward. "Look, Jason, I know you've already weighed the rational measures, and you have two good choices. Now you need to listen to your heart. If you listen carefully when the coin is in the air, you'll know which thing you really want."

Okay, it began to make sense. I went home and pulled out a quarter. I flipped it. I listened to my heart, and I knew to take the Cathedral job, without even looking at the coin when it landed in my palm.

So I agreed to start at Cathedral High School a couple of weeks later, teaching five English classes of sophomores and juniors (128 students) per day, directing one play and one musical, all for a salary of $15,822 over nine months, plus $1,200 for directing the two plays.

A pittance.

And I felt rich.

When I picked up my first bi-weekly paycheck, I could hardly fathom it. Just a year earlier, during my senior year of college, I gave myself a weekly budget of ten dollars spending money. And the spring semester of my sophomore year, nearly broke, I'd allowed myself a scant two dollars a week pocket money. Suddenly, I had money.

Until paid for my first month of teaching, I planned to live at

Mom's. Then I'd get an apartment in the Broad Ripple or Butler area of Indianapolis.

*

During the triumphant month of my return from Europe, my father seemed distant when I saw him. I chalked it up to two things. First, his fear that I sat in judgment against him for finding another woman and leaving my mother. Though I tried not to feel that way about him, he *had* fallen a measure in my eyes. I wondered about this woman but didn't want to bring her up, and I felt like he owed me his side of the story. Second reason for the distance was another failed promise. He had pledged that my never-quite-finished Toyota Celica which I'd driven for a year would be ready when I returned from Europe. It wasn't.

Among my car's idiosyncrasies was a windshield (without moldings) that wouldn't stop leaking no matter how much caulk I gooped around it. Before dates I'd bail water out the floor of the passenger side, dry it with a towel and put plastic down to keep the girl's shoes dry. Before one date, with the most beautiful girl I ever went out with in college, I prepared to bail, but the puddle had frozen solid–a small skating rink on the passenger floor. When I picked her up, I forgot about the ice. As she went to sit in the car, her shoe slipped and she nearly fell out of my car onto the street, skirt flying up, legs sprawled. It was an omen for a long night. Two dates later, it was over.

When I returned to Indianapolis, my dusty Celica sat unchanged, untouched for six months in a corner of the high school body shop. Dad worked long hours in shame (and anger, it seemed) to get it in shape before I started teaching–and I helped. Grinding and sanding alongside him, I thought we might reconnect somehow, but no bridge formed. Disheartened, I spent less and less time helping him with the car.

When it was ready to repaint, we decided to switch from silver to white. The day I went in to see it, I was shocked to find a big

black, triple racing stripe on the lower half of the car, running between the wheels. It was a foot tall. The decal had a bold, italic
GT in the middle. It was a Chevy stripe, something GM put on
hopped-up muscle cars. I hated it. But my old man thought it
looked great, and I couldn't bring myself to say just how stupid I
thought it looked.

With a hokey *GT* on the side of my sensible, yet sporty, Toyota,
how could I put forth the image of the hip and cool, yet tweedy
instructor I'd prepared to play? So I colored over the *GT* with an
indelible black marker. It looked terrible, but it looked better.

Confronting Dad

About the time school started, Dad announced he was moving back home. I don't know if he quit his girlfriend or what.

But my mother said no.

The machinery of divorce was in motion, and she didn't want to slow the gears. They had agreed Mom would buy his half of the house. They'd split other assets, which was no bargain for her since he was the spendthrift and she the saver. But freedom is never free.

Mom's rejection sparked anger. In my father's world, he could choose to break the rules of faith, could juggle agreements, could come and go–with no crack in the china. But no one could disagree with *him* without risking a shatter.

With mounting anger, Dad declared again that he would move home.

My mother dug in. Her determined defiance put him over the top. He made threats. Fearlessly, she held her ground.

I decided to try to reason with Dad, so I stopped by to meet him after school one day. I avoided chit chat and small talk and struck at the heart of the matter. "Look, Dad, you've got to back off. You made a decision to be with another woman. Mom decided to move on. There's no going back from here. You have to live with it and move on too."

"So that's it? That's what you decided?" His eyes narrowed.

"That's what *you* decided." I replied. "You drove this. Not me."

"This has nothing to do with you. Stay out of it." He flexed his grip on a wrench, but I knew he wouldn't try to bury it in my skull.

"I understand it's not easy. But it doesn't have to be ugly. Don't make it ugly."

"Ugly," he mocked. "What do you know about ugly?"

"I know enough of ugly," I said. "I've seen ugly."

We stood facing each other, just beyond reach. Close enough to not back down. To move forward an inch would be an act of aggression. To step back, a sign of weakness. We were rooted in this place, this moment. Him with his wrench. Me with an opinion, an attitude, a diploma.

I was always more confrontational with him than Walter was, hounding him to quit smoking; pushing him to finish projects; needling him about my liberal politics and environmentalism. It annoyed him. I annoyed him. More than I knew. And I saw it now, standing four feet apart on the concrete floor of the vocational autobody garage. For the first time, I sensed he actually might relish a chance to bash in my head with that wrench. Still, he wouldn't. He couldn't. Perhaps my brother was more accepting than I because he knew more of our father's history. Or a different history. I had spent more time alone with him than Walter had. I had confronted and pushed because I sensed a wayward moral compass in him, and foolishly thought I could steer it.

*

When I was a freshman in high school, and loved deer hunting, I'd talked him into a three-day hunting trip at an Alabama state park I'd read about in *Field & Stream*. He didn't care about deer hunting, and disregarding the prey's impeccable sense of hearing and smell, he cleared his throat, blew his nose, ate candy, even smoked cigarettes in the woods. To me these things were offenses against the code of the hunter. And each offense incensed me because I was taking my first real hunting trip seriously. Before long, the old man tired of sitting in the woods and went to the truck to read magazines and nap on the mattress in the camper shell. After a couple of days of seeing nothing, we were getting ready to leave when I spotted a huge hawk in a treetop. Marveling, I thought it might be an eagle.

"Let's shoot him," Dad said.

Shocked, I said, "It's probably against the law."

"Go ahead. Nobody'll find out."

I just looked at him in disbelief.

"I'll do it," he said. "Give me the rifle."

"No way." I held the .30–30 to my chest. He had a shotgun loaded with deer slugs, not accurate enough to down the hawk. "Why do you want to shoot a hawk?" Now he recognized my disgust. Even at the age of fifteen, I was highly principled about hunting, never killing game out of season, never killing anything I didn't eat (except for crows, sparrows, and starlings). And I was judgmental.

"Okay, let's go then," he said, "I just thought it might be fun."

"What's fun about killing a beautiful hawk?"

"That's enough, I said. Let's go. Get in the damn truck."

Now, years after the hunting trip to Alabama, I was far more indignant about Dad's threats against my mother. There was enough of him in me–enough of his teaching about how to face down a threat, enough toughness. So I risked an escalation by telling him to back off.

Confront the enemy squarely.

The enemy? Was my father now my enemy, my foe?

No one could threaten Mom's happiness. No one. Regardless of the cost, I would not allow it. I realized the prices she had paid for me and Walter, and now she deserved her own life.

*

On one of my first weekends as a teacher, I went down to IU to visit a friend in grad school. When I came home, I found out that my father had come into the house, terrorizing my mother, smashing some of her antique dishes. He also took some of her prized possessions, among them an eight–foot walnut table she had designed (based on an antique she'd seen in Williamsburg) and commissioned from a furniture craftsman. My father had brought his chain saw in from the barn and fired it up in the house, waving it around. "This table is half mine," he said taunting my mother. "Think I'll take my half right now." And he held the whizzing teeth just above the rich, dark walnut.

Because my mother has impeccable taste–a love of things beautiful, as I've said–surrounding herself with things of beauty has always been a priority. But my father mistook this love of beauty for materialism. In the larger scheme of life, the table didn't mean a whit to my mother. He could not shake her by threatening items. Not that she wanted to see her beautiful table destroyed, but she wasn't about to throw herself in front of the saw or beg my father not to damage it.

My father tossed the saw aside and hoisted the table and took it out to his truck. He came back and took a couple of her other antiques. As a final threat, he grabbed Mom by the throat and slammed her against the wall, leaving bruises on her neck and shoulder. He left her with warnings of worse–to her and to any of us who opposed him.

All of this while I was in Bloomington having fun with friends.

The guilt of not being there for her hung heavily on me. The thought of my bear-like father slamming my small mother against the wall kept me from sleeping. My heart raced with rage, filling my muscles with adrenaline. My tongue pressed the back of my teeth, my jaw flexing, my hands twitching as I imagined attacking the bully.

In defiance of reason, Dad continued to insist Mom take him back. As if it were still possible. I don't know what changed for him: perhaps the woman he'd moved in with kicked him out, perhaps he feared a weaker connection with his children or his grandchild, all of whom he loved despite his baffling brand of passion. To get away from my father and let things cool off, Mom went down to Evansville, Indiana to stay with her sister for a few days.

A Bar Fight

I stayed alone in my mom's house. One night I was grading papers when the phone rang. It was my brother. Dad wanted to see us, wanted us to meet him at a bar.

"Why?" I asked.

Walter just said, "Let's go find out why. Let's hear him out, see what he's thinking."

"Why does he want to see us?"

"I don't know. But maybe we can cool him down."

I didn't like the sound of it.

And I didn't want to go.

But I couldn't let Walter go alone.

To prepare for the meeting, I went upstairs and selected a shirt that made me look bigger, a polo shirt with stripes across my chest and shoulders. Then I changed shoes, putting on the full-foot wooden clogs I got in Geneva, Switzerland. My father was about an inch taller than I, but wearing the thick-soled clogs, I would be the taller if we stood nose to nose. And I suspected we might. At the same time, the inflexible clogs could be a liability if things got physical. Then I walked through the pasture toward Walter's house. It was a warm September night. Crickets sang and lightening bugs flickered as if it were June, but fall was coming. We took Walter's Volvo, one our father had rebuilt. Driving slowly with the windows down, the dry end-of-summer smell poured in on us.

I said nothing, but I imagined the scene of my father pinning my mother to the wall.

147

Walter kept emphasizing, "We can't make him feel defensive."
Then he added: "Let's hear him out."
And then: "Don't be confrontational."
Quiet anger simmered in me.
"Did you hear me? Let's not be confrontational."
We pulled into the parking lot of the strip mall and paused. Both of us looked at the bar through the windshield. It was in a strip mall, a sporting goods store on one side, a paint and wallpaper store on the other. A once popular place, it had failed to stay hip and had aged poorly, becoming a suburban loser, a leftover from the 1980s, not the type of place my brother and I frequented. Our father waited for us inside. This wasn't going to be easy. We got out of the car and looked at each other across the top of Walter's Volvo.

"God, it's hot," I said.

"Fall will be here soon," Walter responded, knowing it was my favorite season.

I nodded.

"Ready?" he asked.

I wasn't ready. This felt like a bad idea.

At the large, black door, we hesitated. A childhood nightmare about the black door in the basement of the old rented house on 38th Street flashed in my mind, but my adult consciousness stifled it. I could hear the base of the juke box thumping, pounding through the wood. Walter stood behind my shoulder. I glanced at him, took a breath, and pulled the brass handle. The oversized door, deceptively light, flung open in my hand. Again we paused, briefly, before I led us inside, submerging us into the spent air of cigarette smoke and the stale odor from two decades of spilled beer. In contrast to the hot night air, the air conditioned room gave me a momentary chill. I stopped to survey the room. Walter stepped up past me and stopped as well. Dark brown phony barn beams lined the walls, supporting nothing. They emphasized the low, smoke-stained ceiling. The red-and-yellow plaid carpet was unevenly stained and worn to threads near the entrance where we stood. All the lights were red—except for the glowing white island of a lit-from-below fiberglass dance floor. The smeared chrome juke box rattled as it pounded once-popular disco tunes and flashed red and blue over the vacant dance floor. Four or five individuals, separated by stools, hunched over drinks at the bar. Two couples sat in black captain chairs at tables, two other couples at dark booths. If all this darkness and red light was an attempt to imply a sexy context it was an absurd notion in the nearly empty strip-mall bar. The place reeked of failure and disappointment.

I scanned the sprawling, cave-like room again, still looking for our father. There he was in a dark booth at the far end of the room, leaning on his forearms, watching his hands which were wrapped around a glass of beer. A nearly empty pitcher sat in front of him. I caught my brother's shoulder. "Over there." A tingle ran across my brain and down my arm to the tip of the finger I aimed toward the booth.

As my brother moved out of my grasp toward our father, he seemed to stride easily, but I hooked my thumbs in my pockets and walked on my toes. I sensed people looking at us, though I doubted it even as I sensed it. And I felt myself watching us from a distance as I followed Walter across the stained plaid carpet and the glowing dance floor.

The sounds of the bar mixed with my thoughts in a confused murmur. Why were we here, exactly? Some wisecrack from the bartender to a customer about the Chicago Bears. In a mumble, someone ordered another. A waitress laughing in a forced way. What was the goal of this meeting? A Donna Summer disco tune from the late 70's began to thump from the jukebox. Had we come like boys merely because the old man had called us?

Then my focus fixed back on my father, the deep vertical line in his forehead and his fallen eyebrows over his small nose. I recognized this wounded bear look. As we approached, he unfolded his thick, callused fingers and looked our way. He straightened up and tugged at the neck of his navy blue shirt.

"Hey, Dad," Walter said easily and slid into the booth.

I said, "Hi" and was forced to decide which side of the booth to sit on. As I've mentioned, my father was given to feeling slighted, and I didn't want to start our meeting with that. Didn't want him to perceive a repudiation or a two-against-one opposition. But I didn't want to let him feel I was on his side either, didn't want to sit beside him.

So I sat next to Walter.

"Where is she?" our father asked.

"She isn't in town."

"Hell she isn't. Forget it. I'm not talking about anything unless she's here."

What the hell? Walter hadn't mentioned our father wanted us to bring our mother, had expected it. Why didn't Walter tell me? What advantage did it give him, except that it put me at a loss? It caught me off guard, forced me to grapple with that idea in addition to trying to understand the purpose of this encounter and what could be gained by it. It felt like Walter had set me up. But why would he withhold this? What else was he keeping from me?

"Why can't you talk to us about it?" Walter asked.

"Talk to you? It's no use," he said. "Don't you see? God*damnit.*" His large, dark fist pounded the table, and the beer glass jumped, splashing some beer out before it settled. I watched the white globules of foam slide down the glass.

Walter had said something.

I looked into my father's face again as he adopted his quiet, threatening voice, more like a growl than speech. We'd grown up afraid of that voice and what it might mean. "She can have whatever she wants. Anything."

But we were no longer boys. "Anything, except out?" I asked.

He held up two stalwart fingers and waved them in my face. "That's right, she has two choices, take me back or die." He lowered his eyebrows and pointed a finger at us, "I'll kill her. And there's nothing you can do to stop me. I swear to God, I'll do it. I've planned it all summer. I'm not going to do it now, but I'll do it. She won't have a minute's rest while I'm alive. I promise you that. Revenge is first in my mind. Revenge! I can't change, and no one can change me! No one!"

"Revenge?" I snapped. "Revenge for what?" I was conscious of the muscles in my chest, back, and shoulders filling with blood.

"Careful, boy." He jutted his jaw forward. My father's mouth and tongue moiled over his dentures. I'd seen his frustration rise over a rusted bolt, his mouth working like this, just before he smashed out a car's side window. "Revenge for everything," he said.

Walter nudged me a little with his leg. He had seen our father's temper rise to the flashpoint too, and said gently, "Give us an example, Dad."

"Talking to you is–I may as well talk to the wall! You're on her side, so what does it matter?" My father started to get up to leave.

I sprang to my feet and stepped in front of him with a hand on his chest for a moment, only a moment to avoid the affront of a physical confrontation. "You aren't leaving. We're going to talk this out."

"I've said it. There's nothing more. It's finished."

"No," I said. Something was going to come of this even if I had to force it. And I was not afraid to force it with him. "No, it's not finished. There's a lot to say. You can't just leave." To my surprise, he sat. And I pulled a chair up to the booth and sat blocking his bench.

His hand covered his forehead and drew down his face. A deep sigh. When he spoke again his voice neared weeping, "You don't understand how I love her."

"Yeah, I do, Dad," Walter said.

But I did not understand. And his pronouncement angered me–testing my tolerance. I knew I should keep my mouth shut, but I couldn't let him get away with a declaration of great love after he'd left her, had roughed her up, had just threatened to kill her if she didn't do what he demanded. This was the kind of crap my high school students pulled to duck responsibility, their actions steaming off in one direction, then claiming a desire for the other direction as if powerless at the controls of their lives (staying up late to watch Monday Night Football but claiming to want a good grade on Tuesday's exam). Unlike my grandmother, who'd raised my father under the philosophy that we forgive and forget, I sided with my mother's family where one was held accountable for his actions today and tomorrow. So I interrupted, "A few weeks ago you told me you haven't had any life with her at all."

"That's true. No, it's not true, not really," he stammered. "Okay, I haven't been the ideal husband. I'm no angel, but I can change. If she'd take me back, I'd be a kitten for the next fifty years. She can do anything she wants with me." His dark and thickly callused hands opened out to us.

"Except make you leave her alone?" I asked.

The hands turned palms down, "That's right, goddamnit," and his eyes had locked on me.

I felt my heart pounding in my neck, pushing out to my shoulders. I knew my brother's eyes told me to back off, but I wanted to cut through the bullshit now, and I was going to start by not backing down from his stare.

"You left her," I said. "Why do you want to come back now?"

He didn't answer.

I asked again, "Why, Dad?"

"What do you know—you're a goddamn kid. You're twenty-two years old, what do you know about thirty years of marriage? You don't know shit!"

Yes, I was twenty-two years old, but I knew some things. I had lived on my own, gone places he'd never gone, seen things he would never see. When he was twenty-two, he was married, driving for Greyhound, taping rolls of nickels into his boxing gloves. Though our lives were radically different at the age of twenty-two, we both knew a few things and we'd both experienced a bit of life. When he was twenty-two he wouldn't have allowed anyone to tell him he was a kid who didn't know shit. And nobody was going to tell me either, certainly not him.

"Dad," I said, "being twenty-two doesn't mean I can't think." My posture had tilted toward him.

"Watch it, boy. You watch it!" Now he leaned forward, his jaw jutted, mouth working over the dentures, his hands rolled into clubs.

"Okay, Dad, we can hear you, keep it down," Walter said, unable to stay out of it any longer. My brother touched my shoulder and looked at me, as his other hand reached between my father and me. "Let's just calm down a little and talk."

"There's going to be a disaster!" Dad hissed. "You watch. If she doesn't take me back, there'll be a disaster. Life isn't worth living, and I'll kill myself, but not before I kill her. You remember it!"

"Why kill her too?" I said, and the next words flowed out of me unchecked. "Why not just kill yourself if that's how you feel?"

"Because it's her fault, goddamn it!" His eyes began to go bloodshot, and he said in a flat voice to me: "And if you get in the way, boy, I'll take you out too. Without a second thought. With some pleasure, I'll kill you."

I felt my eyes narrow, felt the blood swelling muscles across my back, felt myself leaning forward, felt one foot secure a purchase against the edge of the booth. If that's the way it had to go, his lessons had made me ready to go all the way to the end. All the way.

"Whoa, Dad," Walter approached cautiously, "this is getting out of hand." Walter took off his glasses and set them gently on the table, "Do you really think Mom should take you back now, after you knocked her around and threatened to kill her? After everything that's happened over the years?"

"If she'd just give me one more chance, one chance," our father said, his voice bending to a whine.

"She has given you chance after chance for years," I said. My bullshit detector was clanging in my ears like a tornado alarm. I had to address the reality squarely if no one else at the table would.

The palms flexed into fists again, and he glared at me. Turning to my brother, his face softened, leaning over the table to Walter, hands opening, he said, "I'd be a pussy cat if she'd take me back."

"No you wouldn't," I stated flatly.

"I'm leaving, it's no use talking. There is going to be a disaster!"

"No," I snapped, and stayed in front of his bench. My legs were cocked in the football position, my butt barely touching the seat of the chair.

"Out of the way, boy, or you'll get hurt," he said, shoving me back. I sprang up, the chair tumbling over backward. He pushed past and started for the door.

"Goddamn you," I burst out. "You can't do this to people!"

My father spun and our eyes locked. He came forward and put a finger on my chest. "I'll kill you too! I will tear you to pieces! Come out to the parking lot right now. I'll kill you. I'll kill you! I'll kill you right here, and I can do it!"

I caught his wrist and lowered it slowly. Firmly.

Things were different.

I was different.

From all I had seen and thought about, from my father teaching me about fighting, from my mother's example of hard work and sacrifice, from offensive line in football, from reading literature, from taking to the stage, from coming to Christianity and leaving it, from venturing alone to Cape Cod, from traveling in Europe, from visiting Dachau and World War II battlefields, from contemplating the monuments and lists of the English dead in the War to End All Wars, from this very man taking me to deer hunt in Alabama, from loves that lasted and those that did not, from many successes and failures–all of this had changed me, had hardened me, had made me strong, strong enough for this moment, had made me suddenly stronger than he was, and it was as if my dad had noticed none of it.

It seemed to me he had failed to take stock of his own life, somehow gotten fixed in the delusion that his actions had no consequences he could not undo with enough passion or will or, if necessary, violence. But his threats toward my mother, toward my family, toward me, I would not allow. I was prepared, no matter the consequences, to prove it. I would defend. I would protect.

As I slowly but firmly lowered my father's hand from my chest, I said, "No, you can't." My breathing was even, though my muscles were blood–packed and ready. We stood face to face. My eyes, an inch higher than his with my wooden clogs, fixed on my father's. Our eyes an identical shade of blue, a shade of blue darker than my brother's.

He acted as if he were turning to leave. Then he swung, an old trick he'd trained me to be aware of, one I was plenty ready for, and I ducked it. He grabbed my head and pulled me forward trying to smash my head into the bar. But I was too young and too strong now–my father's days as a weight lifter and boxer too far behind him. These things were different too. I caught the bar and pushed off–then wrenched his arm down, breaking his grip. As I rose up, he grabbed a nearly empty glass beer pitcher, yes, a heavy glass one, and swung it at me. I blocked his arm which caused the pitcher to hit the wall and shatter. I grabbed his arm, shoved it over my head, spinning him around. Before he could turn, I pinned one arm against his back and snapped a half–nelson on him. He tried to fight free, and I yanked tight and pulled him back across the bar room, scattering tables and chairs as if they were empty cardboard boxes.

A part of me wanted to hurt him, to hurt him badly, break an arm, dislocate a shoulder, fling his exposed face into a wall with all my might. And another part of me merely wanted to render him helpless, to end this thing and, more importantly, to make it absolutely clear to him I had both the physical strength and the strength of will to control him and prevent his plans for disaster.

My brother danced around us like a referee, telling us to stop and finally telling the stout bouncer and bar tender who to grab when they rushed over to break it up.

And the confrontation was over.

"Watch it boy. I'll get you." He struggled against the two men. "When you least expect it, I'll kill you," he declared and broke for the black door.

I stood there at the edge of the dance floor, looking after the direction he'd gone, arms cocked at my side, ready for him to rush through the door wielding a crowbar. My father, my dad. The fight did not seem real. And yet, it was vivid and in some odd way felt like the very thing I had been made to do. It must be how a committed soldier feels after a battle.

During this time, my brother looked for witnesses. But as is the case in such bars, no one saw anything until tables went flying. I became conscious of myself and feared some parent or teacher associated with Cathedral might be in the bar. I apologized to the employees and helped upright tables and chairs.

Walter came over and asked, "You okay?"

I nodded.

"Let's go," he said.

He followed me toward the door where our father had just rushed out. I prepared for an attack on the sidewalk, imagined him trying to run me over with his truck as we crossed the parking lot. And of course, he owned a gun. Was it with him, wedged under the seat of his truck? I stepped out first, knees bent, arms cocked. But the sidewalk was empty, his truck nowhere in sight. Outside in the night air there was still no relief from the heat.

The black door closed behind us, and as we walked toward the car, Walter continued to follow me. "Man, you look huge," he said.

My muscles were still pumped full of blood, the way they were during an intense weightlifting workout. My striped shirt no doubt made me look yet bigger. But I felt big.

I felt powerful.

"I don't believe that happened," Walter said.

"Makes two of us," I answered.

"We need to get him committed before he hurts someone. We can't relax about it—we're too close to it to be safe."

We got into Walter's car and started back to his house. "I can't believe it," I said. "That was my dad in there. I got in a fight with my dad—in a bar." We were quiet for awhile. "How does he think Mom would take him back? How did she stay with him?" My throat tightened until I could hardly speak.

"She waited until you finished college."

Yes, she had done that for me. She had sacrificed for her children since she was practically a kid herself. Because I was six years younger than my brother, she had to sacrifice that much longer. The guilt of it set upon me. Though she could not recapture her youth, she could restart her life. If only my father stayed out of the way. And I owed it to her to make sure that was the case after all she had done for me, for us. My thoughts followed this thread until I noticed my brother was driving slowly and taking the back roads. I didn't have to ask why. We didn't speak, didn't need to.

*

The only sound was the rumble of Walter's car and the warm night air billowing through open windows.

I had to circumvent my father's promise by beating him to the destruction. If a fight was inevitable, he'd taught me, get in the first punch and get it in quick and hard. "If you're going to hit a guy, you better try to kill him. Hit him soft and you might never get a second shot." And "If you start it, you sure as hell better finish it." The lesson wasn't lost on me. And I began to steel myself for action. In my head, I replayed every step and shove in the scuffle. I visualized myself from afar pulling my father over tables and chairs.

A "humph" slipped through my tight vocal cords, and my brother responded with a loud hoot and a laugh. "God, I was hoping you'd say something."

"I didn't mean to," I answered, unable to hold back a smile.

"Damn man, you handled that old street fighter. I couldn't believe it. It was like slow motion, and I was tripping around being super cool. 'Okay, Dad, settle down, don't do this.'" Walter went on comparing himself to a hippie putting daisies in gun barrels of National Guardsmen. He joked on, trying to make light of the event the rest of the drive home. I understood his running off at the mouth as a way to diffuse his tension, and he kept chattering. I couldn't let myself go yet, didn't want to talk. Not now. In that moment, he seemed young to me. Though six years older, he seemed younger than I was.

When we arrived at his house, Walter tried to make light of the fight when he told Missy.

Missy didn't laugh, and said, "We need to get a restraining order on him."

"Right," Walter said. "I hadn't thought of it, but yes, right away."

I looked down in silence, feeling their eyes on me.

Then I looked up and said, "You go ahead and get a restraining order. But I'm going to prepare to stop him my way—his way."

Walter got up, "A drink," he said. "Let's have a drink to calm down. You especially," he said pointing to me. "He'll respect a restraining order."

Bullshit, I wanted to say, but didn't. He knew dad never respected authority, why now? Maybe he said it for Missy.

Walter poured the wine, and filled the quiet, talking around what had happened, then moved on to his job and his soaring career. He had begun winning state and national awards for illustration and graphic design. Already, at 28, he was starting his own advertising agency. If ever there was an industry suited to my brother, it was advertising. His creativity, his keen analytical mind, his natural leadership, and his competitive spirit–no one would deny him his future success. More than any other, the advertising industry loves to congratulate itself, to celebrate its members as brilliant stars who are otherwise anonymous. The endless award shows are a device meant to keep would-be painters and would-be poets (Walter was both) from leaving the industry. And the device worked because most artists, my brother included, want recognition. This industry convinced him he was becoming famous. Walter became as driven in advertising as he had been at the age of nine on the football field.

*

On that night, after a fight with my father and threats against my life, I looked at my brother as he spoke, nodding at the appropriate moments, but my thoughts roamed. Dad's threats to Mom and me were real. It could happen. I tried to imagine what had driven him to these extremes. It had to be more than wanting his way; more than a break-up with the other woman if that had happened; more than fearing a split with his family. But I couldn't find a logic to it.

When Walter, Missy, and I decided to go to bed, Walter said he wanted me to stay at their house for the night. That closed the small window of light-heartedness he'd tried to create. We went to bed. All of us very still, hypersensitive to noise. Every sound filled with poignant thoughts. The muscles of my back, chest, arms, and legs quivered as adrenaline leached from them. Once, before dawn, I heard a noise. Silently I slipped downstairs and found my brother peering out a window with a baseball bat in hand. We went outside and circled the house together. My sister–in–law watched us from every window. There was nothing. It was that kind of night–the first of many–eyes nearly closing and then snapping open at a sound. I watched the window that faced the lane all night. Nothing happened. I wondered if my father thought I had beaten him at his violence. And I wondered what it might mean for our next, and inevitable, confrontation if he did.

I watched a red glow of daybreak appear behind the trees to the east. The red yellowing, the blue fading in over the dark sky. And then I heard Connor, my eight–month–old nephew, stir. I walked into his room and watched him wake from a night of placid blue-green sleep.

Shaking the Foundation

Over the next few weeks, things did not cool off. More threats of violence volleyed in from my father. Toward my mother. And toward me. Walter worked with a lawyer friend to establish a restraining order, and he called the cops after threatening phone calls, but they wouldn't do anything without some proof. Meanwhile, I tried to concentrate on teaching and worked hard to prepare for every class. I refused to be as hapless as many rookie teachers, and I struggled against the distraction of Dad and worries about Mom.

I moved from my brother's back into my mother's house, but the family thought it best for Mom to stay with one of my aunts. Though it was my decision to live alone in my mother's house (in defiance of my father's terrorizing), I did not sleep well. The house, still far from the encroaching suburbs, could evoke nighttime bogeymen in the best of circumstances, but add threats to your life, and suddenly the sound of raccoons fighting or wind in the trees sparked fear. For the first time in my life, I locked the doors at night. And I kept my twelve-gauge shotgun next to the bed, a handful of double-aught buckshot shells on the nightstand. But vigilance is wearing, difficult to sustain. Especially when the threats suddenly stopped. After two quiet weeks and Mom safely with my aunt, I relaxed a bit. If disquiet flickered in me, I quelled it.

As I finished grading student papers after eleven o'clock one night, though, an instinctive fear leaped. I listened. Something radiated. Probably a raccoon. I told myself to hit the sack.

That night I had a cinematic dream of my father attacking my mother. My vantage point, fixed at a high angle like a camera on a crane, left me as powerless to stop him as a movie audience is helpless to stop an actor. In the dream, Dad had the waxen-white face of the villain in a recurring dream from my childhood. When I got up the next morning, something felt wrong. Before getting into my car to leave for school, I hesitated. Listening. Looking. Something was amiss, but I chalked it up to my nightmare and went to school.

Returning home that day, I found a trash barrel blocking the drive. A piece of paper said "Jason" with an arrow on it, pointing toward my brother's house. A fear flashed. Without knocking, I walked into Walter's house and called, "Hey, anybody home?"

"In here," came my brother's voice. Home early from the ad agency where he regularly worked late. Another bad sign.

At the dining room table sat Mom, visibly shaken, her pale face forcing a tight-lipped smile. She was safe but scared. I'd never seen that in her, so it unhinged me. Walter and Missy looked addled too.

"What's wrong?"

Walter told the story: Mom had come back to her house to pick up some clothes, to get some more fabric (because she was making the fall line of skirts at Maggy's to fill her orders), and to collect the house bills. She had waited until late morning, thinking it would be a safe time with my father teaching in the vocational school. Then she'd planned to head back to my aunt's. As she got out of the car, Dad, wearing black, sprang out from the garage–like the villain in my childhood nightmare. He slammed her against the car and grabbed her. She tried to break free–and did–but slipped in the gravel, and he pounced on her, his weight pressing her into the crushed limestone.

"This is it. It's all over," he screamed in her ear. "This is it!" A black fabric bag, hit against my mother with the heavy weight of forged metal, and she knew it was his handgun. I imagine his breathing short and choppy, his movements a frantic insanity. Shaking her just to shake her, roughing her against the gravel in a cruel rage, spitting on her as he spoke.

She pleaded, saying she'd do whatever he wanted. She'd let him come back or she'd go with him, whichever. It worked. She managed to reason with him, to calm him. He got off her and let her up. She kept him talking, conceding they should try to save their marriage. And she began planning a course of how they might do that, how they'd mend the rift he'd caused in the family, though in reality she knew all of this was impossible. She managed to get him to take a walk while they discussed it, and, knowing Missy was home, got him to walk the path through the pasture to Walter and Missy's house. Once there, she got him to sit at the picnic table on the patio where she hoped Missy would see her.

At that point Missy interjected that she thought she heard something and looked out the window to see my parents sitting there–that ominous black bag on the table next to my father. Missy didn't know what to do, didn't know if she should call the police about the restraining order violation. She stood near a window out of view with the phone in hand, ready to dial 911.

Mom let out a nervous laugh. "And you had to stand there awhile." It took a long time for her to convince him to leave.

I wanted to know how he'd gotten into the garage, where he'd hidden his truck. My mother explained that during the night, he'd driven his pickup truck down the farmer's lane at the far end of the field and hidden it in the trees. Then he'd spent the night in the garage waiting for me to leave. How he anticipated my mother's return bewildered us. Had he waited to ambush her for several nights? Perhaps he'd assumed, since it was the end of the month, that Mom would return home for the bills.

*

I picture him waiting, playing out his "revenge."

He smokes a cigarette right down to the filter. Then he takes out the .38 revolver, hefting its weight and fingering the smooth, cold steel. Opening the well-machined cylinder, he turns it one gentle click after another, sliding each bullet out of and back into its chamber. After a cycle, he closes the cylinder, satisfied with its mindless and deadly mechanical click. Finally, he burnishes the forged steel with the black fabric bag before slipping it back in the bag and hanging it on a nail by the door. Then he gets up to pace again, urging his rage back to the surface. Conjuring a perception of injustice done to him. He lights another cigarette and blows the smoke toward the joists overhead. He could burn it, this house, the one he has told people he built. Blowing more smoke upward, he recalls how annoying I was as I used to harangue him about smoking. Remembers how he wanted to smack me, remembers the bar confrontation and thinks he should have killed me then. And he considers breaking into the house, slipping up to my bed, and pressing the revolver to my temple just enough to wake me before pulling the trigger. It would be so easy. It would be so impossibly hard. His son. No, he reminds himself, it is her. It is her fault. All of this, all that has gone wrong. How dare she dismiss thirty years of marriage so easily? How dare she not so much as shed a tear when he said he was leaving? How dare she not mind when he left? And most of all, how dare she not take him back? Now she would pay. And pay dearly. Anyone who got in the way would get steamrolled. It was too late now. They all would pay. Goddamn them all, and he would see to it.

Get Out of Town

Because my father knew my mother had been at my Aunt Maggy's, we decided to move her to another aunt's, to Aunt Ginny's in Cincinnati. We agreed. And it fell to me to ride shotgun—literally—on the two-hour trip to Cincinnati. Walter and I went to Mom's house and got my shotgun and a dozen shells. Now I loaded five shells into the shotgun, pumped one into the chamber, and put on the safety. I made sure my old man was gone, checking the field, the garage (a dozen or more of his cigarette butts lay smashed on the concrete floor). Walter went back to his house to call his lawyer friend about enforcing the restraining order on my father. I walked down the lane and checked out Mud Creek Road for a half a mile in each direction. All the while, I held the shotgun across my chest with my finger on the safety as if bird hunting, as ready as I ever was to snap the twelve-gauge to my shoulder if a quail sprang from the brush. Ready to fire. And if he shot at me first, I was prepared to dive for the ditch.

My willingness to fire on my father was unsettling. It was my father. Despite some hard times, I had loved and admired him. Had, for much of my life, modeled myself after him, or my image of him. Now I feared him as I prepared to do whatever it took to protect my mother, myself, and the rest of my family. After I'd secured the road in both directions, I went back to my brother's. Missy drove her van—Walter needed a good night's sleep to prepare for an important meeting the next day, and I wasn't happy about his choice. Mom was in the back seat, and I sat in the passenger seat with the loaded shotgun. I adjusted the side mirror so I could make sure no one followed us. It was a long and edgy ride to Cincinnati. After dropping off my mother and briefly visiting with my Aunt Ginny and Uncle Mike, Missy and I drove back to Indianapolis, arriving around 1:00 a.m. I crashed in the guest room and had to get up early to teach in the morning.

For a couple of days, all was peaceful.

That weekend Missy took my mother's sewing machine and a bunch of fabric to her in Cincinnati so she could work. Baby Connor rode along. Walter had to work. And I had a date.

Missy fed Connor lunch on Aunt Ginny's back patio, right outside the sliding glass doors. When he finished, she took his dishes inside. And that's when my father struck from a stretch of woods along the side of the house. A dark figure flashed across the peripheral vision of those in the kitchen. Before anything could be done, he snatched Connor off the deck and leaped into the back yard. With my baby nephew wailing under his arm, Dad yelled at the house demanding they send Mom out. Missy ran out on the deck. "She's not here." But he knew better.

Panic broke through for Missy when she realized the nightmare my father forced, a choice between the safety of her baby or the safety of her mother-in-law. She wanted to charge into the yard to get Connor, but she knew my father was much bigger and stronger, that he might hurt Connor, that he could hurt Connor in an instant.

As soon as Mom heard his voice she grabbed a sharp knife and dashed to the basement where she opened a small door to the dirt-floor crawl space and dragged herself in among the cobwebs. Dressed in a calico skirt and a white eyelet blouse of her own design, she crawled in the dirt of the damp, twenty-four-inch-high space in fear for her life. From there in the cramped, dark place, my mother heard the muffled voices of turmoil outside and worried.

A neighbor had heard the commotion and called the police. When the sirens got close, my father dropped Connor and escaped into the woods beside my Aunt Ginny's house. Missy told the police about the restraining order in Indianapolis, and they looked for him, but Big Walt was long gone. We feared he might be hiding and follow Missy's van and make an attack, or that he might try to stop Missy on the highway. So Missy drove to the grocery in the van, and my Uncle Mike raced Mom to the airport for the short flight to Indianapolis. That evening, I waited at the airport for a flight to arrive.

Irritated that my brother wasn't with me—something about working late on a presentation for his agency—and that I'd had to break a date, and still had to grade papers and plan lessons, I struggled with my emotions. It was my first trip to the airport since I had returned from Europe, and it gave me pause to think how crazy my world was now. Just a few months ago, I had thought my father faithful to my mother. Though I'd considered their union odd (such different types), I'd assumed them content in their divergent coexistence.

At the sight of my mother emerging from the plane, I had to fight back sobs. She looked wan and drained. Yet she mustered a glassy-eyed smile and one of her crushing hugs. As the hug lingered, I felt each of us reaching for fortitude in the other. She conferred a measure of her strength to me in that moment. I think she knew I'd need it.

*

From the airport we headed straight to my aunt's house, but I was uneasy about it since he had already made an attack at another aunt's house. When I put my mother's small bag in the car, the blanket across the back seat went unmentioned. Under it was my shotgun, loaded and positioned where I could sweep it up in a single, practiced motion.

During the drive, while I eyed the rearview mirror (watching primarily for his pickup but knowing he had access to other cars as well), I said I couldn't understand what Dad was doing. How did he think any good could come from his actions?

My mother said, "I think he's on the drugs again."

"What?" She may as well have said he was from Mars.

"I know this is hard to hear, and I'm sorry."

That's when she explained about his years at Greyhound, how the older drivers had given him speed to keep him awake on those long drives. And how he liked amphetamines. Liked the way he could stay up all night working on cars if he wanted. Liked the way they made him feel, pumped full of invincibility. I was stunned, my brain like a sponge slogged full of mud. Mom went on to tell me about his hospitalizations to dry out. More secrets kept from me but known to the rest of the family. In my naiveté, I'd thought of my father as an upstanding man, never dreamed of the possibility, especially since when I was a kid he'd bragged about never drinking more than two beers.

Much as my mother's news of divorce had made sense of things before, this too ordered a lot of my confusion about Dad's emotional swings. It made sense of what went on during my childhood. The unpredictable temper. The amped–up, all–night work sessions. The unexpected vanishing acts. The glazed–over moments (like unwittingly driving twenty in a forty–miles–per–hour zone). It probably explained his ranting and raging on the sidelines during ball games. And why the family had lost the little bungalow in Fountaintown before I was born. Processing further, I remembered his asking about a teacher selling drugs in the vocational wing of Lawrence North. Could the teacher have been him? Was he probing to protect his own dealing in the high school? Or was he protecting someone else? His source?

I remembered when I was twelve, Tim Parker and I had found a bag of marijuana under the seat of a Jeep Dad had bought. He joked that the dope must have belonged to the previous owner. Then he emptied the contents of the plastic bag onto a newspaper and burned it in the gravel driveway, leaning into the smoke and sniffing with eyes closed, as if in pleasure. It made me uncomfortable with my friend. "So that's what dope smells like?" my father said when he finally opened his eyes. Then he told me not to mention it to Mom. "It would upset her for no reason."

Mom's revelation also explained those times when friends stayed all night, and Dad would explode into the living room bubbling with energy to get a glass of water. He might pause before going back to the garage to tell us one of his wild stories, arms sweeping in exaggerated gestures as he described how in high school he'd spun doughnuts in the gravel parking lot, showing off his hot rod–only to find the principal standing there when the dust cleared. Or how during a football game with Deaf School my father got into a fight on the field when a kid stepped on his hand. Supposedly, my dad grabbed the kid's facemask, jerked his head and punching him under the ribs, until they had to carry the boy off the field.

My friends were amazed and impressed with his vigor. So was I–although I hoped those who saw it would forget how his energy could turn ugly, as it had during that Perry Meridian football game. If possible, I kept his wilder stories secret. I also kept secret outbursts like the night he argued with Mom and slammed his fist on the kitchen table, splintering off a third of the tabletop. And many, many other smaller flashes of what were probably chemically–induced insanity.

Twice I had seen him take a vial from somewhere in his tool cabinet, shake out a handful of pills, and swallow them. I questioned him. "Aspirin," he said.

"But you're not supposed to take so many," I responded.

"I'm a big man, with a big headache."

When I pressured him, he grew angry. "Shut up. It's none of your damn business."

Later I learned from Mom that during Walter's high school days, Dad almost went to jail. When Walter was friends with Lewis Mason, my father became friendly with Dr. Mason, and Dr. Mason became our family doctor. Dad tinkered with Dr. Mason's cars–perhaps in trade for health care, but more likely to befriend and beguile the gullible doctor by seeding a sense of obligation in him.

In time, my father jawboned Dr. Mason into prescribing high-voltage diet pills. When Dad asked for more, the doctor balked. Not to be denied, my father stole prescription pads and began writing his own. Soon a pharmacist became suspicious about the frequency of refills and called Dr. Mason. Caught in a forgery, Dad was going to jail with Dr. Mason pressing charges–until Mom stepped in. She convinced Dr. Mason to drop the charges and promised to get my father professional help.

I recalled Dad being hospitalized and then being bedridden. In a painful rage, he'd punched a hole in the hollow-core bathroom door and split it off its hinges. This was about an ulcer, I was told. But was it? Or was it to break his addiction? If for an ulcer, was it connected to the drug abuse? Perhaps I didn't want to know what I didn't know. After all, the more I learned about my father, the smaller he became, the less he lived up to the image the rest of the family had painted.

I didn't mention my thoughts to Mom as we rode in the car. But then I asked, "Is there anything else?"

"You may as well know," she said. "It was during his days at Greyhound that he began chasing other women."

I shook my head. "I'd always imagined him faithful to you."

"I know you did, Honey. When he first told me, we'd only been married a little over a year, and I couldn't believe it. I mean, I was from a family where people just didn't do that sort of thing. He started going out to the bars with the older Greyhound drivers in Chicago and St. Louis, picking up waitresses. When he told me, I didn't know what to do. Here I was with a baby, and I was so ashamed of him, ashamed about him, that I couldn't tell a soul. He would promise to stop, but then here'd come another confession in a few months. It was almost like he liked to tell me about it, like he had to."

"I'm sorry, Mom."

"It's okay. You know, it didn't ruin my life. I mean, even with all of that, I've had a great life."

"Doesn't sound like it to me," I said.

"But I have, Jason. I just decided, if I can't have a good husband, I can have great kids, and I dedicated myself to kids. And look at you and Walter. I've got a lot to be thankful for, a lot to be proud of. The two of you far outweigh anything negative from him."

"I can't believe he treated you like that. Can't believe I believed in him."

"Don't feel that way. He loved you boys. He really did. Maybe he didn't always show it the way you wanted, but he did. I just think he's gone off the deep end."

We were quiet for a while. I had a lot to think about, plenty to sort out. Yes, it was clear he had loved me, true enough. But his actions of late made it hard to imagine ever wanting him to be part of my life.

I brought in the light bag for myself (just enough to get dressed to teach in the morning), so I could sleep on the couch and guard my mother and aunt. And I brought in my shotgun. After they went to bed, I checked the locks on all the windows and doors. I started to unload my shotgun, but imagining the worst, I left it loaded on the floor next to me within easy reach. Normally a deep sleeper, that night every little noise woke me.

Goodbye to Boyhood

All of this mess with my father went on in the first two months of my first semester at Cathedral. Every night I read the assignments for the next couple of days, made notes for things to discuss in class, and planned lessons, goals, and intended outcomes. I spent a lot of time on this because one of the things I'd been taught at IU, and had seen and experienced first hand, was that a well-prepared and knowledgeable teacher had fewer discipline problems in class. I wasn't about to let anyone accuse me of not knowing my material or of failing to manage my classes. I also wrote tests and quizzes, selected vocabulary lists, conjured writing assignments, and graded papers. God, how I graded papers. I had 128 students, so a two-page writing assignment each week meant I had to read 256 pages of high-school level writing. Beyond reading, I had to correct, critique, and try to teach better writing on each of those pages. I knew teaching was a lot of work, but if the amount of prep time was intense, the volume of grading was a tsunami. And then there were the seven hours a day in front of a frequently hostile audience. (For the most part, my students seemed more interested in grades than in learning, so the hours spent making notes on papers to help them become better writers often felt wasted.)

And those teaching demands coincided with worries about what my father might do to my mother, or to me, or to someone else in the family.

I actually planned how to avoid being shot in front of my students if he came to my classroom. To prevent my students from witnessing my murder. There were two doors in my classroom to the same hall. If he appeared outside one door, I would bolt for the other door and do my best to fight or negotiate in the hall. In a fight I would make a hell of a racket, roaring at him with his own most booming and aggressive voice, trying to take him off balance. "Get the hell out of here. Your drugs make you weak. You're not half the man I am! You got no right coming here!" I practiced the words, the scene, and how to reverse the momentum of his attempted surprise. Of course, another reason to bellow at him was to alert the men teachers near my room for help.

And if he came to the door and leveled a gun at me, I had resolved and mentally prepared to rush him, to die outside my room if possible, and, if he hesitated as he looked down the barrel at his youngest child, I just might have a chance to fight for the gun. I reconciled myself to the reality that Dad had become my opponent, my enemy (he was a level-five nitro) and that a life-and-death struggle, if not eminent, was possible, and I had to prepare for it. Prepare to win it.

At one point I considered telling the school principal about my problems with my father, about the potential trouble so they could watch for him. But I held my tongue when I thought they might fire me to avoid any risk. I told no one about the trouble for fear of who might learn about it and what might result.

These thoughts and events changed me, hardened me. I understood they were not the thoughts of a kid. When I pondered Brian and Rod goofing around in Cambridge and Boston, their lives seemed impossibly far away from me now.

*

We had to find a safe place for my mother. At a family gathering with Mom, Walter, Missy, and me, we talked about it. I felt the responsibility–I wanted the responsibility–to solve the problem. Fortunately her fashion design and sewing business was pretty portable.

"I don't want to stay with any of my brothers or sisters," Mom said. "I'd be afraid of what might happen if he found me." None of us wanted to endanger or worry any of her siblings either.

"And he'd probably look for you there," Walter added.

"Stay with us," Missy said, and I sensed Walter stiffen.

After a split second pause, Mom answered, "No, Honey. I don't think that's a good idea right now. It might not be safe."

"I planned to get an apartment. I can do it now and you can stay with me," I said.

"But he'd follow you home from school," she answered.

"Right," Walter said. "I think you should stay with someone Dad doesn't know."

Then the answer came to me and I said, "You could stay with my friend Sarah Robin in Bloomington."

I explained how Sarah and I had become friends when I observed her teaching English and theater at Bloomington North High School. She lived alone and had extra room at her condo; my father didn't know her; and my mother could sew while Sarah taught school.

Everyone agreed it was a good idea.

My mother's independent streak didn't want to inconvenience anyone or rely on someone outside the family, but she knew there weren't many options and agreed to stay with Sarah.

I knew the answer to the question before I called Sarah and explained the situation following my father's ambush in Cincinnati. "Your mom is welcome to come and stay as long as she wants." Though we had been friends for just ten months, I knew Sarah was the kind of friend I could count on.

Leaving my mother's car behind, I drove her to Bloomington and spent the night. Sarah was as welcoming as family.

Mom and Sarah did get along well, but after just one week, my independent mother began to feel self-conscious, as if she were a burden. And without a car, she began to feel confined. I offered to deliver a car, but she couldn't get past feeling like she was a burden to Sarah. On Friday, after school, I drove to Bloomington to get her. She slept on the couch of my apartment that night.

She had used the time at Sarah's to figure some things out. In the next day's family powwow, she laid out her plan. She'd decided to get a stronger restraining order and to push for a speedy divorce. And then she would leave town, leave the state, and go somewhere on her own until things were finalized. It was best for her to go alone.

That afternoon, Walter, Mom, and I went to see Greg Garrett, my brother's lawyer friend who'd taken care of the first restraining order. A rising star in the legal profession, who'd worked for the prosecutor, this red-haired, tough-minded, and quick-witted Irishman befriended my mother immediately. They understood each other at a chemical level, as if in seconds they recognized their common bond of work ethic, courage, and intelligence, and Mom knew she could trust him.

Greg Garrett was intense. He didn't want to gamble with my father, no need to take any chances. He said the restraining order was a good thing, but the police and courts in 1996 still didn't treat domestic violence as a serious crime, certainly not in Indianapolis. Garrett supported my mother's idea of leaving the state alone. He said she should take a new car because hers was registered in my father's name, giving him an opening to charge her with auto theft if she took it. In my mind, she needed a new car because of the not-so-reliable history of Dad's projects like the one she drove. The next thing Greg insisted on was that Mom stay at his house until she was ready to leave. "He's smart enough not to mess with me," Greg said. "And if he does, Jason'll be there to take care of him." Then he looked at me, "Right, Jason?"

"That's right," I said.

To my surprise, Mom agreed.

As we left Greg's office, he caught my arm before we went out the door, "You'll bring your shotgun."

I nodded.

He patted me on the back.

That night Mom and I stayed at Greg Garrett's, not more than two miles from my mother's house. His wife and two daughters graciously welcomed us. We parked my car in his garage and closed the door. I slept on the couch with my shotgun on the floor next to me–loaded with three double-aught shells and two deer slugs. Those double-aught shells held nine pellets about the size of .22 bullets, hard to find something more deadly.

Greg came in after everyone else had gone to bed and sat on the coffee table in front of me. "Now goddamn it, Jason, I know you're pissed off, but don't you kill him unless you have to. I don't doubt for a second you could do it. But don't." He paused. "Unless you have to." He rubbed his chin. "Unless you *really* have to, like if he's got a gun. I don't want to have to defend you in court." We both sat there for a minute. He looked around at the large bank of windows at one end of the room. "Sleep with your head at that end," he indicated so I'd sit up facing the windows.

"That's what I'd planned."

"Yeah," Greg rubbed his chin again and around the back of his neck. "If he kicks in the door or smashes the glass, you probably ought to take his leg off before you figure out if you'll have to kill him."

I nodded.

"If something happens, I'll be in here like that," he snapped his fingers, "with my revolver."

We sat there another couple of beats. Thinking about it.

"But I really don't think he'll try anything. Even if he knew where you two are. I really don't." He got up and looked around at the windows.

"Just don't kill him unless you really have to, okay?"

"Okay."

He left the room, and I lay down on the couch. He came back in three seconds later and tipped the heavy, wooden coffee table on its side in front of the couch like a shield and left without a word. We both understood why.

The only way to be ready for the worst was to practice, at least in my mind. Testing a few positions for the shotgun until I had it placed where my hand fell naturally to the grip. I could see the front door down the hall and imagined the frame splintering under his heavy boot. That would be a tough angle for me. Picturing the glass windows in front of me bursting forth, I hefted my shotgun. That was the easier angle. Then I looked at the door. Would it be best to roll off the couch behind the coffee table and fire from the floor? I got up and moved the coffee table back a couple of feet.

I got a little sleep that night. Not much, but some. I doubted my father would ever think to look for us at Greg Garrett's, and it seemed unlikely that he would try to attack us there even if he knew. Unlikely, but possible.

Moving Out

On Sunday morning, when car dealers were closed, Walter, our mother, and I went to Roger Blake Honda–yes, one of the dealerships owned by my father's brother–to meet my cousin Bobby Blake. Bobby, eight years older than I, was a born car nut, a wild one rebelling against my Uncle Roger, racing around in hopped-up 1970's muscle cars: GTOs, Camaros, and Firebirds. Surely Bob's being so much smaller than my uncle had something to do with his rebellion, compounded by my Uncle Roger's huge success in the automotive industry, shoes too big for Bobby to fill. This rebellion and love of cars made my cousin friendly with Dad–my old man had been a hot rod show-off as a kid himself. And that desire still lived near the surface in my father. When Bobby needed help, repairing a fender he'd smashed, or jury rigging a loud muffler on one of the few vintage Morris Minis in central Indiana, or trying to find parts to rebuild a '57 Chevy, he went to his Uncle Walt, my father. And I'm sure my dad's willingness to fuel Bob's rebellion against their mutual nemesis, Uncle Roger, sealed the bond between them. Eventually, Bob outgrew his rebellion to a point where he got in line to take over the gold mine of car dealerships my uncle had built. That kind of money has a way of quelling rebellion. Though rumors of Bobby's cocaine use reached my ears more than once, I didn't want to know. Still, I knew he had the resources for that recreation, and he was already wearing his second marriage thin. Perhaps he had drug abuse and infidelity in common with my father too.

Though Bob knew little of the recent problems with my old man, he treated his Aunt April, my mother, with the utmost respect. I felt compelled to tell Bob my father couldn't find out about this car. He understood, he said.

We picked out a new Honda Accord for my mother. It was the first new car any of us had owned. The closest thing had been company cars Dad drove during one or another of his hitches as an insurance adjuster. I rode home with Mom. The new car smell signaled a separation from my father's domain of almost-repaired automobiles and seemed a portent of a new beginning for Mom. At home, I helped her pack bags and sewing machine into the car. The weight of sending her off alone was far heavier than anything I hoisted into the trunk. We hugged a long time before she got in to leave. She said she'd see me soon. Neither of us knew when. And she didn't even know where she was going yet. East, she said. But beyond that, she'd figure out on the road.

I followed her to the interstate to make sure Dad didn't tail her. It was hard not to keep following. At the overpass I pulled over and watched the silver Honda circle the cloverleaf and head east. I watched until her car was out of sight and then some, wishing I could keep an eye on her wherever she went, wanting to be with her.

Then I thought about the classes I had to teach, the papers to grade, the lessons to plan. And soon, I had to select a play for Cathedral's fall production. These responsibilities pushed me back to my brother's house where I was staying for the time being.

Walter and Missy's beautiful house was just up the sloping pasture from my mother's. I stayed in the guest room facing the front, where the long driveway came in from the road and I could see the fork where the lane continued back to Mom's house. When I had trouble sleeping, and I often did during that time, I stood at the north window watching for my father. My shotgun waited in the corner, my once beloved shotgun. Now I dreaded the sight of it.

Since I was fifteen and had special ordered this gun, it had been a prized possession. A classic Remington 870 Wingmaster–a 12-

gauge pump shotgun–it had cost me $300. A left-handed model, it had to be special ordered and not many gun shops wanted to handle it; but I found a place in Bloomington which ordered it for me at no extra charge. My peacenik brother, in college at the time, didn't want to pick it up for me when it came in. But my mother stepped in, and Walter brought it home for me the next weekend. Lifting it out of the box for the first time, the weight and balance of the shotgun, the grain of the walnut stock, the hand-carved wood grip, the sure-sounding snap of the pump, the 32-inch upland bird-hunting barrel with a vented rib–it all felt just right. I felt about it the way a car nut, like my cousin Bobby, would feel about a Porsche. I loved bird hunting with it, and I became a deft shot. But after two harsh winters and two wet springs decimated the bird populations while I was in college, I gave up bird hunting, planning to resume if game-bird populations bounced back. The shotgun had come to symbolize past days afield, walking for miles trying to kick up game in the woods and fencerows around the farmland where I grew up. But I never took up hunting again.

Now my father's violence had turned my bird-gun into a weapon. And I could never look at it as I had before. Another piece of my boyhood gone.

*

In Walter's guest room, with my shotgun standing in the corner, waiting, shells right next to it, I couldn't allow myself to go soft with any sadness about what it had become. Now I had to remain ready to use it as a weapon.

*

One evening I decided to act. Earlier that day I'd found a letter in my mailbox at the school office. All it said in large, hand-printed letters was this:

"When you least expect it."

My father had told me he would kill me when I least expected it: you don't forget it when someone says that. It was time to confront Dad. To let him know his threats and his actions had to stop. Now. Walter came home as I put my shotgun into the back of my car and tossed in a box of shells. Just in case.

"What are you doing?" he asked.

"I'm going to find Dad and have a little conversation. He threatened me today by letter."

"You can't do that," Walter said. "He might kill you."

"Or I might kill him."

Walter rushed in, "If he wrote a threat, we have a clear violation of the restraining order. Let's call Greg Garrett."

"First of all, he didn't sign it, no return address. And with Dad, a restraining order is about as useful as toilet paper."

"He could go on a rampage," Walter said. "He might come straight here, looking for Mom, but take out anyone in his way. You heard him say he would destroy anyone in his way."

"Walter," I said calmly, "that's why I have to go. He can't terrorize us. I can put a stop to it."

"Or die trying and spark a killing spree." Walter stepped between me and the car. "I won't let you go. I can't risk losing you." He must have seen how his words didn't move me. "I can't risk losing them." His chin indicated his house, meaning Missy and baby Connor.

I stood there for a moment, taking in his nice house. He was right. My father had threatened to kill me and my mother. Not my brother, except in his sweeping barroom rage, "I'll kill you all." But even then, his eyes were locked on mine. My eyes went back to my car, to the back seat with the gun.

"Please, Jason," Walter said, "Please don't force the issue. The stakes are too high. For all of us."

That's when it dawned on me that my brother saw me, the one who had confronted our father and who had become the secondary target, as a threat to the peace and safety of his home.

Since childhood, Walter had avoided direct confrontation with our father. Not me. And I'd paid a price. I'd absorbed a few sharp backhands from Dad. Several times he'd shoved my head to the wall and pressed me there by the throat. Many times he'd shaken me by the neck, and tossed me aside. But not Walter. Never Walter.

Even when Dad attacked me in the bar, my brother danced around never touching either of us, offering me no aid or support, merely pointing the bouncers toward my father after I had fought to neutralize him. When Missy and I drove my mother to Cincinnati, where was Walter? Why did I walk the road alone with my shotgun to make sure the old man wasn't there to ambush us? When my mother flew back from Cincinnati, why did I pick her up alone? Whatever it was, he did a disappearing act. When the heat was on, Walter was gone.

Now that Mom had left the state, the chances of my father's rage turning on me escalated. My presence in Walter's house increased the danger to his family. At one point, I'd seen myself as their bodyguard, but now I saw how I could drag them into the violence. I could not shake this nagging thought once I'd hit on it. I might endanger them. I was an accidental threat. So the next day I rented a one-bedroom apartment near the village of Broad Ripple and moved out. Though Walter and Missy never asked me to move out, made every overture to make me feel welcome, wouldn't even accept rent, I had to leave. I'd wanted a place of my own anyway–a familiar trait of independence sprouting.

*

By then Mom had settled in the outskirts of New Haven, Connecticut. She stopped there because she'd remembered my stories about the summer I went to Cape Cod. I had spent some time in New Haven visiting a friend at Yale and had talked about the beautiful Gothic buildings. If she'd asked, plenty of New England towns would have been higher on my recommended list, but that's where she stopped and found a condo to rent. At a furniture store, she snapped up a slightly damaged sofa on clearance which served as her bed and her only furniture. Resourceful as always, she found garage sales which yielded basic dishes, silverware, and cookware. No need for a table with the breakfast bar in the kitchen, she reported, but she found a used coffee table and she was all set. Or so she said. This image of my mother far from family, living alone, living spare, without the comfort of her beautiful antiques and commissioned reproductions and artwork, vexed me. This was my father's fault. This discomfort. This waste of money. This separation. But there was nothing to do about it for the moment. At least she was safe.

I too lived alone in my little apartment, a place my father didn't know about, but it wouldn't take much to find me, so I kept my shotgun and a handful of double–aught shells on the floor next to my mattress. With time to ponder things, a poignancy became clear: a power shift had occurred in my family. My position had changed. No longer was I seen as the baby brother.

Without question my successful solo adventures to Cape Cod and to Europe had elevated me in the eyes of my family and had given me the self–confidence I needed to stand up to my father. But Mom's turning to me for help was larger. I had stepped past my brother to confront my father physically and psychologically. As I thought about it, the lingering hug my mother gave me when I met her at the airport seemed to be my confirmation, a passing of leadership in the family conferred on me. This power, by all rights of history, mythology and legend, should have passed to my older brother, but it passed over Walter to me–with all its risks and responsibilities. And I carried it with pride.

Teaching and Directing

I picked up the ringing phone, "Hello?"

My mother's voice: "Jason, I've decided to come back home."

"Mom, are you sure? I don't think it's safe yet." Only a month had passed since my mother went to Connecticut.

"I've had a lot of time to think about it, and I'm not going to be bullied."

As soon as she put it that way, I understood. No, she would not be bullied. Her strength, her pride, would not cotton it. Neither would mine. The plan was for her to live with Aunt Fern, one of her sisters (there were nine girls in her family and two boys), fifty miles north of Indianapolis, close enough for her to conduct business with the Indianapolis dress shops and far enough away to make an attack from my father less likely. There were other factors. My Uncle Doug had fought in Vietnam, and he was not the kind of man one wants to tangle with–not even my father.

*

At my Aunt Fern's and Uncle Doug's, during the gathering to celebrate my mother's return from Connecticut, my imagination constructed the worst, and I was bound to prevent it. I drifted from window to window watching for Dad, staring at each overgrown fence post where the soybean field met the edge of the yard, watching for motion or a waft of cigarette smoke, and checking window locks. (My aunt and uncle had already secured them.) I left my shotgun in the back seat of my car, covered with a blanket, a box of shells locked in the glove box, three shells in my pocket. The rest of the family seemed truly to celebrate. If any of them noticed my worried watchfulness, no one said so.

When I was called to the table for dinner, I noticed Missy had taken the best seat for watching two walls of windows. When she got a drink before sitting down, I moved her plate across the table.

"Hey, Jason that's my seat."

"Move your feet, lose your seat," I teased, not wanting to explain.

"I saved you the corner so you wouldn't bang your left elbow with anyone."

"That's okay. I'm good right here."

"Whatever," she said.

Typically, time races at our family gatherings, but that day dragged for me. Evening engendered greater fears. My father, a night person, unlike my mother and me, would prefer to strike in the dark, the later the better.

A story Mom told me after Dad's façade fell apart haunted me. When I was just a baby, she had tried to leave and rather than endanger her family or friends, she hid with my father's parents, the three of us packed like refugees in the guest room. One night Dad put a ladder against the farm house and broke into the second floor window by shattering it with the butt of a German army rifle. Mom talked about how he trained that rifle on her, but also pointed the black hole of the barrel at six–year–old Walter's face as well as at mine. Walter carried that memory, but he had never shared it. Eventually my grandmother coaxed the rifle from my father's hands just before the sound of sirens homed in on the house, and my father scrambled out the window and down the ladder, escaping into the night. In the end, my mother agreed to reunite and try again.

But not this time.

As the evening came to an end, something nettled me. I could not be my mother's protector from fifty miles away. Yet I longed to continue to prove myself, to distinguish myself in the family. Was the status I felt, the status I thought the family had conferred on me, just temporary for a job well done?

*

    With Mom at my Aunt Fern's and Uncle Doug's, I poured myself into my teaching. In addition to being a diversion from worrying about my father attacking, my job was compelling. Besides, it was time to choose and direct the fall play. The only edict from Cathedral's administration: select a suitable play involving as many students as possible. In other words, create the most complicated assignment I could give myself. Though I didn't know it yet, a large cast compounded complications because at this small, private school with too many spoiled kids involved in too many activities, dedication spread thin. I soon came to expect unexpected absences from rehearsals, and had to deal with the whims of teen choice. Foolishly, I had assumed I'd find the kind of dedication my classmates and I had given Mr. Goodenough at my high school. For my first play I made a safe selection, the second most frequently produced high school play in the land: *You Can't Take It With You. (Our Town* ranks first). Large cast, screwball comedy, but the romance was way too cornball.

    One choice I made, which shocked many of my conservatively-bred students, their parents, my colleagues, and the administration (and earned me high marks from liberal faculty members)–was to cast color–blind. That meant mixed race families and couples. As with confrontations with my father, I prepared for a confrontation with the principal or the school president. It came. The principal and school president (who was also the head football coach, which said plenty about the school's emphasis on sports, and about where most of the school's scholarship money went) called me into the president's office.

    After a bit of small talk, they started. The president first: "We understand you have a black student and a white student playing husband and wife?"

    "That's right," I said matter–of–factly. I let the discomfort settle on them, basking in the uncomfortable silence.

"Do you think that's appropriate?" the principal asked.

I let the silence fill the room.

"We're a little concerned," the president added.

Before I released my prepared line from the high ground, I took a deep breath and let it out. Then I started slowly, dramatically: "I am the theater coach and, like a football coach," I fixed my gaze on the president/coach, whose eyes fell to his desk, "I cast the player I consider the best performer for the role, regardless of race."

End of discussion.

After another sentence or two of "Thank you for taking the time to explain" and "We hear it's going well," I left.

No one uttered another word of it to me. But I had also sealed my fate. I was an iconoclast, and iconoclastic teachers don't stay in secondary education long, especially at a Catholic high school. The administration simply waits. They've seen it before. They know you'll tire of butting your head against the wall until you walk out the door.

Though I had been told when hired that other teachers would volunteer to support my work in the theater, to assist with the details of set construction, costume design, and organization, volunteers were scarce as hen's teeth when I needed them. So it fell to me. All of it. Directing, lighting design, set design and construction, costumes, sound, and promotion–each facet came with its own set of details and problems. Not the least of these were supervising and teaching groups of kids how to help with each of these things. All of this on top of my teaching load for 128 students.

Once the fall play started, I did nothing but work for the school, and throwing myself into the work did help keep my mind off of my father. Up at 5:30 to finish lesson plans; over at the school by 8:00; teach until 3:00; rehearsals until 6:00; stage crew until 8:30 (and then I'd stay after to clean up); home around 9:30 to grade papers and begin the lesson plan to complete in the morning before hitting the sack about midnight; and start all over again at 5:30 a.m. On Saturday afternoons, I ran rehearsals followed by stage crew before going home to catch up on school work. Sundays I toiled to outline a set of lesson plans that might withstand

the week.
 It was too damn much.

*

 I did have one nice break. A teacher training day sent me to a meeting of the Indiana Council of English Teachers. In a fun afternoon, away from school, I met other teachers, got lesson plan ideas, and gathered survival advice from long-time pros. Waiting in line for coffee, I felt someone nudge me. It was Katie, the student from Butler I'd met a year earlier. A junior now, she said she'd missed me at the spring meeting. When I told her I'd been teaching in England, she wanted to hear all about it. And it turned out she'd gone to Cathedral and remembered most of my new colleagues.

*

 Cathedral High School sits up on a wooded hill about a quarter of a mile from the street, a narrow, curving lane. The auditorium stands at the far end of the main building, surrounded by woods. Each night, after rehearsals and after the evening stage crew left, I followed a routine. I locked the door to be sure my old man didn't sneak in. (Of course all during rehearsal and stage crew time, the doors were open so it would have been easy for him to come in and hide if he wished). I finished cleaning up before leaving. Then I stood at the glass doors to scan the parking lot for his truck or any hint of danger. Then I stepped outside, holding the door ajar, and looked again before I turned my back quickly to lock the auditorium. My car, the white Toyota Celica with my father's *GT* stripe blackened out, waited alone the parking lot near the woods. The wind blew dry leaves scratching across the blacktop. I listened for footsteps and circled my car looking in the windows. Then I unlocked it, putting my briefcase in by the passenger door, checking the back seat again. Every night I half expected Dad to jump me from the woods. I had planned different escape routes. For example, I could sprint west into the woods, down a path, across a small wooden bridge, past the old mansion and down into the neighborhood at the foot of the hill. Or I could sprint south up the hill to the practice fields and across into a neighborhood in that direction. There was a hole in the fence which kids who lived in that neighborhood used.

Even after I completed my safety routine and climbed into my car, I had visions of him running from the trees and ramming the sharp end of a crowbar through the window and into my skull.

Thoughts of my father occasionally followed me as I wandered the auditorium during rehearsals, sitting in the darkened back rows or balcony seats to check the actors' vocal projection. How easy it would be for Walt Blake to slip into the dark auditorium. He could ease up behind me as I paused in a seat to watch the performers, strangle me to death with a wire, and slip out before a single student noticed. Until a couple of them realized I hadn't hollered, "louder," or "good," or "push it" for several minutes. Then it would be, "Mr. Blake?" Hands to foreheads trying to see beyond the lights, "Are you there, Mr. Blake?" And a bolder one, a senior, would yell into the dark, "Hey, JB, what's up, man? You fall asleep or something?"

The Unexpected

Sunday evening in mid-October. Indian Summer and t-shirt warm, hot really. Overhead, a listless sky the hazy blue-white of summer. Mom came down to Indianapolis to deliver skirts to a dress shop and to see her mother–my grandmother–who now lived in an apartment complex. She had called me from the mall, and it was understood for the sake of safety that I needed to get to my grandmother's early, to make sure our father wasn't around. Though I had a heap of papers to grade for the coming week, I agreed. I hadn't seen my mother for about two weeks, and had seen my grandmother only once since returning from Europe.

I drove around the apartment complex slowly. Here and there, people had Halloween decorations, a skeleton, a jack-o-lantern, a scarecrow. The parking lot encircled the three buildings with angle parking nosed in toward the buildings on the perimeter and on the courtyard side. A band of parallel parking spaces made up the outer edge of the blacktop encircling the complex. No sign of my father's pickup and no tell-tale half-finished car with mismatched fenders or quarter panels with flat gray or brown undercoats. After I drove the circuit to make a final check, I parked near my grandmother's and walked around the building.

Rounding the corner near my grandmother's apartment, I had to smile. It looked like a public garden. Though late in the season, her flower beds flooded into the lawn, the walkway lined with mums. And around my grandmother's little porch, hanging pots and planters looked like spillways cascading with flowers. Her passion for flowers clearly hadn't ended when she'd sold her house. If I hadn't known which apartment was hers, I could have figured it out at a glance.

I hesitated on my grandmother's walk, though. Something made me wish my mother were already there. I chided myself for the hesitancy, and knocked on the door. Grandma welcomed me with a hug, and her Kentucky accent twanged, "Oh, well I declare, it's Jay-bo." Pulling my shoulders aside, she craned to see around me, "And where's your momma?"

"She's coming, Grandma. She'll be here any minute."

"Missy called and she and Baby Connor is a comin' over too," my grandmother said. I could hear the excitement in her voice.

She ordered me to sit down and brought me a piece of cake and a glass of milk. Then she started clanging around in her kitchen, getting out cups and saucers, making coffee and asking me, "How do you like the teaching?"

I told her I liked it, but it was a lot of work.

"That's what Andy says too, and did you know he's coaching cross-country this year?" My cousin was in his third year of teaching–another English teacher in the family. Grandma told me that Patrick, another cousin my age, was also working hard in his first year as an elementary school teacher. It amazed me how my eighty-two-year-old grandmother (mother of eleven, grandmother to fifty-two, great-grandmother to a score or more) managed to keep track of them all, and the in-laws as well. Sharp.

When Mom arrived, the conversation really took off. They talked about Connor and the other great-grandchildren, about Uncle Dale's and Aunt Margo's garden, about one family member after another, and the news of each. I couldn't keep up. When Missy and Connor arrived without Walter (Missy said he was working on a painting.) Grandma had to hold the baby on her lap as they talked. I have to admit I grew bored with all the talk, and I began to worry about the papers I had to grade, wishing I'd brought a stack of them along. On and on the visit went. I checked my watch again. Poured myself a second cup of coffee, knowing I'd need it now to grade papers and prepare the week's lessons late into the night. Though I felt guilty for feeling this way, my urgency built to anxiety. But I knew I couldn't leave before the visit ended. Finally, I uncorked it. "You know, I need to leave pretty soon. I've got a stack of papers to grade and lessons to prepare."

What an inconsiderate heel you are, I told myself.

"You can go on if you need to," Mom said. "We'll be all right."

"I think you ought to stay until your mom is ready to leave," Missy said.

"Maybe Walter can come over," I heard myself saying, trying to hold the edge out of my voice, but feeling again I was doing all the bodyguard duty alone, not only for our mother but for his family too. And where was Walter?

"I probably should get going soon anyway," Mom said.

"I'll call Walter," Missy said. Within seconds, she called me into the kitchen, and handed me the phone.

"Yeah."

"You can't just leave Mom there. It's not safe." His tone was pissed-off and I didn't need it. "Don't be so selfish, Jason. She hasn't seen Grandma for a while–just let them visit."

"Look," I said, trying to keep my voice down, "I don't want to end the visit, but I've got a ton of papers to grade and lessons to plan."

"Like that can't wait."

"Why don't you come over here, so I can get some work done?"

"By the time I got there, they'd be ready to leave. Just stay put. They won't be there much longer. All right? Besides, I'm busy trying to get some work done."

"Like that can't wait," I mocked.

"Why are you being so selfish? They will finish soon."

"Okay. Fine." I hung up and went in to rejoin the women at the table. Of course he thought my work could wait. His work was always more important than mine, than me. Meanwhile the clock moved ahead. It was dark outside and my pile of work waited.

Finally, the visit came to an end–sweet good-byes on the small porch and more compliments about the flowers, the giant mums. My grandmother lamented their waning days as fall had come despite the night's heat. October, but it was August hot, one of those nights where the heat and humidity won't break all night. I carried Connor to Missy's car, hoisting him up to ride on my shoulders. Mom lingered to look at the flowers before walking to her car parked farther down the parking lot.

I pulled the flat chrome door handle and opened the heavy door on Missy's gold Volvo. It was a two–door car, making it awkward to climb into the back to put Connor in his car seat. And I had to step around an eight–pack of Coke bottles on the rear floor as well. I put Connor in his seat, pulled the straps over his head and snapped the buckle in place. Gave it a couple of hard tugs to test the security–a sense from days spent in salvage yards with my father among crumpled and bloody cars.

As I checked the belt around Connor's seat, I heard something. Sprinting footsteps.

I was already scrambling out of the back seat when I heard Mom and Missy scream. My hand snatched up one of the Coke bottles. The metal crimp of the cap digging into my palm. And I was after him.

By the time I cleared the car, he had reached her. He hammered her to the ground. Then he snatched up a handful of her hair.

Everything moved in slow motion, every detail vivid. Racing for him, my chest burned. I couldn't get there fast enough.

He was dragging her by the hair as his large, black workboot stomped on my mother. My beautiful, small mother.

I smashed the bottle to the ground. I had to stop this, prevent this, reverse this. I had to take control.

By the hair he jerked and dragged her on the blacktop. Bent halfway over her, ape–like, yanking her around by her hair, holding her head at his hip level as his boot rammed into her chest. His left hand gripped her hair. His right hand was on himself, his chest. He wore dark clothes, a camouflage, insulated sweatshirt. Again and again the heavy black workboot pounded into my mother, his back to me.

My sister–in–law threw herself against my father trying to protect Mom, screaming for help. He shucked her off with a sharp

elbow to the face and she ran for the apartment to call 911. He
still had Mom by the hair. Yanking her head around. Her mouth
agape.

"I'll go with you. I'll go," I heard Mom crying out, no doubt
thinking she could escape him again as she had before.

Mom's arms tried to cover herself against the blows. I heard
nothing now but a constant roar in my head to stop this thing, to
control it.

Closing fast. And finally I was there. I hurled myself into his
back, knocking him away from my mother. Snatching up his thick
sweatshirt in the same motion, I swung him around and slammed
him into a parked car. He tried to fight me off and broke free,
but I was on him in an instant. I yelled at Mom to run. Still he
scratched and hacked, punched and kicked, but I wouldn't let go.
He actually wore two zipper–front sweatshirts on that hot night,
and I recalled even in the struggle his street fighting lesson from
many years before: if you expect a fight, put on an extra jacket for
protection. He had come for a fight–no doubt expecting I would be
there–and I knew I was in a fight that mattered. We struggled on
the pavement, sand and gravel sliding under our feet. He rammed
me against a parked car. Again tried to break free from my grasp.
But I held. He tried to hammer me against the parked car. I turned
him and got low, driving hard, shoving him backward, and digging
in as his weight shifted, plowing him backward and ramming him
over the hood of another parked car, consciously trying to break
his back.

I didn't know where Mom or Missy were, but I was aware they'd
gotten away. I just hoped they were safe and not hurt badly. Hoped
they'd called the police.

Somehow Dad broke my hold, running, and I was after him.
I grabbed him. He took a swing, missing but his arm caught me
across the side of the head and rocked me sideways. He shoved
me against a car and tried to break free but I caught his sweatshirt.
Now I took a wild, haymaker swing at him, missing but the crook
of my arm caught him at the neck and he buckled a bit. Now
I wrapped up his neck and threw him backward against another

car. Bouncing off the car, he rolled with the impact and nearly broke free again. I snapped a half–nelson over his right shoulder, immobilizing his right arm above his head. He tried to yank free. And spun, trying to hammer me against the parked car. All the while, I'm yelling for help, yelling at him, yelling and grunting. I wrenched the half–nelson hard to lock him up. I felt his right hand trying to grab my hair and ducked away. Shoving him one way and then reacting to his pressure against it, I planted him back over the hood of the car.

I heard someone sprinting toward us. A man, hollering at us to break it up.

My father ordered the other man to get me off him.

"No," I yelled, "help me stop him."

The man stepped close. My father gave a tremendous heave, trying to break free, lifting me for a second off my feet. The instant my feet hit the ground I re–squared my stance and gave him a sharp jerk backward.

"He's got a gun!" the other man screamed, and ran back several yards. "Look out! He's got a gun. Help! Help!"

I let go of the half–nelson to grab at my father's left arm with both hands. Under his two zipper sweatshirts, he wore a chest holster. And he grappled to draw his revolver. With his right arm free again, he clawed at my hands, which fought to control the gun.

I battled to freeze the gun, but also to wedge my thumb in behind the safety hammer, so the revolver couldn't be fired. He kept twisting and ripping with his shoulders to break free, but I held tight. And I ripped and yanked at him to counter.

When he went with one of his twists, I sensed his balance shift– just as I had with much larger defensive linemen in football. And I went with it. With all my force, I lifted him and swung him around, slamming him over the hood of a car again, digging my chin into the base of his neck to pin his head down against the car hood. Holding his wrist and gripping the gun with my other hand so he couldn't draw it, I had managed to pin both of our arms. And I had a tight lock on him.

Once I had him in that position, another man ran up. Fuck–he had a gun, and he held the .38 revolver on our faces, its black circle not more that twelve inches from my eye. Nervously he snapped the black hole of the barrel from one face to the other, his hand shaking from his own fear. That black hole ached to do its duty inches from my eyes. "Careful," I said. "Don't shoot him. Just help me stop him. He's got a gun and I'm holding it."

"Get him off me," my father said. "He attacked me."

"Liar!" I screamed and rammed my chin down on the base of his neck. Two more men came out of the apartment complex. None of them knew who was the danger so they combined to hold us both down. The one with the gun announced he was a deputy sheriff, which gave me no comfort at all. Just what I needed, a nervous, young cop, itchy to test his training.

My father and I were both breathing hard. My chest against his back. My father. My enemy. Half of my source for being, for my genetic code. Locked in my arms. At one point, I realized we were breathing, panting, in unison. And I held my breath to break the pattern.

I would not breathe with him.

Would not breathe like him.

I would not be like him.

Every half a minute or so, I bore down on him, squeezing him as hard as I could, wanting to hurt him, wanting to kill him for attacking my mother.

"I ought to break your ribs," I growled in his ear.

"*You* can't break *my* ribs," he responded.

As I felt him exhale, I snapped a hard squeeze and held it so he couldn't inhale. When I eased off, I took satisfaction at his pain, his groaning inhale. Maybe I couldn't break his ribs, but I let him know I could hurt him and I was in charge now. That I was stronger.

Already a thought came over me that would haunt me countless times in my future. Should I have tried to wrest the gun from him in the fight and kill him right there, right then? Could I have done it, killed my own father? Could I have gotten the gun?

The muscles in my arms and back and chest ached from holding him there so long. The blood pumped throbs of pain through

them. Sweat ran down my face, dripped onto my father's camouflage sweatshirt on that hot muggy night. I could smell his sweat,
his aftershave. Where the hell were the police? I refused to lighten
my clamp on my father.

The pain I could live with.

The pain felt good.

The pain felt right.

In a small measure, it freed me. I deserved it. I deserved more
pain than I felt. I deserved the pain he had put on my mother.
That should have been mine. God damn him for stealing it from
me. And I bore down on him again, hard, digging my chin into
the base of his neck, a painful wrestling move, wanting to crush
his face into the hood of the car.

One of the good Samaritans pulled my shoulder back to get my
chin out of my father's neck. "Back off," he said. "It's over. Ease off.
The cops are coming."

That's when I heard the siren in the distance. We heard it coming. For a long time we heard it. The crowd–yes, a small crowd had
gathered around me and my father–the crowd got quiet listening
to the siren. The man still trained the .38 on our heads. And then
the first police car came screaming around the apartment building and the siren wound down with a blip. Everything around
continued to flicker red and white. The crackling static of a police
radio. In the distance I heard two more sirens closing on us. The
cop ordered people to stand back and keep their distance. I wasn't
budging. Neither was the man with the .38.

"Put down that weapon."

"I'm a Marion County Deputy Sheriff, and the man there on the
bottom has a gun."

"Let's everybody calm down here. And you," he said to the
young cop, "put that damn thing away before you shoot somebody."

I felt a hand on my shoulder, "Okay, son, relax now."

I didn't budge.

The other two police cars arrived.

"Okay, back off now." His grip pulled.

As I began to release Dad, he started to stand up. And I was on him, slamming the side of his head down on the hood of the car again, pressing his forehead against the metal with one hand. Then two cops snatched me, roughly pulling me away. "He's got a gun!" I said. I jerked free from one cop. The second shoved me by the chest. I knocked his hand away, and the first one grabbed me more roughly. Strong. And with nightsticks drawn they pressed hard into my chest to let me know they were serious. "Back down. Now. Easy. Just breathe. It's over. Take it easy," they said.

"Don't you tell me easy," I yelled. "That son-of-a-bitch tried to kill my mother."

"Keep him back." This was the first cop, a man about my father's age. His beige uniform taut over a fat belly.

He let my father up and lifted the gun from Dad's chest holster. I heard him say, "Jesus Christ, Walt, what's going on here?"

Walt.

"Don't you get friendly with him," I yelled. Of course my father would know this guy, would be friendly with him.

The fat cop turned around and walked up close to me, striding like one making the most of his power, a living TV cliché of a lousy, fat cop. A finger in my face, "Now, I've heard all I want to hear out of you."

I wanted to spit at him.

Then another police car arrived with a man in a blue uniform who instantly assumed authority. When he asked about my father's revolver, if it was loaded, the fat cop said it was and handed it over. "That's right, it was loaded because he wanted to kill my mother," I yelled. The blue uniform told the younger cops to keep me back. The police talked among themselves and talked to my father. The two young cops kept me at a distance where I couldn't hear, moving with me as I paced back and forth. They held their nightsticks out in front of them. Then I noticed my mother's hair still tangled in my father's hand, and I exploded. Charging toward him, dragging the young cops with me, "Look at his hand," I screamed, "look at her hair in his hand." Dad tried to shake it off, brushing his hand on his black pants.

The young cops threw me back. And the blue uniform came over, "Goddamn it, I told you to keep him back."

"But –"

"Do your job," he said to them. Then he looked at me, "Don't give me any trouble."

"He's the cause of trouble," I hammered, pointing at my father.

"You calm down. Right now. If I have to come over here again, you're going to jail." He pulled one of the young cops aside and whispered to him.

Then the young cops used their nightsticks to press me several more yards away, and they held them against me at chest height to keep me at a distance. "Don't cause trouble. We don't want to hurt you, man. Just stay back. Breathe easy. It's over now."

An ambulance pulled up. An ambulance. I ran over to where an EMT was helping Mom down the sidewalk, Missy following with Connor in her arms.

"Mom? Mom, are you okay?" She was bent over halfway.

She gave me a grim, pained smile, "I'll be okay," she said, her voice a hissing whisper. A second EMT helped my mother into the ambulance.

"You okay?" I asked Missy, her cheek red, swollen.

"He elbowed me pretty hard." She squeezed my arm. "But I'll be all right."

I stood there as the ambulance doors shut. Watched it bump into gear. I blinked when the siren screamed, and I stood alone by my grandmother's, listening to the sound grow more distant. My injured mother speeding away from me. Then I looked over at him. Standing by the police car. A spray of sparks skittered across my brain, and I started toward him, picking up momentum as I went. The two young cops intercepted me again, holding me at bay, jabbing me with their black nightsticks.

Then I heard a voice that calmed me. "It's over now, Jason." Uncle Dale. As I mentioned, he and my mother were the leaders in this large family. He had no children but was a father figure to most of his many nieces and nephews. His hand on my shoulder had the calming effect of a warm blanket. The sparks went out, and

I withdrew a few paces under his touch. Then he strode forward, passing the police officers as if unnoticed. Up close to my father he eased face-to-face, and through all of the commotion, I heard him say to my father in a flat, even voice.

"You really did it this time didn't you, Walt?"

It was the closest to a curse I'd ever heard from my soft-spoken Uncle Dale. And its effect devastated my father. His eyes fell to the pavement, his posture slackened under the weight of my uncle's words. My uncle's statement recalled all my father's other digressions, failures, lies, cheats, cruelties, abuses. Most of which I knew nothing about and would never know. Other wrong-doings which had been forgiven. But not this one. This one had crossed the line.

My uncle came back to me and said, "Go on inside. I'll stay out here."

"The revolver was loaded, Uncle Dale."

"I know, Jason. Now you go on inside."

I walked toward my grandmother's apartment, feeling my father's eyes on my back. Tall and broad and strong, I walked, pronouncing to him with my stride that I had won. That I was the stronger. He may have done his damage but I had won. And if necessary I would defeat him again, would destroy him.

Inside, I saw my grandmother's eyes, red from crying and worry. Missy's too as she rapidly rocked the child held to her chest. Aunt Margo, Uncle Dale's wife, led me by the hand to the kitchen. "Let me get you something to drink," she said. In seconds she handed me a glass of ice water. I took it, and as I lifted it, I saw how violently my hand shook. The ice cubes tinkling together, water sloshing over the rim and running down the sides, dripping on the carpet. I tried to lift it but the shaking got worse as the glass neared my dry lips, then clinked against my teeth, water spilling down my chin.

"Here, honey, let me take that," Aunt Margo said, lifting the glass from my feeble hand and wiping my mouth with a dish towel.

All their eyes were on me. My grandmother. My aunt. My sister-in-law. My nephew. No one spoke. But they all looked at me.

I was sorry I had let her get hurt. They knew I had. It was my fault.

The shaking of my hand moved through my torso and legs. I backed against the wall. My head felt light, and I slid down to sit on the floor.

"Jason? Are you all right?" I heard Missy ask.

I nodded. And then the tears began. Soon I was sobbing.

"Oh, honey," my aunt said, squatting down and hugging my head to her chest. Not knowing what else to say, she just asked, "What is it?"

Now Missy was there, her arm around me.

I couldn't catch my breath.

"I let him hurt her," I blubbered. "I'm sorry."

"No, Jason," Missy said, "you can't look at it that way."

"Yes!" I yelled. "I let him hurt her. I was supposed to protect her. And I let him hurt her!" This all flooded out in hacks and gushes. Connor began to cry, scared to see his uncle like this.

My face burned with shame. The heat of their eyes on me in my shame. I snatched up a dishtowel and covered my face. This was my most important test—my life's most important test—and I had failed my mother.

"How could I let that happen?" I muttered, and grabbed my thick curly hair in both hands.

"Jason," Missy said, firmly cupping my face in her hands and lifting my eyes to meet hers just inches away, "if you weren't here tonight, he would have killed her." She shook me for more attention. "Listen to me, Jason. Listen. Do you hear me?"

I nodded.

"You saved her life tonight. You saved your mom."

Yes, I had saved her.

I knew.

But I had also let him hurt her.

Aunt Margo held a cool cloth to my face, "Calm down now," she said. "Just calm down. Breathe deep and easy. You done your best."

"Better than anyone else could have done," Missy added. "You were there when she needed you. You saved her." Was she talking about Walter? Where was he?

"You done good, Jason," my aunt asserted. She got up, and I heard her say quietly that she was going to get Dale.

I attempted to level out my ragged breathing, concentrating on smoothing the air and slowing the rush of it in and out of my mouth. And then a wave of anguish at letting Mom get hurt, of having to fight my father to save my mother, of wrestling a gun from my father to prevent a murder, of knowing I would never peacefully see him again–and my breathing unraveled in a series of hacks.

Breathe, I told myself again. One, just get one, even, deep breath. Okay, good. Now another, and one more. And one more....

I heard my uncle enter the apartment and my grandmother say, "Oh, Dale, talk to the boy."

And now I felt a new shame, a boy's shame at crying among women, and being caught by a man. I could not look at my kind and gentle uncle. The women backed away to leave me with him. I bottled up my anguish, holding my breath, wiping my face with the wet cloth my aunt had given me, and then trying to breathe through my nose to regain some composure. My muscles, still swollen, continued to shake with spasms as adrenaline leached from them. I did not want to be seen like this. Not by my family. Certainly not by Uncle Dale.

Uncle Dale pulled a chair up close to me and sat down, elbows on his knees and his head down low near mine. He didn't say a word. I looked up just enough to see his hands on his forehead, and then one smoothing his bald pate. I looked down just then so as not to let him see my red eyes. Then his hand on my head, fingers digging into my curly hair and down to squeeze the back of my neck, coming to rest on my shoulder. We were quiet and still like that for several minutes. I felt his strength passing to me, my pain flowing to him. I heard him sniff, noticed him wipe an eye.

He was telling me all I needed to hear without a word. For a long time he just sat there with me. The two of us breathing, two men breathing. Sharing pain. Sharing strength. Eventually his soft voice came to me, slow and easy with his Kentucky accent.

"Ah expect it's time to go on home."

"Yeah, I expect it is," I whispered.

We locked hands around thumbs and he helped me to my feet. We looked at each other. And Uncle Dale said through a tight throat and wet eyes, "You did well by your mother tonight. I'm proud of you." And the power of his words confirmed that something was again different, and that I had succeeded more than failed in that night. I knew I could sleep now. Not easily for a while, perhaps, but I could sleep. Though it was not my uncle's way to display emotion, I hugged him and he embraced me in return.

*

Outside the crowd and police cars had vanished, leaving a silent and still night, a strange vacuum of stillness. Yet a residual aura hung in the air, one full of shouts and struggles and flashing lights. Hot still, and muggy.

I walked slowly.

Alone.

To my car.

Just trying to get there.

Be in the seat.

Turn the key.

And roll away from it.

My car, the one my father had rebuilt, started instantly, and it startled me, as if I expected the car to have as much difficulty functioning as I did. I put it in gear and drove out of the parking lot. Not until I passed under a burned-out streetlight several blocks later did I realize I was driving with my headlights off.

I started south toward my apartment, then at one corner turned in the opposite direction and headed for the interstate. Windows down, I drove north on the I-465 loop around Indianapolis. The three lanes were nearly empty on this Sunday evening. Heat lightening flashed, illuminating the distant horizon as if it were still summer.

My mother was in a hospital.

My father in a jail.

I drove slowly for a few miles and gradually picked up speed until I was flying. How fast I couldn't tell for sure because the speedometer was broken on the car, one of the things my father never got around to fixing. Another glitch was the suspension which still chewed up the edges of tires, making the car unstable at high speeds. Whenever I had mentioned getting the car aligned or having the suspension checked out, the old man had barked it wasn't alignment and he'd fix it. But he never did. Instead, every six months or so, I went to a salvage yard with my father to take tires off smashed-up cars to replace the ruined ones on my car. Whenever I loaned the car to a friend, they'd return it, handing me the keys and asking, "How do you drive that thing?" I'd shrug, feeling defensive for my father, and respond, "Lousy cars make you a better driver. You're just spoiled." But it was dangerous and I knew it. Imagining another disaster that night, I backed off the accelerator and realized where I was.

Unconsciously, I'd driven the long way via interstate to the hospital where the ambulance had taken my mother. At the hospital I checked in at the emergency room, and found the doctor who'd seen her. He explained that she'd been examined and released, that my mother was lucky to have escaped with four broken ribs, no punctures of the lungs, and merely bad bruises and swelling. She'd be sore for a few weeks, he said. None of us will breathe easily for a while, I thought. I didn't know where Mom was, or how she got back to my grandmother's to pick up her car. Maybe Missy had picked her up.

Back at my apartment, I took a cool shower, scrubbing my skin hard. Then I lay in bed exhausted but unable to sleep. There I lay in bed at the age of twenty-two, after preventing my father from murdering my mother and wrestling a handgun from him, focusing my all on Bugs Bunny singing the "Barber of Seville" parody, dressed like a Spanish beauty and toying with Elmer Fudd: "Wwhaaaat do you want with a wabbit? I could be your senorita. I am so so mu-uch sweet-a...."

I did fall asleep for a while. Not long. It was a night of fitful sleep. But knowing Dad was in jail gave me some measure of peace. The next morning, Monday morning, my alarm went off at 5:30, as on every workday, and I dragged myself up into the shower, had some coffee, tried to grade some papers–blocking as best I could the previous night–and went to work. I taught all day and ran rehearsal that night. Right back on the horse.

*

The horror of that night, of that slow motion crispness, remained fresh and vivid in the coming weeks both in waking moments and in dreams. In the dreams, sometimes I got there and sometimes I didn't. I felt the pound of pavement under my sneakers as I chased down my father. The image flickered like an old home movie–of him jerking Mom around by the hair, of him stomping her. My brain tingled at the memory of Mom's hair tangled in his fingers. My jaws locked. My heart pounded in my neck. And I sprang awake ready for fight or flight.

*

I was also staggered and angered a couple of weeks later when Missy said to me, "You know, if Walter hadn't told you to stay there that night, your mom would be dead. Walter saved her life."

Jail and Court

My father went to jail.

Despite a lax view of domestic violence in 1996, there was no way to ignore his attack with a loaded gun and his trying to draw it against his family. That's why my father's policeman friend wanted to know if the revolver was loaded. If it weren't, then the whole night could be buried in the backyard where domestic troubles belonged. An unloaded gun was a family issue to be worked out in private. And for violating a restraining order? Well, it didn't mean much, a stern talking to, maybe a few hours in jail.

But a loaded gun couldn't be ignored, and the old man was trucked off to the county prison.

Greg Garrett, my mother's lawyer, delayed the hearing a couple of times to keep my father locked up, punishing my old man as best he could because he knew the system wouldn't. "Your dad may think he's tough, but let him spend a couple of months with those guys down at the County Jail, and he'll get a whole new perspective on tough," Garrett said.

Maybe, I thought. Or he might face the reality that he's not the powerful young man he still liked to think he was. As for punishing him, I felt ambivalent.

Part of me considered him a murderer because that was his intent, his plan. If one intended a murder and was stopped by an outside force, is that person really less guilty of murder than one who succeeded? I suppose. But a ruthless disregard for life was the same in either case. So sometimes I viewed my father as a murderer.

When I expressed this thought to Greg Garrett, he shook his head. "That's not how it works, Jason. The law can't punish people for bad thoughts. The law judges crimes, not criminal intent."

"Maybe the law is wrong," I said.

"Maybe," Greg answered, "but we ain't gonna change it. So let's work with what we have. Okay?"

That's what you had to respect about Greg Garrett: he wasn't going to entertain my bullshit about "ought to be." There was work to do.

I knew none of us would ever choose to see my father again. Except in court.

*

Six weeks after the attack, we had a hearing before a judge. If this were a fiction, a dramatic courtroom trial might follow in a room heavy with dark and glossy mahogany wood and a railing of substantial turned spindles—all symbolic of the stolid justice system. And in that scene, dramatic truths would come to the fore to reset these lives in place. But this is no fiction. And the event was a small, simple affair in an unadorned and compact courtroom with plastic chairs, florescent ceiling lights, and a polished gray–and–white Terrazzo floor. There was no trial for attempted murder, no charge of assault with a deadly weapon, not even a charge of battery. My father wore pale–blue prison garb, his dark chest hair mixed with gray visible at the neck, and he sat with his head often lowered in a beaten posture.

Next to him sat his lawyer, dressed in a tweed jacket and khaki pants like a college professor. On the other side of the aisle sat my mother, Greg Garrett, and me. Walter was again absent, off at a meeting.

Mom sat composed and straight next to Greg Garrett. The lawyers each explained what had happened on the night of my father's attack from their client's point of view. There was some discussion of the events leading up to the attack. A cursory review of the restraining order. Afterward, the judge asked my mother and me to wait outside the room.

"Why?" I asked with a bit more disrespect in my voice than intended.

Greg Garrett turned and glared at me. "Just wait outside," he told me. "I'll take care of things in here."

After a long ten minutes, Greg came out. "The judge wants one of you to come in and tell your story."

"I'll go," I said.

Mom responded, "I think you should."

I followed Greg back inside, and he whispered for me to keep a cool head.

I raised my right hand, "Do you swear to tell the truth the whole truth and nothing but the truth so help you God?"

"I do."

I sat next to the judge, facing my father.

I glared at him.

His head dipped down a bit, eyebrows lowered slightly, lips tight–the expression on his face was difficult to read. Anger? Sorrow? Compunction? A threat?

He mouthed something to me.

I couldn't tell if it was:

"I love you"

Or

"I'll kill you."

It could have been either one. But not something in between.

In my mind, the heat of my steady glare confronted any threat, rejected any love. He lowered his eyes, moved his folded hands from the table to his lap.

The judge had asked me something. I turned to him, and he asked again that I recount for the court what happened. Which I did, going back over the events since August. Then he asked if I or my brother had ever been abused by my father. Though we had been spanked and shaken, knocked around a bit, I didn't consider it abuse.

"I wasn't. As for my brother, not that I know of."

"We weren't physically abused," my brother declared when I saw him later to tell him what had happened, "but we were intimidated and mentally abused."

I didn't necessarily agree. Intimidated, yes. Abused? I didn't think so. It was a gray area, and my brother was never good with ambiguity.

Either way, he left me feeling stupid for my answer, as if I'd failed the family. But where was he when he might have helped?

My father walked. For a while, I felt my father had been set free because of me. I had blown it. The judge ordered him to stay away from my mother forever, and to stay away from the rest of the family unless one of us contacted him for a reconciliation. And that was the end of it. We left the courtroom.

*

I love you.
I'll kill you.

Playing Ad Man

:60 Radio – Levinson's – Levi's Rodeo

Voice Talent:

I went to Levinson's to pick up a pair of red–label, button–fly Levi's jeans and a Levi's jean jacket. The original denim classics. I stepped into the dressing room to try them on and . . .

SFX:

Space–age warping music.

Voice Talent:

. . . found myself–get this–wearing a cowboy hat with my hand tied to a cow the size of a rhinoceros.

SFX:

Crowd cheering, whistles, the snort, stomping, and bluster of a bull, continue under voices.

Voice Talent (yelling over crowd noise):

What am I doing on this cow?

Voice Talent 2, Bud:

Well that's a Brahma bull partner.

Voice Talent:

Brahma bull?

Voice Talent 2, Bud:

Yep, rodeo strength.

SFX:

Growing intensity of bull snorting, stamping, banging, groaning.

Voice Talent:

He sounds upset. What's his name?

Voice Talent 2, Bud:

Apocalypse.

Voice Talent:

Apocalypse Cow–wow–ouw! (screaming voice fades to background, memory tone comes back)

SFX:

Lowering of crowd cheering, still Pat's voice screaming in the background.

Voice Talent:

With that, I was launched into the ring on the biggest bull in the solar system. I tried hanging on but my Levi's and I got bounced around like a tumbleweed in a tornado. (Voice rising to panic again) I saw my whole wardrobe pass before my eyes. All those great clothes I'd gotten from Levinson's. All those classic Levi's jeans I'd worn as a Midwestern boy. My first Levi's jeans jacket. The Levi's jeans from Levinson's I'd worn through college. Then the furious bull threw me, and I crashed through the dressing room door –

SFX:

Door bursting open. All crowd noise stops.

Voice Talent:

–flew across the store, and was saved by Levinson's enormous stacks of Levi's jeans. (Panic ends but panting speech) Regular and pre-washed, in waist sizes from 26 to 46. Always priced to meet the competition, at Harry Levinson's.

I listened to this radio commercial over the public address system in the Indianapolis Convention Center with 1,200 well-dressed people. I'd written and directed it a few months earlier, in the fall of my first year of teaching. It was being played to the crowd at the Addy Awards as the first-place winner for the best 60-second radio commercial created in Indiana. Just before, they'd played another I'd written and directed which had won third-place. At twenty-three, I was the youngest award winner that year.

The award went to my brother's graphic design and advertising agency, Blake & Patterson. Walter had been joined by his art-director friend Carl Patterson in launching the agency. My brother was strong in graphic design as well as copywriting, but as he got busy, he needed copywriting help, especially for radio commercials. Because I had studied playwriting, I was a natural resource for him.

"Think of it as a very short play," Walter said.

Before long, I was writing and directing one or two radio commercials a week for Harry Levinson's. Walter paid me $50 per finished spot–writing, rewriting, selecting talent and directing–which was gravy for me. As a young teacher bringing home about $1,200 per month in salary, the $200 to $300 additional per month for the radio spots felt like a big cushion. I loved writing and directing, took pride in hearing my work on the radio. Besides, it felt good to help my brother succeed in his new business. Still, I'll admit it annoyed me when I learned Walter charged the client $5,000 per spot, 100 times my fee.

Other teachers who had part-time gigs or summer jobs to stay afloat were waiters or waitresses, house painters, summer secretaries. Two ran small farms. Only a couple of music-teacher/musicians held the kind of jobs I esteemed for tapping their talent. Writing ad copy put me in that category, and I felt good about it.

So a couple times a week, I finished teaching my last class, ran out to my car, and raced to the recording studio to meet the actors, tape the radio spot, and then race back to school to direct play rehearsals. Because of the successful radio commercials, Walter also asked me to write some print ads, and then some brochures. Another graphic designer friend of his needed some copywriting help, and I was happy to assist. Working with Walter over pizza brought us close. We had a lot of laughs, and he came to respect me as a quick study in advertising, and to lean on my creativity. I thrived on his attention as I proved my ability to him and to myself. It was satisfying to produce something as tangible as a brochure, an ad, a radio commercial, after the murky and evanescent efforts of teaching.

At the Indiana Addy Awards my brother did well. The print ads we collaborated on won a number of awards, as did Walter's brochures and direct mail. The award total for Blake & Patterson was surpassed only by the state's two largest agencies. In the end, three of the five finalists for Best of Show were from Blake & Patterson—including my radio spots. The Best of Show award went to an ad series for an optometrist which Walter had designed and I'd helped write under his direction.

It was a glorious night for Walter. I was proud of him up at the dais collecting that Best of Show award. At twenty-eight, he had launched his agency with a big splash. The night reminded me of his success as a football player—skinny, fearless, willing to reverse his field or cut back against the grain, shaking off larger and stronger tacklers by sheer force of will. That night, standing on the dais to collect Best of Show, he heard the cheers as he had heard them from the end zone.

I had been a blocker, less famous than my brother, "Quicksilver," but it was enough for me that night—as it had been when I was a high school football player, coached by my brother and blocking for Tim Parker, protecting Tim from tacklers, opening holes, and then looking up from the dirt to see his long, graceful strides leading to another touchdown.

I had played a key role in the Best of Show campaign, and I was proud of it. But it stung and disappointed me when Walter made his acceptance speech with a list of thank-yous that included the client, photographer, even the photo retoucher, and left me out.

Later, at the post-award party, he apologized for forgetting to mention me when he collected the Best of Show. Though I didn't believe he forgot, I told him it was okay. And it was. Mostly. Linemen don't get thanked much. Even if he left me out on purpose, I understood it was because he needed to establish himself as a top creative talent in the state for the sake of his fledgling business.

What surprised me more was the number of people who slapped me on the back and introduced themselves, and the number of congratulations I received from people my brother introduced me to. Instead of claiming me for his own, Walter told people I was a teacher who did freelance writing on the side.

After Jack O'Brian, the most celebrated copywriter and creative director in the city, especially for radio commercials, very publicly congratulated me for my radio spots in front of about fifteen people around a large table, Walter broke into story about me.

"Jason is hot shit tonight, but you should have seen him at another party when we were kids." He was laughing even as he began.

I saw it coming, "Hold on, hold on–"

"What!? Hey it's the truth."

"Oh, Jason, come on," Missy jeered. She knew what was coming too.

All I could do was lock a grin on my face and endure.

Walter turned back to the gang, to the faces smiling in anticipation of the story. "When our parents built a little ranch in the country, my mom had an open house for the family and friends. And Jason came up to my mother in the crowd and whispered very politely, 'I've got to go to the bathroom.'" He looked at me with the smile of a happy assassin hefting the ax. "So our mom whispered, 'That's fine, go ahead.' And four-year-old Jason runs off to the bathroom. A couple of minutes later, the whole house hears," and Walter's voice rises to a roar here, "'Momma, come wipe me!'" And Walter was laughing so hard and loud that tears flowed from his eyes, his crimson tie pooling on the table before his gaping red mouth, as he pounded the table. The rest of the gang laughed too–though less heartily. Eyes caught mine as if to pity my embarrassment. In my humiliation, I chuckled along, unable to control the heat of shame and embarrassment rising in my face.

But he was not finished. "Everyone in the house falls silent, totally mortified. And here it comes again, Jason yelling, 'Momma, come wipe me!' My mom is so embarrassed she tried to send me in to do it!" He's pounding the table again. "I ran out of the room yelling I wouldn't wipe his poopy butt. Can you believe it?" And he led the laughter like a drum major.

It felt like we were three and nine again, playing on our parents' bed, and suddenly he was launching me backward off the bed. A graphic designer sitting next to me put her hand on my shoulder while she laughed. "It's okay." I knew she was trying to shade me from the glare, but it didn't help much. It occurred to me to throw my drink on Walter, but I took it with a red-faced grin, playing the good sport.

That wasn't the first or last time I'd heard the story. He'd told it to my college roommates once after we'd gone out for pizza and had run into a gang of friends. About a month after I returned from England, and before I'd put a stop to my father's rampage, he'd reminded the family of it at a gathering. And I knew he'd tell it to his son, Connor, and to my kids if I ever had any–whenever it looked like I was winning.

What dawned on me the night of the Addy Awards as I walked to my car was this: what did telling the story tell us about Walter?

*

The "wipe me" story aside, the night of the 1996 Addy Awards (and my brother made it possible) was a wonder. It opened a career opportunity. Soon the phone started ringing from people looking for copywriting help–and I didn't make it easy because I didn't even have an answering machine so they had to catch me at night. First was a solo designer, then a small design firm, then a small ad agency. I had to turn down most of the work because I was still teaching, and at the same time Walter's business was growing like mad, and he needed more and more help from me.

On one of those sunny and warm March Saturdays that always felt like a gift, Walter and I worked at his office in the Indianapolis village of Broad Ripple. It was on the second floor of the stucco Carter Building, built in the late 1930's with a stripped-to-the-bones interior–metal door and window frames, and a dark-brown linoleum tile floor. After Walter and I finished reviewing a radio script together and discussing how to create a print ad to pick up the theme, we went to lunch–a pineapple and Canadian bacon deep-dish pizza at Union Jack's.

Without mentioning it, I watched for our father as we walked, and at the restaurant assumed my place with my back to the wall. I was always doubly watchful for the old man when I was with any family member.

"You know, you're a natural at copywriting," my brother said.

"Thanks," I responded. "I've got a good teacher."

"It's more than that," he said. "You have really good marketing instincts. We have that in common, a way of naturally observing, understanding how to emotionally connect a benefit to the target audience." He let it sit with me for a minute before adding, "Right now, you're one of the best copywriters in Indianapolis, and you're doing it as a hobby."

He could do this at times, take a kernel of truth and nudge it along to where he wanted the facts to stand. He once introduced me to a friend of his as the best English teacher at Cathedral High School, though he'd never seen me teach a class, never met another teacher at the school, and I was not the best English teacher in the school. I'd heard him claim a number of times that one of his friends or colleagues was the most creative, the best designer, the top architect in the state, the best in the Midwest, the best in the nation at this or that, or say that so-and-so was the most brilliant creative thinker he'd ever known. In many ways, this was a wonderful quality. My brother passionately cared about people he liked, was wonderfully supportive. And he desperately wanted to be affiliated with great talent, with greatness. But when that fantastic designer left to join another ad agency, the magnifying glass focused on the chinks in the once glossy armor: "He just couldn't think conceptually, and he always wanted the headline type to be three inches tall."

So I knew to temper my brother's "one of the best copywriters in Indianapolis" compliment. At the same time, I knew I was good at it, and it did come naturally. I could project myself into the mind of the target audience (my training as an actor helped) and speak to the fears and desires of an audience as they related to the client's product or service.

Walter served up another big thick slice of pizza. "Have you ever thought about working as a copywriter?"

"And leave teaching?"

"You could do it."

"It's fun, but I don't know about as a job."

"I wasn't thinking of a job. I was thinking you could go out on your own—be a freelance writer."

"I hadn't thought of it."

"Well think about it. You could make more money and have a lot more time to write freelance pieces, or start a book."

"Think so?"

"Without a doubt."

I shoveled in a big bite of pizza to buy some time before I had to respond to his waiting eyes. It was as if he expected me to make a life decision on the spot. Hell, I was just getting my feet under me as a teacher, and considering whether to go back to graduate school with the goal of teaching college. My professors had complained about their jobs to me: the committee work, the pressure to publish. But they seldom complained about spending six or eight hours a week teaching class (instead of the thirty I taught as a high school teacher) or about the four months of vacation. That life-of-the-mind, as I liked to think of it, looked good, looked damn near perfect. Now, the thought of becoming a copywriter, making a living with my pen, had a certain appeal. But then I'd be an ad man.

Since I hadn't answered, Walter went on, "If you're worried

about making enough money, I don't think that'll be a problem. You'll probably make fifteen thousand or more just from me. From me and Carl."

Walter knew $15,000 would match what I made as a teacher.

"I'll have to think about it," I said.

"Just think about how much time you'll have to write magazine pieces."

Another big bite of deep-dish pizza spared me a response.

"I decided to rent the whole second floor of the Carter Building. Mark Lowman and Diane Connor are sub-letting two offices, David Marx another. Leaves an office for you."

"I don't know if I want to get into renting an office."

"You won't have to, we'll work it out in trade. You do $200 in work for me per month in exchange for the office. You'll be part of a small artist colony."

He'd given this a lot of thought.

Walter pitched me more reasons to leave teaching and to start this new career. Including a 'life-of-the-mind' nod. He did a good sales job.

I had plenty to consider with Walter's vision of my life as a freelance copywriter: more money, more time for writing, and even an artist colony.

A Freelance Copywriter

My brother went out of his way for me, creating an opportunity for a new career. And I felt grateful. But I also felt both of his hands on my back. I couldn't quite keep from wondering–what was in it for him?

For Walter, my career change would supply a writer to fill an increasing need for a staff writer without burdening his business with the cost. Having me next door was even better. A young and inexperienced writer meant low fees. A talented one meant good work. And Walter knew he could make great demands of me, and I'd work my ass off to exceed expectations.

Yes, I wanted to please and impress my older brother, to prove myself to him and to earn his respect. Those Addy Awards meant more to me as affirming my ability to Walter than to the state's advertising community.

At the same time, I was hungry to establish myself as a creative person. I'd never had the visual talents that earned Walter national recognition. The family always celebrated his talent and brilliance. Mine, not so much. Walter's abilities were obvious at a glance. To demonstrate my late–blooming dramatic talents, I needed to get up on a stage, or to get someone to read the page.

But perhaps in advertising I could show my potential. To my brother. To my mother. To friends, and a larger community.

*

While I taught school that spring, I grew increasingly irritable with the antics of my students and disgusted with the priorities of the Cathedral administration. My annoyance made me politically reckless. For example, a memo signed by the principal and president to faculty asked us to review and reconsider grading policies, "because parents don't spend thousands of dollars in tuition for their kids to get C's." Then the memo said we had a much higher caliber student than public schools. That pissed me off. Our students were no better than public school kids. They were merely wealthier, and more parents got involved, and as a result more of them went to college. At the next faculty meeting, I brought up the memo. The president and principal restated their point. My response was, "I didn't think we were in the business of selling grades." There were audible gasps from my colleagues as the principal and president's faces went stony.

It was an act of professional self-immolation. But something in me didn't care.

Salt the fields. Burn the bridges.

*

As the spring semester began, my copywriting workload grew steadily. I could've worked around the clock between teaching, grading, reading, planning class work, and copywriting. It was nuts: if I was awake, I was working.

About then my responsibilities at the high school grew. I had to direct the upcoming musical. I didn't even like musicals. But it was in my contract, and it was a good way to get a lot of kids involved, so I went after it. I selected *Pippin* and had to rewrite, edit or ax some scenes to soften the sexual content. Even if I'd wanted to, I couldn't do the musical alone. I did get good help from a friend on the faculty, Martha Haven, who had studied voice at Indiana University before switching into religion. Another iconoclast, she'd taught religion at Cathedral for two years. She was great because I knew nothing of music, so the kids learned about singing from her.

Choreography help came from Laura Dove, a sexy physical education teacher at a nearby Catholic elementary school, who also directed Cathedral's drill team. I was dating her at the time.

We had some great kids in the show, and they worked hard. Then there was the music director. He should've been my most important ally, but his was another story. Known to be a heavy drinker, he was a big, loud, middle-aged guy who didn't like teaching any more; he taught because it provided health insurance and financial stability for his family when his irregular night-time gigs and summer weddings didn't. The weak link in my team, I knew I needed to push him. Push I did. Throughout the work on *Pippin*, he kept updating me on the orchestra's steady progress. But he also kept ginning up excuses for not bringing them to rehearse with my actors. It smelled fishy. Finally I told him he had to bring his musicians to a rehearsal in three days. When they showed up, the kids didn't know the music. It was clear the big clown had only worked with them for the previous two days.

The next morning, I confronted the music director, a man old enough to be my father. I ordered him to sit down, and I pointed out how he had lied to me, how he had let me down as well as the kids in the cast and his students in the music department. I told him I was disappointed in him and ashamed of him. Tears filled his eyes and spilled down his cheeks as he promised to whip his kids into shape. "Too late," I told him. "I can't work with you. You're fired." I felt bad for the music students because they wanted to participate, but there was no way, no time. I told the music director I'd figure out the music myself. But now I had a new dilemma: where does a guy with zero connections to the music world find a band to play in a high school musical? Fortunately, the music director came to me a day later, hat in hand, and offered to pay a quartet of his professional friends to perform the music. I took the deal. The next night his friends were there, and they managed to save the show.

*

Right after my father's trial—at which the judge granted Mom an immediate divorce and made it clear that anything like a restraining order violation would result in six months of jail time for him—Big Walt Blake vanished. Yet silence didn't mean safety, I knew, so I remained vigilant. Still, his absence did allow me to focus on my increasing mountain of work. And it allowed Mom to take an apartment, a nice two-bedroom unit next door to a friend of hers. Her friend's husband even set up an alarm for her to hit if ever she thought something was wrong. And my father remained out of the picture.

Even during the musical, I kept writing radio spots and print ads. It was crazy. Then after rehearsals I'd go home to grade papers and prepare lessons. To bed by 1:00 in the morning, and back up at 5:00 a.m., to write the next radio spot or print ad. My life went from "when I'm awake I'm working," to "I seldom sleep." And it went on like that right through the weekends—minus rehearsal on Sunday.

Something had to give.

The first thing was the lovely Laura Dove. A few years older than I was, she made two things clear: she wanted to get married soon, and she loved me. Both scared me. From my side, we had fun together and she was nice, but there was no magic, little in common, and ultimately no future. (She'd never even heard of the authors I most admired.) Finally I had to tell her. She still wanted to continue dating, but I told her I needed a break. She didn't take it well, though she told me to call if I changed my mind.

Meanwhile Walter stayed at my shoulder, encouraging me to leave teaching, and demanding excellence on every copywriting project.

The kids, the administration, the actors, the musical director, the parents—as well as the grading and preparation and writing of college recommendations—*all that was school* burned a hole in me by the end of the year. I knew the second year would be easier, that I could build on my lesson plans—and lessons learned—to ease my workload. Year three would be yet easier, as long as I taught the same stuff. But teaching the same material, year after year sounded boring. And even if the teaching got easier, I'd still face a lot of the same issues no matter how many years I taught.

So I decided to leave.

I didn't need to flip a coin this time.

I just took a brisk walk on a beautiful spring Saturday to reflect on the school year and sort out how I was going to leave Cathedral and start my copywriting career. The musical had gone well. I'd done a pretty good job teaching my students about literature and writing–and I'd earned their respect and built positive relationships with most of them. I'd made friends among faculty members if not among administrators. Much of it was fun and fulfilling. So I felt like I would be going out on a strong note. (Maybe I did need to flip the coin.) Walking on, I considered the realities of teaching the way I did, with the workload, which helped me understand teachers who slogged along on auto-pilot, slowly becoming dead wood. I couldn't do that. I wanted to create, to write, to produce from my thinking–and advertising allowed all of that. It wasn't art, but it was artistic and creative. I could make a living with my pen. That's all I had to say to the administrators. They knew I worked hard and made the school better, but they'd feel relieved to see another iconoclast go.

By this time, I'd walked to Holcomb Gardens at Butler University. The Gardens screamed spring with the greens, pinks, yellows, reds, and purples in full bloom. Everywhere I looked flowering trees and flower beds created a spectacular celebration of life. College students wandered around, a few played Frisbee, some read, a couple held hands and walked along the canal. I looked for that girl I'd met at the Indiana Council of English Teachers, Katie, but I didn't see her. After all the trouble with my father and the hard work of balancing teaching and copywriting, somehow I'd lost track of spring, and this explosion of color took me by surprise and brought me back to the beauty and peace of nature.

Spring was happening.

Even if I wasn't looking, here it was. Full of life and hope. In abundance.

When I left the Gardens and headed home, I saw–as if for the first time, and though I was walking the same streets–all the flowers in the yards, the blooming redbuds, dogwoods and magnolias of the beautiful neighborhood. And I began to think about life after teaching.

Soon I would be a freelance copywriter–and writer.

If I was going into business, I'd need a real desk and desk chair. A phone for my office. A better computer. I needed a decent car.

This last thought really energized me. It would separate me from my father.

*

Within a week, I bought a two–year–old Honda Accord from a guy in a hurry, getting a divorce. I wondered if his wife knew, but the car was in his name, so I bought it. And just a few days later I sold the flawed Celica cheap. That nearly–new Honda marked more than a break from my dad, it signaled my career change. I appreciated how different it was from the cars my father had rebuilt. Top of the list was that for the first time in my driving life, I didn't put the key in the ignition and hope the car would start. The snappy little Honda simply started every morning. It had no leaks. Tires wore evenly. Pressure on the brake pedal actually stopped the car–every time. Pure luxury.

During my last days of teaching, I'd go to my new office in Broad Ripple at night and sit on a folding chair at an old drafting table Walter had loaned me, imagining the life to come. How different it would be. The quiet to think, no students hollering or to holler at–it seemed a blessing, yet I already missed the school's energy.

Sitting at the loaned furniture, I decided to buy a new, modern desk and chair to mark my new career. A few days later I found a nice teakwood desk and a decent chair for $900. I put $300 down, the rest was C.O.D. But when the desk arrived a couple of days later, the invoice was red–stamped "PAID." A note in my brother's hand sat next to it: "For Blake Copywriting Company, Incorporated, Unlimited. Happy writing! From Walter." He'd paid off the remaining $600 on my desk, a blessing on my business.

I sat down at the desk and came up with these two headlines for the small–business division of the giant accounting firm Ernst & Young. First, "Your most costly accounting error could be your choice of accountants," with a visual concept of a row of identical accounting nerds. And second, "The wrong accountant could have you seeing red," with an illustration of a falling performance chart dipping into the red across a guy's angry forehead.

Working Alone

I enjoyed the first days on my own, as Blake Copywriting. I appreciated the quiet of my little 10' by 10' office. No bells signaling me to begin or end my work. No more 35-minute lunch hours. No administrator telling me not to leave campus. I felt liberated, living by my own clock. Felt like I was playing hooky every day. For hours I sat in the simple, white-wall office, soaking in the newness of the idea, reading, plinking away at an article proposal, and writing drafts for radio spots and brochures. Concerned about spending money before it came in, I didn't even have a phone for six weeks. My brother, in the office next door, let me use his.

At the end of the day, I'd lock my door, walk down the dark brown linoleum hallway and stairs, and out onto the sidewalk–emptyhanded–and stride along the street to my nearly new and reliable car. I felt free. The evenings were my own, and I spent them reading or visiting friends–especially Frank Bernard, a brilliant young lawyer, who had just moved in next door. Frank and I quickly became friends. Rather than phoning each other, we tapped on the adjoining wall and met on the fire escape; and sometimes we'd walk the mile or so to the local pub and have a beer. Frank was starting his own small law practice, so we talked a lot about how to get things going when you're young and starting out.

With the extra time, I also saw the lovely Laura Dove again. While she was nice, and (this will sound bad) convenient, there was still no special spark for me. She'd moved out of her parents' house, which meant she spent a night or two at my place. I spent a couple at hers, but in the morning I always felt bad. And a little trapped. So I broke it off again, a little reluctantly because the sex was always fun with her and because I didn't have another girl in the wings.

The first weeks of working for myself felt like one long vacation. I wore shorts and t-shirts to work all summer (although I kept dress clothes in the closet to change into for client meetings). Late in the summer, I realized that if I wanted to return to teaching, the time was running thin. I decided to stay with copywriting and felt a little pang of regret, of fear, of loss. The end of August came. The school year started. I stayed away from schools, and for the first time since I was five years old, my life wasn't guided by the academic calendar or class bells. That was a little unsettling. I, who had been an iconoclast throughout most of my school days (including those as a teacher), missed that association, missed my colleagues, even missed the wacky, noisy, annoying enthusiasm of the kids. And finally, I missed performing as the energetic, out-of-the-ordinary, young teacher who stood on his desk (when teaching *The Scarlet Letter* to fifteen-year-olds) to illustrate the ironic symbolism of Reverend Dimsdale looking down on Hester Pryne from his upstairs window; and who wore a fishing hat with "Shakespeare" on it while teaching "Big Bill," and who interrupted the reading of one of Bill's plays with a guffaw at some sexual innuendo. (When kids said, "What? What's so funny?" I'd reply, "I can't tell you, we're not supposed to talk about sex at a Catholic school. You'll have to figure it out for yourselves," and then I'd watch kids dog-ear those pages and pore over them later.) I even missed the yelling and cheering–certainly the cheering more than the yelling–as I tried to coax more out of my students and actors.

As a freelance copywriter, my responsibilities had flipped. Instead of students striving to make me happy or perform to my standards, I strove to please everyone around me, toiling to meet their standards. Suddenly, everyone was my client: the designers (especially my demanding brother) as well as their clients and the final customer. This was new. I had to sell my ideas and writing to both groups. In doing so, I found people reluctant to criticize design–because that was "art" and "Hey, I can't draw." But when it came to words, just about everyone–marketing director, salesman, vice president, CEO, and resident factotum–considered himself a writer. Everyone had taken freshman comp, maybe a creative writing course, written reports, and read Grisham, so anyone armed with Microsoft Word thought himself a writer. *Oy vey.*

When busy, I spent long days alone, writing long–hand and then typing into my Macintosh carefully and slowly, rewriting as I went. When I wasn't busy, I still spent long tracks of time alone. So much quiet. As a social person by nature, the quiet solitude was a real transition for me and one I had mixed emotions about.

During slow weeks, worry set in. I grew certain no work would come along. The erratic income was unsettling. I imagined getting evicted from my apartment and moving in with a family member, having to sell my car, needing to borrow money from my brother or my mother. I also worried about my father who had remained mysteriously quiet. If he tried to make good on his promise, storming into my office with his revolver, there was no escape. The second–floor windows were hard to crank out and even when open, my window was too narrow to squeeze through. I'd be a goner. So if it happened, if he came for me, I decided, I'd just take it. Or charge him and hope for a fighting chance.

This of course was but one of many scenarios that haunted my dreams. The nightmares spun from suspenseful dark shadows to gory bloodlettings with knives. Both were common and mounded up a long, long series of sleep–deprived nights. At one point, after many fitful nights and during a dry spell of work, the blues deepened to black. I slid into a depression. Money was a part of it, and the lack of sleep, but so was the absence of contact with other people. I could have used a dose of Laura Dove, but couldn't bring myself to call her. In addition, I'd failed to meet an important, if unrealistic, goal which I'd set for myself, of publishing an article in a major national magazine (okay, the *Atlantic* or *New Yorker*) by age twenty–four. Add to all this the facts that I wasn't seeing Mom very often, that I worried about her security in her apartment, and that when I did see her I couldn't shake the feeling I had failed her.

Meanwhile my savings and my spirit circled the drain.

I canceled my *New Yorker* subscription for the six dollars they agreed to refund me. I cut back on my food, going to bed hungry most nights or filling up on popcorn. Breakfast became a single banana. Every day.

And I felt too ashamed to share my feelings of failure with anyone. They were just feelings after all–all things I could and should control, all symptoms spilling over from conditions within my control. But while I heard myself telling myself this, I felt like I was swimming underwater among a million minnows, and I was responsible for catching them by hand.

How could I talk to my brother? He was my client. Everyone seemed to be my client. For them I adopted a phony smile and a bright hello that felt entirely detached from me. Pull the strings and show the smile.

How could I talk to Brian Jackson? Whenever he called, he talked about his fun and interesting colleagues at the design firm, or he shared a fantastic adventure story and the laughs he and Rod had as they explored New England. They went to the beach often on Cape Cod or Cape Ann. As I sweltered in the humid Midwestern summer with no hope of a vacation, I pictured them splashing in the surf of the National Seashore off Wellfleet, and huddling around a bonfire under blankets with pretty girls. Though happy for those guys, I sank further into my self–pity.

Any faith I'd had in my father had shattered the previous fall. What else was a sham? All the strength and independence I thought I'd built by going to Cape Cod and Europe alone? Protecting my mother–well, I'd practically let my father kill her, hadn't I? And my writing talent–a handful of advertising awards as consolation and not a single magazine piece, advertising awards I'd won with my brother's help. What a loser.

My fear of abandonment resurfaced during my time of weakness. I thought about Laura Dove. Even though we'd broken up, I feared she'd find someone else. I didn't really want her, but I didn't want to lose a life raft–at least *someone* wanted me. Why would she want me now–me, the one stupid enough to quit a good teaching job to flounder alone? If my professional life was in the toilet, didn't my personal life have to follow? So went the moil of my mind.

When I finally broached the subject of feeling depressed with Walter, his response was a pull–yourself–up–by–your–bootstraps kick in the pants. "Get busy on your next magazine piece. This is the perfect time to write. And just go out there and find more copywriting work. That's all you have to do," he said.

Minnows all around, fool. Just grab some.

When I called on designers, I suspected they sensed my despair, and I believed I presented myself poorly, doing more harm than good. So I quit calling. I sat silently in my small office for hours, staring at the white walls, unable to come up with even a lousy magazine story idea though there was plenty of time for it. I took walks and found myself focused on the ground, missing the beauty of trees and birds, powerless to find a bright side. I wanted to sleep all the time, as if everything would look better in the morning–something my mother had told me as a child. My muscles felt like I'd carried wet sod all day. My weight dropped to 160, a level I had not seen since I was fifteen. Home from the workless office, I didn't want to read anymore. I'd curl up on the couch and study the pattern of the oriental rug my mother had given me until I fell asleep again.

I knew I needed help. But I didn't have the money to pay a professional. And I did not know where to turn. I knew resources existed, but I couldn't bring myself to seek them out. That would mean admitting I was weak or soft, the kind of man my father could crush. At times I imagined him laughing at me. In my dreams, he punched me in the gut and kicked me in the face, grinning as he drew his revolver slowly and leveled it at my bleeding face.

Perhaps, I thought, I deserved to die, and I began contemplating suicide. I had thought about suicide when I was in college during bouts with the blues (though not seriously), and I was drawn to literary figures and characters who had committed suicide. But those thoughts had been in the abstract, a romantic ideal. Never before had I pondered it this seriously. And it frightened me. If the thoughts stayed with me for very long, I'd make myself get up and get busy doing something physical, cleaning the bathroom, waxing my car, going for a run–anything.

On one deadly quiet afternoon, I went to the library to read the *New Yorker* and found myself browsing the shelves of psychology books, thumbing through chapters on depression. With an energy I hadn't felt for weeks, I was soon sitting on the floor with five or six books open around me, reading about myself, about my feelings of failure, of having nowhere to turn, of wondering if the light would ever return to my spirit, of sitting in a dark box or hole with no way out, of being trapped in a dark hall of doors where each door opened to a terrible nightmare, of thinking this life wasn't worth living, of feeling ashamed for these thoughts and feelings. And I began taking notes. I took a break for dinner, walking to a deli for a bagel. I checked out a couple of the books, one a self–help. That night I read until far into the morning hours. The next day I went to work, but only to continue reading. For the first time, I fully admitted to myself I was clinically depressed.

That allowed me to rethink where I was.

It enabled me to recast how I viewed this depression. Rather than an end, a final entrapment in a black box, I could visualize my state as black wall before me. I could look up and see light had extended to the other side and behind me, in my past. I believed I could be happy again, could focus on the positive again, could be psychologically strong. All I had to do was break through this black wall. Or hike around it.

I began pecking at that monolith and found a few hollow places. The first breakthroughs were in my personal life with my family. They were there for me. They had not left me while I looked at the toys in a department store, nor would they. Though I didn't speak to my family directly about the depression, I called some of them, and in short conversations realized I was in no way insignificant to them. When I called Uncle Dale, Aunt Margo answered, and she must have sensed some of the pain in me because she launched into how she and Dale and the whole the family felt indebted to me. She told me I was her hero. I laughed, but she said, "No,

Jason, I mean it. You are my hero. You saved April. To save your
mother, you stood up to danger. You've got your mother's strength,
and it showed up right when it was needed most." Aunt Margo
paused; perhaps she could hear me choking back tears. "So, Jason,
no laughing or dismissing when I say you are my hero. I mean it.
In this big, wonderful, crazy family, you are one of the heroes."

I then called close friends, which I hadn't done for weeks during
my downward slide, and they too cared about me, loved me. I
meant something to them. I recognized I added to the fullness of
their lives as they added to mine. I had value. I mattered. Brian
Jackson reminded me that he and Rod still wanted me to take the
third bedroom in their Cambridge apartment.

Feeling a little better, I went to see Mom for lunch at her apartment. It felt like home, beautifully decorated with her antiques and
oriental rugs. When she asked how I was, I said, "I've been pretty
blue." Noting the concern in her face, I added, "But I'm feeling a
little better."

"You've been through a lot over the last year," she said. "So much
of what you knew was turned on its head." She paused. "Hey, let's
go in the kitchen. I've prepared our old standby." I knew what
that meant: Campbell's Tomato Soup and Velveeta grilled cheese
sandwiches. It was already warming on the stove. She continued
talking as she finished fixing lunch, and I sat at the counter. "You
also started two new careers. In one year! That's a lot for anyone."

"Yeah, it's been a lot. Especially the stuff with Dad."

"I'm so sorry for all that mess."

We sat next to each other on stools at the counter, eating the
comfort food she'd made for as long as I could remember. As
we ate, conversation slid into small talk about how the apartment
was–it's great; about her new book group which was reading Jane
Smiley's *Thousand Acres*; about her routine of power walking for
three miles a day; and about her work on a new skirt design which
was selling well and keeping her busy.

After we finished lunch, I broke the light chat. "Do you ever
worry about Dad?"

"Well," I could tell she didn't really want to answer, "I'm careful, you know. I keep an eye out, and an ear open. It's nice to have Bob and Jan next door, and Bob gave me a couple of panic buttons that call them for help. But I'm not going to live in fear. Your dad moved in with that woman." This was news to me. "So I hope he can be happy with her and just leave us alone. And I know he doesn't want to go back to jail. He hated it. The judge put the fear of God in him, promising a minimum of six months if he so much as said hello to any of us."

"You know," I said, "one of the things I've been feeling bad about is how I let him hurt you that night at Grandma's."

"Oh, Jason, you can't. You just can't feel bad about that."

"Well, I do." I felt my eyes welling up and looked at the ceiling.

"But you really can't." She rubbed my back. "Imagine what might have happened without you there."

"I let him hurt you." I started to cry, leaning over the counter, choking back full-on sobs.

"Jason, Jason, Jason," she said, off the stool and hugging my back. "This is so like you to take this on, but I'm fine. You stopped him. You saved me that night."

"I feel like I failed you."

"You have it wrong," she said, then sunk both hands deep into my curls and gave a tug. "You have to let it go. Get it out of your head." Then she rubbed my neck and shoulders. "Now, listen carefully because I want to put an end to this. You got it?" I nodded. "I was not badly hurt, and I'm fine. And I'm fine because you, Jason, you were there to protect me. You did your job, a job you didn't deserve and never asked for. I have a debt to you—"

"No," I said, "I have a debt to you. I owe everything to you—"

"Enough," she said. "I did my job as a mother. You did your job as a heroic son. And now that job is done. Both our jobs are done, and we both did an excellent job. Okay, so our debts cancel each other out, and it's time for both of us to enjoy our lives. There's so much to do and see, so much fun to have."

Then she laughed and patted me on the back like a drum, "My book group is talking about going to England next summer, and I think I might go with them. So you need to tell me what to see."

I had to laugh too. I couldn't wait to give her a list of places to see.

*

To reclaim my professional confidence, I returned to the work that had won the awards. When I reread the ads and brochures and listened to the radio commercials, I saw the talent and thought, 'That's good work, but you'll never write that well again.' Then I caught myself. 'Bullshit, you're just getting started.' A brighter side spoke up: I had written at this level before, and I could go farther. My best work was ahead of me, and I had better get to it. There was a lot to learn. A couple of small projects came in, and I worked at them as if they were the president's State of the Union Address. A flicker of hope glowed in the effort, in the process–showing up and laying down the words. Chip, chip, chip. Over the course of the next few weeks, I broke through that black wall, growing renewed and strong again. Stronger for getting through the depression.

Feeling vital again, and confident, I pursued more work, determined to keep financial ruin at bay. I called on designers around Indianapolis to show my portfolio. Though I brought in more work and gained a measure of financial stability, I soon realized that some designers saw me because I was Walter Blake's brother, the guy who'd helped him win awards. Other designers refused to see me because I was Walter Blake's brother, the guy who, they feared, might help Walter steal clients. It was difficult to extend my roster of clients beyond the core my brother had built: first Blake & Patterson, then the two independent designers who rented space from my brother, and occasionally another designer friend of Walter's. After this core group, it was spotty: a project here or there. If things got slow for my core clients, they got slow for me.

Working With Walter

Walter taught me a lot about the advertising business, especially how to price my work. When I wrote for him, he set my fees. "That's fine," I'd say, assuming my brother was fair, and it saved me the hassle of trying to figure out what my copy was worth.

But when I worked for other people and had to quote projects myself, I often asked his advice. He recommended fees higher than what he paid me for similar projects. Sometimes much higher. If I didn't ask his advice and quoted a job on my own, he might ask what I was charging for a brochure or an ad and say, "You're giving it away. You got to think about what you're worth and how long it takes with meetings and everything." He also trained me to think about the clients and what they stood to gain from my work. A small women's clothing store made a fraction of what a large corporation made from an hour of my work, and my fee should reflect the value. My brother taught me it was okay to lose business that didn't pay enough. It was okay if the client balked and negotiated for a lower fee. It was a business, and I had to make a profit.

In making a profit there was plenty to learn from my brother. He was good at that too. At one point I saw a proposal to one of his clients. The copywriting fee quoted was five times what he was paying me. We came to words over it, and he rode down hard on the point. He had won the client. He managed the account. He brought in the work. He had to make money from his vendors. And the vendors he selected had better understand it.

Vendor.

For the first time, I realized my brother saw me as a vendor. Something prescient in this echoed the time Uncle Roger tried to help my father when he was between jobs, and hired him to work in the dealership's body shop. When my uncle questioned the quality of my father's work–no doubt bored with a project, Dad had gotten sloppy–Dad exploded. With pride, he boasted of tearing up a paycheck and throwing the pieces in Roger's face. (Even as a kid I doubted the veracity of the story. And if it was true, I didn't grasp how the act benefited our family or why Dad seemed so proud of it.)

Speaking of my father, no one heard from him. The judge's threats must be working, I thought, but maintained a watchful eye.

When I reminded Walter that he'd taught me the industry standard was a fifteen percent mark–up on vendors' fees, he said he was still teaching me to write ad copy, editing me, pushing me. He spent time on the copy and had to make money from it.

All of his points were true, but it still riled me and left a bad taste in my mouth. I left the room, but I couldn't leave it alone, so I came back to say it felt like he was screwing me, and I pointed out how he recommended I charge higher fees to other designers. My quick–thinking brother was ready.

"Do they provide you with free office space?" he asked.

Ouch, even though we'd agreed I paid for the office space in trade.

"Did they create an entire career opportunity for you?"

Ouch again.

"They pay you for a talent you got from me."

This one was off line. He had certainly created the opportunity. He had certainly helped develop my skill. But the talent was mine. As he'd said before, I had a natural ability to pick it up. That's talent. And he had profited from it.

To punish me, my brother didn't hire me for any projects for several weeks. He worked longer hours and weekends to write pieces himself. It hurt me financially, and it drained him. But he was stubborn about it.

During that period, I heard from Brian Jackson, and again he tried to talk me into moving to Boston. I just about hit the road.

*

Then one day, the battle with my brother was over. Snap. As if there'd never been a rift, without a word of discussion to resolve it, he banged on my door and, with his old levity and enthusiasm, he said: "Hey, you want to go to lunch with Carl and me to talk about a new project?" At the end of lunch, he asked me to quote the job. The next morning I gave Walter and Brian a pretty high price, and Walter said, "There's a little more in the budget than that," and added a few hundred bucks to my fee. "Sounds good to me," Carl Patterson said.

And just like that, we were a team again.

But I still knew I was a vendor, and they were the client.

The three of us spent hours brainstorming and developing concepts, talking about visuals, copy organization and headlines. We laughed and joked and worked hard, taking greater pleasure the harder we worked, the way we had when we were kids playing sports, cheering each other for fearlessly diving to catch a ball. During those hours of collaboration, I loved working with my brother. Loved my brother.

But there was always another bump ahead.

Blake & Patterson was taking off. Before long Walter and Carl hired an office manager and a junior designer. Then another designer. And an account executive. Soon, they needed the other independent designers' offices, and my brother had them move out. That left me as the only independent under Blake & Patterson's roof. So much for the artist colony. The company grew to six employees. Then eight, ten. But no copywriters. Except for the few projects my brother wanted to write, I wrote all of the copy for the rapidly expanding agency. During those few short months, I went to another award show with the Blake & Patterson gang, accepted awards for the agency, and attended the first company Christmas party. The line between my solo company and my brother's ad agency grew very thin.

Fewer and fewer outside designers and small ad agencies wanted to work with me. To be honest, I didn't really want to work with them either because I was usually disappointed with their designs. Brainstorming sessions with them drizzled, while those with my brother sizzled. They lacked Walter's unwavering passion to do great work, something he inspired in his employees. In me. Besides, I was busy enough working with Blake & Patterson. By all but the strictest measures, I was Blake & Patterson's copywriter.

Because I recognized my value to the agency, I increased my rates. It was capitalism, and Walter had capitalized on my back. Now it was my turn. We sparred over money. But we had each other over a rickety old barrel. If he rejected my quote, I had to back down because he was my main client. But if I held my ground, he had to back off because I was his only copywriter. It was a delicate balance. Difficult to strike and harder to maintain.

Our tensions were not limited to money. He spoke to me–because I was his younger brother–in the bluntest, gloves–off terms, unlike he did or could with anyone else. "Jason, putting this benefit first is stupid and this headline sucks. What the hell were you thinking? I can't present this." He pulled his glasses off. (He was the only one in my family to wear glasses.) "Jesus Christ, I could lose this account because of you." Other times he came back from a presentation and said, "Zow, I owe you an apology. The client loved your headline. When I told him we were going to rework it, he said he'd fire me if I did." He laughed at himself. But it pissed me off that he didn't have faith in my work when I knew it was good, and that I had to fight to get him to present it.

Like wires in a cable, the tension between my brother and me coiled tighter under stress, and I often felt blind–sided by his attacks. One Spring afternoon Walter and I went to lunch at the little Greek restaurant in Broad Ripple. The topic of money came up and my brother got harsh.

"You've got to stop thinking about money. Don't get greedy," he said. "I didn't get you into this business so you could make a lot of money. I did it so you could make $25-grand a year and write a book."

Who do you think you are? I wanted to ask. Why do you think you get to engineer my life? And what is this about? But you have to be careful how you talk to your biggest client.

"If anyone had done for me what I've done for you, I'd be showing my paintings in Paris by now."

I said nothing. His words hurt like hell. Fuck you, I wanted to scream. It told me so much about what he thought of himself and what he thought of me. As if his greatness was tethered by me somehow, and I wasn't measuring up. Anything short of a National Book Award would fall short of the mark he'd set for me. It recalled those days when I was eleven and he was my private baseball coach. What right did he have to set the bar for my life? My own ambitions were painfully high. I didn't need his as well. And if he wanted to have gallery shows in Paris, why did he produce so few paintings, and why didn't he try to show paintings he had completed? And why was he stuck in his home town? No one forced him to work 60-hour weeks on advertising. His arrogance about his talent, and his assuming it was his place to sculpt a life for me, astounded me.

But I said nothing because his words left me dumbfounded and because he was my client. My brother and my client. He could say anything, and he knew it. So he did.

*

A week later, a group of us played basketball in the driveway of a mutual friend, Scott Washington. This was a regular Tuesday night event, two-on-two or three-on-three, scrambling around on the tight blacktop court. Indiana basketball stuff—a bunch of former high school jocks playing hard. My brother and I matched up against each other in a three-on-three game as we often did. He was six-foot, two-inches tall, and I'm six-feet. I've always been stronger, but he'd put on weight while I'd shaved pounds, so he threw more bulk around. We were both physical players and our competitiveness was intense. Mix that temperament with brotherly rivalry, and with the rising blister of animosity Walter and I felt from work tension, and we were a volatile mixture jarring around on the court.

He had the ball. I guarded him closely, bumping him with my chest. Then he pulled an old trick from his teenage days: looking right at me he jabbed the ball at my face, pulling it back just before it struck me. When I flinched, he shot over me.

To get him back I pulled one of my old tricks on him, a strength insult. I held the ball at arm's length with both hands for him to try to steal. I squeezed it so tight he couldn't knock it away. He slapped it, and I laughed, continuing to hold it out, daring him to try again. He hit it again, harder, and I laughed at him when he couldn't swat it away, taunting him. Still I held the ball out to him for a third try. When he stepped back and came at the ball swinging with all his might, I pulled it away at the last instant, making him miss, and drove around him for a lay-up. The gang laughed.

He was pissed off. I knew he couldn't accept his younger brother making a fool of him before his partner and friends. Next time he got the ball, I was ready when he pulled the same in-my-face stunt, but he actually hit me in the forehead with the ball. I went after it, thrusting my right hand from my waist, but he drew the ball up over his right shoulder and I slapped him hard under the jaw, a kind of open-handed upper cut, knocking him back a few steps.

He exploded, cranking back the ball to throw at me from ten feet away.

My brain slowed everything down. My father's street fighting lessons behind the garage, and Big Dave's bouncer training on Cape Cod came back to me.

I blocked the throw with my forearm. Blood rushed into my back muscles, into my thighs and shoulders, across my chest. I felt my weight rock back, coiling into my hips, knees bending, toes seeking a purchase on the pavement.

Then, deliberately, slowly, I smiled at my brother.

He saw it. I could see the recognition in his eyes. He saw he was in trouble. In the silence, he heard the alarm bells. But he had to go on, "Goddamn you, you slapped me!" he said. He began to move.

I continued to grin. To wait. To see. My eyes followed him, but my toes liked their purchase, and I carried Dad's lesson that a punch rises from your toes through your legs and hips and all the way through the extension.

Sometimes you take on the bully—and Walter was a bully. Since I was a kid and he forced me to eat grass. Since the office where he liked to make me look stupid to others.

So was this the moment of truth?

He was talking again, something about me slapping him and how dare I. And I was lucky he didn't beat the shit out of me.

I smiled again at the thought, felt my fingers roll up and lock into fists.

About then the guys came between us. They put a stop to it.

"I can't believe you slapped me!" he said.

Calmly, I said, and everyone went quiet so he heard it clearly: "I was going for the ball. And it was after you hit me in the face with it." I paused, looking at his eyes, "Did you forget that? That was okay?" I held back from calling him, "Little Prince."

But did I go for the ball? Or had I kept that uppercut hand open because there'd be no explaining a closed fist?

That skirmish ended the night of basketball. After drinking water at the garden hose, a few guys said they needed to get home. I wasn't going to leave before my brother. Why, I don't know. Perhaps because I wasn't going to let him put his spin on what happened for whoever stayed. That was his way. Regardless, I was going to make sure he left first. Even if it meant I had to sleep in the damn driveway. A few of us sat around. Finally my brother left. When his car drifted out of sight, I apologized to Scott and drove to my apartment.

*

After a night of fractured sleep, I walked into the office the next morning on a mission. I had to talk to Walter about our basketball confrontation. I drained my second cup of coffee as Walter arrived.

"Hey man," I said, "you got a few minutes to talk?"

"Sure, what's up?"

"I want to talk about what happened last night at Scott's."

He laughed, "Don't worry about it, Jason. All is forgiven. Just competitive passion flaring."

I wasn't seeking his forgiveness. "I think there was more to it than that," I said. "Walter, it wasn't just competitive fire or brotherly rivalry. Something else was going on."

"Like what? That's all it was for me. I don't know what was driving you. It's been a long time since you hauled off to hit me like that."

I decided to say what I'd thought about during the night. "I didn't mean to hit you. At least I don't think so. But maybe I did. Maybe I felt insulted that you bounced the ball off my face. Or I felt like you were trying to embarrass me in front of friends again, and I snapped."

"What the fuck does that mean? 'embarrass you in front of friends *again*'?"

I'd hoped we could talk, but now it had slipped into a confrontation.

Was this his fault or mine?

Was the basketball skirmish his fault or mine?

Was there a fault to be claimed?

Did blame have to be part of this?

Was I trying to parse blame? For what exactly?

For a flareup on the basketball court? For him being the chosen one in the family? For bullying me when we were kids? For leaving me behind to fall under the influence of our father? For putting me down when I began to rise? For leaving me to battle Dad alone?

What was it? What did I hope to accomplish?

All of this is what I wanted to talk about. All of this was the net I tangled myself in during the long, slow minutes before dawn.

He was still talking, anger rising. "...and those guys, those guys are *my* friends. *Not* yours. You only know them because *I* introduced you to them."

"Walter," I said as calmly as I could, trying to slow him down. "Walter, I didn't mean to upset you with this. I'm not trying to fight, but it feels like there's something bigger here." I started wishing I had the words of a psychotherapist to disarm the moment, but I plowed ahead as best I could. "Maybe there's a lot of stuff. Maybe some of it is tied up with Dad."

"Wait a minute. Wait a minute. Wait a minute," Walter said. "You always do this. You make the simple stuff too complex. And the complex stuff too simple."

Really? Did I do that? Maybe.

"Walter..."

"Is it any wonder you can't find a serious woman to date? Or when you find a serious woman she won't stay? You need to get your shit together, Baby Brother."

His boxing gloves worked me over good now, a roll of nickels taped into each palm. And I simply dropped my guard and let him pound away.

I had started this fight somehow. And against all my father's training, as well as my own instincts, I wasn't going to finish it. I would accept defeat.

Long before that day, I had given up trying to resolve issues with Walter, like the slap on the basketball court, or a flare-up over a copywriting fee, or a disparaging comment about a friend. But as I buried these issues with my brother in the back of my mind, they gradually collected and festered. I knew I could not forever ignore them.

*

The second anniversary of my August return from Europe came and went without mention from anyone in my family. I didn't expect it. But I wanted some acknowledgment.

Since I wasn't dating anyone, I took myself to dinner at the airport. Yeah, the airport. Just like when I was in high school and took girls there to watch the planes come and go, to watch the tearful goodbyes and welcome–home embraces. I sat and took in the flow of emotions. I thought about all that had happened since those high school days. Back then, I'd never ridden a jet. And I thought about all that had happened in the past two years. I'd returned from teaching in England and wandering Europe a kind of celebrated fellow in my family. At least briefly. Like Mom said, a lot had happened in that year. The whole series of disasters with my father. The crush of work as a rookie English teacher trying, vainly, naively, to outshine the veterans. Followed by the copywriting career shift. Then my clawing out of depression. As I sat there, I thought about Septembers and how they'd always brought something new–something told me this one would too.

Becoming a Partner

Carl Patterson came into my office and asked me to go out to lunch with him one day in early September. The leaves had just begun to turn, just at the tips, and the sky held a clear bright blue promise of fall. During lunch Carl said he and Walter had been talking, and they wanted me to join them in the Blake & Patterson partnership. Of course I was flattered. By then it was clear Blake & Patterson, regularly winning regional and even national awards, was a creative rocket ship, soaring for success. It was obviously a great opportunity–would there ever be others? Or others this good? Yes, part of me wanted to instantly say, "No, thanks" and move to Boston. But the offer made me stop and think.

The three of us would make a great team. My brother with his talents for advertising and business, Carl Patterson's immense ability in graphic design, and my own growing skills in copywriting, presentations and business. All three of us were good conceptual thinkers, and we collaborated well together.

Why wasn't my brother at this lunch? I suspected he wanted Carl to extend the offer so I wouldn't take it as nepotism. Yet it seemed Walter should be there when a partnership was offered, even to his brother. I mean, this was an offer to join the company he built. It felt weird.

After stalling Carl Patterson with questions of logistics and such, I knew I should sleep on it, and that's what I told Carl.

*

244

That night, I went for a long walk with my lawyer friend Frank. He helped me think through the list of things I needed to consider–the legal, the personal, the professional. He was great. We ended up at our neighborhood pub for a beer. We kept talking. I knew he wanted me to stay in Indy, but he also wanted me to be happy and make a good decision. After just one beer, I said I needed to think and we went back.

I sat alone in my small apartment and weighed out the options. On the positive side:

The agency was likely to make the partners financially very comfortable, and, while it felt petty to my artistic sensibilities, honestly, I was attracted to financial security. Even though I was not yet twenty-four, I wanted a family someday and I wanted to provide the kind of financial security I never felt as a kid. And I wanted to avoid the money pains I'd known in my first months of freelancing. I knew I was young still, but it was a chance to become part of something great, an organization with high ambitions and the core talent to achieve those ambitions, to be a young star in the Indianapolis advertising and business community. When I thought about the partnership offer, I knew it meant I could buy a house, probably own a lake cottage within a few years, and take paid vacations (something I'd never experienced), including a return to Europe.

On the negative side:

Even if my brother and I could work peacefully with a high level of mutual respect, which I doubted–and even if I could grow to accept his unwillingness to discuss and work through problems in a productive way, which I also doubted–it was easy to imagine a final and irreversible rift over money eventually emerging, with me tearing up a check and throwing it in my brother's face (a sequel to the Roger and Walt Blake falling-out). I didn't want my life to mirror Dad's and how he hated and resented his successful brother. Nor did I want to lug around the nagging resentment, and frequent tension that had become everyday life with Walter.

I loved him too much to hate him.

Could I risk being miserable, struggling with my brother for the rest of my life? Then there was Dad and his threat hanging over my head despite his peaceful silence. Even if my father remained tranquil and work with Walter went well, I'd still be in Indianapolis, my middling home town. I was ready to move on to a more exciting place. Indy was okay and getting better. It was fine to be *from* Indianapolis; but I wasn't excited about living there the rest of my life. A bigger and more interesting world awaited in Boston. But Boston was expensive, and I had no job.

If I turned down the partnership offer and stayed in Indianapolis, I would have to build a business of my own because Blake & Patterson would not be a client forever. I also did not want to compete against my brother. Walter had staked out his leadership in a city and a state which, by advertising standards, was a small and insignificant market. There wasn't room for both of us.

So it was clear I had to join Blake & Patterson, or I had to go.

On and on my positive-vs-negative evaluation went, deep into the night. It was hard. The more I struggled with it, and the more tired I got, the muddier the water. I couldn't see anything, couldn't weigh individual elements against each other. With memories of Mom telling me it would look better in the morning, I finally went to bed.

As I tossed and turned, my thoughts turned from career choices to consequences including the possibility of my father reemerging to threaten my mother. Who would be here to protect her if not me? It was my duty to make sure she was safe. The flipside was the weight I carried of my father's promise to kill me when I least expected. Unable to shake his mouthing either "I love you," or "I'll kill you," I still looked over my shoulder for him even though months had passed without any of us seeing or hearing from him.

*

When I woke up, despite my mother's maxim, things did not look better in the morning. The waters were no more clear. But I didn't feel like I could go to the office and pretend nothing had happened. I took a walk, going down the fire escape from my apartment building. It was another beautiful early autumn day, the colors hinting at a glorious fall to come. I walked in my neighborhood of stately homes, the Meridian-Kessler area, dreaming of one day living in one of these 1920's arts-and-crafts foursquares, or Tudors, or oversized bungalows. With a beautiful wife and a couple of kids, a dog and nice cars. It all seemed suddenly possible—even likely—if I took the partnership offer.

Then I thought of Brian Jackson and Rod Kittle living in Harvard Square. Those guys were enjoying fun, carefree lives. Around them people at Harvard, MIT, and other universities were changing the world. And the girls, my god, the girls. The statistics said there were over 500,000 students in the Boston area. That meant 250,000 college girls. Beyond that, Boston had the youngest population in the US. It was hard not to ache to be there. The history, the ocean, the mountains, the culture, it all appealed to me.

Carefree Boston vs Business Partner.

Back at my apartment, I poured a second cup of coffee and watched the milk swirl into the black. Then I remembered the suggestion from Professor Anne Pain, to flip a coin and let your heart tell you what you want when the coin is in the air.

I figured I didn't have anything to lose, so I did it. After all the lists and the walks and the talk, I had to take a few minutes to clear my mind so I could hear my heart when the coin was in the air. Then I flipped a quarter. When the coin was in the air, my heart hoped for heads, which meant head-out. To Boston.

But I didn't trust it.

"Look, Jason," I said to myself, in a voice that sounded too much like my brother's, "Don't be stupid. When will you get a chance like this again? To become a partner in a business you like, working alongside people you admire and respect and who admire and respect you? Don't be rash. Do you know how many trips you can make to Boston with the financial security this partnership would allow? Plenty, that's how many." Right. It made sense. I could go to Boston every couple of months if I wanted, spend two weeks on Cape Cod every summer.

Besides, Mom needed me. Or might.

The morning after Carl Patterson had extended the partnership offer, I went up to the office Walter and Carl shared.

"How'd you sleep?" Carl said with a smile.

"I slept pretty well, and I made a decision. It's a great offer," I paused, less for dramatic effect than to catch my breath and flinch at the thought I was contradicting what my heart had proclaimed when the coin was in the air. "And I'm ready to do it, ready to join you guys."

"Well, hot dog," Walter said, slapping his desk and holding up his hand for a high five. Carl held his hand up too.

A few days later, I met with Carl and Walter to finalize the terms. I'd make considerably less than they did—and considerably more than I'd made teaching, and I'd get five percent of the company immediately and five more percent at the first of the year. I also had twenty percent of my salary held back to buy into the partnership over the next three years, acquiring five percent a year. But I'd share in the profits with them, and I'd be on a rapidly rising pay scale to catch up to them within five years, depending on the company's performance. At the end of three years, I'd own twenty-five percent of the company. After I had Frank review the documents, I signed and was legally a partner in Blake & Patterson by the end of the week. Already I dreamed of a little cabin on Lake Monroe in Bloomington with a fishing boat on my dock.

Thus it began, my working with my brother and Carl. It was hard and intense and demanding. And I loved it. I genuinely felt like I belonged, and felt like I owned something, that I was building something.

Hello and Goodbye

When the judge finalized my parents' divorce in rapid order after the hearing on my father's attack, he also authorized my mother to buy out his half of their house based on an appraisal Mom's attorney presented. But because of Dad's pledge that Mom would have no peace as long as he lived, she decided to sell the house and keep her apartment.

This meant, despite Walter living a few hundred yards away, I spent a lot of time getting the house ready to sell and maintaining it. Most weekends and occasional nights after work, I cut grass, cleaned, painted, landscaped, raked leaves, and cleaned gutters. My brother had quit doing yard work of any kind at sixteen, choosing to go off with his friends and leaving me, at age ten, to take up the chores. And here I was, still doing those chores long after moving out.

Finally the house sold, not long after I'd agreed to join Blake & Patterson. That granted me time to be a carefree young man again. Or it should have–but I was digging in hard, studying and practicing, and writing and rewriting ad copy, polishing and polishing, trying to become the best copywriter in America, and also become a good businessman at the same time. So go the slings and arrows of outrageous ambition. What the sale of the house *did* give me was another break from my father, and I'm sure it did the same for my mother.

What I missed, what I was unaware of even as I toiled in it, was the connection to the outdoors and nature which I had enjoyed about working at my mom's place. I craved a connection to nature that my work and my in-town apartment stymied.

*

Through it all, Brian Jackson continued to hound me about moving to Boston, but in a friendly, 'Dude, you are crazy to not be here!' way. Then he'd tell me some funny story about them getting caught in a storm. Or, while stuck in the famous Boston traffic, playing Frisbee with other cars and pedestrians in the median. And there were the ski trips and camping trips to the mountains, and the Gang of Twelve (a cadre of designers, writers, artists and musicians) who rented a shack together overlooking the beach in Turo on Cape Cod and pitched tents when they ran out of floor space. He told me how guys and girls shared the outdoor shower openly, stripping down to rinse away the sand and salt, and slipping off to skinnydip in the freshwater kettleholes on cool New England nights. Oh how I wanted to be with them.

But I was becoming a responsible young businessman (perhaps *too* adult and responsible, as Brian Jackson once said). And a creative business person. And an artist–right? Right?

Besides, I told myself, I'd join them on the beach and on the ski slopes in the future. Just as soon as I saved up some money and got some vacation time.

Even as I tried to convince myself, my inner bullshit detector was clanging in my ears.

*

"Patty has got to go." That's how my brother opened my first formal partner meeting for Blake & Patterson, LLC.

I couldn't believe my ears. Recently Walter had gushed about Patty as the most promising young designer in Indiana. He'd spent a lot of time shoulder-to-shoulder at her computer, coaching her, encouraging her, celebrating her. From what I saw, the attractive, twenty-six-year old Patty was smart, good with clients, did strong work, and had a great attitude.

I didn't say anything, I waited for more, waited for Carl to weigh in. Instead, silence.

"Why?" I finally asked.

"She screwed up three things the last two weeks. One for First Start trade show materials cost us a day. It also caused rush charges we had to eat, and it may cost us the account."

"If this was such a big deal," I said, "why didn't I hear about it until now?"

Carl's eyes went from his notepad to the window and back. Walter simply glared at me.

"We can't fire people like Patty. She's too valuable, too hard to replace," I said. "And we don't want an office where people fear for their jobs every time there's a mistake." I remembered Sonny's reaction to me cutting that floor joist too short.

Walter said, "We can't be stupid. She might cost us the account."

"If we lose the account, then we might have to lay her off. But that hasn't happened."

Walter ignored me and began to talk about how we should dismiss her, how much severance we should offer.

"Wait a minute," I said. "You raved about her, and now she has to go? What's going on?"

"Walter," finally Carl spoke, "Jason is not just your brother. He's a partner now, and he has a right to know what's going on."

Walter's glare now fell on Carl.

"He does," Carl said.

"What the hell is going on?" I said, but I had a strong inkling.

"Okay, okay," Walter said. "We had a fling. Nothing huge, no running off to Las Vegas or anything, no surprise pregnancy, but...yeah...." The room went quiet. Waiting. "Now she thinks something more is going to happen, or she wants something more to happen. But I'm not leaving my family. It was a fling. A stupid fling. Just supposed to be fun, but it got out of hand."

"You think?" I said. I felt like I was listening to my father. He glared at me.

"This opens us up to a sexual harassment lawsuit," I said. "You're her superior. Didn't you think about that?"

"Well, since the baby came," Walter said, "Missy has totally checked out of our sex life."

"Please, just shut the fuck up," I said. "You're an idiot. Thanks for the perfect first partners' meeting, Walter." I took a deep breath. "I'm really disappointed in you."

With that we discussed how to stay out of trouble with the law and how to keep Patty or let her go. Finally Carl and I prevailed upon Walter that he had to tell Patty it was over, and he had to swear to us he wouldn't let it restart. Not so much as a goodbye hug. We also agreed to get advice from our attorney Greg Garrett.

Within a week of meeting with Walter, Patty resigned to take her considerable design talents to a competing agency. We wrote her a nice fat check to cover vacation time plus a bonus no one had to call hush money, and we tore up her non-compete agreement. But before we wrote the check, I insisted to Walter and Carl that the money for Patty and Garrett should come out of Walter's year-end bonus, and Walter slowly agreed.

*

I don't know why I haven't told it until now, but to this point, the dreams, the nightmares I've shared placed me as the victim. But it wasn't always so. I said I was prepared to kill my father. And in my dreams I had plenty of practice. Many, many of my dreams became cinematic plays of me rampaging through the night to exact revenge on my father. Whirling from a defensive posture to the offensive—with knives, metal pipes, ax handles, the butt of my shotgun. Hunting him down in the dark. Lying in wait. Ambushing him. Beating him at his own game of promising he'd kill me when I least expected, I attacked when he least expected. Ramming the sharp end of a crowbar through a car window into the side of his head. Firing a rifle through a car window just as he put it in reverse and letting the car roll down the drive into traffic. Running him over in the street. Shoving him off the sidewalk in front of an oncoming bus. Taking a wire to his throat in a movie theater.

Occasionally in these dreams, I would get up from Dad, as he gurgled or rattled out a last breath of life, and I'd look back down to see my brother's face looking up at me. I'd drop down to help, to try to save him, and sometimes, Dad's face came back, laughing and calling me a coward, and I'd have to finish him again, wrapping him in tow chains from his truck and rolling him off a dock into a lake, descending slowly, fading under the murky, greenish–brown water.

I woke from these nightmares and wondered at myself, scared at how gleefully some part of me embraced the savage. What was in me? I hated and feared that part of myself. Yet it steeled me to act–if I had to–in the most intense and final way. All in, or it's all over. No trying to stop him next time. It would be final.

He had set the terms.

*

One mid–October night on my way home from the office in my Honda Accord, I heard a 'thunk' in the front end and thought a stick or rock must have flipped up and hit the door or front fender. When I got home, I found a bullet hole in the left fender. It looked the size of a .38 caliber, the size my old man carried. The bullet had passed through the fender and struck the engine block, doing no further damage.

I didn't want to think too much about what would have happened if it had been three feet back. Right through the door and into me. Or three feet back and a foot higher–right through the glass and Game Over.

It had been about a year. I had wondered if he'd attack again. And it looked like he had.

I didn't want to call the police. Or my family. But I worried my father might have headed for my mom's place after he shot at me. Or, God forbid, before.

I called her. She hadn't heard anything, but she was unequivocal: "You've got to call the police," she said. "I mean now. And I need to call them too."

She got through to me. I promised to call the police and not to leave the apartment. But I did load my shotgun and kept it leaning against the couch.

When the police arrived, two cops in their early thirties I'd guess, looked at the car and agreed it looked like a bullet hole. I told them where I thought it happened, but I wasn't sure. They didn't seem too impressed with my father's history–especially with my lack of evidence.

Mom also got a brush–off when she called the police. Not so much as a drive by. They said to call if anything happened. How helpful.

*

That night, just after dark, someone knocked at my apartment back door, and I snatched up the shotgun. "Who's there?" I said with an intense voice. It was my superintendent come to tell me that a man had come by looking for me earlier that day. Though he gave a poor description, it sounded like Dad. The man wouldn't say why he'd stopped or who he was, except that he was an old friend. I wasn't sure what to say to my superintendent. To let me know right away if the man came back? To call the police? That the man was my father and wanted to kill me? Not to send him up if he returned? But then the super told me he'd shown the man where I lived. At that, my gut instinct was to leave and hole up with friends. But another part of me thought, 'I won't be run out of my place.' So I stayed.

I went to bed late, after grabbing up my shotgun every time a neighbor came up the front or back stairs. My bedroom window faced right onto the back of the fire escape, making it way too easy if someone wanted to kill me. So I moved to the living room couch and wedged a chair under the front door knob.

I didn't sleep much and woke up at the slightest sound. Someone did pause on the back stairs by my bedroom window. I was sure it was him. But by the time I gathered my senses and grabbed my shotgun, all I could see was a figure crossing the back yard of the building toward the street. It was another long night with little sleep.

The next morning, I went down to my car and there was a bullet hole through the windshield and right through the headrest.

Message received.

I was going to call the cops back but decided not to. I did swing by an auto store to buy some body putty (shotgun under a beach towel across the back seat), and I filled in the bullet hole in the fender as best I could. I also picked up some touch-up paint to cover it during lunch. I stitched up the headrest and dropped the car off to get a new windshield–after I smashed a rock through it so as not to have to report it to police. My insurance covered it 100 percent.

When I got to the office, I checked my brother's car. No holes. Inside, I asked him if he'd seen or heard anything out of the ordinary. Nothing. I checked with Mom. Nothing there either. Apparently the old man was focused on me.

I had to be ready.

"So why're you asking if anything happened last night?" Walter said.

I didn't want to tell him, but since my mother knew, he'd hear about it. So I told him about the bullet hole.

He ticked off his points with his fingers the way he did when explaining a concept to a client.

Finger number one: "You've got to call the police."

Finger two: "You can't go back to your apartment alone."

Finger three: "And you can't stay there anymore."

I grinned and returned his finger use:

"When I called the cops, they didn't give a damn because I didn't have any proof. And they're right, I don't know for sure it was Dad. "I'm not going to let him scare me away. "End of discussion."

*

That night I had my shotgun ready if Dad came back. Those nine pellets of the double-aught shell in the chamber. Four more ready.

I sensed he might come back, suspected he was high on drugs and on a rampage, and being reckless in his mission to fulfill his promise: "I love you–I'll kill you." Just after I went to bed, close to midnight, there was a noise on the back stairs. Whoever it was stopped outside my bedroom window. This was it. I snatched up my shotgun and wrapped a beach towel around it, feeling like something out of a *Godfather* movie. I slipped down the front stairs. Then I ran around the building to the back steps, holding the shotgun across my chest and slipped up quietly, slowly. There was someone on the fire escape. I took off the safety.

I could see part of him by my bedroom window.

I could not identify him yet.

Another step.

My heart pounded hard. I could feel it in my neck. In my fingertips as I squeezed the stock and felt the edge of the trigger.

Another step.

I imagined him with his Winchester semi-automatic 12-gauge shotgun. Or his .38 revolver. If he raised a gun, I'd shoot.

I brought the shotgun up, pointing forward.

I was ready to shoot, to kill him.

At the next step, we'd meet. I'd have to leap forward to confront him.

He was still there.

I leaped out with my shotgun pointed forward, watching hands for a weapon. The towel fell away from my shotgun.

A loud scream—a girl. Fuck. A girl. She screamed again. Fuck. And again, fuck, fuck, fuck. What was a girl doing here?

It was Katie, the girl from Butler. The one I'd met at the Indiana Council of English Teachers two years before. I'd last seen her a year ago at the fall English teachers meeting.

I could have killed her. Damn near did kill her.

Another scream, muffled, followed by sniveling and whimpers, and a stammering: "wha–?, wha–?, whoa–? how–?"

"Sush!" I said. Neighbors' lights were coming on all over the building. I scrambled to pick up the towel and wrap the shotgun. "Sussshhh..." I said more gently. "Calm down, Kate. Calm down. Let's go inside."

Now I had to explain. Fuck. "I can explain," I said, but I didn't want to.

"Katie," I hugged her with my free arm, "it's going to be okay." Then louder so the neighbors who'd opened their back doors would hear. "It's okay, Honey. Everything's fine, Honey."

Honey? Oh, Jesus, why'd I say that?

She was still crying quietly as I helped her down the stairs. My neighbors must have thought that nuts too, because we went right past my back door, but I knew I couldn't get past the chair I'd wedged under the knob. So I had to parade her down the steps and around the building. All the while, I was trying to comfort her, trying to keep the shotgun covered, and trying to get her inside calmly. Before someone called the cops.

I took her in through the front door and up the stairs. (I could feel peep-hole eyes on us.) Thank god her head was down, muffling her crying and muttering so no one would think I'd kidnapped a college girl. My neighbors thought I was a nice guy, but here I was with a screaming girl, a loaded shotgun, and wearing cut-off sweatpants.

I brought her in, tossed the blankets aside and sat her on the couch. "Let me get you some water," I said. As I did, those few seconds on the stairs replayed in my head. The safety was off, my finger on the trigger. Thank god I didn't shoot her. Now, once inside, I was shaken. But I had to keep my head; what was I going to tell her?

I opened the fridge and grabbed two beers, thinking I was glad there were plenty in there because I might need more to get through this night.

How the hell was I going to start this conversation? Did it start with, "Why the hell were you outside my bedroom window?" Or did it start with an explanation of me with a shotgun–or rather with a yet–uncrafted lie about why I was out there with a shotgun?

*

When I brought Katie a beer, I realized she was in the bathroom. I sat down on the couch, on the end opposite from where I'd put her, then thought better of it and started to get up.

"No, sit down," she said. And I did.

She sat on the opposite end of the couch.

Katie had changed since I first met her at the Indiana Council of English Teachers in the dingy old gymnasium of Howe High School. She was a senior now. And here she was in my apartment, sitting on my couch. She had gone from pretty to beautiful. Even with the bloodshot eyes.

"I know my eyes look terrible," she said, "but you don't have to look at me like that." She gestured toward her eyes, "Whenever I cry–"

I took a long drink of beer. I decided to start with an apology. And a lie. I was too ashamed to tell the truth, that I had a crazy, drug-using father who wanted to kill me.

"I'm so sorry about what happened out there." I said.

"What did happen out there? Why'd you have a gun?"

She seemed to be settling down fast. There'd be time for my 'what the fuck were you doing out there?' but for now, a story.

I told her there'd been a rash of break–ins in the neighborhood, including one where a woman had been attacked. And I had two single women neighbors upstairs (at least that part was true). Two of the apartments had been broken into, I lied. So when I heard someone outside on the back stairs, I decided to act. She seemed to buy it. And I closed with another apology. "I was so shocked when you jumped out with a gun. Oh..." She went a little white at the memory and leaned back on the couch. I apologized again.

Before I could ask why she was on my back stairs, she poured forth a frank confession–that she'd looked me up and had figured out which apartment was mine. A senior at Butler now, she went by my building often. She'd driven by, ridden her bike past, and jogged by, hoping to run into me. But she'd been too scared to call or knock at my door–until tonight. After a Thursday night out with some of her Butler friends, her fears were mollified enough by a few beers to coax up her courage. So she walked over and climbed the back stairs, only to freeze up outside my bedroom window, afraid to make the final move, to knock on my back door.

The situation was awkward. First it was late, and we were both shaken by the evening's events. I couldn't let Katie walk back to campus alone. Nor did I want to risk walking or driving her back– with my father out there. Instead, I made up the couch for her, and as I headed to my bedroom, she put a hand on my arm, stopping me.

She apologized for the trouble she'd caused and thanked me for the couch before standing to give me a hug that lingered a little too long. Her face rose toward me, perhaps inviting a kiss, but I backed off. I wanted to kiss her, but not if she was drunk or overwhelmed by the evening's events. Either way, I didn't want anything to start on a night like that.

*

In the morning, with thoughts of what I'd done with the shot-gun, and her confessions of a crush, and the lingering hug, I had trouble talking to Kate. But I had no trouble seeing how beautiful she was. Those bloodshot eyes were clear and bright blue now. Making omelets provided a distraction as I struggled for small talk.

Kate was just two years younger, but the age distance felt larger with me teaching and then copywriting while she was still in college.

Eventually, over breakfast and a third cup of coffee, I began to loosen up. Katie made it easy, asking questions about my copywriting and sharing stories of college (she was in an honors seminar on James Joyce's *Ulysses* no less. *Oy!*). She repeated how long she'd wanted to see me. It both flattered me and left me wondering if this was just a passing crush.

We didn't broach the subject of what had happened on the back stairs, but concern about my father hung in the back of my mind.

*

I saw Kate three times over the next week. First for coffee on campus where I made a show of bringing her a cup with real half-and-half in it. Next we went to the art museum. And then to Bennett's Bar and Grille for our first dinner together.

Every night, I continued to sleep on the couch and propped chairs under the front and back doors to slow my father down if he tried to break in. But I spotted no more shadowy figures on the back stairs or running across the back yard. I experienced no more pot shots at my car or me—something I worried about when Katie rode with me. I told her nothing of my father, but it felt unfair to put her in harm's way. In our second week, I made excuses to drive separately and meet at different places after work.

And work ran late most nights. I toiled to grow my skills and accelerate my experience by studying the best work from all the award books, and by writing and rewriting and polishing my work. So I'd work until 8:00 or so, meet Katie somewhere, often just grabbing a deli sandwich and finding a park bench. Then we'd take a walk and talk for hours.

At the end of our second week of dating, and after no rumbles from my father, Katie spent the night in the bedroom of my apartment. Or part of it.

The phone rang and rang, stirring me out of a sound sleep.

"Jason, the phone," Katie whispered.

The clock read two in the morning. Again it rang as I went to answer it at my desk in the living room.

"Jason?" It was Walter.

"Yeah."

"It's Walter."

"Hey."

"Are you awake?"

"Yeah. No. I'm kind of awake. What's up?"

"t's Dad," he said.

That woke me up for sure.

"What–?"

"He committed suicide tonight."

It took me by surprise. And it did not.

Relief washed over me as I leaned on the desk.

Then I felt guilty for feeling relieved.

But the weight of months, two years, of worry vanished in an instant and my legs felt a little weak. I sat on the chair and slumped against my forearm on the desk. I'd expected the tension of constant wariness to last through years of looking over my shoulder, of remembering his promise to kill me when I least expected it. I'd expected years of sitting with my back to the wall at restaurants, of maneuvering in crowds while walking (without explaining why to a friend) to check a man with a gait similar to my father's, of watching for vehicles with mismatched fenders or body putty and spots of undercoat. Now, the alleviation of threat easily outweighed the pity I felt for the suicide of the man who had been my father, my dad. But my forehead went to my arm on the desk. How low he must have been.

Though Dad and I had the same dark blue eyes, I would not see the world as he had. In this I would break from him, as I had in other things.

"Are you there?" Walter asked.

"Yeah," I sat up, "yeah, I'm here."

"You all right?" he asked.

"I'm all right." My voice was flat.

"Can you believe it?" he said.

"Yeah, I can believe it." I thought about it for a moment. "In some ways, I'm surprised it didn't happen sooner."

"Remember when he talked about killing himself at the bar?"

"I remember," I said. "What happened? How'd he do it?"

"Uncle Jim just called me. I guess he drove into Gran's garage, closed the door, and left the car running."

"Oh, god, he did it at Gran's?" I said. "Who found him?"

"She did," he said, "when she got back from a late dinner with friends."

I felt terrible for my grandmother, imagining how she would feel every time she went out to her garage, or came home to face the big square of a closed garage door and recall that one time, behind the closed door, her son, my father, had sat dying.

Of all the garages he knew, and he knew many, why my grandmother's? Was he trying to punish her in some bizarre way? Over the years he had asked my grandparents for money. Had she refused him, and this was his revenge? Was he crying out for help? Could it have been an accident? Did he choose my grandmother's garage because it was a small one-car garage and would make quick work of him? Did he decide to end his life where it had begun, with my grandmother?

"Yeah, and Uncle Jim said there was no suicide note, just a list of accounts he was behind on. I guess he was selling some sort of body-shop equipment and wasn't making his numbers."

"This will be hard on Gran," I said.

"Uncle Jim said the cleaning lady was supposed to come this afternoon but didn't make it. He thinks maybe Dad planned to be saved."

My brother and I were quiet on the phone for a minute. I imagined my father closing the garage door behind him and sitting behind the wheel. Had he wept? Was he enraged? Did he consider how terrible it was to kill himself in his mother's garage? Had he hoped to be saved? Or had he gone there knowing no one would discover him until later?

"You okay?" Walter asked again.

"Yeah."

"How do you feel?"

"I feel. . . ." I wasn't sure I wanted to admit my relief. "I feel several things, but I feel relieved more than anything. Never have to look over my shoulder again."

"That's good," he said.

Was it? Was it good to feel relief above all else?

"And then pity. I feel sorry for him as I would for anyone who would kill himself. And I feel numbed by the news."

Then, thinking of myself and my own fears of suicide, of what might be baked in my genes, I said: "You don't know what's inside you sometimes, do you?"

Then quickly, I asked, "You, how are you, Walter?"

"Like you, I'm relieved," he said. "I kept thinking it would get worse. I didn't want to keep fighting him." When did *you* fight him? I wanted to ask—but this was not the time. Walter went on, "I feel bad for him, for Mom too."

"How is Mom? Did you talk to her?"

"Yeah," he said. "She seemed exhausted by it and wanted off the phone. She said she'll talk to us tomorrow." He sighed. "For myself, above all, I feel glad it's over."

"Yeah, it's over."

The conversation lagged as the numbness seemed to spread over me. Soon we hung up.

I went into the kitchen for a glass of water and sat at the kitchen table for a minute. The light was too harsh, so I turned it off and moved to the back fire-escape stairs and stood, leaning on the rail, looking across the apartment yard where I believed I'd last seen my father, watching the idle blacktop under the glow of the pinkish-yellow streetlight. I took in the musty smell of downed autumn leaves.

"Everything okay?" Kate whispered from the door, wearing one of my flannel shirts.

"Well...no, and yeah."

I came back inside.

"Who was on the phone?"

"Walter. My brother, Walter."

"It sounded serious," she said.

She closed the door and followed me back into the living room. "You okay?" she asked.

I wasn't. I didn't want to hurt her. But I didn't want to talk to anyone or be with anyone. I didn't trust myself in the moment to say the right thing or be able to explain my sense of relief or anger or pity or any of the other less-defined emotions swirling in my soul.

Then I decided to be honest. "No, I'm not okay," I told her.

She put her arms around me and rubbed my back. Her hands pushed ripples of tension off me. "Seems like you need to be alone," she whispered. "That's okay. If you want to talk, I'll be there for you, anytime."

My hand came up as she eased away, part of me wanted to pull her back, to keep her rubbing my back. But I let her go.

In less than two minutes, she was dressed and on her way. She paused at the door and came back to me and kissed me on the temple. Those soft lips lingered a moment. "You'll be all right?" she whispered.

I nodded.

"I'll call later to check in, if that's okay," she said moving to the door.

I followed her, "Yeah, that'd be nice." And we hugged briefly with a quick peck on the lips.

I stood by the front window and watched her go. She got in her car, lights on, and pulled away from the curb.

*

After a time in the late-night quiet, I wanted to talk with someone who knew my father. I wanted to talk to Brian Jackson. He was my best friend and had known my father since he and I were five years old. Brian was also a night owl, but even he was likely to be asleep at 3:30 in the morning. I decided to call anyway. The phone rang four times before the answering machine came on.

"Hey, Brian, it's me, Jason." I paused. Was this the kind of thing one left on a message machine? "Wanted to call you. To let you know–kind of weird to leave this on your machine–I just found out my dad killed himself tonight. Anyway, I wanted to talk. It's about 3:30 here, I'll probably be up for a while. Give a call when you can."

Over the next couple of hours, I wandered around the apartment.

I kept trying to get a handle on how I felt, kept asking myself: How do you feel about this? But beyond the instant relief and stock pity, my emotions were a muddle that continued to leave me numb. I turned my focus from myself to my father.

Connecting his passionate personality with suicide, I would have expected a gun or some other violent means. But he chose a passive method, drifting off to sleep from lack of oxygen. In a car. How else but in a car? Cars had dominated his life, and a car ended it. In his last seconds, did he have his hands on the wheel, recalling those long Greyhound drives from Indianapolis to Chicago to St. Louis and back? Or was it the hot–rod he drove as a high school kid? Or the folly of trying to mate a Dodge and an old Cadillac into a custom beauty–the "Dodge–Cat" fiasco–did he think of that failure and laugh at himself? Did he dwell on one of his victories, like the classic purple 1967 GTO with the white vinyl top? It had crashed and rolled into a lake only to be meticulously rebuilt by my father and sold for a handsome profit; its photo hung on a nail over his work bench for many years. Or did he, facing his more familiar car failures–which precipitated many of his personal failures–impose on himself a punishment involving the automobile which had brought him down? Or did my reckless father merely surrender and sink into the carbon monoxide the way a depressed and failed sea captain might quietly submit to the sea?

My father was a schemer, an optimist without regard for reality. By all rights he should have headed West to seek his fortune–

scratching for uranium in the Utah desert, land-speculating in Nevada, looking to rediscover some lost vein of gold in an arid California mountain, or building custom vans and ogling the girls in Los Angeles. But he was a too-young father, and tethered to a wife who was responsible and diligent to the core. She had reeled in his wildness as best she could, not for herself so much as for the sake of her children. By the time he severed himself from us, my father had lost the power, the wherewithal, and the courage to pursue his schemes, to run away and start over.

I wondered if his suicide was linked to Uncle Roger. As my father fell behind on his accounts while selling autobody equipment, my uncle relaxed on riches from an empire of automobile dealerships. Roger wintered in an ocean-front Palm Beach mansion. Never did my father come to terms with my uncle's success. Never did his resentment fade. Roger was always several steps ahead of Walt, always taller. Did that play a role in Dad's end?

*

Younger brothers spend a lifetime comparing themselves to their older siblings. I was no exception. I related to my father measuring himself against a successful older brother. They both made careers out of automobiles. Walter and I both made careers in advertising. Standing alone in the front window of my modest apartment on the night of my father's death, I connected my brother with my Uncle Roger as similar in their business success, and I couldn't help but connect myself with my father as the less-successful loner.

For all my wishing it otherwise, I knew real threads of my being, both physical and psychological, had sprung from my father and left me irrevocably bound to him. But I had another side to turn to. My days at college had provided the distance from family necessary to begin understanding how I had become who I was, and had given me an inkling of what I might become. I had modeled myself after my mother. I had adopted her work ethic, her early-to-rise discipline; even my choice to work alone as a free-lancer rather than at one of the city's ad agencies came from her. She had had offers from the major New York fashion design firms and turned them down in favor of designing and hand-crafting her own fashions–because she recognized that a simpler life could be a better life. It made me take pause to wonder at myself for having joined the Blake & Patterson partnership. I knew I had a strong independent streak like she did, so I needed to consider her example, reaching for her strength to guide me, and tapping my own strength, recognizing the confidence I'd gained through her and on my own. From her, I would have the resolve to rein in the darker parts of myself inherited from my father–the parts which had steered him over the precipice into darkness. And strength from her would help me leverage the best from Dad too.

The eastern sky began its pre-dawn glow as I thought about these things. A new day.

My father was dead.

And I was alive.

Love and Death

I did not fall sleep until a couple of hours after sunrise and didn't sleep long at that. I wanted to call Kate, to meet her for breakfast or something. To tell her at least some of what had happened with my father. Maybe tell her the whole story. But I didn't want to bother her, I didn't want to risk scaring her off. Not yet.

I took a long shower. I kept thinking, He's gone. Dad is gone. My father is dead. The person who swore he'd kill me, who had shot at me just a couple of weeks ago, is no longer a threat. Mom is free of the threat too. No need to protect her now. I can go anywhere.

When I got out of the shower, I saw my shotgun next to the bed, poorly concealed from Katie with a beach towel. I picked it up and pumped out the shells. Three double-aught, two deer slugs. I tossed them in the trash, and did the same with the rest of the shells. Then I went straight to my Macintosh and wrote a classified ad for my shotgun. I'd loved that gun since I was fifteen, and now I just wanted to get rid of it. I couldn't stand the sight of it, and stashing it in the back of the closet wasn't going to help. Bucolic, pastoral, memories of walking fencerows in the fall, bird hunting with my shotgun—insert a typical October *Field & Stream Magazine* cover here—had all vanished under the weight of seeing my Remington as a weapon to turn on my father. It had become something very different and ugly.

In less than ten minutes, my shortest copywriting exercise so far, I posted this Internet ad in the local paper: "Left-handed, Remington, 870 Wingmaster, 12-gauge. 32" mod. choke. Mint cond.

Asking $300."

And it was gone in a day. A guy gave me $275. It wasn't until I handed it over, looking at the gleaming varnish over the beautifully figured walnut stock, that I thought for an instant I'd miss my shotgun. Then I let it go.

And part of my life went with it.

*

After I placed the classified ad, I didn't know what to do with myself, so I went for a walk around the neighborhood. I had long imagined myself living in one of the beautiful old houses in Indianapolis's Meridian/Kessler neighborhood, and now I imagined living in one with Katie. Almost before I realized it, I was within a block of Butler University. I stood at the gates of the campus and walked in, watching for Katie and trying to figure out what to say if I saw her. But it was still early, the campus quiet. I walked until I came to her apartment at the far end of campus. I stood outside thinking she might happen by, thinking I should call her, thinking I didn't want to wake her after I'd let her go home at about 2:30 in the morning. I felt bad about it, about not explaining.

I started to walk away when I heard a shout. "Hey, Jason Blake, where are you going?" Kate was leaning out the second floor window.

"Just out for a walk."

"Want a companion?"

"Sure."

When she came out, she wore sweat pants and a cool, navy-blue jacket, her hair in a ponytail which reminded me she was a college girl. Everything felt a little weird again. But before the end of the block she took my hand and leaned into my shoulder, "What a gorgeous morning," she said. "Fall is my favorite time of year."

"Mine too," I said and squeezed her hand.

A few steps on I said, "I like your jacket."

"Well thank you very much. I designed it and made it myself."

"Wow. That's very cool." I didn't say anything about Mom, but I was impressed.

Small talk carried us across campus–talk about the autumn leaves and migrating birds, the earthy smell, the angle of the light, and the vivid blue of the sky. We walked down to Holcomb Gardens, and it was there, sitting thigh–to–thigh at the feet of the Aphrodite sculpture, that I felt a strong bond to Katie, and we spoke of my father and the news of his suicide. I had a hard time telling her about the attack, simplifying it, but still I had to choke out the words as the images played too vividly in my memory. I leaned forward as I failed to hold back tears. She silently put her arm around me and rubbed my back.

Then I said, though I'd planned not to, "When my brother called last night, to tell me about Dad's suicide, the emotion I felt first was relief. Relief for me, for my mom."

Katie's hand rubbed my back and gripped my shoulder, "Well of course. You were finally free. A threat on your life was gone. That's normal."

"Then I felt guilty for feeling relieved," I shook my head. "I still do. I feel ashamed of it. I feel ashamed to say it to you."

Katie didn't say anything for a few seconds, and then: "Look, you're just being honest about how you felt and how you feel. Most people can't do that, Jason. It shows how strong you are, what kind of man you are."

To say these things to me, to comfort me with words and touch the way Katie did in those moments spoke to me of her strength and wisdom.

We watched another couple walk down to the gardens in the morning hours, probably thinking they'd have it to themselves. They waved. We waved back.

"You know," I paused and part of me wanted to check these words, but I decided to just let it go, "You know, I was afraid to tell you about my trouble with my father. I was afraid it would scare you off or make you think I might be like him."

"I've seen my share of trouble," she said.

I hadn't expected this.

"Nothing as bad as what you faced," she said. "But my dad was an alcoholic, a mean drunk. After a lot of ugly fights with my mom, he left. Just disappeared one day, and we never heard from him."

"How old were you?" I asked.

"I was ten. So that was over half my life ago," she said. "My mom and I did okay. She worked a lot. I learned to sew my own clothes, which was fun and kept me out of trouble." She shrugged, "And it's really a kind of happily–ever–after story. When I was seventeen she got remarried to a really nice guy, a teetotaler who adores her. He's not who I'd choose for her, but she's happy, and that's what matters. So, yeah, it's good."

I felt myself sinking into something, letting my guard down, feeling like I could say anything. It was a feeling I'd never had with a girl. Deep inside, part of me rose up and felt bright in a quiet and peaceful way.

Was I falling in love with her? I knew my emotions were running high and didn't trust myself to say anything.

*

As we walked back to Katie's apartment so she could get ready for classes, she held my hand all the way. Even when I tried to let go, when we saw people she knew, she wouldn't, squeezing tight. We held a long hug at her front door and parted with a sweet kiss and a promise to talk that evening.

Heading back to my place, I didn't know what to do. Should I go to my brother's? Should I go to work? That felt weird. But I didn't want to sit at my apartment alone waiting for someone to call. Waiting for someone to tell the little brother what to do. Back at my apartment, there were messages from Mom, Walter, and Brian Jackson.

Suddenly, I wanted to be alone, couldn't imagine being with the family.

What was with me? Want to be with my family then away from them, with Katie then away from her. I didn't know how I felt, or what I wanted.

*

At the funeral, because my brother and I had broken with our father a year earlier, and had had minimal contact with his family since, my grandmother as well as my aunts and uncles on my father's side gave us a cool reception. The pleasant smiles, the light hugs, the phony welcoming–the silent shame and heavy blame–it was all there. My mother didn't come, but Missy did. And my father's wife. Yeah, surprise, he'd remarried during the year since the attack. And Brenda wasn't the past-her-prime-sexy-waitress type I would've expected. She was more maternal and plump, in a blue-collar, salt-of-the-earth Hoosier way. She came over with her daughter and introduced herself to us, and she seemed the most genuine, kind, and sincere of the people there. While I sensed my father's family–my grandmother, aunt, and two uncles–felt saddled with embarrassment and shame over the suicide (Big Walt screwed up again), this woman exuded a deep sorrow at the loss of her husband, of someone she loved. We told Brenda it was nice to meet her and we were so sorry for her loss–and all of it rolled out of me as if speaking to a stranger about a stranger, and not my father.

Then, as Walter, Missy and I turned to leave, Brenda said, "He was a good man, your dad. I know you all had some trouble with him, and I don't know details, but he was always good to me. To me and my daughter. And I really loved him," she said. "I just want you to know that."

*

The funeral itself was short, conducted by a man I'd never seen before, speaking a rote service packed with general platitudes as if written by a bad TV screenwriter. A highly polished brass urn sat alone on a table, holding my father's ashes. Its gleaming surface reflected, like a warped sepia-tone photo, the faces of the family gathered there to remember him. For a brief moment I wished I could see my father's body to be sure his death was not staged so he could run away from his debts and start over. Beyond the tight-lipped, semi-smile glares from well-wishers who lay blame with me and my brother, the worst part of the day came when the pastor read from a letter written by my youngest cousin, the only one at the funeral, about how he loved my dad. He was thirteen and, like me and my friends at that age, had fallen under the spell of Dad's charisma and his idea of manhood, entranced by his wonderful, crazy stories. The boy wept as the letter was read. It spoke of his heroic uncle who'd been a professional boxer (matched tales from my childhood); he'd rebuilt beautiful cars from hunks of twisted junk (often true); he'd built a beautiful brick house for his family himself (now we were stretching); and he'd played professional football for the Chicago Bears farm system. (Here was the whopper, new to me, and there was no farm system for the Bears; and it hurt to see the boy weeping as this letter was read, and it hurt me to hear the letter end on a lie. But at the same time, it seemed like a lie was perhaps the only way for my father's funeral to end. For him to end.)

After the funeral, we drove an hour north, up to the family farm in Battle Ground, Indiana—yes, Battle Ground, site of the great Battle of Tippecanoe which spelled the end of the Indian Wars with the Shawnee led by Tecumseh and his brother, The Prophet. My father's ashes were buried in the town cemetery there, alongside my grandfather, who he never liked much, and among generations of Blakes, dating back to my family's first Indian trading post near the confluence of the Wabash and Tippecanoe Rivers—before Indiana was a state.

Finally, mercifully, the day came to an end. Then my brother and Missy wanted to have dinner together. I just wanted to be alone and go to sleep. But we started telling funny stories about my father and laughing, which reenergized us. It felt good to remember his crazy, funny side—it was as if his death released us from our need to remember only the worst.

*

When I got home, it was late. I unlocked the door and was surprised to find the light on. Katie was waking up on my couch. I'd asked her not to come to the funeral, and she didn't, but she was there at my apartment wearing a demur dress with a square neck that accentuated her broad shoulders and lovely shape. My upstairs neighbor, Julie, who had a key and had met Katie, let her in when she heard about my father's funeral.

"How'd it go?" she asked, standing up, smoothing her dress.

"It was weird. It was Dad's funeral. With all the baggage from the last two years. With all the family resentment toward me and Walter. We stuck together with Missy, shields out like a circle of Spartans. Afterward we had dinner and laughed and remembered better days with Dad."

"I'm glad you were there for each other."

Something in her saying this stuck with me because I knew she was an only child from a broken home, and I knew she felt awkward about that as a Catholic kid. Many of her friends came from these large families of six or eight kids.

"You know what, Katie? I appreciate you being here. And you look beautiful." And she did look beautiful, as beautiful as anyone I'd ever seen, really. "I don't mean to be rude. But I'm just exhausted. I really can't sit and talk. I'm all talked out, worn out. It's been a long day, a long year."

She stood quietly in front of me. "Do you want me to leave?"

Now I was quiet, still not trusting my mercurial emotions. "I don't know. My emotions have been swinging back and forth all week. One minute I want to be alone, the next I don't. I–" my throat went tight, and I felt my eyes start to well up as I choked out the next words, "I don't know," and sat back down.

She hugged me and softly said, "Let me be here for you when you want me. And when you don't, I'll stay out of the way."

The words felt like magic to me. Could she do it? Could I?

She kissed me and told me to get ready for bed.

When I came out of the bathroom, I paused to watch her wrestling down her back zipper and slipping off her dress to put on sweatpants and a sweatshirt. She was even more beautiful this

way. And wonderful. She'd already spread a sheet on the couch. I
went to kiss her goodnight.

"Don't sleep out here," I said.

*

I spoke to Brian Jackson the morning after the funeral. He was
the first to give voice to something rolling around in my head:
"Now you don't have to worry about your mom. You are free to
escape to Boston and join us. There's so much going on here, and
so many smart, young people. Jason, you'd love it."

"I know," I said, "but now I'm a partner in Blake & Patterson. I
can't leave those guys high and dry after they welcomed me into
the partnership."

"Sure you can."

I laughed.

"I mean it. You can. You should," Brian said. "Look, being the
dutiful brother, the dutiful son, is admirable. But you did your
duty. Your duty to protect your mom is done. Your brother will
hire another copywriter. You need to live your own life. This is
where you want to be, where you belong."

Before I could offer another counter to this, he went on: "I know
people shouldn't make big decisions when they're under stress or
in a major life crisis. But what happened in the last week relieved
your crisis and stress. Now you're free to do the thing you want to
do."

Although I didn't like being pushed, I had been thinking along
the same lines. I hadn't articulated it yet, but I knew Mom would
be okay, and like Brian said, Walter would find another copywriter.

Now there was Katie to consider. No, I couldn't let myself be
swayed by her, a girl I'd dated for a couple of months, a senior in
college who had a lot of her own exploring to do.

The only real factor to consider was Blake & Patterson. The
agency did promise the financial security I wanted. But did I really
need it? And what's to say I couldn't find financial security in
Boston? I had proven I had marketable talent and skills.

Blake & Patterson was intensely committed to doing great creative work. That passion drove me–I loved the challenge of finding innovative ways to reach people, to motivate them. But there were more good agencies in Boston than Indy, a larger number of talented creatives too. And more interesting clients.

I spent a good part of the day thinking about whether or not I should move to Boston. Whether or not I should leave my brother. And Katie.

As I weighed the options and thought about what was right, I thought about the morning I stood in my kitchen and flipped a quarter and how I'd ignored what my heart wanted and agreed to stay in Indy and join the partnership.

What was the worst that could happen if I went? I'd fail. But I could only screw up my own life, then return with my tail between my legs. There was no family at risk, just one young man's ego, and I'd been kicked around before. I knew how to get up. And I knew how to win. I figured I could win again out there on my own, as I had when I went to Cape Cod, and when I went to England.

I knew I had to go.

Now I just had to tell Walter. Then the rest of my family. Then Kate.

*

First, Walter.

The next morning I asked him to join me in the conference room, trying to find the semblance of neutral turf.

"What's up?" he said as usual, a hint of impatience in his tone.

"Man, I hate to say it, Walter, but I'm leaving the partnership." He frowned at me and dropped into a chair. "I've decided to move to Boston. If I stayed in the partnership, I don't think I'd ever get that life experience." He kept his eyes on the table, spinning a pen as I explained my plan to freelance out there, starting over from scratch, with nothing more than the portfolio Walter and Carl had helped me build.

"If I don't move away, I'll always wish I had. I know this decision echoes my departure for Cape Cod with nothing. And England. Maybe I have to prove again that I can succeed on my own, I don't know." I paused. He said nothing. "If it doesn't work out, I'll come back. But I know I have to go."

"Well," Walter paused, still looking at the pen on the table, "fuck." After several seconds, he finally looked up.

"I wish you were staying, but I think it's a great idea." My brother said this without any of the enthusiasm he normally put behind a great idea. "You'll make it work out. I have zero doubt about it."

I knew he was right—I'd make it work. But my ego wanted either more support from him or more dread that life would be hard without me. I started to sit on the conference table, but decided there was nothing left to say, and turned to leave.

I paused at the door. "I really appreciate everything you and Carl have done for me." I stood tall as I walked out of the room.

In the afternoon Walter asked me to go out for a beer at a dark little pub. We agreed I'd freelance for them until I left in a month.

Then he spoke to the advantages of being in a place like Indianapolis. He said it was better to be in a city that was striving to become a major city instead of being in an established city like New York, Chicago, San Francisco, or Boston, "places that have peaked," he said.

I didn't argue the point.

His tone grew angry as his talk turned to the pie–eyed dreamers who chased glamour and lost their roots as they ran off wherever *People Magazine* told them to go.

By then I was finished listening and decided to talk.

I told him I didn't agree. I granted Indianapolis was improving, but I wanted to live in a talent hub. "I want to be part of something great, and work among the best and brightest."

A hard–to–read emotion rose in my brother's face—part anger, but also a look that might have been jealousy or resentment.

"You know, this means you can't be an employee of Blake & Patterson," Walter said, in an authoritative tone. "You can keep your office, and we'll still use you for freelance. Until you leave.

But effective today, you're no longer an employee."

Whatever. Fuck it. "That's cool," I said, trying to sound as non-chalant as possible. "I appreciate the freelance, and I'll sign whatever papers are needed to return the stock." I didn't want to push it. I was finished fighting with my brother.

Then he was quiet for a minute, and I decided I was not speaking next no matter what. It seemed like minutes passed. Finally, he spoke. "You know," he said, "you mean more to me than the whole business. If I had to choose between you and the business, I'd quit and shut it down tomorrow."

The statement surprised me, and it hung there between us for a moment. It was a nice thing to say. But neither of us believed it.

*

When I told Mom I was leaving, she was very supportive. She even sounded relieved–probably not because she wanted to get rid of me but because she worried about me and Walter working together. She knew there'd been tension. Besides she knew I loved the Boston area.

Then I had to tell Katie.

I waited a while. Because it was going to be hard. What surprised me was how rapidly she and I had continued to grow closer. There was so much in common: a love of literature and writing, a loyalty to family–despite her difficult, alcoholic father. That helped her understand my dad's drug abuse and its impact on my family. She loved art and design and sewing which also bound her to my upbringing and my family. Especially my mother. It turned out the beautiful black dress she wore the night I returned from my father's funeral was one she'd made for herself from a photograph she saw in a fashion magazine. This was something Mom did when she was in high school. Katie also knew financial pressure, different than mine but real, especially among so many wealthy Catholic kids at Cathedral.

When I finally told her, I feared a flow of tears, but instead she told me she was happy for me. She was almost stoic. I wondered if she was breaking up with me. Or did she think I was breaking up with her?

Finally I asked: "Do you think this is the end of us? That it's over?"

"No," she said. "Do you? Are you ending it? Moving on from me as well as your brother?"

"No, but you seemed so stoic, so cold."

"Cold? I'm not being cold. I'm in a little shock here, Stupid. I'm taking it in. This isn't what I expected when you said you had something important to tell me tonight."

"Well, what did you think I was going to tell you?"

"I didn't know, but how the hell was I supposed to guess you were moving a thousand miles away?" She took a deep breath. "And you think my being quiet and taking it in, and feeling sad means I want us to break up?" She paused. "Are you crazy? You want me to tell you what I was thinking?"

I wasn't so sure I wanted to hear at this point.

"I was quietly thinking when and how can we see each other. I figured you'd probably come home for Christmas, and I might be able to come out for spring break and look for a teaching job out there over summer. That's what I was thinking—thinking about how to keep us together. Now it's your turn. What were you thinking?"

I was on my heels. Here were my thoughts: I didn't know. I didn't want us to break up. It had been a long time since I'd felt about a girl the way I felt about Katie. If ever. But I didn't have a plan for after I went to Boston. So I decided to throw caution to the wind, and I pretty much said exactly what I was thinking. "I confess I don't have a plan for us, Kate." I repeated that I didn't want to break up. "But I also feel like I have to go to Boston."

"I know you love your friend Brian," she said, "but before we continue, just tell me if you're gay."

"Gay?" I laughed, "Gay!? Are you kidding me? I may be dense. I may think out loud more than is healthy. But I am not gay. I'd think my attraction to you would nix that thought."

I looked at her. And it came forward: "Katie, I don't have a plan," I said, "but I'm crazy about you. I haven't felt this way for a long time."

Bluntly she replied, "What exactly does that mean?"

"Katie–" I looked at her and was tempted to say, "You know what it means," but I wasn't that stupid. "Katie, it means I love you."

The result was not the storybook, "I love you *too!*" with all the hugs and kisses like in the movies. Like I'd experienced before (sometimes to a degree that awoke me from an infatuation). No, Kate took it in and looked down for a minute. Then she looked up and took a deep breath. I'm thinking, what the hell is going on, and wishing I could take back those words.

"Jason, I love you. I've loved you for awhile now, and you probably know that. But I'm not sure you know if you really love me yet. How could you? There's been so much stress in your life. Your dad just committed suicide–right after he tried to shoot you. You just decided to quit your job. You're leaving your family to move to Boston. There's too much emotion for you to know. I want you to love me, but tell me again after things settle down."

Listening to her talk made me sure. I knew I loved her. But I could wait.

*

Within two weeks of my turning down the partnership, Blake & Patterson hired one of the city's best young copywriters away from a competing ad agency. Then my brother pulled all my freelance work overnight.

But I didn't care. I was finished working with my brother. Done. I had to look forward. On to Boston.

I began shedding my skin, selling or giving away furniture, books (Kate took way too many, stashing them in her mother's basement), dishes, rugs, anything duplicated by Brian and Rod in Cambridge. I got it down to a minivan's worth of stuff, but it wasn't going to fit in my Honda Accord. I puzzled over how to get it all there. Ship it? About then, Katie said she was going to help me move. With her mother's minivan. She'd figured out we should go over Thanksgiving break. We'd caravan out to Boston. Before I could raise a worry about her driving back alone, she said she'd already talked to a friend at Butler who lived near Boston and was going to fly home for Thanksgiving and ride back with Kate. The deal was done.

*

Departure date closed in, and one night, after Katie and I made love, we lay in the quiet, and I couldn't help but think that every minute together was important, and maybe the sand in our hourglass was running out. I suspected Kate had similar thoughts, but whenever we got close to the topic, she remained upbeat as if nothing could come between us. As if a thousand miles were hopscotch.

But I'd had a long–distance relationship before. When I was in college. With Diane, Brian Jackson's friend from the interior design program at the University of Cincinnati. And it didn't last. It was hard and expensive and full of longing and melancholy–and mistrust, and wasted time–all ending in a heap of regret. I'd learned from it. Kate never had that experience. Kate was more stable than Diane by a long shot. Still, I was afraid to talk about it. I didn't want another long–distance romance.

The next day Katie bounded into my apartment. "Guess what?" she said. "I am moving to Boston."

Without telling me, she'd applied to do her student teaching in the Boston area and through an exchange program with Butler and Boston University, she could finish her last couple of classes. And she'd learned of her acceptance that morning. Her classes began in January. She was a force of nature. Thanks to her, we'd be apart for all of about three weeks. We agreed I'd drive home for Christmas and bring her back with me.

Feeling Sunrise

The actual leaving from Indiana was harder than I thought. I was a Hoosier, a country kid in many ways, and I loved all that. But I'd watched rural America changing faster and faster before my eyes. First came suburban sprawl. Then the best people left for cities, or most of them, and behind rose a wake of angry, undereducated people who had the wrong values, as far as I was concerned. Generally, they'd lost their connection to the environment, their love and respect for nature. Stewardship of the land seemed dead. Land had become a mere tool for money-making–the equivalent of a coal mine–something to leverage for a loan on an outsized tractor or luxury pickup. Poisoning water, animals, or trillions of invisible microbes, was all the right of the new corporate land owner in pursuit of extra bushels of corn or beans.

Still, these were my roots, and I was leaving them. Although I'd said I might come back to Indiana, I knew I was leaving for good. All of what Indiana had meant to me, both real and ideal, were behind me.

My future was behind me too–in a literal sense. Katie drove her mother's van behind me. "Every time I flash my brights, it's a kiss," she'd said. She flashed those lights for every possible reason: pulling away from the apartment, passing Butler, getting on the highway, filling up with gas, crossing the Ohio state line, whatever. I loved it.

*

Katie came out to Boston in January as planned, finished her degree, and landed an English teaching job in Sommerville.

My three years of living in Harvard Square with Brian and Rod (with Katie moving just six blocks away) were wonderful. The three of us guys did all kinds of fun single-guy stuff. Spontaneously jumping up from dinner to drive out to Western Mass for night skiing. Taking sailing lessons on the Charles River and then working crew in a sailing race from Boston to New York. Climbing Mt. Jefferson in the fall to see all of New Hampshire make a spectacle of itself with its beautiful foliage. Camping in Acadia National Park and kayaking around the islands of the North Shore. Skiing in Stowe, Vermont. Learning to surf–or trying to–on Cape Cod. Riding bikes around Martha's Vineyard. Bird watching at Plum Island. There seemed no end to our outdoor adventures.

Then there were the cultural opportunities. Poetry readings and political lectures. Art museums and concerts. Street performers and great debates in dark cafes. Wacky restaurants and a looming sense of history everywhere. As well as history in the making.

Then the sports: Celtics, Red Sox, Patriots, Bruins. Boston was even a fantastic sports town–with a sports bar on every other corner, it seemed–as if all the other wonders weren't enough.

My career went well too. I started working as a freelance copywriter, getting a quick start thanks to the work I'd done with Blake & Patterson. Then I decided to join a small, smart ad agency in Boston's Fenway area, an easy bike ride from Harvard Square (and close to Fenway Park). When we lost our largest client, the agency folded. Lucky for me, the client liked me and asked the next agency to hire me, so suddenly I was a hot item at one of Boston's bigger ad agencies. Then that agency was acquired by Omnicom, which made me a tiny cog in a multi-national machine. I focused on doing great work. Won some awards. Got promoted twice. But it never felt like it was enough, like the energy I pumped into the work mattered to the people who mattered. At some point, trying so hard and caring so much makes you feel stupid. Feeling perpetually under-appreciated makes you feel like a slave to "the man" or the machine. Eventually I left.

This time I started my own small agency/design firm with two friends of mine—great designers and great friends. Yes, Brian, Rod and I started our own small agency. We rented a space in a former warehouse, in what was then a crappy part of East Cambridge. It was cheap, and it overlooked the Charles River where we watched the rowers, which inspired the company name: Oarsmen Advertising & Design. As the name and our friendship implied, we pulled together pretty well. It was a fun ride from the start.

*

Ten years later, we're still at it. Still loving it. Still in the same space, which is now a hip part of the city, all renovated and with the cheap rent gone. Our company continues to grow, with 24 staff members now.

Katie and I are still at it too.

We moved in together, living in a little place in Somerville—and two years later—we got married! In the fall of course. Five years after I ambushed her on the back stairs of my apartment building, we married. Now, after traveling together and building careers and both getting master's degrees (me in English and Kate in education), we're expecting our first child. We don't know if it's a boy or a girl, but we know we're bound together to create a new life.

*

Tonight fuzzy dreams of fatherhood disrupt my sleep. Next to me Katie snores like a lumberjack. It has been an easy pregnancy, but we're getting close, and even an easy pregnancy is heavy lifting in the last month. She jokes that she's become a walrus, hoisting herself out of a bed or chair, the baby's head bouncing against her pelvis on the subway.

After drifting for an hour, I decide to get up and go for a drive. It's cold. April cold, damp. Heading north up the coast, it's almost

5:00 in the morning as I get my first glimpse of the ocean, a pool of black on my right. I click off NPR and drive in silence. I think about becoming a father, about my father. I wonder how much of him is in me. More than a decade has passed since he killed himself. I can't imagine a moment of "I love you. I'll kill you." with a child.

But is it possible?

I don't think so. I don't know.

I do know I'm not my father.

Or Walter.

Neither Walt nor Walter.

I have become who I am.

Not like I'm finished. I've got a lot to learn, and there's something deep inside me that keeps me hungry to move ahead, to experience the next thing, learn the next thing.

I'm focused on the driving now, tracking 1–A up past Lynn and Swampscott, circling around the road into Marblehead. A spot of early traffic as I twist and turn through Salem. I swing into the Dunkin Donuts on Salem Harbor to get a cup of coffee. The place is packed. At 5:30 in the morning, it's packed. The smell of donuts, muffins, and sugar tempts me. Lovely, mocha–colored women–from Latin America? Philippines? Middle East? India?– sweep around each other like dancers, like whirling dervishes supplying caffeine to construction workers. Their flashy eye makeup, bold earrings, necklaces, and rings are the only garnish to the otherwise drab, brown uniforms, but it's enough to adorn. To each other, they whisper a foreign language too quietly for me to detect their homeland. To customers, they speak English clearly but with an accent.

The line moves fast. Customers flow in as fast as others leave. The guy in front of me orders a "reg–ya–lah," which is a large coffee with cream and sugar.

I order mine with a little cream. I take it to the car and take a sip. It's hotter than hell, but it's strong, and it's coffee.

Continuing north, I cruise up over the high bridge and down into Beverly, hugging the harbor, then around to the ocean road,

Route 127. I pull over at a beautiful park overlooking the Atlantic and a scatter of islands. Salem lies across the harbor and Marblehead in the distance. I can see three lighthouses from here. Other cars park here, too, in the predawn glow. People drink coffee, read the paper by the car cabin light, listen to the sea and wait for the sunrise. A couple of lobster boats chug out of the harbor to check traps. I notice a historical marker on a huge boulder down near the beach, and my curiosity gets the better of me. I pull my jacket collar up and walk down near the water. It's cold, and I hold the Styrofoam coffee cup in both hands as I read that this is Independence Park, named because this is where the Declaration of Independence was first read to the people of Beverly in 1776. It goes on to say Beverly Harbor served as George Washington's Navy Base, and this harbor was the site of America's first naval battle, when the *Hanna* fought the British *Nautilus* to a draw. I try to imagine the scene playing out in front of me.

I walk the beach with the morning getting bright, and I climb back up the hill to get a view of the sunrise. And here it is. The sun rising, breaking the horizon as an orange line at first, then an arc, then a hump–it's coming fast now, a new day, a new life–a half circle, and you can't stare at it. Lovely orange and yellow mix with gray and white in the clouds between patches of blue.

"Beautiful isn't it?" I hear, and turn to a woman about ten years older than I, pausing with her golden retriever.

"Yeah, it's great," I say.

"I see it most days, walking him, and I never get tired of it."

"It reminds me of where I grew up in Indiana."

"It reminds you of Indiana!?" She laughs out loud.

I laugh too. "There was this field behind my house, and as a kid I used to climb up this small hill in the middle of the field where there was a rock pile. From there you could see a long way to the east across the other fields and watch the sunrise." I didn't mention how I went out there when the field was burned black.

"Well, okay, if you say so, but it still sounds a little crazy to me." She looks down at her dog and says, "Dallas, does it look like Indiana to you?" She smiles at me–because she thinks her dog smarter? "Enjoy the view," she says and sings quietly, "Back home again in Indiana...." Again she chuckles and walks on with her dog.

I turn back to enjoy the view. Okay, it's only a little like my Hoosier home. The tide is going out and the smell of the sea wafts in on the chilly breeze.

April, like life, offers its vicissitudes: warm and cold, damp and dry, colorful and gray. It's a fine time to have a baby. Katie and I will be parents soon. I'd love to bring up a child in a place like this, on the sea, a short train ride to Boston. Maybe we'll move to the North Shore.

We're going to have a baby. I'll be a father.

I stand here on the shore, taking in the sea air and the sound of the gulls and the droning diesel of a lobster boat in the distance, and the sun glaring loudly off the water–and I think I've come a long way. I'm a long way from where I started.

– THE END –

A Word From the Author

If you enjoyed the book, please share your opinion with friends on social media, and add your review on Amazon and GoodReads. These reviews disproportionately impact the success of small publishers and their authors.

You can learn more about John Young and send him your thoughts at: *johnyoungwriter.com*

CPSIA information can be obtained
at www.ICGtesting.com
Printed in the USA
BVHW041115110819
555609BV00020B/716/P